P.O. Box 270014
Hartford, WI 53027

ISBN: 0-9642304-5-3

Distributed by:
Jews for the Preservation of
Firearms Ownership, Inc.
P.O. Box 270143
Hartford, WI 53027
414-673-9745 – Fax 414-673-9746
www.jpfo.org

Cover art by Turner Type & Design, Lacey, WA.

Hope is a work of fiction. Any resemblance
between its characters and real people,
living or dead, is purely coincidental.

"In *Hope*, Aaron Zelman and Neil Smith give us a smorgasbord of broad hints and tantalizing visions of how America could be, and should be, remade into 'the Land of the Free.' The only way *Hope* could be better is if it were longer."

—David Anderson
Freedom Activist
Calgary, Alberta

"*Hope* is an engaging political fairy tale that sets a high standard against which real-life "libertarian" politicians ought to be measured."

-Scott Bisser,
Graphic artist and
proprietor of LibertyArtworx
Riverside, California

"Aaron and Neil have done me a great favor by providing their new novel *Hope* – it's a sort of road map for getting from here (injured and usurped) to there ('sweet land of liberty'). It helped me feel better about the world my grandchildren will inherit."

—Ken Holder
Webmaster and political advocate
Snowflake, Arizona

"*Hope* is a celebration of human potential. Some people will hate it because it rubs our noses in the fact that this country has turned its back on the Constitution, the Declaration of Independence, and, more fundamentally, common sense and human decency. Many of us have done our best to keep the flickering flame of freedom alive. Zelman and Smith are spraying lighter fluid on it. We may have the *Uncle Tom's Cabin* of the 21st Century here."

–Rex F. "Baloo" May
Cartoonist and political observer
Fort Collins, Colorado

"Hope reads like a political manifesto with wings."

–Anders Monsen
Editor emeritus, *Prometheus*
Round Rock, Texas

Hope

How would you feel if you no longer feared your government?

A novel by
Aaron Zelman
and
L. Neil Smith

THIS BOOK IS DEDICATED to all those Americans over the past two and a half centuries who have cared enough – and been brave enough – to defend individual liberty wherever and whenever it was threatened. Our special acknowledgement to James Bovard, who has inspired so many people to embrace the Bill of Rights.

OUR SINCERE THANKS to David Anderson, Scott Bieser, Tom Creasing, Ken Holder, Rex May, Karl Murphy, Roger L. Smith, Rylla Smith, Richard Stevens, John Taylor, Garn Turner, Claire Wolfe, and especially Frank Ney, without whose cheerful help this effort might have been considerably less interesting. And to our muse, Jan Gan Boyd, wherever you are. To Nancy and Cathy for their continued patience.

THIS NOVEL IS A WORK OF FICTION. Any resemblance between real characters and institutions and those depicted herein is purely coincidental. Words (and music, too) to "I Will Be Free" (see Chapter Fifteen) by L. Neil Smith, Copyright 1984.

Printed in the United States of America.

Table of Contents

Do you hear the people sing?
Singing a song of angry men?
It is the music of a people
Who will not be slaves again!
When the beating of your heart
Echoes the beating of the drums,
There is a life about to start
When tomorrow comes!

Herbert Kretzmer
Les Misérables

Chapter One:
SHEILA HENSLEY

> *Painful as it may be to hear it, there's nothing special about the people of this country that sets them apart from the other people of the world. It is the Bill of Rights, and only the Bill of Rights, that keeps us from becoming the world's biggest banana republic. The moment we forget that, the American Dream is over.*
>
> – Alexander Hope, *Looking Forward*

High above the mirror-polished hardwood floor, thickly forested in folding Samsonite chairs, red, white, and blue banners hanging on all four gymnasium walls proclaimed:

HOPE – FOR AMERICA

"A political rally?" Sheila Hensley proclaimed in disbelief. "You've brought me out in this cold and slush to a political rally?" She was a stylishly tall, well-dressed, slender and attractive woman few would have guessed was in her early 60s. It was difficult to see any gray in her ash-blonde hair. The tweed-jacketed man beside her was of about the same age, but he was losing his hair, and was a trifle shorter than she was. "Do you have any idea how many of these I've attended over the past 40 years?"

Hundreds of people were milling around the room or visiting in small groups. The air smelled of wet coats and Chicago in November. The flags that hung around the gymnasium were not the familiar 13 stripes and 52 stars of the 21st century United States of America, but the same stripes and the circled 13 stars of the nation's painful birth years. An enormous blue and white banner over one of the basketball hoops, exhorted:

HOPE FOR NEXT YEAR!

and

HOPE FOR PRESIDENT 2008

"Plenty would be my guess," her companion answered amiably as he fondled his unlit briar. Thornton "Kitch" Sinclair was a professor of history at a private college here in Chicago and a lifelong activist of the libertarian persuasion. He knew that Sheila had once been married to one of the state's Democratic Party movers and shakers. "Although I'd be willing to bet that not one of them was for any third-party candidate."

"Unless you count the Gene McCarthy campaign in '68," she replied, agreeing with him. Recorded music being played from somewhere up near the front of the big room brightened the atmosphere. She thought she recognized something lively from *Les Misérables.*

"I don't count it," Kitch told her. "McCarthy was running for the Democratic Party's presidential nomination."

"About a million years ago," she sighed.

"About a million years ago," he agreed.

More and more people seemed to be entering now, mostly young people, chattering, laughing, some of them stopping at a table to the right of the doors to acquire buttons with the candidate's name and face on them, stickers with winged horses that were somehow associated with the campaign, or little 13-star flags on what looked like teriyaki sticks.

Sheila and Kitch stood just inside and slightly to the left of the two-story double doorway opening onto the recently remodeled gymnasium at St. Gabriel's – the Church of St. Gabriel Possenti of Isola – located in a rather old, comfortable-feeling middle-class Chicago neighborhood. The mini-convention he'd brought her to was being held across a street full of muddy snow at the Piper Arms Hotel, but there was more room here for the public appearance of the candidate.

"And how many of those years, my dear," he went on, "have you had the undeniable feeling that this country is ... well, the expression, I believe, is 'FUBAR'."

She smiled, brightly-colored memories four decades old crowding into her mind. "'Fouled Up Beyond All Recognition'? Only you didn't really mean 'fouled'."

"You're right," he conceded, "I didn't really mean 'fouled'. How many, Sheila, how many?"

"About the same million," she answered thoughtfully. "Or at least for the 40 that I've spent going to political rallies. Kitch, you know it's funny – funny meaning 'grotesque' – that I've always felt that way, starting back when I was a hippie, supporting 'Clean Gene' from the streets, continuing when I became the respectable wife of a Democratic Party kingmaker, and even more so, after the divorce, after John died, and I started being, well, something else, I guess, whatever it is."

He took her hand. "We all started being something else after John died." John Greenwood had been a lifelong friend to both of them, a classmate of Sheila's in high school, a classmate of Kitch's in college, best friend to the latter, the love of her life to the former until – to Sheila's eternal dismay – he'd found his calling. He'd become a Catholic priest and eventually the monsignor here at St. Gabriel's. He'd been killed in Israel by terrorists, but not without giving them a fight.

She realized all over again: this had been his church.

Kitch sighed, "Well, I'm sorry for dragging you here, Sheila, but I had a reason."

"Yeah?" she answered with mock severity. "Well it had better be a good one. I know a place on the lakeshore where we could be eating lobster right now in front of a stone fireplace."

He sighed and shook his head, pretending – at least partly – to be torn between dinner and politics. "It is, I assure you. There was a time, you know, when people didn't feel that way, that FUBAR way I mentioned. There must have been a time like that. Maybe it was before we started hearing all these nasty rumors about the vice president. Maybe it was before the election of 2000. Maybe it was before before Waco, before Watergate, before the War in Vietnam, or before the Kennedy assassination."

"Maybe it was before both world wars or the Depression or the Federal Reserve Act of 1913," she grinned, shaking her own head. She'd heard all of this from him before, many times. But it was one of the reasons she ... she – what *did* she feel for Kitch, anyway? *I won't think about that now,* she ruefully quoted Scarlett O'Hara, *I'll think about that tomorrow.*

"Maybe it was before the War between the States," he went on, startling her. "I don't know where we went wrong and Sheila, I *teach* the stuff! But I *know* there was a time in America when people had greater freedom and a less oppressive life than they do today. A time when the sky seemed to be brighter and the air smelled cleaner and everything, everything tasted sweeter, simply because there was no one to put a tax on it or tell you in minutest detail how it's bad for you and you shouldn't have it."

She started to speak; he went on before she could. "Now there's your *real* pollution, Sheila, too blasted many people-per-million are professional busybodies and do-gooders who believe that everything tastes better if they piddle in it!"

"Like the sophomore senator from New York – and former First Lady – who wants to be the first female President of the United States?" Sheila asked rhetorically.

Kitch nodded. "The *sophomoric* senator, a perfect example of the species. Well, Hope's the fellow to put a stop to it, at least I think he is!"

She arched a cynical eyebrow at him.

"But you couldn't be more wrong about one thing, Sheila," he finished softly. "You never were a hippie, never. To me, you always smelled of bathsoap and yellow roses."

Speechless, Sheila looked heavenward into the rafters of the gymnasium. How could you *not* love a fellow who was this romantic (and in his 60s, no less) and was as cute as a hobbit – which he greatly resembled – besides? Without waiting for any reply from Sheila, Kitch touched her elbow gently and they headed toward a small knot of individuals gathered around a folding table, still at the back of the enormous room, where he thought that he'd glimpsed somebody familiar.

"Father Joseph?" Kitch tapped on a shoulder.

A small, wiry, bearded man in his 30s, wearing a black jacket, shirt, and priest's collar turned toward them. Kitch had always thought he looked rather like Al Pacino. He held up a small plastic cup. "Who do I complain to, Kitch? I believe there's actually *punch* in this punch!"

Chapter Two: *JOSEPH SPAGHELLI*

Chief Justice Oliver Wendell Holmes was wrong. You have an absolute and perfect right to shout "Fire!" in a crowded theater – and to accept responsibility for the consequences.

– Alexander Hope, *Looking Forward*

"I'll give you punch!" a familiar voice threatened mockingly. It was an old man who raised his hand, only to lower it again and thrust it enthusiastically toward Kitch. Most likely in his 80s, he had a long white beard and a yarmulke. The heavy coat he wore had an almost military look to it.

"Ascher!" Kitch exclaimed, highly delighted, but not especially surprised, to see his two old friends here. How long had it been since this extremely odd couple had gone into "business" together? Could it really be almost a decade?

"You remember Rabbi Liebowitz, don't you, Sheila?" Ascher, an ardent anti-Nazi partisan during World War II, had once been fired by a Reform congregation for being politically incorrect enough to openly advocate armed self-defense.

"And his comical sidekick, Father Joe," put in Spagelli. John Greenwood's former assistant, Spagelli now worked with Ascher for the mysterious and controversial Ralston Foundation, dedicated to teaching effective self-defense – including self-defense with firearms – and a special set of ethics to go with it, to inner-city boys and girls. Although the general crime rate, and gang-shootings in particular, had fallen off sharply in areas where it was active, the foundation had been the subject of extremely hostile treatment by the establishment media over the years.

Old Ascher seemed to thrive on it.

"I remember them well," she answered. "A priest, a rabbi – all we need now is for a Protestant minister to show up and we'll have the material for some really classic jokes."

Kitch was about to point out a particular Lutheran clergyman he was acquainted with, up front, addressing a crisp-looking redheaded 20-something female in a severe gray suit whom he felt he somehow ought to remember, but he was stopped by the rabbi.

"If it's jokes you're looking for, young woman," Ascher told her, producing a startled expression on her face, "we have all the jokes we need in this coming election!"

"What do you mean, Rabbi?" Kitch asked with counterfeit innocence, knowing exactly what Ascher had meant.

"It's actually a religious event – the Second Coming of Bozo! To begin with, we've got a possible sexual scandal deeply involving the Republican frontrunner, Vice President Chesley Chambers. (You know, it's too bad the old vice president had to resign and go back home to Wyoming; I rather liked him.) And – dismayingly far ahead in the polls at the moment – an inexplicably charismatic former First Lady whose Senate voting record makes Diane Feinstein resemble a John Bircher, and who now openly promises to take America all the way down the Marxist drain!"

"So much for Socialist Party 'A' and Socialist Party 'B'," Kitch grinned. Maybe that's where America went wrong, he thought to himself, when political parties – the Federalists and anti-Federalists – began to form. Many historians thought so. Then again, how could such a thing have been prevented in a free society?

"Well the election's still a year away, and we've got Hope," said Father Joseph. "No pun intended, of course. A very decent, highly principled guy whose chances of being elected approach those of the proverbial cellophane snowball in a locale that the theologically sophisticated claim not to believe in any more." He finished with a Russian accent, "What a country!"

"Do you believe in Hell, Father Joseph?" Ascher asked.

"Yes I do, Rabbi, I've been there many times."

"What," Sheila asked, "no rimshot?"

"The man's platform," Kitch said, mostly to Sheila and attempting to ignore the theological horseplay, "is shockingly simple. 'Hope for America' consists of no more than one man's promise to stringently enforce the Bill of Rights – exactly like the highest law of the land it happens to be."

"A policy," Sheila replied, her guard up now at the thought of yet another political hero – in a lifetime full of them – inevitably with feet of clay. "A policy you clearly believe will put us back on the 'right track'."

Kitch turned to Sheila, almost pleading. "I think I might weep if such a man could be elected. It's exactly what we were just talking about. Everybody – right, left, and middle – knows that there's something terribly wrong with this country of ours. And that in itself should tell us something."

"Like?" She was frowning at him. Why was this funny little man so easily capable of changing her mind – and turning her head?

"Like maybe," he told her, "it's true. Like maybe it's something really deep and fundamental that went wrong a long time ago, right at the country's beginning. Hope's a history professor like I am, Sheila, only instead of specializing in Middle Eastern literature like I did, his field is American history, which is about as academically popular these days as planetary astronomy."

Pretending indifference, she said, "I'm afraid you've lost me, darling."

"As an historian, Hope 'remembers' a time when you could start your own business by hanging out your shingle, without getting a fistful of permits. When you could write a book that criticized the government and no thug-agency would threaten the retailers who sold it. When you could lock your door and say you wanted to be left alone, without the SWAT team blasting you and your house to bits. When you could dig a hole – even fill one in – in your own back yard without even once seeing helicopters and machineguns sent by the Environmental Protection Agency."

"And as a consequence, he believes that vigorously enforcing the Bill of Rights will go a long way toward fixing everything that's wrong with America?" Still skeptical, Sheila looked Kitch deep in the eyes. "And you agree?"

"My dear, I remember a time like that, myself, although admittedly I was very young. Why, you could leave your front door unlocked, buy unwrapped candy, and let your kindergartner walk to school without an escort because nobody would even dare think of molesting her. And you certainly didn't need a license from the government to exercise your Constitutional rights." He nodded his certainty. "Yes, Sheila, I agree with him."

Sheila sighed, pushed her arm through his, and drew close to him. "Then I suppose I do, too, Kitch. Two great historians can't be wrong, can they?"

Rabbi Liebowitz laughed out loud. Father Joseph exclaimed, "I certainly wish all of my conversions – political or otherwise – came as easily!"

Kitch blushed. "Well, I *have* been working on her for rather a long time."

"I can see that you have!" the priest and the rabbi laughed together.

There was a thoughtful silence.

"Not to change the subject," Sheila told Father Spagelli, "But I thought that you weren't ever supposed to walk on a basketball court like this in your street shoes."

"This is the 21st century. This court's covered in some kind of thick, self-healing polymer. Look down: where we're standing we're half an inch above the paint. All it requires is that every week they ride some kind of little machine over it that warms it up a little and takes out all the scratches."

"Sort like a land-Zamboni." Sheila had always

been a hockey fan. She said it was John Greenwood's fault. He'd played hockey in high school and college, and coached youth hockey as a priest.

Spagelli looked puzzled. "Sort of. I never looked at it that way before."

Sheila nodded. "And that's what you all expect this Hope guy will turn out to be ... "

"What?" she'd momentarily lost them all.

"A sort of political Zamboni."

Ascher laughed. "Let's hope he goes a lot deeper than a few surface scratches!"

"Let's." Spagelli agreed. "There are deep cracks to be fixed, as well, and not just in the Liberty Bell."

"You know," Ascher told Sheila, "I came to this country just as soon as I could after the war. I've been a citizen since 1952. And in all of that time, I've never voted for the man I *wanted* to be the President. I've always voted against the man I *didn't* want. And now I'm tired of voting for the lesser of two evils, my dear. The lesser of two evils is *still evil.* I want to vote for someone who isn't evil at all. Alexander Hope is the first candidate I can support with a clear conscience."

Father Joseph nodded. "Ascher isn't the only one who feels that way. You remember our old friend Albert Mendelsohn?" Albert was John Greenwood's Jewish uncle, another ex-partisan, and a diamond merchant currently living in Belgium. "He can't vote, but he's encouraging all of his American colleagues to contribute heavily to the Hope campaign. In fact, Albert's brother Ruven is here in the States this very minute, actively raising money for Hope."

Sheila was startled. "Is that even legal?"

"As long as it's good old American money," Father Joseph laughed. "I don't think they allow

Chinese government contributions any more, and Hope wouldn't be in line for them in any case."

Kitch shook his head in disbelief. "How old are Albert and Ruven Mendelsohn, anyway?"

"How old, you ask? How old?" Ascher drew himself up to his full height and width. A very big man, even at his age, Kitch wouldn't have wanted to fight with him. "Why neither of those two young fellows is any older than I – "

"Shh!" somebody behind them whispered abruptly. Kitch noticed that there was organized movement at the front, now, not at a podium, but at another folding table where the severe young redhead sat beside a middle-aged man in a gray suit.

"Professor Sinclair, you're wanted up front for the introduction. Mr. Hope's about to speak!"

CHAPTER THREE:
ALEXANDER HOPE

> *Who does this guy Bork think he is? Look closely, for yourself, at the Bill of Rights – the First, Second, Third, Fourth, Fifth, and especially the Ninth Amendment. The whole damn thing is about privacy, and a willful refusal to see and understand that represents the lowest form of intellectual dishonesty.*
>
> – Alexander Hope, *Looking Forward*

Faith-Anne had been right about the suit, Alex thought as he rose to take the battered lectern in the little Catholic gymnasium she'd arranged for him to speak in. (What was the name of the church again? Saint Gabriel Possenti of Isola. Odd, yet oddly familiar, too.) He'd always been a bit frugal (maybe even more than a bit) when it came to buying clothes.

He wasn't a large man (and didn't know that he impressed people that way). At five feet nine, he weighed 175, and, thanks to a health club his daughter had found, and incessant nagging on her part, he stayed in good shape. He had a full, healthy head of wavy brown hair that had to be cut entirely too often, was well tanned – something he made no special effort at – and his eyes were the intense azure of the inside of a sunlit iceberg. One of his female students had said he looked like Mel Gibson. Another had said it was Charles Bronson. At his age, he'd take either as a compliment.

He was also extremely wealthy, but had never managed to get used to it. There were few things he hated more than wearing a suit and tie. A child of the 60s and a westerner, he preferred jeans and cowboy shirts from Sears. But his daughter was right. The more you spend on a suit – in this case, an Oxxford – the more comfortable it is. And if you have your shirts made – an expensive luxury he'd probably never get over – then even ties seem perfectly comfortable.

From moment to moment it startled him to look up and see people watching him in what felt like his pajamas. It was like that dream where he was walking down the street, crawling through the jungle, addressing the board of directors, attending a faculty meeting, or lecturing in the classroom stark naked, and nobody seemed to notice, although that never saved him from waking up shaking and terminally embarrassed.

" ... ladies and gentlemen, it gives me intense pleasure to introduce your candidate and mine, Alexander Hope!"

The audience exploded and rocked the gymnasium with their cheering. He was startled all over again to see that they actually appeared to be interested in what he was about to say.

The introduction had been as brief and modest as he could persuade Kitch to make it. Even as a courtesy, Alex never let anyone refer to him as "the next president of the United States". His old friend and professional colleague of the past dozen years shared his political convictions – had helped lead him to them, in fact – and on that basis had persuaded him to make Chicago one of his first stops after his surprising nomination in Denver by the Free Libertarian Party of America. Kitch was a good man, right to the core. It was a pleasure to accommodate him.

So now it was time to demonstrate to his old friend that he – and thousands of others who'd put their trust in Alex to take the FLPA and its ideas further than they'd ever gone before – hadn't made some horrendous mistake.

"Ladies and gentlemen ... "

Briefly he glanced left. His 23-year-old daughter and campaign manager stood at one end of the little stage watching the audience for their reaction to him. How many Christmas and Easter pageants had been performed here, he wondered, year after year, decade after decade, attended by parents almost as proud of their offspring as he'd always been of his?

At the right, an older friend than Kitch, John Pondoro, was doing the same thing, but for a very different reason. Secret Service protection had never been offered to an FLPA candidate in its 37-year history, nor would it likely have been accepted. (There were no Old Media television cameras here tonight, either, nor even a radio microphone, although his own party would be webcasting this speech live over the internet, and NetPlanetNews.com was carrying it, as well.) But Alex was acutely aware that under the big man's jacket hung a .45 caliber Glock Model 21 semi-automatic pistol – hideously illegal in Chicago – and that John was prepared to use it to save his candidate's life if it became necessary.

Big John had saved his life more than once before, in another country, far, far away. He was another man, like Kitch, whose central values had been tested and were solid.

John's son Cap – 30-year-old Peter Hathawy Capstick Pondoro – was out in the crowd, "watching it from the inside", as he put it. He preferred a hand-built .38 Super automatic. Cap had his own way of doing things, and to his father's occasional frustration, it seemed to work. He and Faith-Anne had already knocked heads because she insisted on organization and efficiency. Cap was only interested in results.

One other person should have been here, but she was still in no condition to travel, and wouldn't be for some time. Those who were responsible for that would be made to pay for it.

Now Alex looked straight ahead, cleared his throat, and spoke.

"Ladies and gentlemen, fellow children of the American Revolution, let me begin by answering the two questions that I'm usually asked first. Yes, Hope is my real name, and, no, I'm not related to Bob Hope."

Polite laughter rippled through the crowd. The remark wasn't very funny, but it had broken the ice reliably in business meetings and first-day classes for years.

He started again. "The next question I'm usually asked is, 'Do you really expect to be elected President?' And if you listen very closely, you can hear three more little words that they'd love to add: 'you silly man'."

This time the laughter was louder and more

spontaneous. Now it was time to make his first real point. "And the truth is, I think, unless some miracle were to happen, that the odds greatly favor the election of the Democratic candidate – "

The hall erupted with booing. He'd expected that and patiently waited it through.

"The odds greatly favor the Democratic candidate, as I said, or the Republican candidate. We're talking about the U.S. Senator, here, the former First Lady. And we're talking about the sitting Vice President, although I suppose I might have chosen some other participle. So let's be as real as we can, shall we?

"What I'm here to do is to spread the FLPA's message of freedom – its heart and spirit – far and wide, in order to make it just that much easier for that miracle I spoke of to transpire *someday*, for somebody who follows me along this particular path. And I'm asking you to help me do that."

Not much reaction there, he thought. Folks didn't like to hear their candidate say he didn't think he could win. But any other opinion would be that of a megalomaniac or a self-aggrandizing liar, and he was accumulating a reputation for the truth, no matter whose ox was gored – even his own.

"So will you help me?" he demanded, "help me spread the FLPA's message of freedom?"

He earned a much better reaction that time. People like to be asked for help. That kind of help, anyway. This kind of people. Now he'd begun to approach that proverbial altered state of consciousness, to feel a sort of warm glow build around him, and a comfortable golden haze, that he usually associated with speechmaking or a particularly good day teaching class. He'd read somewhere that some people would rather face death than address the public in this way.

For him, it was his only real vice.

"I'm a teacher," he confessed jokingly to his listeners, "a college professor. I can't help it, so let's review, shall we? What *is* the FLPA's message?"

Somebody yelled, "Freedom!" Others agreed noisily.

He put a hand up. "Some people might observe tonight, to this particular audience – in this particular place – that I'm preaching to the choir. But my daughter ... " He indicated Faith-Anne with an outstretched hand and people burst into applause and cheering.

" ... my daughter says that the choir are the only individuals who show up for church reliably, and that they deserve to be preached to, if anybody does. So I'll risk boring some of you a little bit by summarizing the beliefs that we of the Free Libertarian Party of America share among ourselves. And then you go out and preach them to somebody *other* than the choir."

He took a deep breath and finally dived in. "Our message – this belief that we all share – consists of two very simple ideas. Two very dangerous ideas in their own way. Or at least King George III thought so."

General, subdued laughter. The sitting president was the third individual named George to occupy that office.

"The first idea is that this nation was built – tacitly, perhaps, implicitly – on the concept of absolute self-ownership. For better or worse, an individual is the exclusive owner – the sole proprietor, if you will

– of his life and of all the products of that life, be those products the sweet fruits of his labors or the bitter smoke from his chimney. The former signifies an individual's rights, the latter, his responsibilities."

That statement got Alex his first real applause of the evening, although it almost certainly wouldn't have done so with any other group, he thought.

"The second idea is that for more than two centuries, the concept of self-ownership has been embodied in and protected by the first 10 amendments to the U.S. Constitution, commonly known as the Bill of Rights."

More applause this time, and some cheering. As usual, his audience consisted mostly of young people – college kids and a handful of high schoolers – and it heartened him. It hadn't been very long since the FLPA had been a graying – dying – group, populated and controlled by those whose interest in politics had originally been kindled in the 60s. And it was said – some people said, anyway – that the change had come because of *Looking Forward,* a book he'd written a few years ago, detailing the ways that stringent enforcement of the Bill of Rights would restore a civilization that was dying, too.

A book he often thought of as having gotten him into this mess.

"One approach, then, lies in reeducating the police and other authorities. They must be brought to understand that the Bill of Rights is not just a laundry list of arbitrary rules that they have to get around somehow in order to do their job. No, no, it is the highest law of the land, and it must be *enforced.*"

He raised his voice and thumped a hard hand on the lectern. The crowd erupted as he knew they would. He'd given minor variations of this speech at least a dozen times so far, and by now he could probably have delivered it in his sleep. That didn't mean he didn't believe in what he was saying – he wouldn't be here if that were the case – it only meant that the unconscious, automatic part of his mind believed what he was saying, too.

And that left another part of his mind free to reflect on the long train of events that had brought him here from his home near Denver, Colorado....

Chapter Four
AMELIA MORROW

> *Some Founding Fathers, like John Adams, were deeply religious. Thomas Jefferson was a "deist" – which is what an 18th century agnostic called himself if he didn't want to be burned alive. Thomas Paine was an atheist, Ben Franklin was a member of the Hellfire Club. A Jew, Haym Salomon, bankrolled the American Revolution. To claim that our counry was founded by Christians alone is to insult the spirit and grandeur of the First Amendment.*
>
> – Alexander Hope, *Looking Forward*

Nobody actually spat on Alex when he came home from Vietnam in 1971. He knew some guys that it had happened to, one serving six months for fracturing the nose and both cheekbones of the spitter with the back of his open hand.

Mostly they just ignored him, out of uniform or in, exactly as they ignored thousands and thousands of his fellow veterans – many of them still teenagers – of a repulsive little war that, even fresh from the heat of it, Alex couldn't make himself believe should ever have been fought.

For a moment Alex looked up and let his eyes

mindlessly follow the foot traffic here in the San Diego Public Library as he attempted *not* to calculate where it would be safe to conceal himself among the ceiling-high racks, and where might be the best place to lay an ambush with crossfire. Didn't those idiots over there by the copy machine know any better than to expose themselves that way? Somebody had told him, on the day he was released from duty, that this would go away eventually. He certainly hoped so, because it was mentally exhausting to deal with.

What the Marine Corps – which in 1969 had bestowed a battlefield commission on him to lieutenant – hadn't known was that he was still a teenager himself. At 13, Alex had lied about his age – what now seemed at least century ago – to get himself a job at Miller's grocery store. Dad had just died of emphysema. Mom had been too distraught to do anything more than just sit at home staring at her dead husband's picture. Dad's pension – he'd been a Union Pacific fireman for 20 years – hadn't quite made ends meet. So Alex had gone to work at Miller's.

He'd let them think he was an undersized 15.

And now here he was, six years later, footloose and fancy-free (or stranded high and dry, depending on how you decided to look at it) here in sunny California, too stiff-necked to feel ashamed of the way that he and his comrades had just spent the last two years of their lives, but at the same time, bitterly disillusioned with the United States government's motives for prosecuting a Southeast Asian war in the first place. Sixty thousand lives wasted – most of them too young to have tasted much of real life – countless more lives forever shattered, And only God knew how many abandoned when the choppers finally fled the jungles, mountains, savannahs, and city streets of Vietnam for the last time.

At the moment – technically still under orders and on termination leave – he was sitting at a long formica-topped study table in a downtown branch of the library, thumbing his way slowly, and without much enthusiasm, through a colorful 18-inch pile of college catalogs, attempting to decide what to do with the remainder of his life. But just at the moment, his eyes were shut. His elbows rested on the smooth, cool tabletop, and his fists against his cheeks. His thoughts kept going back, unbidden, to the insane war that he'd been fighting, unbelievably, only ten days ago.

Ex-President Lyndon Baines Johnson had avoided his own military hitch, putting in a cosmetic and highly-protected six months in the Pacific theater during Work War II before he was conveniently called back to Congress by his mentor, Franklin Delano Roosevelt. Sometimes Alex wished that he were more religious. Truly, he'd enjoy believing Johnson's hairy adipose would eventually end up bubbling, popping, and squeaking in the hottest skillet Hell had to offer.

Whose orders were you "only" following, you alcohol-soaked old butcher?

"Excuse me?" asked a voice, and a very attractive voice, at that. *Oh, no! Had he actually spoken those deliciously seditious thoughts out loud?*

"Er, sorry, Miss." He looked up. A girl – fully as attractive as her voice – was sitting across the table from him, way down at the other end, wearing a pretty, printed summer dress. He wished she were sitting a lot closer. "I was only talking to myself."

"Learn anything you didn't know?" It wouldn't

take him long to learn to love the way her eyes crinkled at their corners when she said something like that. She was tiny, he realized, no more than five feet two, and slender, with a cloud of curly honey-blonde hair around her face. Just now she wore a pair of enormous wire-framed glasses perched on her upturned nose.

He laughed, picked up his college catalogs, and casually – he hoped – moved down the table toward her, carefully staying on his own side. He could see her better that way, anyhow. This was his first prolonged conversation – at least he hoped it was prolonged, and only his first – with a Caucasian female, in over a year.

To his surprise, he noticed as he set his all-but-forgotten books down on the table again, that she didn't have any of her own. What she did have was a long, open-topped box full of paper cards maybe eight inches long and three inches wide. He knew that they were computer cards. She'd been reading them like they were pages in a book. He hadn't known that people could do that.

"I was thinking about Lyndon Johnson," he told her, for lack of anything better to say. Above all else, he knew he didn't want this conversation to end.

Her eyes crinkled again. "Not very politely, I'd guess. Just back from Over There, soldier?"

"Marine," he corrected her automatically. "I'm a Marine. And yes. Last week, in fact." He extended his hand. "I'm Lieutenant – no, *Alexander* Hope."

"Hello, No Alexander Hope. I'm Amelia Morrow." She eyed his college catalogs threatening to topple onto the floor. " Trying to decide what to do with your G.I. Bill, is that what brings you to our esteemed public library?

He liked the way she talked. It sounded like back home, somehow. She certainly didn't sound like a California girl. He liked to watch her mouth work as she talked. Best of all, he liked the way she hadn't asked him if he were related to Bob Hope. He'd seen Bob Hope in 'Nam, on tour for the USO. He could take Bob Hope or leave him. Thanks for the memories.

He nodded, wondering when someone was going to shush them. "How about you?"

"I work across the street." She pointed, but he couldn't make out which office she meant. "It's a zoo over there. I come here to check my cards in peace."

He shook his head in genuine wonder. "You can really read that stuff, Amelia?" He believed he'd never heard such a beautiful name in his life before now. He discovered that he was making one of his famous snap judgements about her character – snap judgements that had seldom betrayed him.

"Yes, Alexander, I can, although we have a new machine on order at the bank that prints the contents of the card along the top edge." She extracted a reel from her oversized purse and unrolled a foot of what was on it. "Paper tape – like for a real skinny player piano?" She laughed with him. "I can read that, too, but you know what?"

The girl's voice dropped to conspiracy level and she leaned in toward him with a look both silly and serious. As she did, she slid a big, square, card-looking thing from her enormous purse. It was manila-colored, with some matte-black something inside, visible through a couple of oddly-shaped holes, and must have been eight inches on a side. "You're looking at the future, Alexander. It's called a 'floppy disk'."

Alex shook his head as if trying to rid himself of ... he didn't know what he was trying to rid himself of. Did Amelia have any idea how irresistibly cute she'd looked when she'd shown him "the future"? She *had* to know.

"Call me Alex." He glanced at his watch – 11:45 – time to take a chance. "Have you had lunch, Amelia?" Then, before she answered, "Will you have lunch with me?"

Her eyes crinkled again, "I'd be pleased to, Alex." He put the catalogs away. She gathered her purse and cards. They left together, and from that moment, they never spent more than 24 hours apart for the next 30 years.

* * * * * *

Even 30 years later, Alex never understood why Amelia had left the library with him that day. The crime rate was horrible, and he might have been some kind of crazy. As it turned out, he *was* some kind of crazy – crazy about Amelia. He'd never known that it was possible to feel this way about another person, and he never really looked at another woman for as long as Amelia lived.

As it happened, Amelia Morrow – soon to become Amelia Morrow Hope – had three great inborn talents. She was good with anything that had anything to do with mathematics. She had a better feel for the future than anyone he'd ever met. And she was an unfailingly accurate judge of character – even better than he was. She told him often afterward that she'd taken one look at him and known with an absolute certainty that he was the man that she would spend the rest of her life with. Nothing mystical about it, she was always careful to add, just an instantaneous preconscious summation of all the factors involved.

"Did you get that bit from *Atlas Shrugged?*" he'd always ask her with a laugh.

She'd always laugh and reply, "No, from Mr. Spock."

Still, Alex never understood why Amelia loved him. He understood precisely – with an absolute certainty – from the first moment that their eyes met, why he loved Amelia. His young bride (a whole six months younger than he was) was both beautiful and brilliant, brimming with untapped talents, with a positive hunger for doing things the right way the first time, and with an energetic enthusiasm that she brought to every aspect of their lives together.

"Look," she told Alex the very first evening, during their first dinner together. He was eating lasagna as if he hadn't had a decent plate of it in years, which happened to be the case. "The people I work for are bankers. They all think that computers are nothing but great big machines for counting things. And they're right – but also, they're wrong. What computers are really for – what they will be for someday – is *communicating*. They're a brand new way of using the telephone that Alexander Graham Bell never dreamed of, and before too long, Alex, everybody will have one."

Alex blinked. He'd read that some expert somewhere had declared that there would never be more than a few dozen computers in the world. Who needed more than that? Now he couldn't help imagining his mother's tiny frame house west of Denver filled from wall to wall with tall metal and glass cabinets with their blinking lights and whirling reels. At least in the summertime she'd enjoy the air conditioning that those monsters couldn't operate without – although how she'd feed the team of PhDs and graduate students needed to keep it running, he couldn't guess.

"I know exactly what you're thinking," she told him, and at least in part, she was right. "The machine I work with is about the size of a large conference table – okay, a *very* large conference table. But only a few years ago, the same machine would have taken up several big rooms and used tens of thousands of vacuum tubes – and it would have been a much, much dumber machine than mine. Every year, Alex, these things get smaller and faster and cheaper."

"And?" He leaned on his elbows and looked at her across the red checkered tablecloth. He loved to hear her talk.

"And if someone *planned* on the assumption that they'd get small enough and cheap enough to buy and use at home, let's say for getting Junior's report card straight from the school, or Grandma's recipe for oyster jelly – "

He sat up. "Yech!"

" – straight from Grandma, or an incriminating picture from the New Year's office party ... "

He nodded enthusiastically. "It'd be like buying Ford stock while Henry was still working on it in the horse barn. Or G.E. when Charles Steinmetz was still..."

"You've got it! Oh, Alex, you're the first person I've ever spoken to who actually got it! By the turn of the century, everybody will do their shopping over some kind of picture-phone-computer network on which merchants will display and describe their goods and services. If someone were to decide right now to become a pioneer in the consumer electronics business – always keeping that future in mind and never swerving from it – then by the time that they'd helped make that future arrive, they'd be rich!"

"Communications, Amelia" Alex asked her with raised eyebrows, seeking confirmation.

"Yes, Alex, communications," she answered.

"Not counting."

"Well, counting, too, Alex, but mostly communications."

"Og understand!" he said in a deep, stupid-sounding voice, and pounded the table. "Og start chipping floppy disk! Have *many* floppy disk when millennium arrive!"

She laughed.

He laughed.

They laughed and laughed together until dawn.

CHAPTER FIVE
FAITH-ANNE HOPE

> *You can't repeal the Second Amendment, any more than you can repeal any of the other nine. It was a package deal, you see, an absolute prerequisite to ratifying the main body of the Constitution. Repeal one, you repeal them all. Do that, and you repeal the whole Constitution – and with it, any legal authority that the government has to exist (let alone repeal the Second Amendment).*
>
> – Alexander Hope, *Looking Forward*

Amelia said, "And do you know what they told me?"

For Alex, the process would always feel like surfing.

"They told me what you always tell me – that moving parts are the enemy! They told me we could be having memory without any moving parts in as little as 10 years!"

Alex snorted. He'd heard that kind of talk before. This time it was something called "bubble memory". He'd believe it when he could hold it in his hand – having bought it for a buck a meg. He hated moving parts, and did consider them the enemy, but for now everybody was stuck with them, and probably would be for some time to come.

He told her so. As always, she listened and (not quite as always) eventually agreed with him. He and Amelia had quickly found their way to the leading curl of the technological wave and had slid right to the top, ten toes hanging over the edge of the future, usually by making the right decisions together.

Amelia would go and talk to her fellow "nerds" everywhere they were to be found in those days, crunching numbers for downtown banks, sorting people for universities, waiting until the smallest possible hours of the morning for share-time on the big machines for their own pet projects.

Everywhere Amelia went, she listened to her colleagues gripe or dream, and then she and Alex would turn those gripes and dreams into ideas for products that made life a little easier for the nerds, while pushing technical progress more and more toward the direction – communication – that she'd outlined for him in the very beginning.

"Okay, then," she sighed, "how about this?" As usual, they were sitting up in bed, with Johnny Carson on the *Tonight Show* making in-jokes that only he and Ed McMahon were laughing at, her steno pad between them, filled with scribbling and doodling it had taken him two years to learn to read.

The programmers and techies that she'd been talking to tonight – programmers and techies who were always ready to talk to a pretty girl because they hardly ever got to see one – had been stealing computer time to play a game that was sweeping the cybernetic underground from coast to coast, loosely based on television's *Star Trek*, a show both Alex and

Amelia had watched ardently and avidly before its perplexing cancellation, and still felt considerable kinship with They believed that they were on a kind of trek, themselves.

Just now they were trying to figure out how to market such a game to a general public who were acquainted only with much simpler items like Pong, the popular new electronic table-tennis game. The trouble was that games like Pong were played, for the most part, in bars and restaurants, or they were smuggled in to play on company computers at work. Very few individuals had computers at home.

"Talk to a couple of programmers," he suggested to Amelia. "Maybe we can have something ready – already written – when the right home machine comes along. I don't think it's going to be that Sinclair thing we looked at yesterday."

The couple's first commercial product had been a new kind of paper tape (they'd found it being used for something else altogether in the textiles industry) that took cleaner punches and was several times more tear-resistant. They'd been about to produce similarly improved punch cards, when Amelia had pulled the plug on that project, and at the same time had adroitly avoided cornering the world supply of eight-inch floppy disks.

Instead, what they now called the Hope Corporation (Amelia had designed a logo using the head and winged shoulders of the flying horse Pegasus) became one of the first commercial enterprises to market five-and-a-quarter-inch floppies.

By this time, however, their main interest was in modems – for "modulator-demodulator" – the backbone of computer communications. Together, they clung to the leading edge of that wave, too, from 300 baud acoustic couplers, through 1200, 2400, 4800, 9600 baud, on up to 14.4, 28.8, 33.6, and 56.2 kilobyte devices. Their little corporation sold communication cards and other kinds of network equipment, and quietly underwrote research in unbreakable encryption. Amelia's original aim was refined: not just computer communication, but communication for private individuals that no government, or anybody else, could ever intercept or interfere with.

Their unusual partnership allowed them to enjoy each other to the fullest. Amelia did the "research" on midnight excursions deep into electronics-filled basements and 24-hour coffee bars all over the region, where a whole new kind of life was being lived on the frontier of what would eventually be called "cyberspace". Southern California was getting to be a more dangerous and crime-filled place to live in every year, so Alex started going with her

Once Amelia told him what to look for, Alex went out and found the product that seemed called for, often by combining items of technology from unrelated areas that had no one had ever put together. More and more frequently, he and Amelia set unheard-of specifications and had new technology created that had never existed before.

Finally, they ventured out into the field together to sell their wares, turning their sales trips into second, third, fourth, or fifth honeymoons. Alex jokingly reckoned that in their first 10 years together, they swam in every motel swimming pool from Fairbanks to Key West and from Tijuana to St. John's, Newfoundland. It had been too cold to swim when they went to England, but they'd taken a hovercraft to see the Roman ruins on the Isle of Wight. Amelia argued that with their mosaics, the Romans had invented the idea of pixels.

Years before that, Alex had earned a bachelor's degree in history on an ROTC scholarship. Subsequently he'd earned his master's degree in the military, through correspondence courses with the University of Maryland. And as they were building their business together, Amelia had made him stay in school. After all, that was how they'd met, she insisted; and it was always important to finish things.

He'd made the mistake, he often joked, of telling her about two men in his company in Vietnam who'd been "Black Muslims", but went on *Hegira* – the religious pilgrimage prescribed by Mohammed – and become full-fledged Moslems. They'd told him that the Prophet had proclaimed, whatever a man's station in life, be he a prince or a pauper, that he should acquire a second trade to keep him centered in the real world. Many years later, Alex had found out that the Prophet had actually meant a manual trade, but by then, thanks to his Amelia and the G.I. Bill, he had a doctorate in history.

Every year, Alex discovered that he loved Amelia more, and he correctly believed that she felt the same way about him. Every year, he enjoyed being married to her more, and although it soon appeared that they would never have children, to them, that was only another reason to keep trying in all of those motel honeymoon suites across the continent.

Every year they made more money, identifying problems, inventing solutions, and selling the result – watching cyberspace expand around them like the Big Bang universe, until nearly everybody they knew seemed to be involved in it.

At the same time that they seemed to be getting richer faster and easier all the time – in ten years their fledgling Hope Corporation went from a smelly, black-widow-infested garage in the back yard of Amelia's maiden aunt's house, to a corrugated metal rental structure in an industrial park just outside the city limits, to a modest office suite in downtown San Diego, to an entire floor in the second tallest building in the city, finally to their own tall, ultramodern edifice with copper-tinted windows in a wholly new high-tech community – it seemed to get harder and nastier in other ways.

It wasn't just that there were local police officials and building inspectors and others like them who had to bribed on a regular basis if they wanted to stay in business. In his youth – and especially after seeing the way that things worked in Southeast Asia – Alex had considered himself a man of the world, enured to a moderate amount of graft and political corruption.

But what got under his skin from the beginning were the "political reformers", mostly in the legislature up north, later on in Congress, who believed that they had some right (and regrettably did have the power) to tell him who he could and couldn't hire – so many of this color, so many of that nationality, so many of this sex, so many of that age – absolutely without regard to whether they could do the job or even speak the language.

Before he knew it, thugs with three-piece suits, hardhats, and clipboards were invading his offices and shops without any kind of Constitutional warrant, prying into everything from office chairs to air-conditioners, forcing him to install special facilities for those whose physical disabilities made them unqualified to do anything more than make coffee for everybody else – for which he was fined when it was discovered. He was also fined if a bathroom sink happened to be an inch too high or too low, or if a toilet held too many gallons in its tank, or if an extension cord was visible on the floor behind a desk, or if a concrete column in the second sub-basement was painted an unauthorized color.

He was even fined because the air in his building had too many molecules of various "hazardous" chemicals (mostly from the Xerox machine), although it contained less than ten percent of the same chemicals that were to be found in the air outside.

When he pointed out that – in order to comply with the government imposed hiring quotas – he'd have to fire great numbers of blacks, Asians, Hispanics, and women, nobody wanted to hear it. Or they simply threatened him with hostile inspections and audits, making it clear that *something* would be found that would allow them to shut him down for good, if he didn't simply shut up and do as he was told. In their bureaucratic arrogance, they didn't seem to care that then there would be no jobs for anybody.

Somewhere along the line, Alex began to sense a growing ... well, one could only call it envious resentment, in those around him and Amelia. But of what? Of the 16-hour days they had put in for decades? Of the risks they'd taken, often with everything they possessed? No, all of that was somehow overlooked and set aside. What people envied, and resented them for, were the *results* of all that effort, as if the results had simply materialized out of thin air, and the effort itself had never been expended,

What surprised, dismayed, and angered him most was *who* it was that seemed to be doing the resenting. The so-called city fathers didn't disturb him. They were nothing more than a dreary collection of tax-consuming parasites who couldn't have been elected to be cesspool cleaners if the voters had known the least fact regarding their lives and careers. They were constantly at him, accepting the gifts he gave the city – parks, playgrounds, libraries, even a giant concert hall, intended mostly for his employees – while viciously attacking the profits that made such gifts possible.

But that wasn't what astonished him. After all, what was politics itself, but a process of stealing what people earned or created, and then giving it to those who were incapable of earning, or unwilling to earn, for themselves? No, not welfare mothers, but the bureaucrats who spied on them and handed out the checks.

There were his many competitors and fellow businessmen who made it worse for everybody by being everything that Karl Marx might ever have accused them of (several made a practice of finding pretexts to fire senior workers near their 19th anniversary, to avoid paying them their full pensions), while simultaneously sucking up to the very politicos who pretended, publicly – especially around election day – to be their class enemies, but played golf and went to cocktail parties with them the rest of the year.

Alex didn't play golf. He and Amelia went hunting, mostly in Wyoming, and didn't talk about it in San Diego.

No, what bothered Alex most were his own ungrateful, brainwashed employees, people he'd thought enjoyed working for him, but who had organized a labor union against him, and then found every possible excuse as individuals to sue him and his corporation for everything from on-the-job-hang-nails to the sexual inequality "implied" by his having provided them with separate bathrooms. On the day that the Hope Corporation was reported by the media to have made its first billion dollars (strictly on paper – everything was tied up in inventory and "receivables") the number of these evil, bloodsucking lawsuits had quadrupled.

Always, his lawyers advised him to settle.

Always he refused to give in to blackmail.

Usually, he won.

Even so, Alex soon began to regret not having gotten his college degrees in the law. He also regretted having chosen to start their business here in California where they'd met, especially since Amelia was no more a Californian than he was. He'd been born and raised in Morrison, Colorado, a little town just west of Denver best known for having given its name to a geological layer full of dinosaur bones stretching from Canada to Mexico.

Amelia had been born and grown up in Laramie, Wyoming.

Both of them considered themselves westerners, and understood perfectly that California wasn't a western state at all, but a colony of the socialist east coast – or of some European communist police state.

And then, in the spring of 1980, everything changed.

One Sunday morning, Amelia had awakened

him, informing him she had coffee waiting for them in the living room. He put on a bathrobe and followed her. By now they had a roomy apartment with an ocean view that they used as much for work as for living. However this Sunday, they'd vowed to swear off work altogether and go see the ocean liner *Queen Mary,* anchored permanently in Long Beach, and Howard Hughes' gigantic seaplane the *Spruce Goose,* something they'd talked about doing for years but had never done.

Amelia let him drink his first big cup of coffee and his second. Then she'd taken his hand gently, saying, "Come here, darling, there's something I want to show you in the bathroom. He'd gone, having no idea what she was up to – and why the bathroom? – and what she'd shown him was a pregnancy test.

"When I missed my period, I took the test the first time just to see. That was yesterday. This was to make sure." She threw her arms around him. "Alex, you're gonna be a daddy!"

For every one of the nine years that they'd been married, Alex had believed that the happiest day of his life – the happiest day that could ever possibly *be* in his life – was the first day that he'd made love to Amelia.

He discovered now that he was wrong.

Their tiny baby daughter had been born early in December of 1980. They'd brought her home, placed her under the Christmas tree, and taken pictures of her that they'd always treasure. Their Christmas present to themselves, she was, not nine months in the making, but nine long, hopeful years.

They'd named their little girl for Alex's mother Faith – still back in Morrison but planning to fly out as soon as possible – and for Amelia's mother Anne, dead for the past five years. She'd known Alex (and never quite decided if she approved of him, he thought) but would never know the granddaughter whom she would have adored and spoiled thoroughly.

Having watched with a kind of slow-motion horror what had become of government education in the state of California – propaganda camps for socialism and breeding grounds for illiterate criminals – they vowed that their little Faith-Anne would never so much as set foot in one of them.

Over the next years, however, any thoughts they'd had of leaving California had gotten set aside, somehow, and Faith-Anne gradually became an integral part of the family business, contributing ideas that were increasingly less childish, and startling people who didn't know her (and even some who did) with her wisdom and maturity. Friends who were enthusiastic about Frank Herbert's **Dune** half-jokingly called her an "abomination".

Eventually, one of her precocious ideas developed into a highly popular combination home cordless and cellular telephone that made the Hopes ten times as wealthy as they had been (and earned them ten times the resentment from the media and politicians). Faith-Anne finished UCLA at 16 and, recognizing the family's vulnerability, went on from there to law school.

For Alex, it seemed only a moment between those happy successes (and the struggles that went with them) and the sudden loss of Amelia in 2001, to breast cancer. For three decades, she had given all of her bright energy to his life. She had also given him any meaning his life had ever possessed. For a year afterward, the only thing that kept him from simply joining Amelia in death was his only child, his grown daughter, Faith-Anne.

Then he had an idea. Faith-Anne had inherited all of her mother's sharp-minded business sense. The company didn't mean as much to him as it had before. In fact, without Amelia, it meant nothing. Therefore – in a move harshly criticized from coast to coast in newspapers and trade journals – Alex handed control of the Hope Corporation over to his 21-year-old daughter.

And moved back to Colorado.

Chapter Six: *CHANCELLOR VAN CLEAVE*

> *The Second Amendment was written expressly to intimidate government officials and keep them in their place. The fact that politicians and bureaucrats, regardless of their party, detest it and want it obliterated proves that it works.*
>
> – Alexander Hope, *Looking Forward*

It had been six years and it still hurt every day.

If anyone had ever thought to ask Alex, before Amelia died, what she meant to him, he would immediately have told them "everything". And he'd have meant it. And he'd have been right. But before Amelia died, he hadn't known what "everything" meant.

He found, after she was gone, that he unconsciously associated Amelia with his "rebirth". The world before he'd been shipped off to Vietnam didn't seem real to him – it hadn't seemed real a month after he'd arrived in Southeast Asia. Emerging again into the bright, noisy, colorful "real" world of the United States, of southern California, of a new business, and above all, of Amelia, Vietnam no longer seemed real.

Alex had been literally living a new life.

And now that life was over, because the partner,

the lover, the best friend he'd lived that life with – the scent of her hair, the sound of her voice, of her laugh, the face that he adored and had come to know better than his own – was gone. All that Alex could see ahead of himself now was bleak and one-dimensional – a cold, gray world of overcast and ashes.

For a longer time than he thought possible, Alex went through a process in which – regarding some event at work, regarding a movie or a piece of music, regarding something he'd seen in a newspaper or heard on the radio – his first reflexive thought, a habit of 30 years, would be, "Just wait'll I tell Amelia!"

Then, before that thought was quite completed, the unthinkable truth, the unbearable truth (no adjective was adequate) would hit him, and it was a little like losing her all over again – although not quite as bad as waking up every morning, expecting her to be there, and discovering in a heartbeat that she wasn't and never would be again.

Alex had fled the west coast and the memories it evoked without very much thought about where he would go or what he would do. Almost instinctively – like a salmon or a migrating bird, he thought – he'd headed back home. There wasn't much objective reason to do that. Both of his parents had died years ago. He had no brothers or sisters. And somebody had subdivided the foothills he'd wandered happily as a boy, .22 rifle hanging from his hand, following his dog after rabbits and rattlesnakes. There was only his folks' little frame house in Morrison that he'd held onto, mostly out of sentiment.

And that was it.

Of course he didn't have to *do* anything. As the wheels of his corporation's LearJet had touched down on the asphalt at Jefferson County Airport (Denver International Airport, far to the east of the capital city, was nothing but a monument to political arrogance and corruption; he avoided it whenever he could), his daughter had called him by internet video to inform him that his net personal worth had just crossed the billion dollar mark.

Alex would have given every cent of it – and gone a billion times further into debt – to have Amelia back. But to whom do you make an offer like that? He wished he knew. He'd have made it to the Devil himself, if he'd believed in the Devil. He looked out the little airplane's window as it taxied to a rental hangar without seeing what was outside.

"Now you're absolutely sure you're going to be all right, Daddy?" Faith-Anne asked him in their personal realtime chat area, hidden securely within the depths of the Hope Corporation website. Her expression on the laptop screen before him was worried. "Isn't there anything I can do for you?"

Was there anything *she* could do for *him?* Suddenly, Alex felt hideously guilty for abandoning his little girl to fend for herself at the corporation headquarter in San Diego. After all, Amelia had been her mother, and Faith-Anne's loss was at least as great as his – in all probability, far greater. Although their Faith-Anne was 21, and an unusually mature 21 at that, at this particular moment, her father kept seeing her in his mind at age four, all orange pigtails and freckles, valiantly fighting back tears when she'd taken a spill at the local ice skating rink.

"Nothing, dear, thank you", he spoke softly into his laptop – a product of his company, ironically, a model called the "Amelia" – as the jet slipped into what was now the Hope Corporation hangar. It was all he could think of to say to her, although he desperately wished it could be more. "Come see me when you can, Boss."

"LOL", she replied, a very old internet expression meaning "laughing out loud".

He'd taken the company car he'd arranged to be there, a 1999 peacock blue Dodge Durango with the restrained Hope Corporation logo stenciled on the doors in yellow. From the hangar, he'd driven himself from just northwest of Denver to just southwest. He'd always hated I-25 where it passed through the city, but there wasn't much choice. On the other hand, catching sight of Coors Field, home of his beloved Blake Street Bums, always seemed to cheer him up. To him, they were the home team. He'd never really felt at home in San Diego.

But Alex had never been suited to inaction, and doing nothing only made him dwell on his unbearable loss. Amelia wouldn't have liked that, not at all.

Alex had arranged for power, gas, and water to be turned on during the flight out here. He'd picked up some groceries at the local King Soopers (Miller's was long gone.) and mooched around the modest two bedroom house he'd grown up in for less than 72 hours before he decided that there had to be more to life than sitting here and watching the hairsprayed mouth-breathers on Denver's various TV news broadcasts make even bigger idiots of themselves than they were already. They wouldn't have lasted another day on the air if only 10 percent of their viewership had even the most elementary education in subjects like logic, economics, Constitutional law, history –

Suddenly, he knew what he had to do!

He glanced at his wristwatch – an original Omega Speedmaster Professional with a winged horse engraved on the back – a gift from Amelia on their 10th anniversary. There was a lot of history, one way or another, associated with that watch. It was too late today. He'd start first thing in the morning.

Amelia would have loved this!

* * * * * *

Gallatin Memorial College suited Alex perfectly.

It was private, conservative-leaning-to-libertarian, and small. It had originally been constructed from native sandstone well outside the city limits, just about a century ago, but now found itself entirely surrounded by quiet, green, tree-shaded residential communities. Best of all, it was here on the west side of the city, less than ten miles from his boyhood home in Morrison.

Taking no chances, he'd called his daughter the same evening he'd had his idea. "Faith-Anne? Hi, honey. I'm just fine – or as well as can be expected, anyway. You're doing your hair differently, aren't you? Look, kiddo, I guess that there's something I want you to do for me, after all."

Delighted, she'd tried to fill him in on the details of current company operations, but he didn't care, and he wasn't very subtle about saying so. He had every confidence in her, and he had this idea he found himself suddenly excited about – when he'd thought that he'd never feel excited about anything again.

"Okay, Daddy, shoot!" Faith-Anne had every confidence in him, as well, and on top of everything else, she still called him "Daddy", a title he felt he'd earned and was far prouder of than other titles he'd worn,

"Sergeant", "First Lieutenant", "Chairman of the Board", "President and CEO".

"Okay, kiddo, I want you to use one of the dummy corporations I had set up – I think the Ralston Foundation would be a little too blatant; use something else; make it up if you have to – to endow an academic position at Gallatin Memorial College west of Denver. Here are the details ... "

Faith-Anne was good at details, just like her mother. And unlike her mother, she was also a lawyer. Together, by phone and laptop for the next two hours, they revised and refined the qualifications of the endowment until they had become so narrow they could only fit one man: Alexander Hope, PhD.

For the next two weeks, as half a dozen grey-suited, power-tied, briefcase-wielding attorneys for a California something-or-other that called itself the Thomas Paine Scholastic Foundation arrived at Denver International Airport and helicoptered across the city to bestow its corporate largesse upon the astonished administration of Albert Gallatin Memorial College, Alex allowed himself the first real vacation he'd taken in 30 years.

Thinking of Amelia every step of the way – showing her the sights of his hometown as if she were walking with him or sitting in the car beside him – he went off to see the Denver Zoo, the Natural History Museum, the Botanical Gardens, and the tall, gray art museum he could remember as a kid. He even went to see the new ocean aquarium and the Butterfly Pavilion and the poor, pale ghosts of Elitch's Gardens and Lakeside Amusement Park.

He drove the peacock blue Durango, and his memories of Amelia, down to Colorado Springs to see the Air Force Academy, Cheyenne Mountain Zoo, the Will Rogers Memorial, the former home of Robert A. Heinlein, the Rodeo Cowboy Museum, the cliff dwellings, Seven Falls, the Bug Museum (where he thought about getting himself a cute, furry, pet wolf spider – and then rejected the idea; the only thing in the world that terrified Faith-Anne was spiders), and the Cave of the Winds. He found that he missed the Clock Museum, which had been shut down many years ago, and what he'd always called the Hall of the Wax Presidents.

He even saw a couple of Rockies games, both of which they lost.

And finally, it was time.

One morning he got up, showered, shaved, ate a healthy breakfast, put slacks on instead of the jeans he'd grown used to again, found a conservative shirt and tie, a professorly corduroy jacket with leather elbow patches, and went to claim the job he'd created for himself. One of many bright spots: nobody at conservative Albert Gallatin Memorial College would be offended when he drove a great big peacock blue SUV into their parking lot.

* * * * * *

"*The* Alexander Hope?" As in, *the* Howard Hughes, or *the* Bill Gates.

"Dr. Van Cleave," Alex told the man behind the desk, "I assure you that I don't expect to be treated any differently than any other applicant."

On the wall behind the fellow's desk there hung an enormous color photograph of the damaged Apollo XIII service module. Alex didn't know what that flight meant to Van Cleave, but it had always been important to him as the supreme example of courage under fire and the ability to "think on one's feet".

The Chancellor of Albert Gallatin Memorial College, and the head of its philosophy department was a tall, thin man of about Alex's own age, with snow white hair, a beard, and a moustache that belied his otherwise youthful appearance. Surprisingly, the man wore cargo slacks and a tan bush jacket.

"But you're a unique individual, Mr. Hope – "

"Call me Alex."

"Alex, then. You're a unique individual, Alex. You *have* to be treated differently – and so does everybody else." He glanced through Alex's papers once again, those associated with his three degrees in history, as well as perhaps the briefest resume he'd ever seen. It mentioned Alex's educational background, the Marines, and the Hope Corporation.

"Besides," the Chancellor went on, "we have something that may interest you. It's an endowed chair in history, but it has to be given to a man with a military background who's also been successful in business."

"Which is defined as ... ?" Alex knew perfectly well.

"Having made," Van Cleave grinned at him, and Alex knew that the man understood exactly what was happening here, "more than a billion dollars."

Alex grinned back. "Would you care to see my Dun & Bradstreet or my tax returns?"

* * * * * *

The college catalog referred to it as "The Meaning and Spirit of the American Revolution."

After teaching the course for five years, Alex had been surprised and delighted to learn that it was one of the most popular classes on campus.

Of course Albert Gallatin Memorial College was no ordinary campus. Still, it pleased him that they'd had to find a larger venue for this section every year, and that the young faces in the first several rows continued to be bright and eager.

"Today, ladies and gentlemen" he opened a book he wouldn't look at again for the next hour, leaned over the lectern, and told them – all 250 of them – "is the fifth anniversary of my arrival here at Gallatin Memorial, as well as the fifth anniversary presenting this class, which, in turn, was a major reason for my wanting to teach at Gallatin in the first place."

They occupied what used to be a dissection theater, a splendid hall from another era, built of golden oak, with a 60-foot skylighted ceiling, brick floors, and granite tabletops. Before him, the seats rose in a horseshoe shape and stadium-style, for 30 rows. Then there was a balcony with another 10 rows. Students entered there, or through doors on the landing beneath the balcony on either side of the hall. There were doors behind him, as well – for a fast getaway, he always joked – at either end of a wonderful set of enormous blackboards made of genuine slate in several oak-framed layers, sliding up and over one another. The acoustics were absolutely perfect. There was no need for a microphone, or even to raise his voice.

"A lot of individuals these days," he said, "both in academia and politics, pretend to have difficulty understanding what the Founding Fathers meant when they wrote the Constitution, and especially the Bill of Rights."

He heard a sort of rustle go through the class as they settled down to listen. At that, it was a lot better, he thought, than hearing them snore.

"It seems to me that you have to be desperate to advance your political agenda – pathetically desperate – if you're willing to appear so dullwitted and ignorant that you're unable to comprehend the clearest thinking and the cleanest writing ever, in the history of the English language."

He'd once read through the Declaration of Independence, inspired by H.L. Mencken's silly 1920s street-slang translation of it, with an eye toward rendering it more accessible to the 21st century ear. What a mistake that had been. He hadn't been able to think of a single substitute for the common – and uncommonly beautiful – words that Thomas Jefferson had chosen, even as tweaked painfully afterward by the Continental Congress.

"So for the benefit of mental malingerers like that, as well as our own, for just a minute, let's put ourselves where the Founders found themselves after the Revolution and see if we can't figure out for ourselves just what they were getting at."

He stepped out from behind the table where his book lay and began pacing slowly in front of it.

"Let's give it a try: following a 20-year cold war, and a shooting war that lasted for nine years, you've just completely flabbergasted yourself, and everybody else in the world, by humiliating the regular military and the mercenary forces of the most powerful and ruthless empire the world has ever witnessed, a culture that has pretended for centuries to be the most refined and genteel civilization known to mankind, but which has raped and pillaged and enslaved its way across the face of this poor, suffering planet since Henry Cabot rediscovered Newfoundland in 1497."

Alex always enjoyed throwing that in. Newfoundland had been the very first dominion of the British Empire, founded in 1688 by Sir Cavendish Boyle – the funniest name Alex had ever heard. He and Amelia had been to Cabot Tower on one of their sales trips, a big stone chess rook of a building, standing on a coastal hill high above old St. John's, from which Guglielmo Marconi had sent his first historic wireless signal in 1901.

That had been a good trip. His mind returned to Colorado, and the present. "Now, Founding Fathers and Mothers, you find yourself writing a document – the basic legal foundation for your new country – hoping to make sure that the abuses of power that caused you to fight the Revolution to begin with can never happen again.

"Let's start with what's often regarded as the most outdated and least important of the first 10 amendments to the Constitution, commonly known as the Bill of Rights, the Third Amendment, which forbids the quartering of troops in people's homes in times of peace, or in times of war 'but in a manner to be prescribed by law' – which necessarily implies just compensation; considering the nature of the 18th century practice, that pretty much precludes quartering of any kind under any circumstances.

"If you're the "beneficiary" of this kind of government attention, you can bet that your livestock will be slaughtered first, to feed the troops you're quartering, or herded off to grace some officer's estate, along with any rolling stock – wagons or carriages – you have. At the same time, your crops will be pulled from the ground – even if they're not ready it will deny them to the enemy – and your orchards cut down for firewood.

"Of course all of your furniture and personal property will meet similar fates, the smaller items – the gold locket with hand-cut silhouettes of your mother and father – vanishing into the voluminous bulk of the military uniforms of the time, the larger items hauled away to that officer's estate, on your wagons, pulled by the oxen you'll never see again.

"But that's only the least of it. And you can pretty much expect your daughters, your sisters, your aunts, your wife, and even your mother to be bringing more English babies into the world in a few months – that is, if they aren't simply beaten to death, or gutted from crotch to sternum by British bayonets, once they've been used by the officers and thrown to the troops afterward."

He always listened for a reaction at this point, and was usually rewarded with a few gasps or groans, followed by a shocked silence. Over the past two centuries, British redcoats had almost become friendly figures, like Canadian Mounties, or Smokey the Bear, instead of the European-style army of rape and pillage that they were.

"Remember, we're not speaking of Nazis, here, or of Cossacks, or even of the Mongol Horde. We're talking about the "kindest, gentlest" empire in the world. Does the Third Amendment seem so obsolete and insignificant now?"

Murmuring, of a sort that told him he'd gotten through, filled the room.

"Okay, then, maybe you're ready for this one.

If you'd just been through all of this – you, your

neighbors, and friends – would you write yourself a Second Amendment guaranteeing a right to own and carry weapons to a state-approved militia? Or would you try to safeguard the natural and inherent right of any human being to defend yourself and your family *against* the state – no matter who disapproved of it or how hard they tried to twist and distort your words and intentions afterward?"

Somebody yelled, "You bet your ass I would!" Alex suppressed an unprofessorly grin. He knew who the shouter was and would deal with him appropriately later on. When the laughter had finally died down, he went on.

"Obviously, at least one of those among us has learned something from history. Now despite all of the sighs and lies of the so-called news media, despite the blithering of Hollywood "personalities" so empty of mind and spirit they have to be filled with other people's words and ideas – and even movements from place to place on a set – despite the posturing of a judiciary that's a national disgrace and desperately in need of scouring out with flamethrower and firehose, despite all of that, anyone who holds to the former interpretation of the Second Amendment, and denies the latter, simply admits to the world that he's ignorant, stupid, crazy, or every bit as evil as the English atrocities that forced the Bill of Rights to be written in the first place."

He closed the book before him.

"No formal assignment today, ladies and gentlemen. Go home and think about what I've said."

CHAPTER SEVEN:
THE AUSTRIAN MAFIA

> *Any politician who won't trust you with the weapon of your choice clearly cannot be trusted with the power he desires over your life.*
>
> – Alexander Hope, *Looking Forward*

"You want to *what?*"

Sitting at his desk, Alex peered up over his reading glasses at his four favorite – and brightest – students, who had crowded themselves into his tiny office. In a transparent attempt to flatter him, each of them carried a copy of *Looking Forward,* the book he'd written his first year here at Gallatin Memorial. He wondered where they'd come by their copies. The book was currently "O.P." – meaning "out of print".

Before him, spread across the blotter, was his lunch: an open tin of difficult-to-get tiny sardines, packed in two layers in soy bean oil (these days, most of the sardines you could buy in grocery stores were big enough to reel in on a hook and line), a box of saltines, and a plastic screw-topped bottle of Coca-Cola.

Now if only this cubicle had room enough for his four young guests to sit down. As it was, the quarters were so close that they probably couldn't *fall* down. At least he had a window, looking out at "garden level" onto the college commons. (In the summertime, a classical Greek play was always performed here, invariably billed as "The Tragedy of the Commons"; it was an economists' joke.) That window was the only thing that kept him from believing that his office had once been a broom closet.

Ernie Hanover answered him. "I was just listening to the MP3 recording I made the other day of your lecture on the Third Amendment – I wanted to preserve whatever version of it you delivered on your fifth anniversary here. Professor Hope, nobody else has your unique take on history and the issues of the day. We want to nominate you for President!"

Ernie was an energetic, perpetually pink-faced young man with short, curly hair that wasn't quite red. Uncaring of current fashion, he wore bleeding Madras shirts he must have inherited from his grandfather, black rimmed glasses, and hushpuppies, Unlike most people who rattled on at 300 words a minute, he almost always made sense.

This time, his history professor thought, might prove to be an exception.

Alex mused out loud. "President? Of Albert Gallatin Memorial College? When we already have a fine Chancellor in the person of Dr. Van Cleave? You know we don't do things democratically here, Ernie. Is this an armed mutiny? Are you aware of what a good shot Chancellor Van Cleave happens to be? We've been antelope hunting together, and believe me, I know."

He raised his right hand, made a pistol of it, pointed it at Ernie, and dropped the hammer – his thumb – simulating recoil.

Ernie clutched his chest and groaned dramatically.

"No, no, Professor Hope!" Katie Harris shook her head. She was a pretty brunette with fascinating eyes, bouncy ringlets around her face, too sexy a voice for someone of her years, and the highest grades in any of his classes. She was usually quick on the uptake, and would someday be valedictorian, but she didn't seem to understand that he was joking with them now. "President of the United States!"

Alex had seen the local news this morning. (He usually turned the sound off and turned the closed captions on; for some reason it was easier to take that way.) He knew exactly what they'd meant. He even had a pretty good idea what they were up to.

Together, these four and a small handful of others constituted what everybody on campus referred to as the "Austrian Mafia". On their own time, they all studied and discussed the ideas and works of the famous Austrian-school economists Ludwig von Mises, Friedrich Hayek, and Murray Rothbard. Sometimes they would publicly debate the equally ardent followers of "Chicago monetarists" like Milton Friedman, whom the Austrian Mafia infuriated to insanity by loftily dismissing as "Neo-NeoKeynesians."

"Are you involved in this conspiracy, Mr. Thomas, Mr. Douglas?

Rick Thomas and Mick Douglas – commonly known as "Rick and Mick" – nodded their heads enthusiastically. "Guilty as charged!" Mick told him, grinning from ear to ear. He was a broad-shouldered kid with a crewcut and would likely have been on the football team, if Gallatin had had one. Instead, he played tennis and golf, games Alex didn't care for or understand the appeal of.

"With oak leaf clusters!" Rick agreed. He was the oldest, having served in the Air Force before starting school. Rick was a fifth year undergraduate creating his own course in "praxeology", a formal study of "human action" of which Austrian economics was a part. With long, prematurely white hair, he was the usual ringleader when these four were up to no good. "And with a Republican candidate apparently up to his neck in some kind of internet nastiness, and a Democrat candidate who happens to be the most thoroughly hated woman in America, you might even stand a chance, if we can get you the nomination."

"And how do you propose to accomplish that?" Alex asked, although he knew perfectly well. These were good kids, he thought. There was more character in this room than in the entire state legislature.

"At the Free Libertarian Party of America's National Convention," Rick said.

"This coming Labor Day weekend," Mick added.

"Right here in Denver!" Ernie shouted.

"Be there," said Katie, "or be – "

"Somewhere else," Alex finished for her, forked a sardine onto a cracker, salted it, and took an icy swig of Coke to wash it down.

* * * * * *

Alex had only been to one political party convention before, in 1964, when he was 12 years old. He'd spent part of that summer with an aunt and uncle. Among other adventures he'd had with them, they'd taken him to the Alabama state Republican Party convention that had helped place Senator Barry Goldwater's name in nomination as the GOP candidate for president.

He could still recall Goldwater's stirring words (which he learned later were written by Karl Hess) spoken at the GOP national convention that year: "Extremism in the defense of liberty is no vice. Moderation in the pursuit of justice is no virtue." He also recalled the squeals of outrage those words had elicited from network commentators and Goldwater's most bitter enemies – liberal Republicans. Alex even had some campaign buttons from that year – one said "Goldwater-Miller", another, "AuH2O" – and an unopened can of "Gold Water", a lemon-lime drink of some kind, he'd always assumed.

The candidate himself hadn't been in Alabama (Alex had almost seen him the following September in Denver; his parents, both Democrats, had forbidden it). His Republican uncle joked for years afterward that Alex's father had warned him if he voted for "that insane warmonger" Goldwater, America would end up in a land war in Asia. Sure enough, his uncle had voted for Goldwater (Lyndon Johnson had been elected in a 60-40 landslide), and that's exactly what had happened in Asia. So much for conventional wisdom.

Alex could still remember the giant concrete indoor arena, most of it underground, in which that state party convention had been held. He recalled the noise and the music, the bright lights and the bunting, the balloons and the bumper stickers – and thousands of individuals gathered together for the first time, every one of them hot, sweaty, and exhausted (in a building which wasn't air-conditioned), but filled to bursting with enthusiasm and good cheer, looking forward to a future they believed would restore ownership and control of their own lives to them.

Now, to Alex's disappointment, this convention wasn't anything like that. It was being put on in a hotel ballroom in downtown Denver. Most of the attendees were over 50, graying, bored, and tired of life by appearances, still going through the motions for reasons they probably couldn't have articulated. Now that he thought about it, he knew dozens of individuals who'd been active in the FLPA and dropped out, including his own daughter and the Chancellor of Albert Gallatin Memorial College.

Looking around, he began to understand why, and wondered, all of a sudden, if he was doing the right thing. The Free Libertarian Party of America had been around since 1971 and had never won more than 900,000 votes for its presidential candidate – most of the time it was less than half of that. Everybody he saw looked as if they understood that nothing revolutionary was happening here today, nothing revolutionary had ever happened here, and nothing revolutionary was ever going to happen.

A conspicuous exception seemed to be the Austrian Mafia: Katie Harris, Ernie Hanover, Rick Thomas, Mick Douglas, and a handful of friends their own age, who greeted them delightedly as they entered the hotel.

Wandering through the high-ceilinged hotel lobby with his favorite students, Alex was shown a dozen sales tables laden with political pamphlets, books, magazines, DVDs, VHS cassettes – *The Fountainhead* with Gary Cooper, *Harry's War,* Edward Herrmann's anti-IRS movie, Michael McNulty's documentaries about Waco – and CD ROMs containing the Declaration of Independence, the Constitution, the Bill of Rights, the Federalist Papers, the Covenant of Unanimous Consent, the original Articles of Confederation, and other documents vital to the freedom movement.

He also saw tables heaped with healthfoods, megavitamins, amino acids, enzymes, and other substances whose purveyors asserted to be life-extending.

Most of all – something he found both amazing and gratifying – Alex saw his own book, *Looking Forward,* not just stacked on tables, but in people's hands as they sat and read in the lobby, tucked under their arms as they went from place to place. He made a mental note to contact his publisher – where were all these copies of a supposedly out-of-print work coming from, anyway?

Thanks to a photo of the author printed on the back of the dust jacket, he was recognized immediately, and spent the next two hours at three different booksellers' tables signing books for their customers, as well as for those who'd already purchased the book and wandered by. It was the first time he'd ever signed books for people he didn't know and he enjoyed it immensely.

Meanwhile, Ernie and his cohorts had disappeared for a while, probably buttonholing likely allies, Alex thought, getting a feeling for the floor of the convention, attending to the formalities (and vastly more important informalities) of entering his name as a contender for the 2008 presidential nomination of the Free Libertarian Party of America.

Abruptly, an extremely shapely female 10 or 15 years his junior, handed Alex a copy of his book to sign, and pronounced, in a deep, breathy voice, "This is a gift for a dear friend of mine, Professor Hope. Please sign it, 'To D.G.M'. I'm utterly fascinated with your ideas, Professor. Maybe after you're through here, we could go have a drink and discuss them."

She wore a tight black sweater with a deeply plunging neckline and a pleated peasant skirt, with a concho belt. She also wore turquoise and silver earrings, necklaces, bracelets, and rings. Alex had always liked southwestern jewelry very much, but... He signed the book as requested, raising an eyebrow, "In the bar over there?"

She shrugged, giving him what she must have imagined was a sly, sexy expression. It probably worked on others; it didn't work on him. She wasn't unattractive, but she was wearing too much perfume and too much bric-a-bac. Her fingernails were absurdly long, painted black, and trimmed square on the ends. In classical China, those nails would have betrayed her as an aristocrat, helplessly dependent on the useful hands of others. A bigger problem, of course, was that she wasn't Amelia. "I have a fifth of Chivas in my room."

"I appreciate the offer," he told her, "but I have a meeting in a few minutes with the people I came here with, and I don't know when it'll be over. "Perhaps we can have a drink in the bar some other time." He handed her the book he'd just signed. "Thanks a lot, I hope your friend D.G.M. enjoys it." She nodded, mumbling something he didn't understand, and left.

After a while, he discovered that he was signing fewer books and was encountering, instead, all sorts of people who, it gradually dawned on him, had gotten wind of what his students were up to, and had come to check him out. As he stood beside the table of "Invisible Hand Books", speaking with a young woman passionately interested in a free market space program, a paunchy, middle-aged, balding figure approached and curtly interrupted her. He was fairly tall, and wore a neutral tweed sports jacket and glasses.

"You know," he said to Alex, ignoring the young woman altogether, "I've talked to thousands of libertarians over the years. I've never met a single one that your book brought into the movement." Although he didn't look like the cartoon character, the man's petulant, nasal tone somehow made Alex think of the overweight ponytailed guy on *The Simpsons* who ran the comic book store.

"Is that so?" Alex replied, thinking of the dozens of tattered, dog-eared copies of *Looking Forward* he'd signed this afternoon. He'd seen a million of this guy over the last 30 years. The computer industry was full of them.

"Oh, I'll admit that you're a moderately decent writer – although not in the top 100 pro-freedom writers of all time – probably not even in the top 250. Everywhere I go, I look in bookstores and I never see your book in any of them. It's very unusual, seeing so many copies of your book in one place. Do you think they're actually *selling* any of them?"

"I didn't know you cared," Alex laughed. "Who the hell are you?"

The man looked wounded that Alex didn't recognize him. "Why, I'm Forrey Nadalindov," he replied. "Despite the fondest wishes of your little children's army, I'm the next presidential candidate of the Free Libertarian Party of America."

Children's army? Alex wondered how Ernie and

his friends would care to hear that. He rather liked the sound of it, himself. This party looked ready to start guzzling Geritol and collecting Social Security checks. It needed fresh blood desperately. It needed "children" like his students – and the young woman Nadalindov had just treated so rudely.

Momentarily ignoring the man, Alex turned back to the girl. "Have you read my book? I've proposed shutting NASA down and repealing any laws and regulations that prevent private space launches."

"No, Dr. Hope," she told him, a little embarrassed. She wasn't quite pretty, but Alex thought he saw something in her eyes – call it a thousand light-year stare. "I'm an electrical engineering student at Colorado State University and I don't have much time or money for outside reading, right now."

He picked up a copy of his book from the table, nodding at the proprietor and leaving a 20 dollar bill in its place. Opening it to the title page, he signed it, and added, *To my newest friend, the electrical engineer: Ad Astra per Ardua*. "Read it when you have time, on me."

Nadalindov sniffed. "So that's your secret, Hope – you *give* them away!"

Alex grinned. "I'd be happy to give you one, Forrey."

"I already have one," Nadalindov sniffed. "A first edition. I bought it wholesale at Discount-Books.com."

Another fan heard from, Alex thought. He parted company with the engineering student and Nadalindov and was heading to the bar for a Coke – nothing more than that today – when he heard his name being pronounced behind his back.

"Dr. Hope? Alexander Hope?"

He turned to see a very pretty young Asian girl smiling at him, carrying a laptop computer, a tiny handheld recorder, and a copy of *Looking Forward.* He surprised himself by noticing, as well, her uptilted nose and prominent cheekbones, her beautiful almond eyes, and that her short skirt and light sweater revealed a nice little figure. Her big wire-rimmed glasses made her look impossibly cute (about a nine on what he thought of as the "Mighty Mouse's Girlfriend Scale"), and her glossy, shoulder-length ebony hair was filled with reddish highlights.

Alex shook off a strange feeling of guilt. What's wrong with me, he thought, it's been six years; can't I even *notice* a pretty girl? This one's at least 30 years younger than I am, he answered himself. She's barely older than Faith Anne. Nevertheless, he smiled back at her – it wasn't that difficult. "Is there something I can do for you, Miss ... ?"

"Oh, I hope so, Dr. Hope! I'm Dana Li, NetPlanetNews.com. Katie Harris told me I might find you down here. May I have a few minutes of your time?

"For the record, you mean?" As the former head of a billion dollar corporation, Alex had plenty of experience with the media, all of it very bad. He felt especially on his guard because this reporter was so attractive and ... well, the only word for it was "perky". He was a sucker for perky.

"For the record," she replied. "I've done my homework, and to my knowledge, nobody's interviewed you yet as a candidate for the FLPA nomination. I'd like to be the first, if I may. Don't worry, Dr. Hope. I'm New Media, I won't bite." Her eyes crinkled at the corners when she smiled, and she smiled with every sentence that she spoke. He was a sucker for that, too.

Now he was doubly on guard.

"Well, be gentle. Where do you want to do this, in the bar?"

She shook her head. "Wrong climate altogether," she told him. "Katie said you've taken a suite for the weekend. I suppose that we could – "

Alarm bells went off! Alex thought of at least 16 different horrible outcomes to that suggestion. "Why not do it right here in the lobby? It isn't as noisy as the bar, and there are lots of comfortable chairs."

"Great!" Her eyes crinkled again. They crossed the lobby, found two overstuffed chairs at right angles to each other, and sat. She opened her laptop and typed a few strokes, then held up her recorder, a familiar-looking palm-sized silver instrument. "The most expensive two words in the English language are 'cellular modem'. I'm online right now to NetPlanetNews.com. This chip recorder is just for backup. Do you mind?"

"That chip recorder, a Hope Corporation FA-18, I see, is just in case I deny what I've said to you later on. Okay, I don't mind at all. Go ahead and interview away."

She laughed, and that was even better than her smile, tinkling and melodic. This kid was positively *dangerous*. Happily, he made a point of never saying a word he didn't mean, seldom changed his mind, and had nothing (that he knew of, anyway) to hide.

She nodded and was suddenly serious. "I'm sure you know by now that you're a newcomer in a field of seven contenders for the FLPA presidential nomination. Only two other candidates really count, Abe Horrwyrn, who was the FLPA nominee back in 2004, and Forrey 'Nada' Nadalindov."

"'Nada'?" Alex asked, unable to suppress a chuckle.

"Not a nickname he's very proud of, but it's what everybody seems to call him. Dr. Hope, each of those two, Horrwyn and Nadalindov, has a much longer history in the FLPA than you, and, at this point, many more supporters. Is it fair to say that what you bring to the party, so to speak, is that you're a billionaire who can finance his own campaign?"

Alex laughed. "Is that what they're saying in there?" He indicated the ballroom where the business of the convention was supposed to be happening.

"It's what they're saying in the hallways – " She typed for another few seconds.

"Where the real business is going on?" he asked.

Several people drifted up to listen where they sat in the lobby. The internet reporter didn't seem to mind, and Alex had no objection. One of them was Rick Thomas, who quietly set a Coke before Alex on the low table in front of him. Little by little, they began to gather a crowd. Alex suspected it was as much to look at the highly decorative Miss Li as to hear him speak with her.

"And your answer is?" she persisted, fingers hovering over the keyboard.

"What I bring to the party, Miss Li, is whatever knowledge and experience I've acquired as a businessman and academician. I have a reputation, which I've earned, for truthfulness and integrity, and unlike many FLPA candidates I've seen, I'm not afraid to deliver the ideas this party was built on to the public, without euphemizing them or pulling any punches."

She grinned a little. "That may not be quite as popular a quality around here as you think, Dr. Hope. Do you think you can you run on the current FLPA platform?

"I read the 2004 platform last night." His tone was neutral.

"And what was your impression?" She looked up at him expectantly. Her eyes were black, as if they had enormous pupils, and they sparkled.

He shrugged. "I found it cautious, timid, even a little cowardly, – all of those the very last things the platform of a third party ought to be."

"So what platform will you be running on, then, your own?"

"Something really radical and confrontational. My platform will be the first ten amendments to the Constitution, commonly known as the Bill of Rights."

She raised her eyebrows. "But even that needs some interpretation, doesn't it? Haven't people wrangled over the meaning of the Bill of rights for two centuries?"

"Only judges, lawyers, and politicians, who fear the freedom it guarantees, and are willing to deliberately misinterpret – willfully misunderstand – every single line of it, every sentence, every word, to take that freedom away."

"So what's your plan to keep them from doing that?"

"Well, just for starters, every time I speak publicly, or give an interview like this, as a candidate or as president, I'll remind you of your 1000-year-old right and duty as a juror to weigh not only the facts of a case, but the law. If you think it's unconstitutional, unjust, or just plain stupid, then you can refuse to convict and throw the law out.

"And my administration, Miss Li, will help you as much as it can."

CHAPTER EIGHT:
DECLAN GHILLIE MOURE

> *You can have a Third Amendment, protecting your home and property from being looted by the government, or you can use RICO and asset forfeiture to illegally deprive drug dealers, and others you happen not to care for, of access to their "scumbag" lawyers. Your choice.*
>
> – Alexander Hope, *Looking Forward*

The fifth ballot had just been cast and counted.

The numbers stood almost exactly where they had the previous four ballots: Abe Horrwyrn 40%, Forrey Nadalindov 35%, Alexander Hope at not quite 20%. The remaining 5% was distributed between a retired Special Forces officer, a female Olympic weightlifter, a hairdresser from El Rancho Cucamonga, California, and "None of the Above" – not necessarily in that order.

It was quite a field, Alex thought, watching the proceedings on the hotel's closed-circuit television channel. He'd heard that C-Span was covering parts of the convention, as well, but he didn't know what parts. He'd traded a couch in the lobby for another upstairs, and was now observing events from a large suite he'd taken on the top floor of the building.

Despite the fact it was September, to Alex, it felt like spring. He wished he didn't consider it improper – it would have been a conflict of interest on her part – to ask Dana Li up to watch with him. It would have been a perfectly respectable invitation: the whole Austrian Mafia, Ernie, Katie, Rick, and Mick, were in and out of the suite from moment to moment, conferring with him or simply taking a break from the convention floor (or the more-important hallways) and getting a bite to eat. He'd ordered several cases of soda and a dozen pizzas from the only company he could find–Rocky Mountain Pizza Belly– that didn't forbid their delivery drivers to carry weapons for self-defense.

Still, Dana – Miss Li – had a job to do, he supposed, and she was doing it. A few moments ago he'd caught an enjoyable glimpse of her, interviewing the lady weightlifter whose platform, as near as he could tell, consisted of nothing but a threat – at least that was the way that he interpreted it – to get the Free Libertarian Party of America back in shape.

Or else.

"Oof!" Ernie startled Alex, landing on the couch beside him as if he'd fallen from the ceiling. The young man had been wheeling and dealing downstairs for hours, but except for a slight sheen across his forehead, appeared as fresh and energetic as if he'd just arrived at the convention.

"Sorry, Prof! I thought you'd appreciate a quick summary of what's going on down there on the floor. Say, are those smoked oysters I see on that pizza?"

Alex nodded. "We have some with anchovies, too. You're right – at the moment they look deadlocked to me, and they have been all day. How many ballots will they cast before they just – "

"Give up?" Ernie waggled his eyebrows. "They won't do that. They can't do that. They have to decide tonight. And there are some rumors down there – "

"Carefully placed in circulation by you?" Alex raised his eyebrows.

"Prof, you wound me!" Ernie laughed wickedly and picked up a slice of pizza. "Both sides are pretty rattled by now. They never figured on any more competition than the one-percenters are giving them. They know each other pretty well, and the gloves are well and truly off. They're spilling every dirty lie – or dirty truth – about each other they've been saving up for 30 years. The trouble is, all they know about you is good. You're rich, committed, a widower for the ladies, and a veteran for the men.

"He hasn't much to offer the FLPA's smattering of pacifists and gays," Katie answered, entering the room. She sat in the big chair opposite Ernie and inspected the pizza closely. "Smoked oysters? Yuck! But he isn't any threat to them, either. And he hasn't said word one about abortion."

"And he shouldn't, if he can avoid it," Ernie said.

Alex shook his head. "I'm right in line with traditional FLPA policy on that one. Abortion remains legal, but not one penny of tax money ever gets spent on it again. Not that it matters, but I've seen opinion polls indicating that 85% of Americans would go along with a compromise like that, just to end the perpetual wrangling and get on with other things."

"'Abortion,'" Ernie quoted his favorite professor around a huge bite of oyster-laden pizza, "is the issue the left counts on to keep the freedom movement divided.'"

Katie said, “By the way, Dana Li said to tell you hello.”

“Er, why not have some root beer with that pizza?” Alex suggested abruptly. “It’s from Hop’s – they just started bottling it this week.”

“Dana said,” Katie persisted, “be sure to watch NetPlanetNews, because – “

“Look at this!” Mick Douglas burst into the room, followed by Rick Thomas. “Somebody out there – in cyberspace – likes you!”

Mick held out his PDA – his handheld “personal digital assistant” – but had to wait as Alex found his glasses and put them on. It was a wireless internet device, logged on to NetPlanetNews.com.

FRESH BLOOD AT LAST

By Dana Li <mailto:danali@npn.com>

EXCLUSIVE TO NETPLANETNEWS.COM

Regular readers of this column know that I make no secret of my philosophical convictions. Like most of those who earn their living and live their lives in cyberspace, I am an unabashed libertarian. And like most philosophical libertarians, I have been unhappy, for quite a while, with the slim pickings that the Free Libertarian Party of America has been inclined to offer us in the way of presidential candidates.

This election year promised to be no different. The contest was to be between one of the half dozen original founders of the FLPA, and the FLPA’s candidate from last time, both bone-weary has-beens, any imagination, enthusiasm, or magic they ever possessed used up long ago. It was almost enough to make a person want to vote Republican

Almost.

But at the very last minute, along came a knight in shining – if virtual – armor, an individual with experience creating and running a multibillion dollar high-tech corporation, a father and husband (sadly widowed some six years ago), a former soldier who has now become an author and a teacher.

The subject that he teaches is individual liberty.

The man I'm punching these keys about, of course, is Alexander Hope, author of *Looking Forward,* which has reenergized the movement by reconnecting it with its radical Revolutionary roots, author, as well, of the Hope Corporation, whose products have given us all a new ease, mobility, power, and freedom, here where we work and reside in cyberspace. I'm writing this on one of his "Amelia" series of laptops now, named after his late wife, who he modestly insists was the real genius of the Hope Corporation.

Here is a man who – unlike that increasingly bizarre recluse Bill Gates has become – understands liberty and wants it for others, as well as himself. Here is a man with a program, taking time-honored treasures like 10th century jury nullification and the 18th century Bill of Rights to new heights in the

> 21st century.
>
> Will the FLPA exercise the socialist virtue of recycling its worn-out hand-me-downs, or will it try something shiny and new?
>
> Only time – and internal party politics – will tell...

* * * * * *

"Hey, Prof?"

Alex stirred, realizing he'd fallen asleep where he sat, waiting for the next ballot to be taken. Katie and Mick and Rick were gone. There'd been some kind of parliamentary delay while procedural votes were taken on the floor: whether to extend the balloting process to tomorrow, Sunday, which had narrowly failed; whether to break for a long overdue lunch, which had passed almost unanimously.

"What is it, Ernie?"

"They've adjourned for lunch – and extracurricular politicking. Declan Ghillie Moure would like to see you."

Alex blinked. "Who?"

"Declan Ghillie Moure, Abe Horrwyrn's personal aide. Some people think he's the real brains of the operation and that Horrwyrn is just window-dressing."

"Okay, give me a minute. Would you mind stacking those pizza boxes and putting the empty ones out of sight?" Alex stood and stretched, grateful he'd carefully draped his jacket over the back of an upright chair. He went to the bathroom, checked to see how wrinkled his shirt and tie were, inspected himself for pizza stains, then ran a hand through his short hair and rinsed his mouth out with water.

He emerged and shucked into his jacket, still basking in the glow of kind words from a pretty lady, grateful that after today he could go back to his western shirt, bluejeans, and his comfortable Montana's Yellowstone Trail cowboy boots – his "MYTs" – of water buffalo calfskin.

"Okay," he told Ernie, as he went to the Mr. Coffee. It was empty. Alex began looking for paper filters and the coffee packets. To his delight, the filters were in a cabinet under the counter, atop a freshly-opened can of Chock Full O' Nuts, "the heavenly coffee". That would be Katie, he guessed. "Let him in."

The figure Ernie invited in was that of an over-aged preppie, with odd, chipmunk-like jowls. He was a head shorter than Alex (who wasn't very tall, himself) and wore dark slacks, a navy blue, brass-buttoned blazer, and collegiate tie. He stepped – nervously, Alex thought – across the room, eyes darting this way and that as if he expected to be ambushed by Viet Cong. *Somebody should tell this little guy the war is over,* Alex thought.

Ernie raised a hand to let Alex know he was leaving.

"Great to meet you at last, Mr. Hope!" The newcomer, carrying a copy of *Looking Forward,* extended a hand which Alex had to set the coffee can down to take. He went back to making coffee. "I'm one of your biggest fans, Declan Ghillie Moure," he said almost breathlessly. "People call me Ghillie. As Hanover has probably told you already, I work with Abe Horrwyrn."

"That's what Ernie tells me, all right," Alex answered. "I'm making coffee. Would you care for some? You're sure? Then what else can I do for you,

Ghillie?"

"Just like that?" the little man blinked. Apparently Moure was accustomed to doing business in a more roundabout – "devious", Alex thought – manner. He noticed the way Moure fidgeted and couldn't seem to stand in one place for more than a second or two, and wondered exactly what that signified.

"Just like that," he repeated. He hadn't become a billionaire by being roundabout. His Japanese customers and vendors, who made being roundabout a way of life, hated bargaining with Alex, but they loved doing business with him.

Moure was silent for a moment. "Okay," he said at last. "Okay, Abe and I would appreciate your help breaking the ballot deadlock down on the convention floor. It's about to set an all-time record for the party and we don't like it. Abe's willing to offer you the Vice Presidential position in exchange for your delegates. Is that straightforward enough, Mr. Hope?"

The coffee machine had finished its gurgling and Alex had been pouring himself a cup. Now he nearly spilled it in an attempt to keep from laughing out loud. He turned, as slowly and carefully as he could, and retrieved the little carton of half-and-half out of the minifridge.

"Maybe it helps that I've come to the party from the outside," he observed thoughtfully. "Do you remember who Cactus Jack Garner was, Ghillie?"

Moure wrinkled his brow in momentary concentration. "Cactus Jack – you mean John Nance Garner, one of Franklin Delano Roosevelt's vice presidents."

Alex nodded, exactly as he would have to one of his students who'd answered correctly. "Do you remember what he said about the vice presidency?"

"I do," Moure winced. "That it wasn't worth a bucket of warm spit."

Alex laughed. "Only he didn't say 'spit', did he, Ghillie? And if that's true, can you imagine what a vice presidential *nomination* is worth – from a third political party that's never gotten more than 900,000 votes?"

"But, but ... " Moure was speechless. Alex didn't realize, as yet, that it was an uncharacteristic condition for the little man. "I don't get it. Why would you even want the FLPA presidential nomination, then? You're rich and famous enough that you could – "

"Could what? Run as a candidate for Socialist Party 'A', the Democrats, or for Socialist Party 'B', the we-try-harder Republicans? I want the FLPA nomination because I promised my friends that I'd try to get it."

The expression on Moure's face changed to ill-concealed disgust. "Hanover, you mean, and his little playmates. Well I can tell you, Hope, they're going to be sorry that they did this to Abe...and you are too!"

Alex shook his head. "Can't you see they're doing it *for* the FLPA, Ghillie? For the cause of individual liberty – remember that old thing? They think Abe shot his bolt last time when he only got 384,000 votes from 100,000,000 voters. They think it's time for somebody else."

"Just you wait – " Moure stopped abruptly as they both noticed on the television that the sixth ballot had just taken place downstairs. Horrwyrn had received the same 40% as before, Nadalindov's 29% was six points fewer than he'd had for most of the day – and Alex now stood at 25%.

The deadlock had begun to break. Without another word, Moure turned on his heel and left the suite. The copy of *Looking Forward* that he'd brought with him to flatter Alex with lay forgotten on the countertop beside the coffee-maker.

Alex opened it to the title page. It had been signed, in his own handwriting, to "D.G.M." Of course it had. Maybe he should have Ernie return it, Alex thought. Then again Ghillie wouldn't want the book. He made a mental note to find out what he could about Moure and his overdressed girlfriend from Dana.

Er, make that Miss Li.

* * * * * *

"So how about it, Hope? Accept my offer of the veep nomination, break Horrwyrn's hold on the FLPA, and I'll give you a clear shot at the top spot in 2012."

Nadalindov had followed Moure to Alex's suite by less than an hour, during which he'd had a number of phone calls. The Special Forces colonel unceremonially announced his withdrawal, ceding the votes of his tiny group of supporters to Alex, an ex-Marine he said he could respect. Alex had thanked the colonel as graciously as possible, asking him to dinner later in the week. Morrison was famous for The Fort, which specialized in exotic game. The colonel had thanked him and accepted.

He'd also heard from the lady weightlifter, who wanted the number two position on Alex's ticket. Prompted by Katie and Rick, who were taking a break, he'd informed her that he regretted that the FLPA was unique in voting for their vice presidential nominee separately, and that, lacking the well-oiled machinery of Horrwyrn and Nadalindov, he had little to say about who his running mate would be.

The guy from El Rancho Cucamonga had asked Alex where he stood on professional licensure and homosexual rights, his two pet issues. Alex had said he opposed all professional licensure, and that he believed homosexuals had exactly the same rights as everybody else – and no more – see the first ten Amendments to the Constitution. Apparently he'd said the right thing. The guy became excited and promised to throw his support to Alex. Alex thanked him – and invited him to dinner at The Fort with the colonel. The table conversation should be interesting.

He'd invite his students, too, and possibly Dana.

Better make that, "Miss Li", he corrected himself again.

He'd fielded other calls until Ernie, Katie, Rick, and Mick came to tell him that they were talking downstairs about extending the late lunch break into an early dinner. Alex suggested that they all go to a nearby Japanese restaurant where the chef cut everything up and cooked it at your table. He could see that Ernie, at least, deeply regretted telling him that he had "places to go and people to kill" before the seventh ballot.

The other three all pleaded similarly and left with him. It's true, Alex thought, gazing out the suite's 30-story window, it's lonely at the top.

Then Nadalindov had come. He'd dismissed the Cactus Jack Garner quote. "You can make anything you want of the vice presidential nomination, Hope, that's the beauty of running with a third party. I'll campaign my way, you campaign yours. When it's over we'll go back to our lives."

"You make it sound very attractive, Forrey," Alex lied. "But what could the next presidential candidate of the FLPA possibly want with the leader of a little children's army who's only a moderately decent writer, not in the top 100, not even in the top 250, who's never brought a new member into the movement, and whose book is never in any bookstores you visit – although you seem to have a copy yourself? Want me to sign it for you?"

"I ... er ... uh ... "

"My very thought, Forrey, and eloquently put. Clearly you don't need me. Your three or four delegates from the Mensa Society should be more than enough to put you over the top, and you shouldn't miss the support that you threw away when you were needlessly rude down there to a bright and committed young woman who's here representing the Space Colony Foundation. I just had a call from her, by the way. That was her five percent, for the most part, that I took from you on the sixth ballot."

Nadalindov gasped. "You haven't heard the last of this, Hope!"

"That's what Ghillie Moure said. Why don't *you* two get together?"

Nadalindov started to say something, but was interrupted when Ernie broke excitedly into the room. "Prof – " He stopped when he saw who else was there. "They're about to start the seventh ballot."

"I should be going," Nadalindov said, sarcastically adding, "Good luck."

"Sure," Ernie said before Alex could. "Break a leg, Nada."

As the door slammed shut behind the angry man,

Ernie sat down on the couch to keep an eye on the TV. Alex joined him. "I talked to lots of people down there just now, Prof, who are fed up with Tweedle-Dum and Tweedle-Dumber. They think that you could get the FLPA up above the million votes mark for the first time in history. It wasn't very hard. I just refer them to your book, to the Bill of Rights, or to Dana Li's column."

"Or to my credit rating?" Alex laughed.

"Hey, it's like chicken soup," Ernie replied, "it couldn't hoit." He turned to greet Katie and Rick, just coming in. "How's it going down there?"

Rick shrugged. "Can't tell, Ern. Just say it looks interesting – in the Chinese meaning of the expression. Say, Dr. Hope, isn't that your girlfriend on the tube? You know half the people I talked to were taken by that item she did on you. She can do one on me any time she wants!"

Katie hit him over the head with a sofa pillow.

Girlfriend? Ridiculous! Alex didn't know what to say. It was a crazy kind of day all around. Sure enough, Dana Li was down there on the floor, interviewing delegates who were about to vote.

"It's now or never," Katie declared, leaning toward the screen.

This time, probably because he was paying attention now, the balloting seemed to take forever. On the first ballot, he knew, voting had proceeded alphabetically, beginning with Alabama, then Alaska, and so on. The second ballot reversed the alphabet. It had alternated that way until, on the seventh ballot, they were back to plain old alphabetical again.

Ernie leaned over his PDA, hurriedly making notes as the spokesman for each state FLPA's delegation came to the microphone to announce their vote. Under longstanding national rules, a state's delegation could divide its vote, and "None of the Above" was always an acceptable choice.

"Horrwyrn's losing some support," Ernie told them as the fifth or sixth state voted. "I don't know if it's enough. Nadalindov, too. More 'None of the Above' votes, though. Somebody down there doesn't like you, Prof."

Alex let it pass. He was getting nervous and it bothered him. He arose with as much dignity as he could, went to the bedroom he'd claimed, took his shoes off and lay down atop the coverlet, pulling a pillow from under it before he put his head down ...

* * * * * *

"What?" Alex sat up in a kind of shock. Someone outside was pounding on the door he didn't remember shutting. He could hear all three of them out there (he remembered wondering what had become of Mick) screaming as if the building were going up in flames. "Wait just a minute!"

He put his shoes on and opened the door.

"We did it! We did it!" Katie was jumping up and down. She threw her arms around him and kissed him on the cheek.

Ernie thrust a hand at Alex. "Congratulations, Prof. You got 52% to Horrwyrn's 25% and 'None of the Above' beat Nadalindov."

Alex was astonished (and more than a little dismayed) at how childishly pleased the victory made him. He was about to say something when Mick crashed into the suite, as agitated as his three friends put together.

"We know, we know!" Rick told him.

"No you don't. Alex, Dana Li's been found in one of the service corridors, beaten half to death!"

Chapter Nine:
DANA LI

> *The assertion that "driving is a privilege, not a right," is pure statist drivel. Given the way Americans have come to use and feel about their cars, the right to own and drive one ought to be protected, either by the Fourth Amendment or the Second.*
>
> – Alexander Hope, *Looking Forward*

They'd restarted her heart in the elevator on the way up here.

Saint Androcles Hospital's "LifeFlight" lifted Dana Li's nearly lifeless body from the landing platform on the roof of the hotel in a throbbing, deafening, mind-consuming roar of helicopter blades that brought back old, bad memories to the veteran in Alex. Bright lights battered at their senses in the dusky Rocky Mountain twilight. Dana wasn't breathing and had shown no signs of consciousness from the moment she'd been found lying in a service stairwell by one of the cleaning staff.

Being no relation to the terribly injured young woman, Alex and his friends weren't allowed aboard the machine, but he was grimly determined that she was going to pull through this, no matter what it cost him in terms of money or anything else. The young and pretty internet reporter had almost certainly suffered this horribly brutal beating because of the complimentary column she'd written about him, and, perhaps even more than that, she was the first female he'd really noticed since his Amelia had died.

As he and Ernie, Rick, Kate, and Mick followed the paramedics back across the asphalted roof and back into the elevator, Alex used his phone. He called the hotel garage and asked them to bring his Durango around to the front. Then he made a long-distance call to a certain North Carolina number that he knew by heart. They kept walking. The software that allowed him to continue his conversation, even wrapped in the steel and concrete of the elevator shaft, had been Amelia's final pet project.

"John? How you been? You did? I didn't know that FoxNews had covered it. I watched it on the hotel's closed circuit system. John, something has come up. It never occurred to me I was going to need security, as a third party candidate, but an internet reporter – that's right, Dana Li – has been beaten up and nearly killed, and I think it's my fault, or at least on my account. You want to come out and keep an eye on us for a while? Sure, bring Cap along. Maybe we'll find time to drop a line in a trout stream, too."

Ernie raised an eyebrow but didn't ask. The elevator doors slid aside and they found themselves in the hotel lobby at street level. Not only was his peacock blue Durango waiting for them out front, it gleamed and glittered at them in a million brilliant city lights, having been washed, waxed, and filled with gas. Even the simple Hope Corporation Pegasus, with its wings spread wide, looked fresh and new.

Alex tipped the attendant generously and they all piled into the big blue machine.

As soon as they were underway, Alex offered an explanation to Ernie. "That was John Pondoro, an old war buddy. He saved my life so many times in Vietnam that he's obliged, under Chinese customs, to keep doing it forever."

Ernie gave him a funny look.

Enjoying it, Alex went on, "His grown son Cap – Peter Hathaway Capstick Pondoro, named after a famous African elephant hunter – is eventually going to inherit the obligation, of course, so he's coming, too. John knows more about helping people avoid getting kidnapped, beaten up, or killed than anybody else I've ever heard of, let alone actually met."

At a stoplight, he glanced around carefully, than separated the keys hanging from the ignition, leaned over to the right across Ernie, unlocked the glove compartment, and took out a large, heavy, black and stainless steel automatic pistol in a stiff black plastic holster. He slipped it under his suit jacket and fastened it on his belt. He then dropped each of the two spare magazines that had been with it in the glove box into his jacket pockets.

"And believe me," he went on as if nothing extraordinary had happened, "I've checked around. When you're a corporate CEO with a wife and daughter, especially in southern California, you educate yourself in these matters."

"I hope to shout," Katie observed from the back seat. She was sitting there with Rick. Like a little kid, Mick had climbed into the third row of seats and was enjoying the slightly extra height and better view it afforded. "So this man and his son are going to come out and watch your back?"

Alex cursed the downtown Denver traffic before answering Katie. Even at this hour, it was among the nation's worst, the difficulty apparently springing from several city administrations that loathed the automobile – for the privacy and individual freedom that it afforded – and childishly refused to adjust themselves to its existence, let alone embrace it as the most efficient form of mass transportation ever developed.

America's socialist mayors would rather play with their toy buses and trains, he thought, which ran empty most of the day, consuming bushels of the taxpayers' money for fuel. Too bad he wasn't really going to President – despite himself, Alex had been having thoughts like that more and more frequently – he knew exactly what he'd do about that.

"They're going to watch all of our backs," he told Katie at last. "Assuming, in the light of what's happened to Dana – Miss Li – that you all still want to stick with the campaign. It looks like it could be a dangerous thing to do."

Katie said, "Can I have a gun?"

"Do you want one?" Alex asked her.

"Actually, I have one, Professor Hope. I just stupidly left it at home today."

He laughed. "Then if we're going to bear arms and go in harm's way together, call me Alex from now on – at least outside the classroom. That goes for all four of you. Here's the hospital. And I can actually see a parking place."

* * * * * *

So far, the five of them had endured more than

three hours in the Saint Androcles emergency room waiting area, and understood that they might have to wait many hours more. Two sides of the room had windows reaching from the floor to the ceiling, affording them a view of a well-lighted driveway, the helicopter landing pad, and the perfectly groomed hospital grounds, beginning to turn brown in the dry Colorado autumn.

Dana Li was still in surgery.

"I guess any one of her injuries wouldn't have been so bad, Mr. Hope" the ER doctor was telling them. "But there were so *many* of them! She doesn't have a skull fracture – I don't know how she avoided that – but she has a concussion, a broken cheekbone, and a broken nose."

Alex hated to think of any damage to that lovely face, but he was overjoyed that the brain behind it was intact. The hospital people had initially refused – and properly so, he'd agreed – to give him any information about her. Alex had handed Mick his laptop to find Dana's parents. Her editor at NetPlanetNews.com had informed him they lived in Manitou Springs.

The editor had already alerted her parents of her injuries and they'd been almost out the door when Alex called. He'd promptly sent his company helicopter to pick them up, instructing the pilot to land on a neighboring golf course. In flight, they'd given their permission by internet picturephone to the St. Androcles ER to tell Alex what they could of her condition.

The ER doc went on. He was a tall young man, with a long blond ponytail. "In addition, both of her arms are broken, humerus, radius, ulna, the whole nine yards. Two of the fractures are compound, and there's a lot of bruising and crushed tissue. If I had to hazard a guess, somebody struck her repeatedly with a section on one-inch black iron waterpipe, not more than two feet long. Any longer, and the added leverage to the blows would probably have killed her."

"Doctor ... " The girl had lost some blood, mostly to her internal injuries. Alex and his students had offered blood, but none had turned out to be the right type.

"There's more. How she escaped major spinal or skull injuries is totally beyond me. It almost had to be deliberate on the attacker's part. Was that merciful or sadistic? She has severe bruising to the hips, several broken ribs, a broken femur, and on the other leg, a broken fibula. Also defensive injuries in the form of assorted broken fingers and toes."

She'd fought back. The feeling, deep inside Alex, of churning, acidic, blinding fury was almost uncontrollable. All he could do for several long heartbeats was stand in one place, swaying a little, deliberately *not* clenching his fists at his sides, breathing as deeply and slowly as he could.

He felt the doctor's hand on his elbow. "Are you all right, Mr. Hope? You're looking a little pale, there."

Alex blinked. "Yeah, doctor, I'm fine. Just mad."

"Well this will make you madder, Alex."

He turned to see Ernie standing beside him. "What is it?"

Ernie looked disgusted. "The cops have just arrived, like D-Day. They say they want to know where you were when Dana Li was getting the slats kicked out of her."

* * * * * *

"No, sir, I can't," the police officer said. "I can't tell you who put us onto you, Professor Hope. And even if I knew, it's strictly against department policy. I didn't have any part in writing it, I just follow it."

Alex replied amiably, "So I don't get to face my accuser, and you get to use the same excuse the Nazi concentration camp guards did at Nuremburg."

Rick, Mick, Katie, and Ernie were down at the far end of the room, each of them getting to know a new friend. As soon as he'd arranged the flight for Dana's parents, Alex had made another call, to a local computer outlet he'd recently done business with. He'd ordered four of his own company's machines, the latest version of the same model he used – an Amelia Octium 5E – with all of the bells and whistles, and had them delivered here, to the Saint Androcles Emergency Room, for his four young campaign workers.

He'd taken some pleasure in that, as well as in sending his helicopter to Manitou Springs to fetch Dana's parents. A good thing he'd ordered it here from San Diego for a fishing trip with Van Cleave. It was nice to have money when you needed it, he thought, not for the first time – although it wasn't much different in principle, he supposed, from the simple convenience of having change for the Coke machine.

As the man's bulky two-way radio chattered away on his hip, the uniformed Denver Police sergeant gave Alex the pained look of a man who's just been compelled by circumstances to listen to an unpleasant truth. Alex cast an eye on the long, black, L-shaped bludgeon on the man's other hip, the canister of incapacitating chemical spray, the 9mm Glock automatic pistol with the high-capacity magazines that it was still illegal – despite eight long years of so-called Republican government – for civilians to purchase.

Maybe, Alex reflected, this cop would have reacted differently to someone else – someone who didn't happen to be a billionaire. He was certainly equipped for it. Then again, maybe he wouldn't have. It all depended on the man, which, in six short words, was the problem with the law today.

Twenty-five minutes later, having interviewed the Austrian Mafia separately and together, the sergeant stood, obviously relieved to be going. "I guess I'm finished here, for now. You have four witnesses that put you in your hotel room fast asleep – in the middle of the afternoon? – when the victim was being attacked." He handed Alex a card. "We may need a statement from you later."

"Well, I was under some stress, Sergeant. You see, I'd never been nominated for Presidency before." In return, he handed the sergeant a card – his lawyers' card.

The cop grinned. "Yeah, right. I know all about that from my kids. Free Libertarian Party of America? The sex, dope, and weapons party is what I've heard. But good luck, Professor. You sure as hell can't be any worse than the other two who're running – the former First Lady and the Vice President – they both make me wanna puke. Hell, I may even vote for you, myself!"

The sergeant started to turn and walk away, then suddenly stopped, as if struck by a thought. He turned back again, leaned down to Alex, and whispered, "Declan Ghillie Moure". Then he straightened up and carefully pronounced, in a louder, public tone, "And let that be a lesson to you."

Alex nodded soberly. "It will, Officer, believe me." He wondered how the good sergeant would have reacted if he'd known about the highly customized .40 caliber EAA Witness automatic he carried in the kydex holster under his coat. Denver's history of official hatred for the Second Amendment was even worse than its hatred of the private automobile.

"Professor Hope?"

He turned. It was the emergency room nurse he'd first dealt with when they'd arrived, a tall, blond, almost pretty, heavyset young woman with a permanently harassed expression. In his experience, hospital nurses tended to be like that, harassed and heavyset. He understood the former; he often wondered about the latter. She'd adjusted to talking to Dana's parents through his computer pretty well, he'd thought.

"Professor Hope, I see that the patient's folks haven't gotten here yet, and I understand that you've been acting sort of *in loco parentis.*"

That stung a little, Alex noticed. It was perfectly true that he was old enough to be Dana's – Miss Li's – father, if his estimate of her age was correct, but he didn't have to like it. "They should be here any second."

Unaware that she had wounded his vanity, the nurse replied, "Well, she's waking up right now and will want to see somebody she knows. Will you come in and talk to her?"

Alex nodded, his heart suddenly thundering in his chest, and got up, signaling to his students that everything was all right and he'd be back. He followed the nurse through half a dozen glass doors into the depths of the Intensive Care Unit, stopping there at the first room they reached.

Inside, a shockingly bandage-swathed form lay in a complicated mechanical bed, surrounded by plastic plumbing and electronics. The dressings across her face, stained yellow-pink by leaking plasma, left her almost unrecognizable. Sections of both of her arms and legs were in casts, particularly disturbing, somehow, because they were applied asymmetrically.

The girl's left eye was covered with thick gauze. He approached her from the right side of the bed, found a leatherette-topped wheeled stool there, moved it up to the bedside, and sat down. He didn't know if he should lay a hand on hers, although he wanted to. It, too, was criss-crossed with bandages, stuck with a big needle, held down by tautly-stretched clear plastic tape.

She opened her right eye.

"Alex," she sighed wearily, and then gave him her killer smile. "It's so good to see you!"

She'd called him by his first name! (He wondered what it meant.) "It's good to see you, Dana," he answered. It was all he could do not to break down and sob. A tear fell from his face onto her bandaged hand.

* * * * * *

"Daddy?"

Groggy and confused for a moment, Alex glanced up from where his head rested on Dana's hospital bed. What a day! Had he fallen asleep again? He didn't think so. But standing in the door, where he hadn't seen or heard her approach, was his daughter.

Faith-Anne wasn't a very tall person, but she was good looking enough, shapely enough, redheaded and authoritative enough, that people generally didn't notice. She resembled her mother so strongly, Alex often thought – with her blue eyes, slightly uptilted nose, and high, prominent cheekbones – that it was sometimes painful for him to look at her. But she had coppery hair to go with her blond mother's freckles, and her body language was more graceful and certain than her mother's had been. Amelia had raised her well, and he hoped that he had helped.

He stood up a little stiffly. Dana was awake, now, too. Standing behind Faith-Anne was an ICU nurse he hadn't seen before, with a highly disapproving scowl on her face.

"Dana Li," he found himself saying automatically, "this is my – " He'd almost said little girl. " – this is my daughter, Faith-Anne. Faith-Anne, Dana."

Dana tried to turn her head, but failed, and spoke to the ceiling, she could see instead. "Pardon me if I don't get up, Faith-Anne. I've read a lot about you and it's good to meet you. I seem to be having kind of a melodramatic day. Right now it's a lot like a scene from *The Mummy.*"

Alex chuckled dutifully, then tore himself away from the bed and went to his daughter. "I'm not complaining, mind you – but why are you here?"

Faith-Anne's eyes got very large when she saw the red rims around his, but she threw herself into his arms and hugged him as hard as she could. "Hey, it's not every day that a girl's daddy gets nominated to be president," she told him. "I was kind of wondering if you needed a campaign manager."

The notion filled him with joy – and cold foreboding. "I'd be delighted – as long as you're willing to do everything John Pondoro tells you to do, without complaining."

"Uncle John's playing, too? Is Cap coming? This is going to be fun!"

"Who's Uncle John?" asked Dana, from the bed.

The nurse had finally lost her patience. She pushed past them and rushed to Dana's side. "You people have got to get out, right now!Miss Li has to rest!"

"Uncle John," Alex told Dana, ignoring the nurse and stepping to the bedside again, "is the closest thing I have to a brother. He'll make sure this kind of thing never happens again. I wish to hell he'd been here earlier." He leaned over and kissed her on the small patch of bare cheek he could find. "I'll come and see you first thing in the morning, Dana."

"I'd like that very much, Alex."

It was very hard to leave.

* * * * * *

The waiting room, in his absence, had become a madhouse. Something was obviously up with Ernie and his three friends. The four of them were sitting against a back wall, staring wildly into their laptops, typing like demons, and speaking to each other rapidly, in low but urgent tones.

Dana's parents – at least that's who he assumed the well-dressed, middle-aged Asian couple were – had finally arrived and were having an almost equally energetic conversation with the big blond Emergency Room nurse.

The Hope Corporation helicopter pilot, Fred

Gorski (Alex privately thought of him as Scrooge McDuck's pilot Launchpad McQuack, whom he resembled in some way), wearing crisp coveralls with the flying horse corporate logo on the back, was arguing with a man in a hospital security uniform. Alex could see the company aircraft on the landing pad outside. He was willing to bet they wanted it cleared as soon as possible.

At some point, somebody had apparently ordered pizzas – probably Ernie, who was now completely preoccupied with something else – and the poor unhappy delivery person from Rocky Mountain Pizza Belly was looking around desperately for that somebody to pay him, so he could leave.

In the corner by the floor-to-ceiling windows, stood a tall, muscular, crewcut young man in clean new bluejeans, a tan sportscoat and a colored T-shirt. Something about him made Alex think of federal employees he'd known. He was looking across the room, directly at Alex, in a way that made Alex feel uneasy. He'd seen eyes like that before, in Vietnam.

First things first: he strode across the room to the pair of uniformed figures and asked the pilot, "You have something for me to sign, Fred?"

"Sure do, Mr. Hope!" The tall, gangly pilot thrust a legal-sized transparent clipboard at Alex, with an attached form acknowledging the safe and timely arrival of his passengers at their destination, as per standing corporate procedure. "That's them right over there, Boss." He indicated the Asian couple, who were looking a bit lost. "Nice folks, but real worried about their kid. Is she really that pretty internet reporter?"

Alex said she was and signed the form. "Thanks a

lot, Fred." He glanced at the security man, who was waiting impatiently, "Now take my favorite chopper back to the barn and get these people's landing pad clear, ASAP."

"Right you are, Boss! I *love* this job!" The helicopter pilot waved and ambled out of the Emergency Room, headed toward his waiting machine.

Next order of business: "How much do we owe you?" Alex asked the pizza deliverer.

"You Ernie Hanover? Three Sampler Deluxe, $63.50"

"Ernie works for me." He counted out three twenties, a ten, and a five and took the stack of boxes. "Keep the change. Thanks a lot for coming out here, son."

He took the pizzas and put them in the chromium and plastic seat next to Ernie – who never noticed – then went to the Asian couple, again interrupting a conversation. "I'm Alex Hope," he told them. "What can I do to help?"

"This woman won't let us see our daughter," the mother complained, "although I'm told you've been in to see her."

"And wore her out," protested the nurse. "She's sleeping now."

Alex turned to her. "If you'd been seriously injured like Miss Li and gone through several hours of surgery, wouldn't you want to be awakened to see your mom and dad?"

The nurse got that look. "Five minutes."

He grinned and patted Dana's mother on the shoulder. "We'll talk later," he told them both.

Now let's see, he thought, was that everything? No, he had to find out what was up with his students.

"Daddy?" It was Faith-Anne. He'd almost forgotten his daughter. She was standing in front of him, now, with that crewcut young man at her side.

He took her hand. "What is it, honey?"

She hesitated. "Well – I did fly out to congratulate you, and to apply for that job I mentioned. But I also wanted to introduce you to Chip, here."

The young man thrust a hand out, took Alex's, and gave it a good, firm shake. "Harmon Sheridan," he told the older man. "Glad to finally meet you."

"Chip is more or less fresh out of the 82nd Airborne, in western Siberia." Faith-Anne explained. Western Siberia was the Republicans' latest idiotic foreign adventure. "I met him last year at a meeting of the California FLPA." She held up her left hand, on the third finger of which glittered a modest diamond. "We're engaged to be married!"

CHAPTER TEN:
CHIP SHERIDAN

> *If the Fourth and Fifth Amendments were enforced, every last judge and prosecutor in America would be in jail – and America would be a cleaner, healthier place for it.*
>
> – Alexander Hope, *Looking Forward*

"The internet!" Jessie Li exclaimed to her husband. "Don't you see, William, if it weren't for the internet, this would never have happened to our Dana! They wouldn't have taken her seriously, whoever they are! They could have afforded to ignore her!"

If Alex had been a drinking man (which he happened to be, on occasion), he could have used a stiff one now. What had begun as a polite conversation he'd been having with the young reporter's parents had swiftly evolved into an argument between them, in which he now found himself trapped as an involuntary witness. They reminded him of his own parents.

William and Jessie Li had something else in common with him. Both were instructors at Colorado College, a two-year institution serving El Paso County, including Colorado Springs and Manitou

Springs. Dana's mother's attitude – blaming the internet for a vicious physical attack on her daughter – was predictable. She taught classes in print journalism. Dana's father was a professor of mathematics.

"Would you *want* our daughter to be ignored?" He disagreed with his wife. "You are mistaken upon this subject as you always are, my dear, blinded by a medieval prejudice favoring wet soot on woodpulp. Were it not for the internet, this sort of thing would be happening all the time, as it does in the bad old country we fled. The internet is all that makes it possible today for the so-called 'little people' to stand up against corporate abuse and government terrorism."

"The internet," Dana's mother insisted, "makes it possible for 'little people' to get injured or killed for expressing unauthorized opinions. What's so terrible about 'wet soot on woodpulp', anyway?"

"It's a weapon of the enemy," William told her. "That and network TV are the reason the internet had to be invented, so that people could have the truth, instead of 'authorized opinions'!"

"Nonsense!" She folded her arms and turned her back.

Alex could see, now, that Dana's mom was absolutely frantic over her little girl's injuries – as what mother wouldn't be – and that this apparently longstanding argument with her husband allowed her to let off steam without completely breaking down. He could also see that Dana's dad was a wise and kindly man for steering their attention in this relatively harmless direction. He wondered if he'd be getting to know these people better in the future. He thought he might like to.

William shook his head. "Without the internet,

our daughter would most likely be a junior reporter on some city daily – she'd never have sold her soul to television; she's no socialist lapdog, like Connie Chung. And when she wrote something that those in power didn't like, she could have been hurt or killed without anybody knowing about it. Instead, her people at NetPlanetNews.com are raising hell all over the world about what happened, Matt Drudge is reporting her condition hour by hour, and they're even talking about it on FoxNews."

Jessie looked up with tears starting in her eyes. "FoxNews?"

William took her in his arms. "That's what his students say."

Realizing that Mrs. Li was in the best possible hands, Alex walked across the waiting room, quieter now than it had been earlier, to his students, who were still typing away frantically. "Okay, Ernie. I'm sorry for the delay. What's happening that has you guys all upset?"

Ernie looked up from his computer to Rick and Katie and Mick, and took a breath. "Well, in an unfortunate fit of consillyitis – "

"Consillyitis?" Alex raised an eyebrow. He moved the pizza boxes and sat in the plastic and chrome-tubed chair next to the young man.

"A foolish, futile and, unwonted desire for conciliation," Katie said without looking up. She was intent on her laptop. Alex leaned over and saw that she was playing Solitaire. She grinned up at him.

"'Con-silly-ation'," Rick chuckled. "A pathetically submissive attempt to make peace where, within principle, there can be none."

"And probably wouldn't be a good idea if it

could," Mick finished.

Ernie went on. "The convention delegates have nominated one of the candidates you defeated – Forrey Nadalindov – as your running mate. Prof – Alex – please believe we did everything we could to prevent it. These laptops helped a lot. We contacted every state delegation we could, but except for Arizona, it was no go."

Alex nodded. The news gave him an odd sense of foreboding. "Did we make a mistake being here instead of at the hotel?" It made no difference; he'd have been here if the world were coming to an end.

Ernie shook his head. "They're convinced they did a good thing. That kind of stupidity is unstoppable. What did Lenin call them?"

"It was Joseph Goebbels," Mick told him. "Hitler's clubfooted minister of propaganda. He called people like them 'useful idiots'."

Alex laughed.

* * * * * *

"I flew out commercially," Faith-Anne told her father. "The flight itself was nice, but as usual, slogging through the airports was like a tour of Communist Bulgaria – 'your orifices, Comrade!'"

Alex had loved flying commercially as a youngster – still loved the flight itself – but on the excuse for tyranny the word "security" always provides, they'd turned the experience into something unpleasant. Too bad he wasn't really going to be president.

He was driving the peacock blue Durango back to the downtown hotel to prepare and make his acceptance speech later this evening. Needing leg room, Chip Sheridan occupied the seat beside him.

His daughter sat behind them with Rick and Katie. Ernie shared what he insisted on calling the "hindmost" seat – Alex gathered it had something to do with a Larry Niven novel – with Mick. The peculiar thing was that Faith-Anne and Ernie already seemed to know each other.

"I figured we'd take the corporate jet back to the coast," she concluded. It was her right; she was head of the company now.

"Too late, baby, sorry," her father told her. "I sent it to North Carolina to get John and Cap. You know the way they always bring more politically incorrect hardware with them than the airlines like dealing with."

"Well," she replied cheerfully, "of course it depends on when Chip has to get back to San Diego. He got here ahead of me, on business for the past couple days, but maybe we'll stay until Uncle John gets here. I haven't seen him since... " She trailed off into bleak silence. She hadn't seen him since her mother's 2001 funeral.

Alex reached back to pat his daughter's arm. "Stay in Morrison, with me, kid," he told her, "at Grandma's house. I have lots of spare room ... " He glanced over at Chip. "It's closer to JeffCo Airport where John will be landing and you'll be taking off. And you two can play on the swingset in the back yard."

"Oh, Daddy!" Faith-Anne exclaimed.

Alex threw his head back and laughed. "You know I finally figured it out, you know. The conspiracy between you and Ernie."

"Conspiracy?" Faith-Anne's tone was a mockery of innocence.

"Conspiracy. Ernie told you – it had to have been months ago, a long time before he told me – that he was planning to tap me for the FLPA nomination. You arranged for a new edition of *Looking Forward* to be printed well in advance of the convention. How much did it cost us, kiddo – and is it legal?"

Faith-Anne was proud of herself. "It didn't cost *us* anything. It was my contribution to the effort. And it was almost a year ago, before you were a candidate for anything, so it's perfectly legal."

Her father was proud of her, too. "Well, thanks, dear. It was lots of fun seeing them stacked on tables and signing them. How about it, Chip? Can you stay a couple days? What is it in San Diego you have to get back to?"

"Property management, sir." Chip's voice was deep and pleasant.

"Don't 'sir' him, darling," Faith-Anne laughed. "He hates it. Maybe he'll tell you why, someday. Chip's a slumlord, Daddy."

"Hey, I'm *not* a slumlord!" Chip protested amiably. "I only work for slumlords. I used to manage slums on Rodeo Drive in Beverly Hills. Now I do the same thing – for a lot more money – in the Horton Plaza development area in San Diego." The young man finished, laughing. Apparently this was an old joke between him and Alex's daughter.

Faith-Anne said, "Tell him what you did before that."

"Faith-Anne!"

"Tell him."

Chip sighed. "Yes, sir. Before that, I was a lieutenant in the 82nd Airborne, freezing my, er, toes off in western Siberia. It's a pretty place in the summertime – which was on Wednesday this year, they tell me – but it's not so pretty when the snow flies."

Alex nodded, grinning at what Chip had said. He was beginning to see what Faith liked about this young man. Ex-G.I., good looking, well-spoken, ambitious, good sense of self-deprecating humor, and a libertarian. He tried to relax. Faith-Anne had never had a steady boyfriend her father was aware of. Alex was grateful Chip didn't have any visible tattoos, a Mohawk, or a safety-pin through his nose.

* * * * * *

He'd given speeches before, mostly to trade associations, and he'd been on television. He'd had brighter lights in his eyes, but just now, couldn't recall when. He'd had a vaster unseen audience, but just now couldn't recall where.

On his way to the podium he'd caught a glimpse of his old friend Kitch Sinclair in the Illinois delegation – Kitch had been an FLPA member since the party's founding – flanked by a young priest and an old, bearded man in a yarmulke. There were supposed to be 3000 people out there in the darkened hotel ballroom, although it had sounded like less than that when he'd been introduced by the party's chairman, a doughy little man with watery eyes, and ushered to the platform. Then again, he wasn't this group's first (or even second) choice for president, and their lack of enthusiasm for him was a palpable thing.

"Mr. Chairman. Ladies and gentlemen of the Free Libertarian Party of America, fellow children of the American Revolution," he began, speaking without notes. A small, faint cheer went up, but died a lonely and embarrassed death.

"Please accept my thanks for your nomination." There was more applause that time. He'd planned to thank them for their confidence in him, as expressed by the nomination, but at the last minute couldn't bring himself to utter those words. Now he was glad he hadn't.

"I want you to know I get just as fed up as you do of everything being decided for us in advance. I want to be the candidate you want, not some clown you have to accept because he was shoved down your throats by the power boys and the backroom dealers."

That actually elicited a few cheers.

He looked up, straight into the pair of television cameras being trained on him from a platform in the ballroom's center. "Ladies and gentlemen of the United States of America, let me tell you why I'm here today, and why you should choose me to be your president."

The audience stirred and fell silent.

"No nation that enshrines a First Amendment to its Constitution – forbidding the establishment of a state religion, guaranteeing free exercise of your personal faith – no such nation has any place for the police state policies of an Internal Revenue 'service' that forces you to prove that your beliefs, and the group you share them with, constitute a state-approvable belief system, to file official papers every year to renew that approval, or to refrain from expressing whatever political conclusions your faith may move you to make."

The reaction to that was a little confused. There were religious libertarians, of course. But historically, the FLPA sprang from the writings of Ayn Rand and others who were not religious, or who even felt that religion was harmful to individual liberty. It was something party members had long agreed to disagree on. Alex was confident that they'd see where he was headed in another minute.

He went on. "No nation with a First Amendment to its Constitution – protecting freedom of speech and of the press – no such nation has any place for the police state policies of a Federal Communications Commission, whose unconstitutional purpose is to *ration* free speech. Nor has it any place for the police state policies of a Federal Elections Commission whose implacable purpose is to *prevent* it ... "

Here, he had to stop. The audience, which for decades had viewed the FEC as its mortal enemy, had erupted with applause and cheering. As it died down, he continued. "Nor has it any place for police state policies forbidding those whose products happen to be out of political fashion – alcohol, tobacco, firearms – to advertise themselves."

He paused for a moment, shifting the context. "No nation with a First Amendment to its Constitution – guaranteeing your absolute right to assemble peaceably and petition for a redress of grievances – no such nation has any place for police state policies that require you to apply for permission to exercise those rights."

More modest cheering that time, but he had clearly begun to win them over. What he planned to say next would help.

"No nation with a Second Amendment to its Constitution – a pledge that the unalienable individual, civil, Constitutional, and human right of every man, woman, and responsible child to obtain, own, and carry, openly or concealed, any weapon, rifle, shotgun, handgun, machinegun, *anything*, any time, any place, without asking anyone's permission, will never be interfered with to the slightest degree – "

He had to stop again; nobody would have heard him. He was suddenly aware of a weight dragging at his right hip. He still wore the same clothes he'd had on when he'd rushed to the hospital: jeans, MYT boots, informal shirt, light sweater, sports jacket. He hadn't left the .40 in the car as he'd planned, How appropriate to the occasion, he thought with a grin, and to the words he was about to say. (He made a mental note to have the Oxxford suits Faith-Anne had just persuaded him to order provided with a reinforced gun pocket.)

" – no such nation has any place for the police state policies of a murderous gang of Alcohol, Tobacco, and Firearms terrorists, nor for 20,000 gun laws, each and every one of which is unconstitutional!"

When the noise died down, Alex changed contexts again. "No nation with a Third Amendment to its Constitution – forbidding the peacetime quartering of soldiers in any home without the consent of the owner – no such nation has any place for police state tax laws that accomplish exactly the same thing, depriving individuals of half of what they earn, sacking their fondest dreams, looting the futures of their children, pillaging their hopes, reducing them all to bitter ashes."

He could tell that few of them had ever looked at the Third Amendment that way before. It had become a specialty of his.

"No nation with a Fourth Amendment to its Constitution – securing your person, home, papers, and personal property against unreasonable search and seizure, mandating that warrants can only be issued 'on probable cause, supported by oath or affirmation, and particularly describing the place to be searched, and the persons or things to be seized' – no such nation has a place for police state policies like John Doe warrants stacked two feet high in some hack judge's office to be taken and used freely by uniformed criminals more intent on enforcing unconstitutional laws than on keeping the peace – "

They started to roar, but he held up a hand. "Nor has it any room for midnight battering rams to smash in your door, followed by dozens of screaming, jackbooted thugs with black body armor, ski masks, Nazi helmets, and machineguns."

It took almost five minutes for his audience to quiet down. In the midst of it, somebody started chanting, *"Hope! Hope! Hope!"*, and a dozen, a hundred, a thousand voices joined his, *"Hope! Hope! Hope!"*

"No nation with a Fifth Amendment to its Constitution," Alex persisted, "defining due process of law, forbidding private property to be taken for public use without just compensation – no such nation has any place for a police state policy of 'civil forfeiture', under which government thieves steal your home, your car, your business, your savings, anything else they want, long before you're proven guilty of any crime, with the open purpose of denying you an adequate defense in court; then, even if you're proven innocent, the thieves keep what they've stolen."

The ballroom erupted with cheerful boos and catcalls, against a counterpoint of *"Hope! Hope! Hope!*

... Hope! Hope! Hope!"

"Nor has it any place for federal 'civil rights' prosecutions – violating the spirit of the Fifth Amendment's prohibition of double jeopardy – against those who've been declared innocent by a jury of their peers. Nor has it any place for civil suits when criminal trials don't go the way the government wants, or for laws forcing manufacturers to advertise against themselves."

"Hope! Hope! Hope!" exclaimed the audience, *"Hope! Hope! Hope!"*, and in the break between each triplet of words, some began shouting, *"FOR AMERICA!"*

"No nation with a Sixth Amendment to its Constitution – promising a speedy public trial by an impartial jury – no such nation has a place for the police state process of *voir dir,* a phrase best translated as 'jury tampering' by judges and prosecutors, letting them hand-pick jurors to ensure the conviction of innocent defendants. Nor has it any place for schools and media and judges who refuse to inform juries of their 1000-year-old right and duty to evaluate the law, as well as the facts of the case."

More cheers. Jury nullification was popular with this crowd. The chanting started again: *"Hope! Hope! Hope! FOR AMERICA! Hope! Hope! Hope! FOR AMERICA! Hope! Hope! Hope! FOR AMERICA!"*

Alex had to wait it out. "No nation with a Seventh Amendment to its constitution – protecting the right to a jury trial in civil cases, limiting the power of federal trial and appellate court judges, setting a standard of due process, proclaiming our heritage of jury trials, and reminding the world of our culture's commitment to citizen control of the legal process – no such nation has any place for a vast, proliferating horde of federal welfare state agencies and their administrative law courts that apply their own rules and impose their own penalties, with no jury of the people to evaluate the facts or to ensure that justice is served."

"Hope! Hope! Hope! FOR AMERICA! Hope! Hope! Hope! FOR AMERICA! Hope! Hope! Hope! FOR AMERICA! Hope! Hope! Hope! FOR AMERICA!"

"No nation with an Eighth Amendment to its Constitution – forbidding excessive bail, excessive fines, and cruel and unusual punishments – no such nation has any place for judges who set bail or levy fines intended to cripple their victims, who let white collar defendants be restrained by manacles, leg-irons, and belly chains to make a Marxist political statement, or who countenance consent decrees that punish targeted individuals without proving their guilt."

"Hope! Hope! Hope! FOR AMERICA! Hope! Hope! Hope! FOR AMERICA! Hope! Hope! Hope! FOR AMERICA! Hope! Hope! Hope! FOR AMERICA! Hope! Hope! Hope! FOR AMERICA!"

"No nation with a Ninth Amendment to its Constitution – reserving to the people all the rights *not* mentioned in the Constitution – no such nation has a place for thousands of police state agencies and millions of agents interfering with every aspect of your life, telling you what to eat, what to drink, not to smoke, what car to drive, how to drive it, how to fuel it, how to bring up your children, what crops to raise, what crops not to raise, how tall your lawn can be, even how many gallons of water your toilet tank may contain."

"Hope! Hope! Hope! FOR AMERICA! Hope! Hope! Hope! FOR AMERICA! Hope! Hope! Hope! FOR AMERICA! Hope! Hope! Hope! FOR AMERICA! Hope! Hope! Hope! FOR AMERICA! Hope! Hope! Hope! FOR AMERICA!"

"No such nation has any place for police state monsters who blow the heads off mothers holding their babies in their arms, or burn and machinegun whole churches full of women and children, and tell low, cowardly lies about it afterward and give each other worthless coward's medals.

"Hope! Hope! Hope! FOR AMERICA! Hope! Hope! Hope! FOR AMERICA! Hope! Hope! Hope! FOR AMERICA! Hope! Hope! Hope! FOR AMERICA! Hope! Hope! Hope! FOR AMERICA! Hope! Hope! Hope! FOR AMERICA!"

"No such nation has any place for the increasingly prevailing police state philosophy of government under which, as E.B. White warned us, everything not forbidden by the state is compulsory and everything not compulsory is forbidden."

"Hope! Hope! Hope! FOR AMERICA! Hope! Hope! Hope! FOR AMERICA! Hope! Hope! Hope! FOR AMERICA! Hope! Hope! Hope! FOR AMERICA! Hope! Hope! Hope! FOR AMERICA! Hope! Hope! Hope! FOR AMERICA!"

"No nation with a Tenth Amendment to its Constitution – reserving to the states and the people all powers not given to the government by the Constitution – no such nation has any place for police state agencies like the Bureau of Alcohol, Tobacco, and Firearms, that cruelly trapped, confined, and tortured 80 helpless men, women, and children in their church near Waco, Texas, for the purpose of improving its public relations problems.

"Hope! Hope! Hope! FOR AMERICA! Hope! Hope! Hope! FOR AMERICA! Hope! Hope! Hope! FOR AMERICA! Hope! Hope! Hope! FOR AMERICA! Hope! Hope! Hope! FOR AMERICA! Hope! Hope! Hope! FOR AMERICA!"

"Nor has it any room for a Combat Assistance Group – popularly known as 'Delta Force' – that helped the ATF – or a Federal Bureau of Investigation that finished the victims off with flammable chemicals, shoulder-fired missiles to set the chemicals ablaze, and machineguns to make sure they stayed in their church and were poisoned or burned to death.

"Hope! Hope! Hope! FOR AMERICA! Hope! Hope! Hope! FOR AMERICA! Hope! Hope! Hope! FOR AMERICA! Hope! Hope! Hope! FOR AMERICA! Hope! Hope! Hope! FOR AMERICA! Hope! Hope! Hope! FOR AMERICA!"

"Nor has it any room for a Drug Enforcement Administration whose unconstitutional predations have all but destroyed the Constitution, corrupted government at every level, transformed our once-fair cities into combat zones, and turned America into a banana republic.

"Hope! Hope! Hope! FOR AMERICA! Hope! Hope! Hope! FOR AMERICA! Hope! Hope! Hope! FOR AMERICA! Hope! Hope! Hope! FOR AMERICA! Hope! Hope! Hope! FOR AMERICA! Hope! Hope! Hope! FOR AMERICA!"

"Nor has it any room for a Department of Housing and Urban Development that was among the first to ravage the Bill of Rights, obliterating hundreds of thousands of mostly inner urban residential buildings, forcing their occupants into so-called public housing, then lawlessly shaking its captives down whenever it feels the urge.

"Hope! Hope! Hope! FOR AMERICA! Hope! Hope! Hope! FOR AMERICA! Hope! Hope! Hope! FOR AMERICA! Hope! Hope! Hope! FOR AMERICA! Hope! Hope! Hope! FOR AMERICA! Hope! Hope! Hope! FOR AMERICA!"

"Nor has it any room for an Occupational Safety and Health Administration, and an Environmental Protection Agency that, more than any other, have 'exported' millions of American jobs by making the manufacturing industry all but impossible here.

"Hope! Hope! Hope! FOR AMERICA! Hope! Hope! Hope! FOR AMERICA! Hope! Hope! Hope! FOR AMERICA! Hope! Hope! Hope! FOR AMERICA! Hope! Hope! Hope! FOR AMERICA! Hope! Hope! Hope! FOR AMERICA!"

"Nor has it any room for a Food and Drug Administration which causes thousand of deaths every year with unnecessary bureaucratic restrictions on new and badly-need medicines.

"Hope! Hope! Hope! FOR AMERICA! Hope! Hope! Hope! FOR AMERICA! Hope! Hope! Hope! FOR AMERICA! Hope! Hope! Hope! FOR AMERICA! Hope! Hope! Hope! FOR AMERICA! Hope! Hope! Hope! FOR AMERICA!"

"Nor has it any room for a Federal Emergency Management Administration which capitalizes on human misery in the wake of natural disaster to control the lives of millions and take away their property and their rights.

"Hope! Hope! Hope! FOR AMERICA! Hope! Hope! Hope! FOR AMERICA! Hope! Hope! Hope! FOR AMERI-

CA! Hope! Hope! Hope! FOR AMERICA! Hope! Hope! Hope! FOR AMERICA! Hope! Hope! Hope! FOR AMERICA!"

"Nor has it any room for an Interstate Commerce Commission which makes the most of a deliberate misunderstanding of the Constitution to control and oppress the lives of millions every day.

"Hope! Hope! Hope! FOR AMERICA! Hope! Hope! Hope! FOR AMERICA! Hope! Hope! Hope! FOR AMERICA! Hope! Hope! Hope! FOR AMERICA! Hope! Hope! Hope! FOR AMERICA! Hope! Hope! Hope! FOR AMERICA!"

"Nor has it any room for a Law Enforcement Assistance Administration which has militarized police all over the country, endangering the lives of millions.

"Hope! Hope! Hope! FOR AMERICA! Hope! Hope! Hope! FOR AMERICA! Hope! Hope! Hope! FOR AMERICA! Hope! Hope! Hope! FOR AMERICA! Hope! Hope! Hope! FOR AMERICA! Hope! Hope! Hope! FOR AMERICA!"

"Nor has it any room for a National Endowment for the Arts – the Art Nazis – who want to force you to pay for crucifixes exhibited in jars of human excrement, and call it 'art'.

"Hope! Hope! Hope! FOR AMERICA! Hope! Hope! Hope! FOR AMERICA! Hope! Hope! Hope! FOR AMERICA! Hope! Hope! Hope! FOR AMERICA! Hope! Hope! Hope! FOR AMERICA! Hope! Hope! Hope! FOR AMERICA!"

"Nor has it any room for an Army Corps of Engineers which, with or without the permission of the owners, rearranges whole vistas, in a way that often renders them more dangerous to human life and enterprise.

"Hope! Hope! Hope! FOR AMERICA! Hope! Hope! Hope! FOR AMERICA! Hope! Hope! Hope! FOR AMERICA! Hope! Hope! Hope! FOR AMERICA! Hope! Hope! Hope! FOR AMERICA! Hope! Hope! Hope! FOR AMERICA!"

"Nor has it any room for thousands of other agencies riding roughshod over the duly constituted authority and the sovereignty of state and local governments and the American people themselves."

"Hope! Hope! Hope! FOR AMERICA! Hope! Hope! Hope! FOR AMERICA! Hope! Hope! Hope! FOR AMERICA! Hope! Hope! Hope! FOR AMERICA! Hope! Hope! Hope! FOR AMERICA! Hope! Hope! Hope! FOR AMERICA!"

There came a hush. All ten Amendments had been mentioned; the ritual seemed complete. No one knew what to expect next – except for Alex.

"No nation with a Thirteenth Amendment to its Constitution – outlawing slavery after 6000 bloody years of the vile, disgusting practice – no such nation has any place for conscription of any kind, no matter the emergency, no matter the excuse."

It began again. *"Hope! Hope! Hope! FOR AMERICA! Hope! Hope! Hope! FOR AMERICA! Hope! Hope! Hope! FOR AMERICA!"*

He raised his voice at last. "Nor for income taxation!"

"Hope! Hope! Hope! FOR AMERICA! Hope! Hope! Hope! FOR AMERICA! Hope! Hope! Hope! FOR AMERICA! Hope! Hope! Hope! FOR AMERICA!"

He shouted over the crowd, at the top of his lungs, "Or for those death-camps for the mind, the public schools, spewing their ceaseless *crapaganda_* all over our precious children, converting them into our political enemies, and enlisting them in the socialist destruction of individual lives!"

"Hope! Hope! Hope! FOR AMERICA! Hope! Hope! Hope! FOR AMERICA! Hope! Hope! Hope! FOR AMERICA! Hope! Hope! Hope! FOR AMERICA! Hope! Hope! Hope! FOR AMERICA!"

The uproar seemed to last for ages. Alex held onto the lectern and let it wash over him. It was like standing three feet from the tracks as a heavy freight-train passed by at 75 miles an hour, exhilarating and frightening at the same time.

At last he raised both hands again. "It's time to ask, what *does* such a nation have a place for?

"The total obliteration of socialism?"

"Hope! Hope! Hope! FOR AMERICA! Hope! Hope! Hope! FOR AMERICA! Hope! Hope! Hope! FOR AMERICA! Hope! Hope! Hope! FOR AMERICA! Hope! Hope! Hope! FOR AMERICA! Hope! Hope! Hope! FOR AMERICA!"

"Government of the Bill of Rights, by the Bill of Rights, and for the Bill of Rights?"

"Hope! Hope! Hope! FOR AMERICA! Hope! Hope! Hope! FOR AMERICA! Hope! Hope! Hope! FOR AMERICA! Hope! Hope! Hope! FOR AMERICA! Hope! Hope! Hope! FOR AMERICA! Hope! Hope! Hope! FOR AMERICA!"

"And zero tolerance – for tyranny!"

"Hope! Hope! Hope! FOR AMERICA! Hope! Hope! Hope! FOR AMERICA! Hope! Hope! Hope! FOR AMERICA! Hope! Hope! Hope! FOR AMERICA! Hope! Hope! Hope! FOR AMERICA! Hope! Hope! Hope! FOR AMERICA!"

The chanting and cheering lasted 20 minutes.

CHAPTER ELEVEN: *JOHN PONDORO*

> *Look at the Ninth and Tenth Amendments and Article I, Section 8 of the Constitution, which spells out and sets limits on what government's allowed to do. Use a magnifying glass, Coke bottle spectacles, a jeweler's loupe, or a scanning electron microscope, you'll* NEVER *find a word in there about public schools.*
>
> – Alexander Hope, *Looking Forward*

"Tell me, Nada, are we simply going to let this ... this... *billionaire* buy our party's nomination?" Abe Horrwyrn demanded rhetorically.

Horrwyrn was a bizarre figure of a man, Forrey Nadalindov thought. To start with, he was ludicrously tall and thin, reminding Nadalindov of the character Jack Skellington in *The Nightmare Before Christmas.* What was more, he had a very odd, waxy-gray complexion and mechanical mannerisms exactly like those of one of Walt Disney's audioanimatronic dummies. Slap on a beard and a top hat and you'd have another Abe – Abe Lincoln.

However strange they may have seemed in person, though, Horrwyrn's appearance and eccentric behavior – as well as his excruciatingly slow delivery

– worked very well on television, and that was all that counted.

"Buy our party's nomination? As opposed to stealing it, the way you did the last time?" asked Nadalindov. He'd just arrived in the convention hotel's Presidential suite, having been curtly summoned here by its present occupant. Horrwyrn sat near a window, in the same position made famous by Rodin's "The Thinker", with the city's lights twinkling behind him in the night. "Anyway, I thought we were in favor of things like money and billionaires and, well generally, acts of capitalism between consenting adults."

"Don't get smart, Nada!" Declan Ghillie Moure entered from an adjoining room. It was the end of a long, hard, discouraging day, but the little man looked as if he'd just been washed and pressed, with his blue blazer, gray slacks, and striped red tie. "You're not built for it, and it certainly isn't why we arranged for you to have the Vice Presidential nomination."

"You arranged – ?" Nadalindov was outraged and bewildered. "But I spent *hours* down there, wheeling and dealing, pulling in every favor I ever – "

"While we spent hours undoing the damage you'd done, cajoling, threatening, blackmailing, and twisting arms – not to mention all the two-penny bribes we shelled out in the hotel bar and on the floor." Moure made a snorting noise. "It's gratifying – and disgusting – how little these simps will sell themselves for. Do you really imagine you could have done it without us? Imagine again – you're our man, Nada, bought and paid for!"

Horrwyrn said, "Now, Ghillie..."

Moure's face was suddenly scarlet. "Shut up, Abe! Just sit there and try to look all statesmanlike and telegenic while I give Nada, here, his marching orders."

"Give me one good reason," said Nadalindov, a ball of red-hot fury growing in his stomach, "why I should take orders from you, Ghillie Moure."

"Because after this is all over, we'll see that you're appointed executive director of the FLPA with a six figure salary – low six figures, mind you."

Nadalindov gulped. "What do you want me to do?"

"Simple. Run as hard as you can for *Vice* President – we'll help with the logistics – but run as if you want to be *President*. Wage an independent campaign as the self-declared libertarian moderate that the voters can rely on to be 'realistic'. Whenever Hope goes overboard with his publicly-stated policies and positions, tell the media things like, 'He doesn't really mean it – and if he does, trust me to talk him out of it.'"

Nadalindov shook himself like a wet spaniel. "Let me get this straight. You want me to continually undermine our own Presidential candidate?"

"Nada, Abe and I want your unspoken campaign slogan to be, 'Elect us – then impeach him.' Hope will be noble and try to ignore you as best he can, but the media vultures, who are always on the lookout for conflict of any kind, can be counted on to give you considerable play."

"Elect us, then impeach him." Nadalindov rolled it around in his mouth. "Sounds good to me."

* * * * * *

"Crapaganda?"

Alex laughed out loud, glancing briefly to his right, where his old friend John Pondoro was taking up a lot of room in the front passenger's seat of the peacock blue Durango. All around them, the open prairie countryside, the fields and trees, had long since turned to gold and amber.

They were leaving the Jefferson County Airport where the sleek little Hope Corporation LearJet had arrived on time. Now they were headed back to the Alex's modest little house in Morrison, bearing his old war buddy, his buddy's grown son, and a lot of rather heavy, lumpy baggage – exactly as Alex had predicted to his daughter. It was September 4th, the day following Alex's FLPA nomination and acceptance speech.

The day following the vicious attack on Dana Li.

"I was speaking without notes," Alex explained, "and the word just came out of my mouth. I didn't realize you made a practice of watching C-Span."

Pondoro was an exceptionally large man, six feet three or four, Alex estimated, and built like an old-growth oak. Just one of the man's hands was the size of both of Alex's, and he recalled the way, during the war, that it had swallowed up a Colt 1911A1 .45 and made it look like James Bond's tiny Walther PPK. They used to make a joke about John not needing a gun at all – he could just push the bullets in with his thumb.

John wore his silvery hair in a crewcut, and like Alex, preferred bluejeans and cowboy boots to any other kind of clothing – although his pet brand of boots was Lucchese. While Alex liked western shirts and sportscoats, at the moment, John chose a khaki bush jacket like Chancellor Van Cleave's.

"Well it's a good word," John said. "Let's keep using it. I don't watch C-Span, I started with FoxNews, like I told you on the phone, but I was also logged onto NetPlanetNews.com and I actually watched your acceptance speech that way. Very preferable to having a couple of talking heads doing voiceovers and telling me what they want me to think you're saying.

"Say, isn't that the same outfit your cute little girlfriend works for, Uncle Alex?" John's son Cap, sitting immediately behind them, was as tall as his father, but only about half as wide, wiry, quick, and strong, with a perpetual sardonic grin. Life seldom got the better of Cap Pondoro; if he'd been tortured by the Spanish Inquisition, he'd have found some way to enjoy it – probably by making jokes at the Inquisitor's expense.

"You know perfectly well it is," Alex replied, feeling a sudden heat rising along the sides of his neck. "And she isn't my girlfriend, Cap. She's probably younger than my daughter, and I'm certain that she's younger than you are. The truth is," he admitted sadly, "I hardly know her."

"Ah, your voice says no, no, no, Uncle Alex, but your eyes say yes, yes, yes," Cap laughed, patting Alex on the shoulder. "That's your story, and you stick with it – as long as I get to be a flower girl at your wedding."

"He's got it bad, all right," John laughed with his son. "I gather she's the reason you wanted us out here."

Alex sighed wearily. Were his feelings about the young internet reporter really so obvious to everyone?

If they were, he wondered what his daughter was thinking – my father's a dirty old man, probably. And he was afraid she might be right. "Only indirectly. She's with the media, not with my campaign – boy, doesn't that sound funny, 'my campaign'? – and your being here couldn't have prevented what happened to her."

"That much we'd figured out," John nodded.

Alex went on. "But it got me thinking. In nearly 40 years of trying, the FLPA has never won more than a few hundred thousand votes for its Presidential candidate. So you wouldn't think I'd represent much of a threat to anyone. Certainly no point in making a martyr of a loser. But somebody nearly killed Dana – Miss Li – and apparently over that piece she wrote about me."

"Apparently," John emphasized the word. "Your Dana – our Miss Li – makes a professional practice of telling the truth in public. A very antisocial habit, if you ask me. And she probably has a lot of enemies of her very own as a result. I took it upon myself to have a couple of operatives start looking into it. Are you all right with that, Boss?"

Alex nodded his approval. "Now as far as I can determine, John, no FLPA Presidential candidate has ever asked for or been offered Secret Service protection – "

"And you would have refused it in any case," John finished for his old friend.

Alex laughed. "You're right, I would! Consequently, hiring the most competent security consultant I know – a Marine Corps war buddy who also happens to be my closest friend – seemed the only sensible thing to me."

"Not to mention his batboy, Robin," Cap said.

John nodded. "Gotcha, Boss. And thanks for the testimonial. Coming from you, Professor, it means a bundle." Reaching under his jacket, he extracted a large, black, bulky automatic pistol, and pinched its slide back a quarter of an inch with his big thumb and forefinger to assure himself that gremlins hadn't unloaded the chamber since the last time he looked. "So are you ready now, for my first professional piece of advice?"

That sounded particularly ominous. Alex's eyebrows went up. "Uh, sure. Go ahead."

"Get rid of this car. It's like wearing a blue neon target on your back. If you really need a big car, get yourself a neutral-colored Suburban."

"I *like* my Durango," Alex groaned. "I *hate* Suburbans. The badguys use 'em."

* * * * * *

"Good afternoon, dear friends," the heavily hair-sprayed synthetic blond gushed at the camera. The makeup she was wearing, Alex thought, must have been put on with a cement trowel, and her perfume made her a walking violation of the Geneva Convention's international prohibition against chemical warfare. "I'm Marla Towers, your host for *Hot Fresno Afternoons.*"

There was no studio audience here, but the room suddenly filled itself with artificial applause. That was a first for Alex, so far on the campaign trail, and he hoped sincerely that it was a last, as well.

"We're speaking in our downtown studios today," the woman said, "with Professor Alexander Hope, billionaire high-tech industrialist – eligible bachelor, ladies – and the newly nominated Presidential candidate for the ... "

She glanced down at a slip of paper in her hand.

" ... for the Free Libertarian Party of America. Professor Hope – may I call you Alex? – libertarians have recently been described in the media as 'childishly selfish geriatric adolescents', and by somebody else as 'just a felony waiting to happen'. Does it ever embarrass you, given your own extreme wealth – and the terrible burden of guilt that must inevitably go with it – to be associated with a political party that seems to idolize money and personal pleasure above everything else?"

"Watch where you point that cheat-sheet, Marla," Alex took a cue from her and grinned at the camera, 10 feet from where he sat. "It might go off and hurt somebody." Ernie had calculated, when he saw them off at the JeffCo airport, that this was his 200th television appearance since Labor Day, and Alex was used to this sort of thing by now. "I'm curious, did you *learn* to load questions like that, or is it a natural talent?"

The television hostess blinked stupidly. "Excuse me, Alex? Isn't this my show? Aren't *I* the one who's supposed to be asking the questions, here?"

As if, Alex thought to himself and laughed. "Okay, Marla, fair enough. We libertarians are just like any of our fellow Americans. We want to keep what we earn, and to live our lives for their own sake, without police state interference. If the FLPA 'idolizes' anything, it's the individual liberty to become anything you have the moxie to make of yourself. And if that happens to mean accumulating a great deal of money – or becoming a local television personality – then so be it."

The hostess smiled as if her shoes were too tight. Alex could see fine cracks in the makeup around her eyes and mouth. "With us today, as well, is Forrey Nadalindov, Alex's running mate, the FLPA candidate for Vice President. Forrey, what do you see as your role in Alex's Presidential campaign?"

His exposed scalp beading visibly under the bright studio lights, Nadalindov folded his hands across his vest. "Well, Marla," he intoned with a ponderous complacency, "my dear old friend Alex is rapidly becoming famous all over the world for his tremendous passion where the defense of liberty is concerned, and his extremely straightforward expression of it."

"I see," fluttered the hostess. "And ...?"

"And sometimes – as we've seen here today, for example – that extreme passion seems to carry him off into the clouds. I see it as my job to be the reasonable partner, and to try to bring him back to earth again."

As he had on previous occasions like this for weeks, Alex fought to remain calm. His concerns about Nadalindov's candidacy had proven all too well-founded. The former Young Republican seemed to believe that it was his mission in life was to sabotage the Hope campaign wherever and whenever he could. Alex didn't have to wonder who'd put him up to it, that had been clear from the pattern of votes cast for Nadalindov on the FLPA convention floor. It had to be Abe Horrwyrn – or even likelier, Declan Ghillie Moure – who was pulling Nadalindov's strings.

Alex glanced over at the mighty John Pondoro,

standing off-camera with his arms loosely folded across his massive chest. The expression on his big face would have soured milk. Then he looked at his daughter and campaign manager, Faith-Anne, very tiny beside her "uncle" – but no less disgusted.

At the other side of the studio, Cap appeared to think the whole thing was funny, but Alex knew exactly what each of them was thinking. It wasn't the first time that his running mate had said something like this in public. Alex was growing weary of it. The idiot reminded him of his mother.

The television hostess spoke to him again, jerking him out of what had almost threatened to become a reverie. "As a lifelong student of history – according to your official biography – as well as a college professor of it, you've stated that you plan to campaign, more or less exclusively, on what you like to call a 'Bill of Rights enforcement' platform." She fluttered her artificial eyelashes at him. He could almost feel the breeze. "Can you explain what that means for our viewers?"

Alex nodded. "Yes, Marla, I think I can do that. I believe that putting legal teeth in the first ten amendments to the Constitution – which were written by the Founding Fathers to protect us all from the police state interference in our lives I mentioned – will cure most of this country's many political ills. It will eventually eliminate every last remaining trace of that alien philosophy, socialism, from America."

"I see," Marla lied. "It says here that you're also an advocate of jury nullification. Isn't that where juries will be able to decide if they don't like a law?"

He grinned. "Not 'will be', Marla, juries have that power here and now, and have for a long time. As a sort of a trademark – echoing the ancient Roman senator Cato's remarks about destroying Carthage – although I missed a chance in my acceptance address at the convention, I make a practice of trying to end each and every speech I make, whatever else it may be about, with as firm an endorsement of jury nullification as possible."

The interviewer simulated alarm. "But Alex, won't that lead inevitably to anarchy?"

"It hasn't over the past 1000 years, has it, Marla? That's how old our jury system happens to be, and it's the best thing we inherited from the body of English law. In fact, the way that prosecutors and judges have taken over our courtrooms today has brought us much closer to anarchy – in the sense that it's all but destroyed the rule of law."

Nadalindov loudly cleared his throat. "Now Marla, here's a perfect example of what I've been talking about. Alex's heart is in the right place, of course. Nobody can dispute that for a minute. But he always takes the most extreme position he can on issues like this one. I ask you, how on earth can the rule of law be destroyed by judges and lawyers? It seems to me that anything that judges and lawyers do *is* the rule of law."

Marla giggled. "Well, I don't know much about the law, but that certainly seems obvious to me!"

"Marla," Alex said, as sweetly as he could, "what's obvious to me is that the individuals in your, er... profession make a point of not knowing much about the law, or about history, or about science, or about much of anything else, for that matter. Maybe that's why they've acted for so long as if they believe that there's only *one* Amendment to the Constitution "

Marla sniffed. "Oh? And what Amendment would that be, Alex?"

"The First Amendment – and that it applies to them and nobody else."

"Now, Alex," she changed the subject. "We're hearing today that Vice President Chesley Chambers may be indicted later this week on absolutely shocking charges – trafficking in child pornography over the internet. We've even seen some of the pictures on TV, poor, naked little boys and girls – properly censored, of course. Now isn't it fair to say that this is something you libertarians would actually approve of?"

Alex leaned toward the obnoxious-smelling woman. "Marla, I have a daughter of my own. She's all grown up now. In fact she's my campaign manager, Faith-Anne Hope, right over there. But she was little once, and vulnerable. Also, it's true, the First Amendment right to freedom of every possible form of expression – including those that plenty of other people don't approve of – is of sacred importance to all libertarians."

She nodded toward the camera as if to say to her viewers, "Didn't I tell you, ladies?"

But Alex wasn't finished. "If somebody had used my daughter when she was five or six to make pictures and movies like that – long before she was ready to choose wisely for herself – he wouldn't be alive today."

Marla gasped, "You mean you'd actually – "

"The world is full of predators," Alex answered her, "and it's a parent's proud right and solemn duty to preserve his children from them. The libertarian culture I want to reestablish – a culture rooted in stringent enforcement of the Bill of Rights – would support him in that."

"Don't you mean he *or she?*" For a single frozen moment, lacking any other recourse, the hostess had reverted to mindless, robotic political correctness. Then: "How old would you say a child has to be to choose wisely?"

Alex shook his head. "I don't say, Marla. I won't say. It has to be different for every single individual human being. That's one of the things that makes us human."

Nadalindov spoke up. "Be careful, Marla. You know if Alex had his way, they'd let two-year-olds have guns and drugs, and five-year-olds would be allowed to vote."

Alex held up a hand. "Nada's – I mean, Forrey's first assertion is absolutely *not* correct. Poor fellow, he's never understood this issue and possibly never will, although I've tried to explain it to him many times. As to giving five-year-olds the vote, he may be on firmer ground. Look what we've got in office right now. Given the vote, could children possibly do any worse than adults have, over the past two and a half centuries?"

Instead of replying, she said, "Whatever else, Alex, you'd have to agree that the Vice President's troubles mean that the former First Lady now has a lock on the election. The opinion polls this afternoon put her at 75% to the Vice President's 20%. Do you have any comment about that?"

"It would be a tragedy of historic proportions," Alex replied. "if that woman were to become President. The former First Lady has a long track record in government. Every nanosecond of it demonstrates her grim and utter commitment to imposing a socialist dictatorship on the people of America."

"Oh, Alex! Isn't that a little strong? True, the former First Lady is a liberal – "

"There's no such thing as a liberal, Marla. There hasn't been for a long, long time. I never use the word, and you shouldn't either – nobody should. 'Liberal' is what socialists call themselves when they don't want you to understand that they plan to take away your rights, your property, and eventually your life. Any politician who would have you imprisoned for paying your own doctor in cash certainly fits into that category."

The hostess glanced toward Nadalindov for support, but the man turned his palms upward helplessly and shrugged. "I gotta confess, Marla, that where the former First Lady is concerned, I agree with Alex completely."

Apparently resigned, she inhaled deeply and exhaled. "One final question, Alex. We all thought we'd gotten meaningful campaign finance reform a few years ago. Nobody ever counted on a billionaire running for the Presidency. Can you comment on the news stories we've all seen in the past few days that you're willing to spend as much of your own money on your Presidential campaign – something close to 100 million dollars, according to the stories – as the other two candidates combined?

Alex grinned. "I've never been a Republican, who values the contents of his wallet more than he does freedom. Can you think of anything better to spend money on than making America a free country?"

* * * * * *

"Alex, he called me a 'slope'," Dana whispered quietly. "He called me a 'gook'. He called me a 'zipperhead' – and I don't even know what that means!" A tear emerged from the corner of her eye and ran across her cheek.

"I never did, either, to tell the truth." Alex couldn't remember being angrier. He looked out through the big window he'd insisted on when they'd moved her to a private room, at an enormous decorative pond populated, even in October, with ducks and geese, and tried to calm himself, watching the ripples. "I assume you told the police what he said and looked like."

He'd tell her later about the "operatives" John had put on the case. Up in a corner near the ceiling, the television babbled softly to itself. The pictures were of the former First Lady making an appearance at a federal daycare center. Poor Dana, forced to watch the competition.

Dana smiled up at Alex and lit the room. They'd taken most of the bandages off her face by now, although her cheeks and forehead were still covered with livid yellow, purple, and green bruises. She was still in her body cast (he certainly didn't envy her the itching), and had some kind of brace – a small splinter of aluminum and fabric – across her nose, which the surgeons had assured him would be pretty again.

"Yes to the former. No, I'm greatly ashamed to say, to the latter. The guy came at me from behind, at first, wearing one of those black ski-mask things."

"A balaclava," Alex told her absently. "All kinds of thugs use balaclavas, freelance and governmental." He'd been holding her least injured hand since he'd arrived (her left index finger, middle finger, and thumb hadn't been hurt) and squeezed it now, reassuringly. She squeezed back. As usual, he wondered if that meant what he wanted it to mean.

Even bruised and broken, lying in a complicated hospital bed with electric wires and plastic tubes plugged into her everywhere, Dana was the most exotic and beautiful thing Alex had ever seen in his life. Her warm, dark, wonderful eyes were powered from the inside by her lively and perpetually cheerful personality, and he loved to hear her speak. At the same time, Alex was alarmed that he could feel this way so quickly about anyone.

And there was no denying that he did.

The worst – or best – of it was that he knew with a certainty beyond question that Amelia would have liked Dana and approved of his interest in her.

"The very first thing I'm going to do when I get out of this place – aside from showering for about 12 hours – is taking up martial arts," she told him. "Katie tells me that you might consider teaching me to shoot."

"Dana, it would be my pleasure." He squeezed her hand again, not knowing what more to say to her, not needing to say anything, happy just to be here with her.

And again, Dana squeezed his hand in return. He hadn't felt this content since –

"Alex! Alex!" Suddenly, Katie rushed into the room. She skidded at the corner and nearly fell on the tile. Dana had told him she'd been here every day to visit.

"Katie! Katie!" he responded jokingly, rising to help her steady herself. "I'm glad to see you, too!"

"No!," she exclaimed. Her face was flushed and

she was breathless. "Turn the TV to channel – whatever it is here! The Communist News Network! I was watching it out in the lobby just now. You'll never believe what's happening!"

Dana pushed a button, raising the head of her bed a little and used the remote control Velcroed to the safety rail. Sure enough, CNN was showing a dozen federal marshals in brightly-lettered Navy blue raid jackets dragging a struggling and sobbing Republican Vice President Chesley Chambers from his Washington campaign headquarters – as Alex had once put it – in handcuffs, belly chains, and leg-irons.

CHAPTER TWELVE: *THE FORMER FIRST LADY*

> *If the prospects for liberty are so bleak, if so many "sheeple" are happy living in a police state, why is it that each time there's a technical improvement in communication, each time there's an upward increment in interconnectivity, each time it becomes possible to feel the national pulse more accurately, the pressure for individual liberty _increases_?*
>
> – Alexander Hope, *Looking Forward*

The middle of October had arrived, unusually cold and snowy in Colorado, and they were headed for Houston, suffering an unusual heat wave.

It was surprisingly quiet inside the little jet plane. John was sitting up in the cockpit behind the pilot and co-pilot, "expanding his education", as he put it. Alex and Faith-Anne and Cap had just finished microwaving themselves some lunch. Alex loved a certain brand of frozen stuffed bell peppers, never failing to top them off with a slice of American cheese for the final minute. Now the three of them were sitting back, trying their best to relax before the big event facing them in Texas.

Against the stone gray of her favorite suit, Faith-

Anne's long, straight hair looked almost scarlet in the brilliant high-altitude sunlight. Tens of thousands of feet below, the entire world seemed shrouded in a thick, unbroken cloud-layer. Alex knew it was snowing hard in Colorado. A screen at one end of the cabin was tuned to the Weather Channel, showing ominous-looking maps to that effect.

He'd also had an internet videophone conversation with Dana an hour after taking off from the JeffCo Airport. Her old laptop had been smashed by her assailant. Alex had given her one of the company's best as a get-well present. She'd turned her new laptop's CCD camera to the window of the St. Androcles' Hospital room she'd finally be leaving behind next week, and shown him the great big, wet, thickly-falling snowflakes outside.

Alex was looking forward to seeing Houston, even though it was an incredible 90 degrees and raining cats and dogs there. A attractive, Hispanic-surnamed conservative Congresswoman from New Mexico, who'd been Vice President Chesley Chambers' token female running mate, was now half-heartedly campaigning for the presidency, and had violated every precedent by volunteering to publicly debate the FLPA candidate. The former First Lady was now at 80% in the polls and the GOP must be desperate. Ironically, the New York Senator was headed to Colorado today, for some kind of fundraising event among the Hollywood airheads in Aspen.

Alex took another look at his redheaded daughter. He'd been lucky, all his life, to be surrounded by women with beauty and brains. There was an item he'd been meaning to discuss with Faith-Anne – a highly personal item – and this was the first time they'd come even close to being alone together in weeks.

Even so, he hesitated. Cap was back here with them, his nose stuck in an aviation magazine. But the subject was important to Alex, even he dreaded what she might have to say about it. In all her 28 years, he'd never been able to tell his daughter adequately how much he loved her, although he'd tried again and again. This, he thought, wasn't going to be any better.

Abruptly, Cap got up, went aft, and shut himself in the head. When he'd been there for more than two minutes, Alex began, "Hey, kiddo – ".

Faith-Anne turned toward her father, away from the window. "Daddy, there's something I need to tell you. I've needed to for a long time. Do you mind?"

He blinked. "Not at all, Baby, is it about Chip?"

She shook her head. "No, Chip and I are just fine. It's about you and Dana."

Uh, oh, he swallowed. *She's beaten me to it. Here it comes.*

Faith-Anne got up from her seat near the window and sat beside him, sideways, on the little sofa he'd occupied. She took both of his hands in hers. The gesture was Amelia's, when she'd wanted to make sure Faith-Anne was really paying attention. It had always worked pretty well on him, too, he thought.

"Daddy, I know you better than I know anybody. I know you're in love with Dana, and I know you're worried about it, partly because of Mom, partly because of me, partly because Dana's so much younger than you are."

Straight to the point, he thought. He'd certainly handed his business over to the right person.

"I'll plead the Fifth," he told her, his heart racing,

"until I know where this is headed."

She smiled at her father lovingly, and to his surprise, a pair of small teardrops trickled down her cheeks. Faith-Anne wasn't the crying type. "Where it's headed is this, Daddy. Mom loved you and would never have wanted you to be lonely. Me, it's easy to see that you're happier now than you have been in the past seven years. And Daddy, all adults are the same age."

"All adults are the same age?" He shook his head. "What is that supposed to mean?"

She pulled his hands to her heart. "It means you should follow your feelings, Daddy – at last in this one thing. It means I think you're overdue for some romance in your life. Some love. Dana's all grown up, Daddy. I've always been a big fan of hers. She's honest and straightforward in her reporting. She's very pretty and she's even smarter. She's also slightly older than you think. She's 32 – she told me. We've had quite a number of little talks in the past few weeks, Dana and me."

Shocked again, Alex exclaimed, "What?"

"Hey, I gotta check out my future step-mom, don't I? Dana loves you, Daddy, but she's afraid you'll think that she's a gold-digger, or that she's too young for you. And no, she didn't put me up to this. She'd be mortified if she knew I was doing it. She's also a little worried about her folks, especially her mother."

Alex sat beside his daughter in utter, speechless astonishment. On the other hand, a faint sensation of relief – and perhaps even joy – had began to trickle through him. Half sarcastically, he asked her, "Anything else?"

Cap chose that moment to emerge from the tiny

head. He saw that Faith-Anne had been weeping. "What's the matter, F-A? A little motion sickness?"

Faith-Anne told him, "Come over here where I can throw up on you, and we'll see."

They'd been like this, Alex reflected, whenever they happened to be together, since they were little children. Cap stuck his tongue out at her, settled into his chair again, and picked up the magazine he'd been reading.

"There *is* something else," Faith-Anne smiled brightly through her tears as she leaned in and whispered to her father. "Dana says she wants to give me lots of little brothers and sisters!"

* * * * * *

Ten of thousands of feet below, back along the Rockies west of Denver, the former First Lady's convoy wound its way higher and higher into the mountains.

In her limousine, the sophomore Senator from New York was fuming at the weather – as if it were doing this to her personally, and on purpose – and as usual, she wasn't suffering silently. By now her Secret Service escort – in this instance, Agents Mitchell Case and Betsie Hull – were accustomed to the constant barrage of obscenity the woman kept up in private. She was a child of the 60s she told them from time to time, especially when she'd been drinking. They knew she'd lived a relatively difficult life, with a husband whose only lasting legacy was his chronic, unceasing treachery against everyone and everything, from the betrayal of his nation's safety to Communist China, to ravaging the armed forces he famously despised, right down to destroying his own family. For the

Senator and former First Lady, humiliation was a way of life, and had been for 30 years.

Maybe some people felt sorry for her. Maybe they even voted for her, because of that. For some reason, it failed to make Agents Case and Hull – not to mention their colleagues in this detachment – feel any more sympathetic toward the New York Senator. After a while, they all had come to understand clearly that the woman was planning to make up for every bit of the humiliation she'd suffered, no matter who had to pay the price.

Sure, they'd leap in front of a bullet meant for her, every last one of them, but it would be because of a professional duty they felt they owed to themselves, not for the sake of the former First Lady, herself.

Two big black Chevrolet Suburbans filled with large men, a quota's worth of women, and tons of ugly black weapons preceded her limousine as it slowly climbed toward the Continental Divide. The wind-driven snow made it hard to see. (She hated riding backwards, but she'd been given no other option.) She knew that her car was being followed by a pair of rented stretch-cars full of print reporters and their unkempt camera nerds.

Two more black Suburbans followed behind the press cars. Twenty Secret Service agents altogether, the former First Lady thought. That hardly seemed adequate in the middle of a country full of guns – 750 million of them at the BATF's last shamefaced estimate – and 100 million rednecks and genetic culls who stupidly hated her for trying to help them.

Take away those guns and they'd learn to love her. They wouldn't have any choice.

The original plan had been to land the presidential campaign's 737 at D.I.A, east of Denver, then take a smaller chartered plane up to Aspen, one of the smallest towns in America with its own jet-capable airport. There the former First Lady would be greeted on the runway by cameras of all kinds, and an enormous double handful of worshipful movie and TV celebrities. But the Great Plains weather had spoiled everything. Now all she could look forward to was skulking into town in a blizzard, having endured several hours of uncomfortable and dangerous car travel.

The former First Lady pushed a button and a small wet bar revealed itself. Careful in the moving car, she poured herself a big highball glass of scotch and soda. The soda spritzer seemed much livelier at this altitude, she noticed; she nearly splashed liquor on her $5,000 traveling outfit, the last of her original Versaces. Then she found a pack of cigarettes – her brand, she noted with grudging gratification – lit one, inhaled luxuriantly, and settled back to fill the car with the thin reek of tobacco smoke whether little Mitch and Betsie cared for it or not.

She'd made her secretary and personal assistants travel with the press today, while she relaxed in relative privacy. There was nothing she could do about the bodyguards. She'd once demanded that they – whoever it had been at the time – leave their guns in one of the other cars, and they'd refused, while unsuccessfully attempting to stifle laughter.

It was too much to hope that she could catch up on her sleep – not on this winding, slippery road – but at least she could rest. She'd just endured a complete facial in Washington and the scotch fumes burned her upper lip where her moustache had been waxed off. Some idiot of an internet columnist had once called her the Woman with One Eyebrow. He hadn't known the half of it. She'd have complained that it was no fun being 61, but she'd had exactly the same trouble when she was 16.

Nevertheless, the internet, and the untutored and seditious vermin it was infested with, were right at the top of her list of items to take care of, once the mere formality that this election had become was over with, and she was back in the White House, in full control, this time.

The former First Lady and sophomore Senator from New York snuggled down into the folds of her full-length mink coat (better not let the animal lovers see that when she got to Aspen) and tried not to think for a while.

* * * * * *

"Ruven Mendelsohn!" Alex held the phone to his ear. The connection (if that's what one called a telephone conversation conducted without wires) was poor. He supposed it might have something to do with the vast storm they were flying over.

"Is this who I think it is?" the voice on the other end asked faintly, and a bit incredulously. It didn't sound to Alex like the voice of an old man in his 80s.

"That's right, Ruven, this is Alexander Hope, the next former presidential candidate of the United States of America! Unless you want to count the Republican Congresswoman who replaced the vice president."

Faith-Anne sat at a table at the other end of the cabin, doing her own communicating by means of her laptop. Looking over her shoulder for a moment,

Alex had seen messages addressed to Ernie Hanover, Kitch Sinclair, somebody named Sheila Hensley, and now she was chatting with Chip Sheridan in real time. John had emerged from the cockpit in order to microwave himself some lunch. They were only half an hour away from Houston.

Although they'd had many telephone conversations like this one, Ruven complained amiably that they'd never met face to face and probably wouldn't get to before the election, which was now only a few days away.

Alex glanced at his daughter again and thought about his earlier video contact with Dana. Technology was wonderful. "Well, you should get yourself a computer, Ruven, with a camera, so we could see each other when we talk. They have computers there in Belgium, don't they?" He got the rise out of Ruven he'd expected. "Of course I'm kidding – do you think I'd waste an international cellular telephone call on serious business?"

Ruven laughed and Alex laughed with him. He'd grown to like this old man very much.

John waved a cold plastic bottle of Coca-Cola in his direction and Alex nodded, accepting it. Flying always made him very thirsty. The cabin was pressurized to 8000 feet, so he had to be a little careful unscrewing the cap, but it was almost welcome, like the inconveniences of being on a picnic. He took a long drink while he listened to Ruven describing some of his political fundraising adventures here in the States.

Ruven, his brother Albert, the Rabbi Ascher Liebowitz, and Father Joseph Spagelli were soliciting contributions to the Hope campaign all over the country. Alex didn't quite have the heart to tell any of them that he didn't need the money. In fact, their efforts on his behalf made compliance with the election laws vastly more complicated than it would have been.

Instead, he let them spend whatever money they collected (with minimal legal supervision by Faith-Anne), on the possibility that they might hit upon a better strategy than he was following, himself. He'd learned long ago that gracefully accepting people's well-meaning help was a big part of leadership. And in the meantime, their success at raising money gave him an estimate of how the campaign was going in general.

"And you say that none of the general circulation magazines would accept your ads?" He'd repeated Ruven's words because he wanted John to hear them. "We had pretty much the same experience at our end. We wound up placing ads in special interest publications, instead – gun magazines, car magazines, magazines for long haul truckers, motorcycle magazines, computer magazines, smokers' magazines. It seems to have worked out pretty well."

He listened to Ruven again, then replied, "You were bound to get rebuffed, even condemned, by some Jewish leaders, Ruven. These are folks whose commitment to socialism is greater than their commitment to Judaism. You'll find that exactly the same thing is true with the National Council of Churches and most big religious organizations. If it were really all about God, Ruven, they wouldn't need a corporate headquarters."

Ruven laughed. *"No, they wouldn't, Alex, would they? Say, I'm flying to Wisconsin next week to confer with some people in a group called CCOPS. Do you know them? Is there anything you'd care to have me say to them?"*

Alex nodded, realizing as he did that Ruven couldn't see him do it. "CCOPS – Concerned Citizens Opposed to Police States – I've heard of them. You can tell them that within my first week in office (if disaster struck and I were actually to get elected) I'd create a commission to demilitarize, decentralize, and reform police practices all over the country."

"And what should I tell the gun people I'm meeting the week after that? As if I didn't know."

Alex grinned. "Tell them we'll have a commission to investigate the Thomas Dodd/Nazi Germany connection with regard to the Gun Control Act of 1968. Tell it to the Mass-Murdering Mothers, too, if you can get them to listen. Every law they steamroller through costs thousands of lives. They know it, but they don't care as long as they win the legislation game."

Ruven sighed. *"It used to be different, Alex. Your country used to be different."*

"I agree, Ruven. Freedom used to be important. And people used to be ashamed, once upon a time, of alcoholism, drug addiction, things like shoplifting, and living off the charity of others. It's a painful thing to contemplate, but they're going to have to learn to be ashamed all over again. Maintaining civilization is a relatively simple matter of self-respect, and respect for others."

"So where would you start, Alex?" Ruven asked.

"One of the first things I'd do is address the nation and explain the significance of December 15, 1791, when the Bill of Rights was ratified. Believe it or not, the Franklin Roosevelt Administration once called for a week-long period in school dedicated to studying the Bill of Rights, including a national Bill of Rights "bee". We'd do something bigger and better. Can't let ourselves be one-upped by New Deal socialists, can we?"

"No, you can't," Ruven told him. "I'll come for the first celebration, Alex. Will you let a shabby old man like me into the White House?"

"Don't you 'shabby old man' me, Ruven Mendelsohn. I saw you on NetPlanetNews.com, at the Space Colony Foundation fundraising banquet, wearing a fancy tuxedo and escorting a good looking blond. You're welcome in any house I live in, my friend. Thank you for all you've done for me."

"And the country. You're welcome, Alex. Say hello to Kitch and Joe and Ascher for me, will you?"

* * * * * *

Eustace Barlow was a thinker. He most enjoyed thinking of himself as the Last Living Hippie. His snow white hair and beard made him look like the world's skinniest Santa Claus, a Santa Claus who took a huge drag on the joint in his left hand, held it for several seconds, and exhaled, fogging the windshield. The van was filled to overflowing with the sound of "Stairway to Heaven"

Sure, there were thousands – probably even tens of thousands – of long-haired, tie-dyed, bell-bottomed dope-smokers living up here in the Rockies. Some of them may even have possessed vintage Volkswagen vans like his, equipped with all the necessities of life – his bhong, his mongrel dog Mr. Natural, his old lady Beamer (her name predated the nickname for the automobile by a decade), a little propane furnace to make up for the VW's inadequacies in the heat department, and a sound system worth ten times what the car was – and painted with all of the symbols and sentiments appropriate to the 1960s.

But Eustace *was* the 60s. He'd been 62 years old in May, having been born in an overcrowded hallway at Denver's Mercy Hospital during the original baby boom of 1946. He'd seen it all. He'd been one of the first intrepid souls to move into the Haight in '61, and probably the last one out…when was it? Sometimes he had trouble remembering things. He'd been in Chicago during the violent summer of '68 and to Woodstock where he'd actually shaken hands with Joe Walsh. He'd thought long and hard about going to Canada during the war – his generation's "*the* war", but he'd contracted hepatitis just in time to save him from the draft.

Eustace hadn't only seen it all, he'd done it all twice, bought the T-shirt, and sent a postcard to his mother. He took another long drag on his bomber, held it, and exhaled.

Not for the first time, Eustace wished that they weren't out here on the road today. The pavement was already icing over and it was slicker than snot on a doorknob. The VW's tires were old and bald. But they had to make their way from Snowmass to Denver somehow, he, Mr. Natural, and Beamer. It was necessary. They had to get to the free women's clinic in Denver before they could refill Beamer's hormone replacement prescription. She got real cranky without it and didn't want to cook or fool around. She was cranky with him now. But was it his fault the doctor wanted to see her before reordering her prescription?

Eustace took another toke on his doobie – California stuff – to settle himself down. Then he offered to pass it to Beamer, who shook her head crossly and went on trying to peer through the increasingly snow-covered windshield into the blizzard. She was getting fat in her old age, and he didn't care for that. So was the dog, for that matter. He looked forward to scoring some of that great Cambodian when they were down in the city. He'd share it with his old lady and blow some smoke into Mr. Natural's nostrils, and that should smooth things out all around.

Outside, the visibility was down to a few dozen yards now, and even if it hadn't been, the Volkswagen's windshield wipers were only working intermittently. He considered pulling over onto the shoulder and clearing the blades manually, but that would only help a little. Besides, they were on a steep downhill grade at the moment (he'd always wondered what it meant, 6%) and it was frigging *cold* out there.

Once they were past this mess, maybe he could persuade his old lady to deal with the wipers.

It was at this precise moment that the master brake cylinder he'd just rebuilt gave a peculiar little sigh and spilled brake fluid all over the floor underneath the brake pedal. Eustace smelled the fluid, but it was a long moment later, about halfway down the mountain grade, approaching a vicious right turn, that he consciously realized that he didn't have any brakes.

The VW's speed mounted from 35 to 55, and from 55 to 80. Eustace was hard pressed to keep it from fishtailing on the black ice. Then the speedometer pegged as the bus exceeded any velocity its little engine had ever been capable of driving it to. Both he and Beamer were screaming, now, a full octave apart. The VW was doing more than 120 when Eustace saw the former First Lady's motorcade coming around the curve, up the mountain toward him.

Eustace was steering the best he could, trying to brake with his gear box. He thought he might miss the first three cars, two huge black SUVs and a long black limousine, and hit a similar car behind them. But at the last minute, another SUV surged up from behind in the other lane and deliberately tried to hit him. The VW bounced off its front bumper, directly into the path of the first limousine, striking the vehicle broadside.

Even through heavily-smoked glass, Eustace glimpsed a strangely familiar-looking woman's face in the back seat of the limo, her eyes wide, both hands on the window glass, and her mouth a great black "O" of terror. The last words Eustace ever heard came at him through 12 speakers: *"And she's buying a stairway to heaven"*.

That was all he had time to see. Eustace was wearing a seatbelt, but his old lady Beamer wasn't. At the moment of impact – even above his own screaming, Eustace heard the hollow thunk of colliding cars – she smashed, at 100 miles an hour, through the windshield, and was splattered against the side of the former First Lady's car. At the same moment, Mr. Natural, who weighed 75 pounds, rocketed over the driver's seat and out the windshield, snapping Eustace's neck on the way and killing him instantly.

Both cars, the limo and the bus, crashed through the log and metal roadside barrier as if it weren't there. Amidst the hideous cacophony of tortured, screeching metal, and the roaring of engines suddenly deprived of a load, the limo half-rolled and half-fell 2000 feet, the VW following after it. Somewhere near the bottom, the VW's liquid propane fuel tank broke open, mixing the highly flammable gas with the air around it.

As both cars struck bottom, the propane ignited in a fuel-air explosion that rocked the valley from end to end and reduced every trace of both cars and their passengers to fingernail-sized bits and fine, white ash that mixed with the newly-fallen snow and melted it – but only for a little while.

* * * * * *

"It is not the role of a libertarian president to formulate his own tax policy."

It was blistering hot in the Houston Senior Center's auditorium and as humid as a steambath. Alex's fashionable and expensive suit felt like the inside of crockpot full of Hungarian goulash. He knew that outside, it was even worse. The same gigantic weather system that was blanketing his home state with three feet of snow was dropping rain in buckets here in Houston. He could hear the stuff slamming down on the roof.

Meanwhile, as each of the debaters stood at his (or her) own lectern at the opposite ends of the low stage, he was answering a point his opponent had attempted to make about the FLPA's "lack of a governing plan or philosophy".

"I mean to leave formulating tax policy to Socialist Party 'A'," he said, "and to Socialist Party 'B', so that people will know who did it to them. Taxation, Ms. Moderator, is *theft*, and theft, as we all try so hard to teach our little children, is morally repulsive. It is a libertarian president's role to veto, repeal, nullify, or otherwise eliminate every tax he can."

Half of the audience erupted with applause and cheering, the other with boos and catcalls, while the moderator from what Alex thought of as the League of (Socialist) Women Voters banged her gavel, trying to get both sides to quiet down.

Alex thought she was banging a little harder than the situation called for, but he understood. The blue-haired ladies of the league were upset because the former First Lady, whom they tended to think of as their own, had flatly turned them down for this event, remarking through a representative that she didn't have a real opponent any more, so why bother?

So here the ladies were, stuck here with a conservative Republican Congresswoman from New Mexico and their worst nightmare come true, a third party – for which read loose cannon – candidate doing as well in the polls, now, as she was.

At the back of the audience, Alex saw a handheld placard that read, "ABANDON AL HOPE". Pretty funny, he admitted to himself. He'd have suspected Forrey Nadalindov's not-so-fine hand in this, but he didn't think the man was up to the wordplay, and he happened to know that his so-called running mate was in Oxnard, California for the day, at an FLPA rally, exhorting voters to choose the Hope-Nadalindov ticket on the grounds that, after the election, Hope could be impeached, leaving a "mature and moderate" leader in his place.

Alex had watched him say it. Wonderful thing, the internet.

The audience here gradually settled down again, and the New Mexico Congresswoman opened her mouth to say something. But at that very moment, Faith-Anne surprised him by leaping up onto the debate stage – a nice trick, he thought, in that long skirt and those four-inch heels – approaching him to whisper urgently into his ear, while the audience buzzed with puzzlement.

"Ladies and gentlemen," Alex told them, as his daughter remained standing beside him. "I've just learned that the Senator from New York, the former First Lady, has been killed in an automobile accident in Colorado."

Chapter Thirteen: *LINDA ALVAREZ*

> *Put any kind of face on it you choose, taxation is robbery at gunpoint. And no function of government is important enough to threaten anybody's life over.*
>
> – Alexander Hope, *Looking Forward*

Ernie said, "Somebody pass the guacamole, please!"

It was the strangest election night Alex had ever experienced, and the fact that he was one of the candidates for President was only a small part of it.

Alex's election night headquarters, courtesy of Chancellor Van Cleave, were in the campus gym at Albert Gallatin Memorial College. That would have caused a lot of problems at a state institution like CU or CSU. It was one of the many advantages, Alex appreciated, of a private school. If he had any real chance of being elected, he'd do everything he could to see that sooner or later every *school* in America was private.

It was a strange election night in another way. Faith-Anne and Dana had conspired to decorate the place with fresh flowers, rather than flags, balloons, and bunting. It was almost as if this were a meeting place for the Green – and yellow and blue and red and white – Party. The carnations made the room smell wonderful, instead of smelling like a gym.

Both of them were here, of course, Faith-Anne greeting guests at the door, dipping punch for them, dealing with what little media had chosen to show up. Alex had established the dress code by wearing his MYT cowboy boots, bluejeans, and an olive green Albert Gallatin Memorial sweatshirt fresh from the campus bookstore. Faith-Anne had answered her father by wearing bluejeans herself, and a sweatshirt of her own, bright red, emblazoned in white with the flying horse of the Hope Corporation logo.

Chip Sheridan was here, too, following Faith-Anne around in a charming, puppy-like attempt to help her, but mostly getting in the way. Cap Pondoro sat back in a corner and watched them.

Meanwhile, Dana, who had only been on her feet for two days – all four feet, she insisted, indicating her aluminum crutches, the kind that wrapped around her upper arms, with bicycle grips for handles – was hobbling about the room, cheerfully talking to everyone she could, the long skirt of her pretty Hawaiian-print dress concealing steel and fiberglass braces. She was scheduled to be in physical therapy for the next eight months.

Except for Faith-Anne, the Austrian Mafia, and him, she'd told Alex, her time in the hospital had been like a prison sentence. She was speechlessly grateful it was over with, and she was out and among people once again.

Ruven Mendelsohn had brought his brother Albert, and Albert's wife Rachel all the way from Belgium to be here tonight. It was a gallant gesture,

Alex thought, considering that somebody else was going to wind up being President in the morning.

From Chicago, Kitch Sinclair had brought his lady-friend Sheila Hensley, Father Joseph Spagelli, Rabbi Ascher Liebowitz, and a young black law student named Blake Chapman. They'd also brought Julia Greenwood, mother of the late John Greenwood in whose honor an award banquet was being given a few weeks from now in Portland, Oregon, by the Ralston Foundation. Alex, whom they didn't know was bankrolling the whole thing (only Faith-Anne knew that), had been asked to be the keynote speaker.

The whole crowd from Albert Gallatin Memorial was here, too, of course, including Chancellor Van Cleave and the Austrian Mafia – Ernie Hanover, Rick Thomas, Katie Harris, Mick Douglas – and they'd even invited the Neo-neoKeynesians, who despite their friendly theoretical rivalry, were just as interested in seeing a libertarian elected as the Austrians. A handful of FLPA members mostly from western states, was here, as well. He remembered seeing some of them at the convention.

Nobody from the rapidly-failing traditional networks – ABC, NBC, CBS – had bothered to show up. Nobody from CNN or MSNBC, either. Alex had rented a dozen television sets and hooked them up to the college cable system just for tonight. Network anchors from the Old Media were interviewing each other, for the most part (a reason they were failing rapidly) and occasionally airing brief moments on videotape with the replacement candidates from both of the major parties, the senior Senator from New York the Democrat, and Linda Alvarez the Republican. Socialist Parties "A" and "B".

Someone else who hadn't shown up was the FLPA Vice Presidential candidate, Forrey Nadalindov. Alex hadn't heard from him directly since the death of the former First Lady, although he'd seen the man pontificating on one of the sleaze-shows practically every day: Rosie O'Donnel, Geraldo Rivera, Larry King Interactive, Oprah Winfrey, or Jerry Springer.

Each day Nadalindov's message became more hysterical: Hope is a filthy rich but very dangerous nut who, by a stroke of misfortune, was able to buy the FLPA nomination. An ethically and morally questionable relationship with that Chinese dolly internet snoop had made him even nuttier. Yes, elect him, but then get rid of him, and you'll have me. Alex wondered vaguely where Nadalindov was tonight, but he really didn't care.

Alex had asked Faith-Anne to rent a lot of comfortable sofas and chairs for the evening, but Van Cleave had overheard him and had the students bring furniture from their dormitories and the faculty lounge. Now the gymnasium looked like a cross between a hotel lobby, a florists' shop, and a bus station.

Someone had said Matt Drudge himself might show up tonight – Alex would believe that when he saw it – and there were people from C-Span and FoxNews wandering around with tiny, unobtrusive cameras that seemed to work in ambient light. Dana's boss, Alan, from NetPlanetNews.com, was a former senior columnist from a big Orange County daily newspaper. He'd shown up before any of them with a tiny camera of his own, and a gigantic bouquet of flowers for his star reporter, who would be returning to limited duty next week.

The television sets all babbled on in a dozen voices about the lowest election turnout in history – all except for one set that everybody in the room was crowded in front of – showing reruns of *The X-Files.*

Alex wanted something to drink. He wandered toward the back of the gym where a small kitchen held all the supplies for tonight's offbeat festivities. It had a long counter-window, presently closed, that worked something like a garage door. He entered through a door to the right of the window.

Inside, he found Dana standing in front of an open refrigerator, wrestling with the heavy door and her crutches at the same time, while trying to get an enormous bowl of something out of one of the crisper drawers. Striding forward to help her, he was just in time as one of her crutch tips slipped on the tile floor. She started to fall, but he caught her in his arms.

She hardly weighed anything at all. Dana turned in his arms and looked up at Alex. She let the crisper drawer slam shut, let go of her crutches, and threw both arms around his neck. She smelled wonderful to him, very faintly of ginger and cinnamon. Alex lifted her up – suddenly she felt so tiny and delicate – let the refrigerator door swing shut, closed his eyes and kissed her.

She returned his kiss with a passion that astonished him.

When they came up for air, she told him, "I've been waiting a long time for that, Alex."

He felt dizzy. "I have, too, Dana. And I believe there's something I need to tell you."

She grinned up at him and her eyes crinkled. "What's that, Alex?"

He took a deep breath. "I love you."

She kissed him that time, longer and harder, and then whispered, "I loved you first."

* * * * * *

"You answer the door, yourself? Don't you think that's a little dangerous?"

The woman on the doorstep was in her early 50s, Alex knew, but she looked at least 10 years younger than that, despite the soft touch of gray at her stylishly-coiffed temples. She was obviously Hispanic, and very easy on the eyes. He'd recognized his erstwhile debate opponent the instant he saw her.

"Everybody else is watching Mulder, Scully, Doggett, and the cigarette-smoking man," he responded. He didn't tell her about the heavy .40 caliber pistol under his sweatshirt, or the large man with the Glock .45 who was watching them. His head was still spinning, even though he'd been hoping for months that he and Dana would end up together. "If it isn't Congressperson Linda Alvarez, Republican, New Mexico. Fancy meeting you here."

"It's Congresswoman, Professor Hope, I don't care how the National Organization of Women wants to distort our language. But I'm not a Republican anymore. I wanted to get here and tell you before the polls close, so you won't think I'm a crass opportunist. I'm a *principled* opportunist. I quietly resigned from the party this morning and lost all of my committee appointments. I don't plan to give up my seat. The constituency that elected me – I'm from the southern part of New Mexico, not the Welfare Belt up north – would only approve of what I've done. May I come in? It's cold out here."

Alex ushered her in. Across the room, he saw Dana struggling to get up from the borrowed sofa where he'd just left her, her reporter's instincts afire with the sudden appearance of the Republican candidate for President.

Alex took the Congresswoman's black seal coat, hung it on a brass hook by the door, and then escorted her directly to meet Dana. It was the least he could do. He was ruining the girl's career. She *really* had a conflict of interest now. He wondered what she was planning to do about it.

He'd ask her about it once they were alone again.

On the other hand, after tonight, it wouldn't matter. He'd just be another retired businessman again.

Dana came across the floor to meet them and the women shook hands, the reporter shifting her right crutch to her left hand to accomplish it. Apparently they knew all about one another and liked what they knew. They returned to the sofa Dana had just left. The Congresswoman took a comfortable chair facing the couple. Faith-Anne materialized with a drink for their guest, then sat down on the sofa on the other side of her father.

"I'd appreciate it if you'd embargo this until the polls close on the west coast," the newcomer told Dana. "That oily creep is probably going to win this election, but there's no point making it any easier for him."

Dana smiled. "I'll embargo it until the polls close in Hawaii, if you like, Congresswoman Alvarez – "

"Call me Linda, please. And I'll call you Dana and Faith-Anne and Alex." She repeated what she'd told Alex about having quit the GOP. Faith-Anne and

Dana were delighted, but not surprised. "After tonight, I'm taking a little vacation from politics. My house seat is safe. The Democrats didn't run anybody, and I'm better on all of the important issues than the stiff the FLPA ran this time. I'm going fly-fishing for three weeks, and when I get back, I plan to enjoy being the first libertarian in Congress."

"Okay, that's one," Faith-Anne responded. "How many does that make to go?"

* * * * * *

"Alex! Alex! Come here, quick!"

He'd been sitting on the sofa holding hands with Dana, their eyes locked, talking about things that couples holding hands usually talk about. Linda Alvarez was huddled in another corner of the room with Cap, some of the Austrian Mafia, Faith-Anne, and Chip. God only knew what they were talking about.

By shortly after nine o'clock Rocky Mountain Standard Time, the polls had been closed everywhere but Alaska and Hawaii for more than an hour. National interest in the election had been minimal, even the networks seemed unusually reticent, but everyone expected a long night nonetheless.

Alex stood and helped Dana to her feet. Together, they went to the bank of television sets that Ernie was watching.

Sara Michelle Gellar, formerly "Buffy the Vampire Slayer" and the latest in a string of "celebrity commentators" networks were employing in a last, desperate attempt to slow the crumbling of their ratings was just winding up: "And there you have it: 23% of those eligible – the lowest turnout in American history – have cast their votes. And to the utter discombobulation of every 'expert' everywhere, 53% of that 23% apparently have voted for billionaire industrialist libertarian Alexander – "

He couldn't hear the rest. The gym erupted in cheers of disbelief and celebration. Emotionally he was as numb as if he'd just been shot full of Novocaine but the mind that had built a multibillion dollar empire was still working.

Discombobulation?, he thought. There were still technicalities to get past – in these corrupt times, would the Electoral College and the House of Representatives actually allow a third party candidate to occupy the office? – but from here it looked like he was the next President of the United States.

He turned to look at Dana. She looked up at him, tears streaming down her lovely, exotic face. He hoped very much that they were tears of joy. "The next four years may be hell," he told her, brushing her tears away as best he could. "And I may have fatally damaged your career. But there's something I want to ask you, Dana, now, before it gets really confusing."

Softly, she asked, "What is it, Alex?"

"Heads up, people!" Ernie suddenly shouted. "The media creeps who ignored us before are gonna be all over us in the next few minutes. Let's get ready!"

Damn!, Alex thought, how will I ever work up the courage again? "It'll have to wait. Would you like the first exclusive interview with the President-Elect?"

"Only if he remembers later what he was going to ask me – and I can have some Kleenex!"

A sudden pounding on the door shook the entire gymnasium. Before it could answered, the door slammed open and two dozen figures wearing dark blue raid jackets marked SECRET SERVICE in bright yellow pushed their way through, carrying Heckler and Koch MP5 submachineguns which they leveled at Alex's guests.

They were followed by half a dozen young men in black suits and dark glasses – it was 9:30 P.M., Alex thought – and earphones. Outside, he heard the roar of helicopters. One of the suited young men strode to him.

He flashed an I.D. "Secret Service, Mr. Hope. I'm Agent Smith. We're here to protect you!"

Alex pushed Dana behind him. John had appeared at his side. "Have your people point their weapons somewhere else immediately, or you can all get out!"

The young man ignored him and reached for the pistol on Alex's hip. His sweatshirt had ridden over it when he wasn't looking. "I'll take this, Mr. President-Elect. You won't be needing it. We'll be taking care of you."

In a swift, smooth gesture, Alex reached across, turned his left hand over, seized the young man's thumb and bent it toward the back of his wrist. The young man went to his knees, agony written across his face. It was a trick John had taught him. He placed his right hand on the grip of his Witness and half-drew it from the holster.

John said, in a low voice, "Touch that piece again, son, it'll be the last thing you ever touch." He pulled his jacket back to expose the grip of his Glock .45. "Now you tell your little playmates to stand down and get out."

Alex looked around him. It was a tenser moment than he'd known. The raid-jacketed troops had their machineguns pointed everywhere in the room, at everyone but him. He must be causing them severe nervous confusion. They were supposed to protect him (unless they were here to assassinate him), but both he and his bodyguard were threatening their commander.

His own people, the Austrian Mafia, the Chicago group, some of the FLPA, Chancellor Van Cleave, Chip Sheridan, even the rabbi, had their own pistols and revolvers out – a bewildering variety – and pointed at the Secret Service. Even Faith-Anne had drawn her little Chief's Special .38 from wherever she kept it. Someone was going to hiccup and they'd all be ankle-deep in blood.

"Mr. President!" It was Linda, flowing across the room toward him as if she weren't surrounded by half a ton of lethal hardware. "I'd like to take this moment, if I may, to concede the election to you! Congratulations!"

Somebody – one of the Secret Service guys, he thought – laughed, somebody else joined him, and soon the room was filled with merriment instead of gunfire.

* * * * * *

"I'm Dana Li of NetPlanetNews.com. I'm standing in the election night headquarters of the Alexander Hope campaign, here on the campus of Albert Gallatin Memorial College near Denver, Colorado. Professor Hope, as we all know by now, was the candidate for the presidency of the Free Libertarian Party of America. He is now, to every appearance, the next President of the United States."

Dana stood on her crutches before a small camera in the hands of her boss, looking more beautiful than ever, Alex thought, and sounding just as good. He'd always enjoyed the sound of her voice. Outside, the helicopters were gone, having taken most of the machinegun-toting boys and girls with them. Alex had generously allowed a small handful of them to stay, but he wasn't through with them. From now on, the President would set an example for the nation by conspicuously taking a hand in his own protection.

"In a moment," Dana continued, "we'll hear from Professor Hope himself, but first, a little catching up. The Republican Presidential candidate, Congresswoman Linda Alvarez of New Mexico was here tonight as a welcome guest and has now conceded in person. Rumor has it that she may be considered for an important cabinet post in the new Hope Administration."

Glancing across the room, Alex could see the surprise on Linda's face. He grinned at her. Quick thinking on her part had probably saved 200 lives tonight and he wanted that kind of thinking in his immediate political family.

"At the same time, the New York senior Senator who replaced the deceased former First Lady as the Democratic candidate, has refused to concede the election and is now said to be in seclusion in his upstate vacation home. Meanwhile, FLPA Vice Presidential candidate Forrey Nadalindov, who was not here at headquarters tonight, has, as he says, 'reported for duty' and will meet with his new boss Professor Hope as soon as possible, 'to lend a firm and steady hand of moderation'."

A few feet away, Alex heard Ernie mutter, "I've got a bad feeling about this."

At her signal, Alex joined Dana on her mark

before Alan's camera. He kept his hands folded in front of his belt, at a sort of parade rest.

"Professor Hope," she began. "What do you think about the historic events we've witnessed tonight?"

There were reasons that he loved this young woman standing beside him. Nine hundred ninety-nine out of a thousand others news people would have asked him how he felt. This one wanted to know what he *thought*.

"Dana, I'm as surprised as anyone else about the way this election turned out. I'm sorry it may have been because of the Vice President's shameful – alleged – conduct and the former First Lady's death. The hard part is still before us. I'll begin on January 20th of next year enforcing the Bill of Rights as if it were the highest law of the land – which is what it is. For now, as President Elect, I'll continue to 'campaign' exactly as if I were still a candidate, making speeches and spelling out my policies wherever I can so that everyone will have a chance to understand them."

She nodded. "I see. Will you be appointing a transition team and making some preliminary selections for your Cabinet? And will you be keeping the group of individuals together who helped to put you in office?"

Alex shrugged. "To be quite truthful Dana, although I've given it a little thought, I never expected to win this election, so I don't know exactly who I'll be working with. I'd like to keep my daughter on as chief of staff or something, but she's got a corporation to run. Likewise, most of the people closest to me are students who should go back to their studies. And a lot of it, of course, will depend on confirmation by the Senate. I don't expect they'll give me a very easy time about my appointments."

"I don't expect you'll give them a very easy time about the laws they pass," Dana replied. "I'll bet you wind up vetoing more than any President in history."

"Could be," Alex nodded. "There is one appointment I can make that the Senate doesn't have a word to say about. I'd like to make it right now. Dana Li of NetPlanetNews.com, would you consent to be my First Lady?"

* * * * * *

It was December 15th, five weeks after the election of 2008, Bill of Rights Day. Alex had yet to be confirmed in his victory by the Electoral College. That wouldn't happen for another three days. But the Austrian Mafia, instead of meekly returning to their studies as he'd suggested, had done a little research, and he no longer anticipated any problem about that.

Nevertheless it wasn't right for people (including Dana) to call him President-Elect Hope just yet, although they (including Dana) wouldn't stop doing it.

For the past five weeks, anticipating some of the many problems he knew he faced once he was in office, he'd kept the promise he'd made to Dana and the country to keep campaigning for support for his ideas. He'd granted all the interviews he was asked for by broadcast and print media, made audio and video recordings for distribution through a variety of channels, and appeared on talk shows where, unlike any other President-Elect in history (there – he was doing it himself!) he was harassed by other guests. The establishment media did their level best to insult or ignore him.

At the same time, the "New Media" – talk radio and the internet – bubbled over with enthusiasm for the first President they believed genuinely represented them. Ratings for traditional network radio and television shows plummeted – it was the end of the "Old Media" era – while sales of computers, PDAs, and internet connections soared. Wherever he appeared in person, greater numbers came to see him.

Now here he was, in the best hotel Portland Oregon had to offer, preparing to make a pivotal speech at the Ralston Foundation's annual John Greenwood dinner to award conspicuous courage in the face of tyranny. In the suite that his own people and the Secret Service had carefully inspected beforehand, he finally gave up and shoved a stack of 3x5 cards into an inside pocket of his tuxedo jacket. This speech was too important to make off the cuff.

Rising from the desk, he headed toward the door, feeling naked. The suit was too close-fitting to conceal his big EAA Witness .40. Maybe he should get a smaller gun – or have the tux retailored – or simply resign himself to appearing lumpy.

John was waiting outside the door, wearing a suit that had been properly cut to hide his big, blocky Glock. His son Cap stood beside him. To his surprise, Father Joseph Spagelli, who'd be presenting tonight's award to a recipient unknown to Alex was there, as well, looking more dapper than any priest he'd ever seen.

Agent Smith (Alex wondered if he'd ever seen *The Matrix)* looked like exactly what he was. He even resembled Agent Doggett from *The X-Files* a little. The young man spoke into his sleeve and they gave Dana and his daughter a few moments to join them in the corridor before they started to the ballroom. Alex hated all of this security stuff and meant to do something about it when he had time.

At long last, he heard a noise up the hallway – several noises: footsteps, rustling gowns, happy voices. Annoying Smith, he strode up the corridor to meet Faith-Anne, Chip, Dana, and their own security detail. Dana – who had tearfully accepted his "appointment" on national television – wasn't here tonight in her capacity as a reporter, but as what the media were calling the "First Fiancee".

He saw them. Dana was incredibly gorgeous with her dark glossy hair up, in her crimson ball gown. Crutches and all, he could hardly believe this beautiful creature had agreed to be his bride.

Faith-Anne, to whom he owed this miracle to some degree, wore a saffron yellow gown that was just as impressive, although he didn't think he'd ever get used to seeing his little girl in a low-cut dress.

Chip was wearing his Army officer's "mess dress" uniform with a chest full of combat medals. It made him look like a tall, crewcut head waiter.

As the three of them and the four agents escorting them came within 10 or 12 feet, Chip dropped back a step, pulled a standard military issue 9mm Beretta 92F from under his short white jacket, and aimed it straight at Alex's face. In the odd light, Alex could see the glint of a hollowpoint bullet deep inside the chamber.

Instinctively, he stepped to one side and slapped his hip, shocked to be reminded that his Witness wasn't there. Behind him, John and Cap yelled at Agent Smith to get out of the line of fire. One of the agents with the women made a long dive for Alex, inadvertently pushing him back into Chip's pistol sights. Alex saw deep into Chip's dead eyes, as well, and then a two-foot ball of pale pink and blue flame blossomed at the muzzle of the Beretta.

Alex never felt the bullet hit him, he simply couldn't get up when he tried to – and didn't remember falling.

At some timeless point, Dana screamed and suddenly she was rid of her crutches and down on her knees hovering over him protectively. That didn't seem right somehow, he thought. He heard a lot more yelling, male and female voices, and three very loud shots.

A heavy figure stumbled over Dana where she lay. There was a thump, and suddenly Chip was on the carpet between them. His last word, gurgled as he choked on his own blood, was "zipperhead!" He collapsed in a rapidly spreading pool of scarlet. Standing over Chip's body, her little snubby revolver still smoking, he saw Faith-Anne, grim-faced and flushed.

John Pondoro, Glock .45 in his hand unfired, knelt beside Alex's body, Cap was on the other side of Dana with his .38 Super. And a stunned Father Joseph Spagelli started to administer last rites.

Now prostrate, Dana sobbed.

Alex wanted to tell them, especially Dana and Faith-Anne, that he was all right, that wherever he'd been hit, there wasn't any pain, and in fact he was beginning to feel very warm and cozy. But he couldn't speak.

Then someone turned the lights out.

And the sound off.

Chapter Fourteen:
FORREY NADALINDOV

> *In declaring "war on drugs", America declared war on itself, not because recreational drugs are an especially valued or indispensable part of our national culture (they're not) but because you can't declare war on any Ninth Amendment right without declaring war on all of them – and along with them, on every other individual right under the first ten Amendments to the Constitution.*
>
> – Alexander Hope, *Looking Forward*

"Miss Hope! Miss Hope!"

The weather outside was terrible today, the air in the room damper than she was used to, even living in San Diego. The place smelled of everybody's wet overcoats – or everybody's wet dogs. It was pretty much the same smell, she thought.

Whenever the door at the back of the room opened, she could hear the monotonous clanging of a Salvation Army donation collector stationed beside his pot and tripod, just outside the main entrance of the hotel. Out in the lobby, cheerful holiday melodies were playing over the hotel Muzak system. What a time for something like this to happen, she thought.

Christmas would never feel the same again – but then it hadn't really felt the same since her mother had died seven years ago.

"Miss Hope! Right here, Miss Hope!"

The strobe lights weren't quite as painful and annoying as the flashguns would have been a generation ago, but the television lights made up for them, and who would ever have thought that a tiny sound – the click of a 35 millimeter shutter followed by the brief whine of an automatic winder – multiplied a hundred fifty times, could have been so distracting? And maddening? It was like being overrun by noisy crickets.

One of the reporters shouted, "M.C. Raker, CBS/NBC." There was some justice in the world, she thought; the two networks had finally been forced to merge in order to survive collapsing ratings. "Who did it, Miss Hope, and why?"

With all the shoving and hollering, it also felt like a day at the commodities exchange. This was the first real question they'd managed to ask her in the ten minutes since she'd stepped to the lectern the hotel had thoughtfully provided, here in a ground floor room decorated in muted, telegenic colors, reserved for what she increasingly regarded as "press confrontations". (Its neoclassical decor clashed, she thought, with the three dozen Samsonite chairs.) The slant-topped wooden box had a colored decal on the front, the presidential seal, and that may or may not have been appropriate. The alternative was the hotel's logo.

At the front of the room, on either side of her stood a pair of Secret Service agents, heavily armed and wired into one another. One of them was Agent

Smith, in charge of this detail. He was taking what had happened to her father very hard – which was only right, she thought. She had more faith in Uncle John, a wall of a man standing at the back of the room, his eyes moving over the crowd of reporters and cameramen, his big right hand never far from his left armpit.

Or for Cap, for that matter. He may have been a clown, but he was a reliable clown who could shoot almost as straight as she could.

Faith-Anne conspicuously said nothing until the noise died down. "There are plenty of reasons," she said, "why people sufficiently afraid of individual liberty might want my father killed, Mr. Raker. Freedom can be frightening, a terrible burden. And slaves, as we know, may come to love their chains and resent anyone who would offer to take them away. As to Chip Sheridan, the assassin, that should be obvious – but then you mean who was behind him, don't you?"

More pandemonium, pushing and shoving, jostling equipment, shouted obscenities and impertinent questions, gave her a chance to think. Old Media people, it suddenly occurred to her, were like a roomful of ugly, spoiled children with nasty little teeth, filed to a point. What was that old journalist's expression? "If it bleeds, it leads." And if it didn't already, then they'd *make* it bleed. The atmosphere today – for them – was almost festive. Nothing like a good old-fashioned assassination. Faith-Anne was deeply ashamed that she had ever taken any of these creatures seriously.

With her father's blood still wet on the hallway carpet upstairs, Uncle John and the Secret Service had both insisted that she talk to these carrion-eaters as soon as possible, before they started making the story up for themselves. There probably wasn't anything that could stop them from doing that, she'd told them, but she'd reluctantly agreed on the condition that it would only be for five minutes. It already felt like half an hour. Unfortunately, she didn't dare be photographed looking at her watch.

The plain truth, then: "I have no idea whether anybody else was behind Sheridan. There's no way I can think of to find out. There are other people, supposedly qualified, working on that, but I don't know how much good that'll do. Nobody ever really found out who killed Jack Kennedy, did they? All I know is that Sheridan shot my father and now he's dead."

Somebody toward her left, wearing a terrible toupee, said, "By your own hand, Miss Hope! How does it feel – "

"You mean what do I *think*, Mr. Donaldson?" Faith-Anne shrugged and shook her head. "Because that's all you're going to get out of me. What I *feel* is my business – private, off limits – and it would be a much cleaner, far better world if everybody else followed the same personal policy."

She waited for that to sink in and, to her astonishment, the room grew quieter. "What I *think* is that I'm very glad I spent so much time at the Hope Corporation's company shooting range just outside San Diego. The three shots I put into Sheridan weren't more than an inch apart."

Agent Smith's mouth dropped open; the buzzing in the room dropped an octave. Uncle John and Cap both shook their heads and grinned. She'd refused to answer their favorite question, answered one of her own, instead, and made them angry because she was able – and willing – to use deadly force to defend herself and others. Well, what did she care what they thought? The election was over and her father – she wished Dana were here, asking the questions.

Or helping to answer them.

Another voice: "Christiane Amanpour, CNN. So you're proud of what you did, Miss Hope?"

Faith-Anne exhaled. "Are you proud when you do the things – wash the dishes, cut the lawn, repair the car, step on a cockroach – that are necessary for survival and a decent life? I suppose I'd be proud of what I did, if I'd given it any thought before now. Ask me the same question tomorrow. Next?"

She pointed to a middle-aged, overweight female with extremely short hair and adolescent skin problems, sitting on a folding chair as close to the lectern as she could. "Parva Poverish, Miss Hope, WiccaNewsDaily.com. While it's true that you've empowered women by your act, it could hardly be described as heroic, since you took him by surprise, from behind. He never had a chance – "

Faith-Anne nodded. "You're right. He'll *never* have a chance – to hurt anybody else. Are we speaking the same language, here, lady? Are we even on the same planet? It all happened in about four seconds. The guy was shooting my father, *had* shot my father. Your next president. I shot him to make him stop. What would you have done, diaper him and powder his nose? Take his picture?"

* * * * * *

"You've got to be kidding – or insane."

Faith-Anne brushed a strand of copper-colored hair off of her forehead. She wore no makeup – she didn't need to, ordinarily. Her eyes were red-rimmed and bloodshot from tears and lack of sleep. She wore a gray UCLA sweatshirt from her undergraduate days and faded jeans. At the moment, her mouth was set in an expression of angry resolution.

Outside, "unusually seasonal weather", as Ernie had put it, was attempting to plaster a layer of wet snow across the huge plate glass hotel windows. Faith-Anne was sitting on a sofa in the living room area of the large suite her father had paid for in the Portland hotel where he'd been shot the night before. Among those with her were Dana, John, and Cap, along with the original Austrian Mafia, Ernie, Mick, Katie, and Rick.

The mood they shared was tense and unhappy.

On their feet and facing Faith-Anne, their backs to the hall door, were Forrey Nadalindov, who had just arrived despite the blizzard, one of his official Secret Service escort, the Nomex-covered suppressor of an Uzi machine pistol conspicuously hanging at an edge of his damp, lightweight topcoat, and a well-dresed older man carrying a briefcase. None of them had been invited to sit down.

"I assure you, Miss Hope, that I am neither," Nadalindov replied. "I am merely doing what I consider my duty as Vice President Elect, under Section Four of the 25th Amendment to the Constitution."

He glanced at the man with the briefcase as if for confirmation, then shifted his gaze to focus on John, seated in an upright chair to Faith-Anne's left. "I believe this matter could be settled more easily and quickly if you were to ask this thug of your father's to step into the other room until we're finished. Otherwise, well, I feel he might attack me at any minute"

"You don't get it, Mr. Nadalindov, do you?" she smiled sweetly. "Uncle John is here to keep *you* from being attacked. By *me*. Believe me, if I had even a microscopic shred of evidence to support my suspicion that it was you – and your buddies Horrwyrne and Moure – who arranged for my father to be assassinated, you wouldn't be standing there right now. You'd be lying in a steaming pool of your own blood!"

Nadalindov's government bodyguard stiffened visibly at her words, while John laughed out loud. "You'd better take her seriously, Nada! After all, she's the one who plugged the assassin – and he was her own fiance!"

"Half a second too late," Faith-Anne sighed, shook her head with regret, and looked ruefully at Dana sitting beside her. In her heart of hearts, she was chagrined at having been taken in, cruelly used by a cold-blooded killer who merely saw her as a way of getting at her father. But she had sworn to herself never to let anybody see it.

She went on. "In any case, Mr. Nadalindov, the 25th Amendment doesn't apply in this instance, as I'm sure you must be aware. You're not the Vice President Elect, because my father wasn't the President Elect when he was shot – the Electoral College won't meet until day after tomorrow. And even then, the law only applies to a sitting President, not the – "

Nadalindov protested, "But under the precedents established following the election of 2000 – "

She cut him off. "There *weren't* any precedents established following the election of 2000!"

Ernie and his friends laughed heartily. "You

know before 2000," Cap observed, "I'd always thought that 'dimpled chad' was some kind of surfer dude."

"Are you an attorney, Miss Hope?" asked the older man with the briefcase. Under an expensive camel-colored topcoat, its shoulders still damp from the snow outside, he wore a dark blue suit worth at least 3,000 dollars, and a red "power" necktie that screamed "lawyer" at hundreds of imaginary decibels. His tone implied that that question usually stopped the opposition cold.

"Last time I looked," she replied evenly, "Yes. And if you were any good, you'd already know that. Are *you* an attorney?"

The man didn't acknowledge her question. "An officer of the court should know better than to make death-threats, especially against the Vice President Elect."

Ernie said, "An officer of the court should know that it isn't a genuinely manly threat for manly men as long as it's couched in the subjunctive mode."

"And that this pompous ass you're working for," Rick added, "is *not* the Vice President Elect! As Faith-Anne just told you, the Electoral College – "

"Besides, counselor" a new voice came from a corner of the room, where a slender young man in black was seated in a comfortable chair, idly playing with a pair of dark glasses. A coiled bit of wire led from beneath his jacket collar to a plug in his ear. "If she tried to shoot the Vice President Not-Quite-Elect, I'd have to shoot her first – that is, if Agent Sanchez, there, didn't do it with that Buck Rogers Blart-and-Bonkus-gun he's not concealing very well."

Sanchez, the younger man standing beside

Nadalindov, tucked the business end of his machine pistol back under his coat and scowled at his colleague, his expression plainly saying that Agent Smith had learned entirely too many bad habits from this disreputable collection of anarchists.

"You'd *try*, Agent Smith," Pondoro chuckled. "You'd try."

Smith nodded amiably. "Count on it, Uncle John."

Nadalindov shouted, "This is absolutely *infuriating!* You're all nothing but barbarians, shooting this person, shooting that person, as if it were all some kind of video game! Don't you understand that this is serious? Don't any of you have even the slightest regard for the future of this country?"

"Without Alex Hope," Dana spoke for the first time, addressing the not-quite Vice President Elect in a voice so flat that it sent chills up the spine of everybody in the room, "this country *has* no future. And you know it."

Ernie and the rest of the Austrian Mafia sobered abruptly and muttered their agreement.

Dana had been sitting on the sofa beside Faith-Anne, holding Alex's daughter's hand in both of hers. Now, waving off the gallant help of Mick and Ernie and Rick, she struggled to her feet and got her crutches under her.

"If you'll all excuse me," she said, indicating Nadalindov, "I've had just about as much of this man's company as I can take, and there are some arrangements that still have to be made." She turned to touch Faith-Anne's cheek briefly, nodded fondly at Katie, sitting at Faith-Anne's other side, then at John and everyone else in the room she considered friends.

Then, pushing past Nadalindov and his small entourage, she stormed out of the suite.

"Besides," Nadalindov wasn't about to give up the floor. He'd started speaking before Dana slammed the door behind her. "You don't have the time or energy to spare, Miss Hope, for a foolish and futile attempt to keep your father's idealistic dreams alive. I'd think your hands would be full enough, with the criminal charges that are being pressed against you."

When the police had finally arrived, 20 minutes after her father's shooting, it had appeared their first and only priority was to arrest Alex's daughter for carrying a concealed weapon and discharging it within the city limits. Until this moment they'd been shoved aside by the Secret Service as far as next-presidential security was concerned, limited to manning street barriers. They resented it, and now they meant to make up for it.

At the same time, the Portland city government was as famous as that of Denver for its lack of tolerance where individual rights were concerned. It had required a battery of Hope Corporation attorneys, and the full weight of the United States Secret Service, to keep Faith-Anne from being taken to jail then and there.

By telephone, a judge had been persuaded to "release" her on her own recognizance, pending her arraignment shortly after the first of the year.

Under pressure, the police had surrendered her little revolver to Agent Smith, who had handed it, then and there, in front of their noses, back to Faith-Anne. She would always treasure the expressions on the officers' faces as she reloaded it and tucked it back into her handbag. A little later, John had told her that if the police had seized her weapon, he'd have given her his backup – a short, stubby miniaturized Glock .45 – to defend herself with. This morning, Agent Smith had informed her, a bit shyly, that he'd have gladly taken "credit" for shooting Sheridan, sparing her the legal difficulties, if only she had been using the same caliber ammunition he did.

"Mine is .38 Special," she'd replied. "What's yours?"

He'd pulled his jacket back to reveal the webbing of a shoulder harness and the butt of a SIG-Sauer P220 autopistol. "Same as Uncle John's," he'd grinned at her, ".45 ACP."

Now she stood and took a step toward Nadalindov. "It's a little early to pronounce my father's idealistic dreams over with, don't you think? No matter how much you wish they were? In any case, they'll never die as long as I'm alive, or anybody else whose life my father touched! Now I suggest that you leave, Mr. Nadalindov, before I do something you'll regret!"

"If I leave now, young lady," he pulled himself up to his full height and puffed out his chest, "without some negotiation in good faith on your part, it will be to file a lawsuit, get an injunction that will allow me to seize control of this campaign organization, and then call a press conference to demand that I be declared President Elect!"

John sat up suddenly and started to get to his feet. Agent Smith rose with him and for a moment the two stood face to face with their eyes locked.

"You do that," Faith-Anne told Nadalindov. She then turned to his attorney. "Have you bothered yet to inform this goof that no legal provision exists to let him do what he wants? Or are you the other goof, who led him to believe there are applicable precedents from the election of 2000?"

The man took his client's elbow and steered him toward the door. "We'll be leaving now, Miss Hope."

As the door swung shut behind them, John suddenly reached inside his coat, startling Agent Smith, who almost – but not quite – snatched for his pistol.

The big man pulled out a cellular telephone which was vibrating visibly. "Tickles," he told Smith. "Hello," he told the phone, then waited to hear what it had to say.

Faith-Anne went back and sat down on the sofa, punching buttons on her own phone as she opened up her laptop computer. She was finished as her father's campaign manager, but she still had his multibillion dollar corporation to run.

For a while, Agent Smith listened as they each attended to their separate chores. Then he decided it was time to attend to his, pulled out his own telephone, and began checking informally with members of his security detail, stationed outside the door, along the corridor, and in various other places in and around the hotel. He preferred to reserve their Secret Service-issue radio frequencies for more formal occasions.

He'd starting to call the other half of his detail, far across town, when suddenly, John swore aloud. "Say that again!" he shouted into the phone, paused, and then, "Agent Smith, have your men let a lady through their ranks downstairs. They'll recognize her right away, she's a *professional* lady, if you know what I mean. And she's taking a terrible risk coming to us here, so make sure she gets up here in one piece."

"Professional lady?" Faith-Anne mouthed the words silently, with a questioning expression on her face. At the same time, something in John's demeanor made her terminate her phone conversation, close her laptop, and stand up.

Agent Smith nodded at John and, taking what comfort he could in the fact that those he was charged with protecting had proven pretty good at protecting themselves, hurried out the door and toward the waiting elevator.

Still holding his phone to his ear, John approached the sofa to stand beside Faith-Anne. "I'll stay with our friend on the phone until she walks through that door over there. I'd go fetch her myself, but that would leave you unguarded. You still there?" he asked the phone.

Apparently he got the answer he wanted.

"Professional lady?" Faith-Anne repeated her earlier question aloud.

"Right," John told her. "She says she was with Ghillie Moure the evening the former First Lady was killed, when he and Abe Horrwyrne interviewed – "

"Whose story is this, anyway?"

The door to the hallway slammed open. Striding through it, Agent Smith immediately behind her, came an extremely blond young woman wearing tight designer bluejeans, a red gingham plaid shirt tied in the front so that it exposed her flat, smooth midriff, an elaborate diamond necklace and dangling earrings, six-inch patent leather pumps, and a floor-length blue-gray chinchilla coat.

She still held a cell phone to one ear.

Faith-Anne took a step toward her. "Interviewed whom?" she asked.

"Chip Sheridan, honey." The blond young woman was chewing gum. "Cute, but it looks now like they were hiring him to kill Mr. Hope. Say, you're his daughter, aren't you?" She threw an enormous purse on the floor, ran across the room to Faith-Anne and threw her arms around her. "I voted for your daddy, you poor baby!"

* * * * * *

Thirty-six hours later, John shoved his big Glock Model 20 .45 back into the nylon holster under his left armpit, overcame a temptation to leave his half-frozen hand there with it, and watched Agent Smith go through similar motions with what John was certain was a Sig-Sauer P220 not officially sanctioned by the Secret Service. Weren't they all supposed to carry little politically-correct 9mms?

At arm's length, they could barely see each other, and that was about all that either of them could see at the moment, concealed in a night- and storm-darkened corner of an old concrete airport apron, hidden between enormous stacks of abandoned, rusting, ice-dripping cargo containers. The weather in this place was horrible, incredibly cold, wet, with a bitter Maine nor'easter coming straight into their faces off the Atlantic Ocean. Huge flat flakes of snow sailed all around them, drifting up in dirty piles on the oily runway surface.

The air smelled quite strangely, of Christmas past, seacoast, and diesel fuel.

The mind-shattering roar of a small business jet plane taking off on afterburners was just beginning to fade from their ears, so that conversation was possible again. John rather liked the smell of jet fuel in the air. It had always meant the beginning of a new adventure to him. Overhead, much larger aircraft than the one they'd just "seen off" crossed the starless sky beneath the clouds with vastly greater grace and dignity.

"Well," Agent Smith observed with a grim satisfaction that belied his words, "we just missed them, didn't we, Uncle John?" He brushed his hands off on one another, obviously happy to be finished with this particular dirty job. Together, they'd just watched a terrified Declan Ghillie Moure, Abe Horrwyrne, and Horrwyrne's wife, hurrying aboard a hastily chartered aircraft, just one step – they had been encouraged to imagine – ahead of the Secret Service, federal marshals, and other unforgiving types with guns and uniforms and badges.

And warrants.

A great deal of effort had been expended – on a purely unofficial basis – to give them such an impression. Gratifyingly, they'd reacted as expected and "taken it on the lam". It had been Smith and Pondoro's job to observe them from hiding and make absolutely sure they all got on their little rented airplane and that the airplane took off for faraway places, preferably never to return. It was easier this way, Faith-Anne had insisted, than prosecuting them, and at this critical point in history, it was probably better for the country, too.

The culprits were headed, according to sources Agent Smith refused to name, for a grimy and impoverished little colony, in Rumania of all places, of expatriate actors, producers, writers, and directors who had decided they needed to "flee" the country shortly after the last President had been elected in 2000.

Lacking the Hollywood cachet of those who'd arrived before them, Moure and Horrwyrne would probably wind up washing windows and waiting tables for handsome, empty-headed movie stars and their bleached-blond wives, while Horrwyrne's wife changed their bedsheets.

If all went as planned, Sheridan would soon be written off as the usual "lone nut". The historic template for that old canard was well established, the Old Media would happily shout it from the housetops. They'd have to find out what his middle name was, of course – Lee Harvey Oswald, James Earl Ray, Mark David Chapman – assassins always had three names. An internet investigator here and there would have his suspicions, but nothing would ever come of it.

On the other hand, apparently invited by his erstwhile allies, Nadalindov had steadfastly refused to run. John had listened to the surveillance tape several times (Alex would never have approved of that). To the Secret Service, he'd insisted on a having polygraph test, which might mean, in Pondoro's estimation, that he didn't know anything about the plot to kill Alex.

"Reckon they outfoxed us and escaped us fair and square," John drawled. "A darn shame, too. We coulda thrown 'em to the possums, or whatever's customary in these parts. We couldn't have thrown them in jail – we don't have any evidence that's admissible. But, 'the guilty flee where no man pursueth", and it's time to get ourselves back to Portland. It isn't a whit warmer or drier here in Bangor, is it?"

The normally stoic Agent Smith permitted himself a modest shiver. He even reached up and touched his left ear – it felt naked without the earphone –

wondering if it was frostbitten. "No, it isn't," he replied. "Not at all. Nor does one have the warmth of friends and family to comfort one here, as one presumably does in Portland. How long before we can go?"

"Very carefully put, Agent Smith," John laughed, "very carefully put. Two minutes, if our little motor scooters are still where we stashed them earlier. I gave my pilot instructions to keep the getaway plane running."

Chapter Fifteen
LONG JOHN SILVER

> *As a juror, I will exercise my 1000-year-old duty to arrive at a verdict, not just on the basis of the facts of a particular case, or instructions I am given, but through my power to reason, my knowledge of the Bill of Rights, and my individual conscience. When needful I will judge the law itself.*
>
> – Alexander Hope, *Looking Forward*

He looked so pale lying there, Dana thought, even against the billowy white fabric enveloping his head and shoulders. He'd been a somewhat darkly complected man, like Cary Grant or Mel Gibson, but now his face – the face she had learned to love so dearly – was the color of death.

The others would be arriving soon, it suddenly occurred to her. She might not get another chance. She bent down, and without a moment's hesitation, gave him a small kiss on lips that seemed impossibly cold.

"We've got to stop meeting like this," Alex told her, opening the one eye that she could see. The left was covered with a piratical eyepatch.

Dana's eyes crinkled at the corners. Putting her arms around him as best she could, with all the wires and tubes attached to him – wires and tubes exactly like those she'd spent several weeks attached to, herself – she laid her cheek on his. At least they'd shaved him, today. She'd had to work her way up here through a dozen layers of government security, and she never could have done it without Faith-Anne "escorting" her every step of the way by cell phone and laptop video. "Does that mean you'll remember seeing me, this time?"

Somewhere, an electronic chime went *bong* and the PA system chanted, "Dr. Basow, Dr. Teumer, Dr. Lalipandresh, please report to the ICU stat. Dr. Basow, Dr. Teumer, Dr. Lalipandresh, please report to the ICU."

"You mean we've done this before?" He struggled to sit up and failed. "I must have been pretty sick if I've forgotten that. Here I thought I was in heaven and you were an angel. Probably the head angel."

"Alex... "

"No uncalled-for modesty, here. You're the most beautiful girl I've ever known. You have a wonderful face to wake up to. I'd like to do a lot more of it. What are you planning for the next 30 or 40 years?"

She whispered, "Well, I'd sort of had my heart set on having a lot of babies and being as politically obnoxious as possible in public. I can tell you I'd rather not go on trading shifts in the hospital with you."

"What are you talking about?" he laughed – and cringed because it hurt. "This is a completely *different* hospital. That was Denver, the Mile High City, this is Portland, the Home of Cement. You know, it's kind of funny, kid, I remember being shot with perfect clarity – it didn't hurt – but I don't remember much of anything else. How long have I been here?"

And why didn't I think to ask that before now, he wondered. Blinded by the light, I guess.

Dana said, "You were shot the evening of the 15th – happy Bill of Rights Day. This is the 18th – by the way, the Electoral College met this morning in state capitals all over the country and cast their votes. You're now officially the President Elect of the US of A." Was that a tear on her cheek? "I don't know whether to congratulate you or not."

"Better make your mind up," he told her, reaching between them to dry her face with his fingers, "because that makes you the First Girlfriend."

She dimpled; he could feel it with his hand and against his cheek. "First Fiance, thank you very much – unless you're planning to withdraw that offer you made to me on national television in the gymnasium kitchen on Election Night."

"I'd sooner tear my tongue out with a pair of Vise-Grips." He pushed her up, back into his range of vision, allowing himself a moment to take her beauty in all over again. "No, I'm afraid you're stuck having babies – lots of babies? – and being politically obnoxious. I plan to be a lot of help with both projects. By the way, can you give me an idea what's wrong with me? I didn't lose anything important, did I?"

She laughed, a wonderful sight and sound to him. "Only a couple of gallons of blood! I ought to leave this to the doctors – but I won't. You were shot through the left lung, Alex. The bullet passed near your heart and lodged under your shoulder blade. That's why it hurts when you laugh. You were also shot in the right thigh. I think the Secret Service did that. Nine millimeter, so it wasn't Agent Smith. And you have a ricochet injury, plaster from the wall, to your left eye from which you're expected to recover fully."

However she was weeping by the time she finished. She'd come so close to losing him!

"In other words," he said, "I'm a mess: crutch, eyepatch, all I need on Inauguration Day is a parrot on my shoulder and it'll look just like Long John Silver's being sworn in – *aarh!*" He hesitated.

"You know, I just remembered the oddest dream – that it was Chip Sheridan who shot me."

She shook her head. He enjoyed watching the way it made her dark, shiny hair move, showing off the reddish highlights. "Oh, Alex, I'm afraid it wasn't a dream!" She quickly told him everything she knew about the matter, including details about his daughter shooting Sheridan, how they'd found out who had hired him, and what they'd done about it.

"My poor Faith-Anne. She must feel like she's been run over by a truck." Dana was surprised and pleased that it was the first thing he chose to comment on. Here was a man who would make – had already made – a good husband and father. Did he know she'd have loved him if he'd been a clerk or an auto mechanic or garbage collector, instead of a billionaire and President of the United States? Somehow she had to make sure he knew.

She nodded. "She's blaming herself for everything that happened and feeling especially bad for having been taken in by Sheridan. I'm trying to help, but on top of that, she's having a tough time staying out of jail."

"*What?*"

Dana explained to Alex what was going on in that

connection. Then she told him about what she termed "Nadalindov's attempted *coup d'etat*".

The chime rang again. "Agent Smith, please report to the first floor entrance, Agent Smith."

"That will be your daughter," Dana said, "and probably Cap and Uncle John."

* * * * * *

But Dana was wrong. The first four faces through the door were those of the Austrian Mafia, Katie Harris, Rick Thomas, Mick Douglas, and Ernie Hanover. Ernie was struggling with an irregularly-shaped package almost as big as he was, wrapped in red, white, and blue tissue paper.

"Hail to the Chief!" he exclaimed as he entered the room.

"Hail, yes!" Rick and Mick answered him.

Katie started to add, "Congratulations, Mr. Pres – "

"Don't say it," Alex warned her. "I told you what to call me, back at the beginning of this circus. Mr. Hancock, what's that you're carrying?"

Mick said, "He's going to give himself an Ernia!"

"Ha, ha, ha," replied Ernie. "It's a gift – something I hope you'll find useful over the next four years." He plopped it on the foot of the bed. The package was at least five feet long, two feet in diameter – although it seemed to taper from one end to the other – and weighed at least 30 pounds.

"Dana," Alex said, "can you help me with this?"

"Sure thing!" As if she knew what was going on, she turned the large end toward him, and parted the colorful tissue paper to expose a black nose and whiskered muzzle under bright eyes set in a fur-covered but earless head. It was an exceptionally large stuffed animal, a toy made to resemble a familiar marine mammal. Over its shoulders, it was wearing a large blue square of cloth showing an official coat of arms – the same one (although Alex had no way of knowing it) that had been on the lectern his daughter had used the day before at her press conference.

"It's beautiful!," Alex said. "But what does it mean?"

"It's the Presidential Seal," Ernie told him, obviously proud of the bad pun. It earned him some moderate laughter, two groans, and a healthy *Boo!*

Katie added, in a stage whisper, "I keep telling you, it's a sea lion, dope!"

That got even better laughter from everyone, including Alex who then squinted and tensed with pain.

* * * * * *

Cap, John, and Faith-Anne weren't far behind. They came to Alex's room accompanied by Agent Smith, who stood conversing with Dana and Faith-Anne – and listening to the voices in his earpiece.

John moved the Presidential Seal to the chair beside the bed and sat down near Alex's feet. "I thought you might like to have this," he told Alex, handing him a zippered, roundly triangular case made of something that looked like leather. "Although I've never understood what you see in such an inexpensive toy when you could afford anything your heart desires."

Alex recognized the case immediately and enthusiastically took it from his friend. He zipped an edge open, pushed his hand into the case, and, glimpsing at the door of his room to make sure it was shut, withdrew the weapon he'd decided not to carry the night he was shot.

It was the European American Armory "Witness" he'd owned for years and usually kept in his car. Alex had other handguns. This was the one that seemed to find its way onto his belt most of the time. The model designation was "longslide sport", with a matte-chromed frame, a black slide about the same length as a government Colt .45, but with a high capacity magazine that held a dozen .40 cartridges, each about as powerful as .357 magnum. The weapon had a big adjustable sight at the rear of the slide, an oversized thumb safety, and rubber grips. When cocked, its trigger had been honed by a professional to "break" cleanly at two and a half pounds.

Alex thumbed the black button at the root of the square-faced trigger guard and let the loaded magazine slide out and fall heavily into his left hand. He grasped the serrations at the front of the slide and pulled it back far enough to expose the cartridge in the pistol's chamber. He let the slide move forward again, replaced the magazine, briefly inspected the two spares in the case, and then put the gun away.

"Thank you, John," he said. "I chose this piece because it's the best – and most underrated – handgun on the market. I doubt you could do better if you spent $1500. This cost about a fifth of that."

John shrugged. "To each his own, I guess."

"I'm very happy to have it – although I don't know where I'm going to keep it here, where the nurses and doctors might see it. It wouldn't have done me much good the other night. I never even saw it coming."

John shook his head. "Neither did I. Guess I was

too impressed with Chip's credentials from the 82nd. They were genuine enough – I'd checked. What a waste!"

Cap said, "But you don't have to hide it from anybody, Uncle Alex. You're the President."

Alex laughed – and grimaced. "Oh, yeah. I keep forgetting."

* * * * * *

Before Alex had a chance to speak with his daughter, Agent Smith approached him. "Mr. President El – sir, I've just heard that Congressperson Linda Alvarez is downstairs and wants to come up. Do you want to see her?"

Alex nodded. "I certainly do – and it's Congress*woman* Alvarez, Agent Smith. Better get that straight before she gets up here if you want to live."

Agent Smith almost grinned. "Right you are, sir, Congresswoman Linda Alvarez." He spoke into his sleeve. "Send the Congresswoman on up, Louie."

Minutes later, Linda came into the room, leaving her dark suited, sunglassed escort waiting outside. She was wearing light blue jeans and a short fur jacket. There were crystal drops of rain or melted snow in her dark hair.

John got up off the bed, moved the Presidential Seal to the top of the dresser, and pulled up the chair it had occupied for the latest guest. Cap helped by taking the Austrian Mafia downstairs to the hospital cafeteria for a Coke.

She shook her head. "No, thanks, Mr. Pondoro – John. I won't be here that long. I've never been shot, but I had an appendectomy once, and I remember quite vividly how tired a little thing like that left me feeling."

She turned to Alex. "I just came to see how you're feeling, to congratulate you, and tell you that for the next two years, at least, you have the full support of the one and only libertarian member of Congress."

Alex took her hand. "Thanks, Linda, I can't tell you what that means to me. But please don't go just yet, I'm just about to attempt a somewhat silly stunt, and I'd appreciate it if you were here when I do it."

She raised her eyebrows, but nodded. "You've got my very raptest attention."

"Good deal." He signaled to his daughter and to Dana, who came to see what he wanted. "How much effort," he asked, "do you think it would be for me to make a statement from this room on national TV within the hour?"

Agent Smith's head whipped around toward him at those words. John nodded understanding and agreement, as did Faith-Anne. Linda Alvarez laughed out loud.

Dana said, "I don't know whether the traditional Old Media will go along – "

"To hell with them – Faith-Anne, I guess it's your job, at least for now – tell the networks if they aren't ready to take a feed within the hour, that I'll make my first statement as President Elect exclusively to NetPlanetNews.com."

Everyone in the room cheered and applauded. It took a while to quiet them down. Even Agent Smith seemed tempted to give Alex a look of approval.

"Dana, please get in touch with your boss somehow and ask him to get a mike and camera up here ASAP. If he wants somebody else to ask me questions – other than you, on account of conflict of interest –

he'd better send them up, too. I'm very sorry about that, my darling, it's the one aspect I truly regret of having been bewitched by your charms."

"You regret having been bewitched by my charms?" Dana repeated, an entirely false pout on her face. "I said yes, didn't I? I knew what I was getting into, didn't I? I'm a grownup, aren't I? I'll bet my boss is downstairs right now in that drizzle-covered crowd in front of the building."

* * * * * *

Dana pulled the heavy collar of her coat up, hoping no one would recognize her. She kept her crutches hidden, as much as she could, in its folds. She wasn't exactly afraid, even after what had happened to her in Denver, and the people here in the hospital parking lot were very clearly on Alex's side – and therefore, she hoped, on hers, as well.

In fact, she was stunned at this gathering which, as far as she knew, was completely spontaneous, and she was a bit worried about being mobbed.

She looked for Alan. There were thousands of people here, maybe even tens of thousands – he would have obtained a count by now. Every sort of person she could imagine was here, too, black, white, brown, and yellow. Men and women, old people, children, and everybody in between. She saw furs and expensive topcoats standing right next to t-shirts and ragged jeans covered with improvised slickers made of green garbage bags.

Candles hadn't worked out too well in the Portland winter drizzle. The streaming asphalt was littered with them. Instead, people held up flashlights and cyalumes, filling the otherwise dreary parking lot with a soft, multicolored light that reminded her that Christmas was only a few days away.

She'd gotten her present, already: Alex was alive and would recover.

The people stood peaceably, shoulder-to-shoulder, dripping and cold in the light but constant rain. Many of them were praying, some were openly weeping. Somebody in the far corner of the lot began to sing:

Tell the parasitic bureaucrat,
Tell the looting politician, as well,
That their days are numbered and about to end,
That the fight for liberty has found a friend,
And its enemies are headed straight for Hell,
Because the friend that it's found is me!

I will be free, I will be free!
Free to choose, to win or to lose!
I will be free-ee-ee-ee,
I WILL *be free!*

Tell the scum I won't be satisfied,
'Til I've taken back the city street,
'Til they've stopped creating poverty,
And the whole world's private property,
Or their blood is running at my feet,
If that's the way that it's got to be ...

I will be free, I will be free!
Free to choose, to win or to lose!
I will be free-ee-ee-ee,
I WILL *be free!*

I've been silent for 200 years,
Since they took the Declaration away.
Losing all my freedoms Left and Right,

Now they're gone and now it's time to fight.
The Declaration's back, today's the day!
The flag's unfurled, O can you see?

I will be free, I will be free!
Free to choose, to win or to lose!
I will be free-ee-ee-ee,
I WILL be free!

I'm an army unto myself,
Each friend of Liberty's an army, too.
Blood and fire, I will find rebirth.
Lever and fulcrum, I will move the Earth!
No tyranny will stand when I am through,
No trace remain of the enemy ...

I will be free, I will be free!
Free to choose, to win or to lose!
I will be free-ee-ee-ee,
I WILL be free!

The singing began to spread until it filled the parking lot, and people inside the hospital came to the windows to see what was going on. The song itself, she'd heard before. It had been written by one of the Austrian Mafia at Albert Gallatin Memorial College – not one of the four she knew, but a friend of theirs. The melody, especially of the chorus, was lovely, but the words were a bit bloodthirsty, she thought, in a manner that reminded her of the French revolutionary anthem *"La Marseillaise"*, which was all about the tyrant's foul blood running in our furrows, or words to that effect.

Maybe that was the way a revolutionary anthem had to be. She was willing to bet that Ascher Liebowitz and the Mendelsohn brothers would approve. The point, however, was that these people apparently loved Alex, and wished him well.

Almost as much as she did.

* * * * * *

"Ladies and gentlemen," Alex said to the camera, "fellow children of the American Revolution ... "

In the end, it was decided that there wouldn't be any questions. Not tonight. By the time the arrangements had been made, Alex was very nearly used up. He tried to pretend otherwise, but his daughter, his fiance, and his best friend weren't fooled. He had to promise to keep it under ten minutes.

The camera – surprisingly tiny and mounted on a single-legged support – belonged to NetPlanetNews.com, and it was being handled by Dana's boss, who, at least to Alex, greatly resembled Edward G. Robinson. What he saw through his viewfinder would be shared out to all the traditional Old Media networks, but it would have the NPN logo in the lower right hand corner.

Alex inhaled. "Please permit me to introduce myself, as I will not assume that you already know me. Fewer than an eighth of the eligible voters in this country cast their votes for me. I am Alexander Hope, of the Free Libertarian Party of America, and I've just learned that the Electoral College has named me the winner of the general election of 2008."

In a chair at one end of the bed sat Faith-Anne, Alex's daughter, campaign manager, and, for the time being, at least, chief of staff. In another chair, at the other end of the bed, sat the Presidential Seal – Alex had insisted. On the opposite side of the bed from the camera, behind Alex as he spoke, stood John, Cap, the Austrian Mafia, Linda, and Dana.

Alex had insisted on that, as well.

He spoke without notes. "The first thing I want you to know is that nobody could be more astonished than I am to be addressing you this evening as the President Elect – hopefully, in time, *your* President Elect. Like those of you who consider themselves Republicans or Democrats or Independents, I sincerely wish that Vice President Chesley Chambers had turned out to be a better man than it appears he is. Likewise, I wish that the former First Lady had not been killed, along with more than a dozen others, in that horrible accident in the Rocky Mountains."

The nurses had done a fair job hiding the drainage tube from his lung and the intravenous line to his left arm. They'd been persuaded to temporarily remove the wires attached to the sticky snaps on his chest and abdomen. They'd covered him, as requested, with a cheerful southwestern-patterned blanket from his car outside (a plain gray 2008 Durango – he couldn't let John have his way with everything).

There was nothing they could do, however, about the eyepatch he was wearing. Ernie and Mick and Rick had been making piratical noises all afternoon, and John had said something to his son about shirt advertisements. Alex just thought about Long John Silver and soldiered – or pirated – on.

"This is where we stand, however. These are the cards we've been dealt. And the second thing I want you to know is that I will take my duties as President of the United States as seriously as – perhaps even more seriously than – if I had been elected overwhelmingly in a landslide."

It was as close as he dared come to saying he'd act as if he had a mandate.

"The third thing I want you to know is what happened day before yesterday. For reasons known best to himself, a young man in whom my staff and I had placed considerable trust chose to betray that trust by attacking me. You can see the result. I am injured, but recovering. My daughter Faith-Anne, of whom I am extremely proud (and to whom I am extremely grateful), put an admirably efficient stop to that attack by shooting my assassin dead, as a consequence of which I promise you that I will take my oath of office, standing on my feet, on January 20th in the nation's capital."

He didn't say anything that would exclude the use of crutches. He and Dana would make quite a pair, for a while, on their extra aluminum legs.

"The fourth thing I want you to know is that, on my inauguration, I will immediately begin to keep the one and only campaign promise I ever made. I will energetically and stringently enforce the first ten amendments to the Constitution – commonly known as the Bill of Rights – exactly as if they were exactly what they are: the highest law of the land."

He tried not to rearrange his blanket while he let that statement sink in – or at least he hoped it sank in. The socialist media would be howling at the moon tomorrow, for his blood – what he had left.

Let them howl.

"Look them up," he went on, referring to the Bill of Rights. "You can find them in any encyclopedia or almanac. I plan to ask that they be printed in the telephone book, as well. See for yourself what the future holds. Don't rely on television pundits or government lawyers or judges to tell you what your rights are. They're there for you in black and white. Read them for yourself. The Founding Fathers meant for you to understand what's possibly the clearest use of language in human history."

He paused for a moment, then went on. "To begin my policy, I'll expect any bill that crosses my desk to include a citation of the Constitution to justify its passage, and an argument that it doesn't violate the Bill of Rights. Otherwise, I will veto it. Of course it may be passed over my veto but it will take a two-thirds vote of Congress to do that, which is progress in itself: it will bring us that much closer to the unanimous consent this country requires to run decently and justly. Of course the names of those who vote *against* the Bill of Rights will be posted on the internet and receive the full attention of their irate constituents.

"In the opening week of my administration, I will also require every federal employee and every department head to justify his job and its activities with reference to the Bill of Rights."

He was beginning to tire badly, it was difficult to breathe. But he hadn't gotten to the important part yet, and he was determined to.

"Nobody who works for a living – no member of the productive class in general – has anything to fear from such a policy. Nor does anyone who can live without initiating force against others or having it initiated for him. Even those who have subsisted, heretofore, at the involuntary expense of others, will find reason to be grateful for the establishment of this policy, because it will set them free, it will enable them to stand up on their own, and to be proud."

He took a deep breath, trying desperately to avoid wheezing. "What I mean to do is return ownership and control of your life to you. In the end, each and every one of us will know with certainty where he stands, under the law."

This time, he paused for a long while, until one of his nurses started forward from behind the camera, a worried look on her face. He put a hand up to stop her, then turned it into a five-finger count.

"The fifth and final thing I want you to know is that you can help me to return this country to the rule of law by remembering your 1000-year-old right and duty, when called upon to be a juror, to judge the law, as well as the facts of the case or the instructions of the judge. If it doesn't match your understanding of the Bill of Rights, the law must be discarded."

Finished at last. "I'll speak of this again. For the time being, thank you, and good night."

* * * * * *

The lights and camera were gone, and so was nearly everyone who had crowded this room an hour ago. Only Dana remained, sitting in the chair beside the bed, holding Alex's hand, and touching his injured face the way he had touched hers what seemed to both of them such a short time ago. Her own sore feet were propped up on the Presidential Seal.

They had both been silent for most of that hour, listening to Christmas music playing faintly on the hospital's sound system. "There is something we need to know about each other, Dana," he told her, suddenly serious. "Something we need to get straight right at the beginning."

She looked alarmed. His voice was wearier than she'd ever heard it. "What is it, Alex? Are you absolutely sure it won't wait until tomorrow morning?" Would it end with his saying they could always be friends?

He shook his head. "No, it won't wait. You know this will be our first Christmas together, my love, and there are only seven days left until then. Geez, I never even got any shopping done. But I have to know ... "

"What, Alex?"

"Does your family open their gifts Christmas morning or Christmas eve?"

She laughed and grinned. "Silly, I'm a Buddhist!"

Chapter Sixteen:
THE CHIEF JUSTICE

> *Right-wing myth to one side, "republic" and "democracy" mean the same thing, one in Latin, the other in Greek. The thing to remember is that they're both just another form of collectivism, of socialism, under which your neighbors may vote you into the poorhouse – or the grave – if they want what you have. Those who profess to care about their nation and its place in history must expend every effort to limit this possibility or to eliminate it altogether.*
>
> – Alexander Hope, *Looking Forward*

The Chief Justice of the Supreme Court wore an expression that was appropriate to the occasion, but there was encouraging, conspiratorial light in his eyes. He'd had trouble himself, over the long, rocky course of his career, from those who hated him, not so much for the color of his skin, but for daring to cherish ideals that his enemies had decided – for him – were unsuitable to a man of his color.

"Place your left hand on the Bible, raise your right hand, and repeat after me" 'I, Alexander Hope...'"

Alex tried to exhale evenly. "I, Alexander Hope..."

"'Do solemnly swear ... '," the Chief Justice continued.

Alex repeated, "Do solemnly swear ... "

"'That I will faithfully execute the office of President of the United States...'"

"That I will faithfully exeecute the office of President of the United States..." Alex was relieved; he'd been afraid he fumble that part, under the pressure of the occasion.

"'And will to the best of my ability, preserve, protect, and defend the Constitution of the United States...'"

"And will to the best of my ability, preserve, protect, and defend the Constitution of the United States." That was exactly what he'd come here to do.

"'So help me God.'"

"So help me God."

Alex wasn't certain to what degree he believed in God. If there was one, he could use His help. He found it difficult to keep a tremor out of his voice this morning and it was only partly due to his still-healing wounds.

Taking this oath in public should make anybody nervous, he thought, especially knowing that thousands present here today, friend and foe alike, and perhaps a billion others on the other ends of all those television cameras, would be watching his every move for the least mistake or sign of hesitation.

How did that old bluegrass song go again, about "The Great Speckled Bird"?

Add to that the awkwardness of placing his hand on the big black book that George Washington himself and every President after him had sworn the oath on – a hand that stuck out of a sling on his left arm intended to keep him from reopening his chest wound – and raising the other hand, while trying to keep his crutches from slipping out from under him.

Then there was the damp, bitter, January cold that only the former swamp known as the District of Columbia was capable of producing. He could well believe that another President, William Henry Harrison, had caught pneumonia at this very ceremony and died in office only a few weeks later.

He turned stiffly on his crutches and put his good hand on the lectern. The platform where he stood, ringed with Secret Service agents and a sprinkling of people John had called in for the occasion, was raised a dozen feet above the street. He glanced across an ocean of faces below, consisting mostly of various VIPs and the press, the latter having been expressly denied places on the platform. Not all of them were friendly. Alex was beginning his term of office at about the same level of popularity, he calculated, according to this morning's polls, as Richard Nixon when he had resigned.

Maybe it was the eyepatch. He could see perfectly with that eye now, indoors, but sunlight, even through the overcast, was still painful.

Seated in one of the front rows where she was easy to see, was Dana, her trim little figure wrapped in a long, quilted coat. Her crutches lay on the ground underfoot, where the camera couldn't see them. Her cameraman knelt on a chair in the row before her, where he could shoot her with an instrument no bigger than his fist, then turn easily to the ceremony. Alex had wanted her on the platform with him. But she'd insisted that this was the last chance she'd have to be an "infobabe".

Alex's other friends were evenly divided between the President and the First Girlfriend. Cap was watching Dana's back; Alex was glad to have him there. John was on the platform with him, of course. Just to keep the DC police off his back – they actually required a special permit for a camera tripod – Alex had written John a very slightly postdated note this morning asking him to carry any weapon he wished. John and Agent Smith had come to some agreement. Alex often saw them together, the older man more than likely laughing, the younger trying to learn how.

Forrey Nadalindov, Alex's Vice President, and Linda Alvarez, the FLPA's only representative in Congress were here, too. The Austrian Mafia were in the row behind Dana, trying to resist a temptation to make faces behind her back when the camera was on the "infobabe".

Only an instant had passed. Alex cleared his mind to speak.

"Ladies and gentlemen, fellow children of the American Revolution, Mr. Chief Justice. It is astonishing how much torture and abuse people can become accustomed to, provided it's done to them gradually. In the darkest of the Dark Ages, there was a law, universally respected throughout the civilized world even by the blackest of villains, that no peasant could be taxed more than ten percent of what he earned by the sweat of his brow."

He could hear them buzzing out there. This was beginning like no other inaugural address in memory. But what else could they expect?

"In 1913, as he was imposing an income tax on this country (after the Supreme Court had declared Abraham Lincoln's income tax unlawful), Woodrow

Wilson promised Americans that it would never go any higher than five percent, and that it would never affect anyone but the very wealthiest two percent of the population. Almost certainly this is where the observation first came from, that you can tell when a politician is lying – because his mouth is moving."

Timid laughter. Hadn't anyone ever told a joke on this occasion?

"Today, by a gradual process, punctuated from decade to decade by wars that serve as an excuse to tax Americans more and more – and limit their freedoms in the bargain, using 'National Security' as an excuse – we've reached a point where the rate at which they're taxed can only be regarded as obscene.

"Not only is an American forced to give up a third of his income to the federal government each year, but other taxes – state, county, and municipal, property, sales, and excise, fire district, water district, and road district – raise the burden to half of what he earns, *five times* what any medieval serf was ever required to sacrifice.

"In exchange for the money that's taken from them – whether they want them or not – Americans are 'offered' a range of 'services' that generally fall into one of two categories: things the private sector could do more competently, cheaply, and safely; and things that nobody, least of all the government, should do at all."

"Seven-eighths of everything in America is tax. Half of what you earn is taken from you by one tax or another, so right away, you're expected to keep running on half of your economic capacity to survive.

"Companies that provide you with goods and services pay half of what they earn to government, as well, except that they don't pay it, you do, built into the prices of what you buy. So, given the taxes you part with directly and those you part with indirectly, you're really living on only a *quarter* of what you earn.

"Finally, it costs something to comply with regulations and fill out paperwork – in fact, it doubles the price of goods and services again – and those costs are passed on to you, as well. So now you're struggling to get by on one *eighth* of what you earn.

"It's as if the purpose of government is not just to take away your hopes and dreams, but as many of the remarkable benefits of individual liberty, private capitalism, and the Industrial Revolution as it can. Certainly if people kept what they produced, the contrast between the world that would create and the consequences of socialism advocated by my political opponents would be too high to mistake. Nothing but total economic and political freedom would ever appeal to them again. Maybe that's the whole point to something like the IRS.

"The victims in the pink bathtubs in the 2000 film *The Matrix*, hardwired into the system, drained of their vital energies from a dozen outlets, they had it easy, compared to the American taxpayer. All they had to do was lie back and dream. Americans are expected to work and worry themselves to death paying for 'services' many of them find morally repulsive, their dreams smashed by a voracious state.

Stunned silence. He'd expected at last a timid cheer or two.

"As you may know, I'm an historian by trade. For decades I've been hearing stories about the 16th Amendment, passed in 1913 to override provisions of the Constitution that made Lincoln's wartime income tax unlawful. The stories hold that the 16th Amendment was never properly ratified, and that the federal income tax structure, and the Internal Revenue Service that enforces it, are themselves illegal. I admit that I was disinclined to look into these stories, because, even if I believed them, there wasn't anything I could do about them.

"I still don't know if the stories are true, but now that I can do something, I mean to find out. The first thing tomorrow morning, I'll appoint a Presidential commission, consisting mostly of historians, to investigate claims that the 16th Amendment was never properly ratified and, if it wasn't, make recommendations regarding what should be done about it. Those of you who are forced each year to surrender half of what you work so hard to earn may rest absolutely assured that this administration will *not* try to reinstate the 16th Amendment.

"Which brings me to a broader point. During my campaign, all kinds of people – mass media, even members of my own party – were after me to describe my 'tax program', if I were elected. They should know that it's not the role of a libertarian President to create his own tax program. In the words of the late humorist Roger Price, that would be like the people who believe the world is round, gathering up the people who believe the world is flat, and shoving them off the edge.

"It's a libertarian President's role, not only to resist new taxes or increases in old ones, but to repeal, nullify, or otherwise dispose of every tax he can. The idea is not just to cut them by a few points here and there, but to abolish them altogether.

"As I said, government 'services' fall into two categories: things the private sector can do better, cheaper, and safer; things nobody, especially government, should do at all. If you're tempted to call it 'anarchy', you reveal a tragic ignorance of history. It's simply the way things were, for the most part, before Woodrow Wilson – a pious mouth-mover who got elected by promising not to send American boys to fight and die in a European war, and then broke his promise as quickly as he could – before Wilson did his part to convert the land of the free and the home of the brave into a socialist dictatorship.

"Don't be alarmed, however. The President's powers have limits. Those of you concerned with government functions you believe are necessary – the military, the courts, local police, the National Weather Service, the Bureau of Weights and Measures – need look no further than the many Democrats and Republicans in Congress certain to stand in my way with regard to abolishing taxes.

"In a sense, you have more to say about it than I. At the moment, the IRS maintains its own courts and judges because it knows what would happen if the tax code had to face a real jury of your peers, fully informed of their 1000-year-old right and duty to judge the law, as well as the facts of the case. I will put an end to that police state practice immediately, with an executive order I wrote this morning and am signing as I speak to you. The same order will abolish withholding, so that you will be able to see more clearly what's being done to you, what's being taken from you, and help me put a stop to it once and for all.

"When you are called to jury duty in a tax case, remember those medieval peasants who paid a fifth of the taxes you do, remember the burden you suffer under, remember the peace, progress, and prosperity being taken from you with every tax you're forced to pay. Remember that seven-eighths of everything is tax.

"Remember and vote. If you really desire freedom from fear of the government, remember and vote. No one can stop you."

x x x x x x

They bundled him into a limousine for the ride to an address on Pennsylvania Avenue. To his delight, he found himself sitting beside Dana, still wearing her heavy coat and a smile that lit the inside of the big black car and filled it with summery warmth. In the privacy of tinted windows, he leaned over, crushed the coat, and gave her a kiss.

John handed him a Thermos with the Presidential seal ("the one with the eagle, not the flippers," Cap pointed out) enameled on its shiny stainless circumference. Alex raised his eyebrows at John.

John shook his head, "Hot chocolate only. Sorry."

"January 20, 2009," Alex recited dramatically, "a day that will live in infamy."

"Because I didn't spike the cocoa?" John tried to look hurt.

Alex shook his head. "Because for the first time in more than 200 years, this country's going to run by the rules that were written for it. Which seems to make me some kind of radical. Judging from the reaction of my audience – or the extreme lack thereof – you'd think I was announcing they were all about to be beheaded."

"Not a bad idea," John laughed. "But they'd probably like that. We both know the weird, sick mentality of liberals."

"There's no such thing as a liberal," Dana intoned with a scowl, imitating Alex at his academic best. "Like 'environmentalist', it's an obsolete word used to cover the ideological backsides of socialists."

Alex said, "I hate to interrupt, but this Thermos is half empty."

"Or half full, depending on how you look at it." Dana held up a stainless cup – also with the Presidential seal – and tipped it in salute. "I've applied for the position of food taster. John's giving me a tryout. Anyway, I deserve something, don't I, for being banished to the ground with the rest of the Earthlings, while you share a platform in the sky with the pretty Congresswoman from New Mexico?"

"I like Linda fine," Alex assure her, "but she's not my type."

Dana replied, "Oh, what is your type, Professor President Hope?"

"Chinese dolly internet snoops." Alex shook his head. "Anyway, I was up there with the Chief Justice, too, and this ugly lug." He nodded toward John who was extracting another Presidential Thermos from one of two black nylon traveling bags. The other bag, Alex knew, held spare Glock magazines and a shotgun with a folding stock.

"And Agent Smith," John added. "And your pretty daughter."

Alex peered at Dana. "Are you really jealous of Linda?"

"No," she answered, her eyes crinkling at the corners, "but I had you going pretty good there for a minute, didn't I?"

* * * * * *

"Good evening, ladies and gentlemen, fellow children of the American Revolution, I'm Alexander Hope."

He was sitting at a desk in the Oval Office, a room he'd only seen before on TV. On the desk before him, a presentation model Government .45 automatic pistol was displayed for the viewers to see, gold plated and engraved with the words of the Founding Fathers, in celebration of the Bill of Rights.

"It's six o'clock on the west coast where I lived and worked for 30 years. People are getting home from a hard day at work and an even harder one on the freeway. They're trying to relax, and beginning to think about what they'd like for dinner. They're probably not in much of a mood to hear a political speech, even – maybe especially – from the man who just took the oath of office earlier today."

At the other side of the room, out of the camera, both Dana and Faith-Anne nodded encouragement at him. John gave him a thumbs-up, and Cap made bunny-ears behind Faith-Annes's head.

Alex struggled to ignore him. "On the High Plains and in the Rocky Mountain west – 'flyover country' where I grew up, where I returned to teach history at Gallatin Memorial for several years – it's seven o'clock. People are eating and wondering whether there's anything good on TV this evening.

"In the midwest, it's eight o'clock and I'm interrupting some of those TV shows. I apologize for that. In the future, I'll do my best to confine these monologues to Saturday evenings, when there's nothing much worth watching, anyway."

He took a deep breath. "Here on the east coast, it's nine o'clock. On almost any other Inauguration Day, I'm told there would be scores of noisy gatherings in the District, celebrating the electoral success – or mourning the failure – of this or that party's candidate. While there are a few such celebrations underway, they seem to be mostly somber occasions – even among the victorious Free Libertarian Party of America – and it feels to me like a time for contemplation.

"That's why I've chosen this evening for my first address to you – since the inauguration this morning – as President of the United States. Somebody once said if a new President wants his programs to get through, he'd better manage it in his first 100 days in office, before opposition from other parties and the socialist media sets like concrete, and he spends the next 45 months bashing his head against the wall they've built around him to confine him.

"As an historian, I've never given that notion much credence. But I want to get off on the right foot, and do it quickly. So my first official act in this room is to sign these papers granting executive clemency to my daughter, Faith-Anne, who has been criminally charged (an expression that can be taken two ways) by the city of Portland, Multnomah County, and the state of Oregon for carrying a concealed weapon in their jurisdictions and discharging it in the defense of her father, who had just been shot by an assassin and was lying, bleeding and unconscious at her feet, in a hotel corridor.

"This document absolves her of any statutory wrongdoing, as well as any future charges arising in this connection.

"To allay any suspicion that I'm granting my daughter a special favor by enforcing her unalienable individual, civil, Constitutional, and human right to own and carry a weapon, observe the stacks of paper behind me. Six of them reach 11 feet toward the ceiling. My staff took all afternoon to put them there, before they unpacked the rest of my office. They're executive clemency forms I'll sign and they'll send you if you've been arrested, arraigned, tried, convicted, fined, or imprisoned for violating any of this country's 25,000 unconstitutional gun laws. Simply call the office of the White House general counsel at 1-800-FREEDOM. If you qualify, you'll receive orders for your release and full reinstatement of your life, your property, and your rights, including financial restitution.

"I'd like to extend special thanks to the city fathers of Portland for making this act necessary. If anyone wonders where I get my authority to do this, to violate what they may mistakenly believe is a state's right to violate the rights of others, I refer them to Article VI, Paragraph 2 of the US Constitution, which states:

> *This Constitution, and the Laws of the United States which shall be made in Pursuance thereof ... shall be the supreme Law of the Land; and the Judges in every State shall be bound thereby, any Thing in the Constitution or Laws of any State to the Contrary notwithstanding.*

"The outgoing Secretary of the Interior, as you may already know, used to be the Attorney General of my home state. By all accounts, she's a competent lawyer and as decent a human being as you'll find in politics. I don't mean to single her out, I wouldn't mention her at all if she hadn't made herself a textbook example of what's wrong with this culture's current perception of rights.

"Once, years ago, I heard that the Attorney General was wondering aloud at just what age the Bill of Rights – in particular, the Second Amendment – began to apply to children. I confess I was as shocked as I've ever been by anything political happening around me. I was aware law schools are hopelessly inept at teaching the meaning of the first ten amendments to the Constitution. They seem unaware there's any history, any moral philosophy, or even any purpose underlying them.

"Nevertheless I assumed the Attorney General could *read*, that she might have noticed the Bill of Rights isn't about children; it isn't about her or you or me; it doesn't concern any of us at all. Above all, it isn't a list of things the government allows us to do. It's terribly misnamed: it isn't really a 'bill of rights' at all.

"What it is, is a list of things the *government* is forbidden to do: establish a state religion; abridge freedom of speech; interfere with peaceable assembly; quarter troops in people's homes; search or seize people's persons, houses, papers, and effects unreasonably; try them twice for the same offense, make them testify against themselves, take their property without compensation... It isn't about us, it's about what the government can't *do* to us.

"One thing government is forbidden to do is infringe the right of the people to keep and bear arms. Decades of historical and legal scholarship have established beyond a shadow of a doubt that the Founders were referring to a pre-existing individual right. The Second Amendment says government can't interfere with that right, even in the slightest little degree – that's what 'infringed' refers to.

"They had reasons: people were to remain armed to keep government contained, meaning that government interference with the right to own and carry weapons is the grossest conflict of interest. Note also that, since the Second Amendment limits government power, and isn't really about people or their rights, there's no minimum age someone must attain before they mysteriously acquire this right not to be infringed upon. They're born with it; it's up to their parents – not governments – to assure they learn to exercise it wisely.

"Interference with this process amounts to state terrorism and cultural genocide. That's why the severest penalties await any official, at any level of government, who willfully continues to misinterpret or misunderstand this or any other article of the Bill of Rights. Let me repeat that, so it's clear: under this administration, the severest penalties await any official, at any level of government, who willfully continues to misinterpret or misunderstand this or any other article of the Bill of Rights.

"The 27-word text of the Second Amendment reads, 'A well-regulated Militia being necessary to the security of a free State, the right of the people to keep and bear Arms shall not be infringed.' Despite massive volumes of historical and legal scholarship to the contrary, those who oppose enforcement of the Second Amendment often point to its first clause, 'A well-regulated Militia being necessary to the security of a free State,' as evidence that it refers to collective right, or a right of the states to organize militias.

"What they seem to have missed is the clearest implication of that phrase, that anyone who seeks to infringe the *necessary* right of the people to keep and bear arms, in the view of the Founding Fathers, is placing the security of that free state in peril. There is a technical term for this: *treason.*

At least two and a half million Americans defend themselves with guns each year, most of them pistols and revolvers. The number may be as high as four and a half million. It's impossible not to conclude that those who favor 'gun control' – call it by its proper name, 'victim disarmament' – actually *want* those two and a half million Americans injured, or killed.

"In the end, advocates of victim disarmament have a question to answer which, with the help of corrupt politicians and the even more corrupt mass media, they've so far evaded. From this moment on, they must be confronted at every turn, everywhere they appear, everywhere they speak, everywhere they try to rally, until they are compelled to answer it, and expose themselves for what they truly are.

"Why would they rather see a woman raped in an alley and strangled with her own pantyhose, than see her with a gun in her hand?

"As you may be aware – although every effort is been spent to keep it from you – violent crime has been plummeting for decades in states with 'must issue' weapons-carry permit laws. Unfortunately, under the Second Amendment, requiring people to obtain such permits is illegal. The least violent crime is found in Vermont, where permits are not required, and people may simply arms themselves and go about their business. We call that arrangement, 'Vermont Carry'.

"America must go 'beyond Vermont Carry'. The collapse of violent crime we're witnessing is such an unquestionably valuable thing that offering significant tax credits – money that would ordinarily pay for law enforcement that's no longer needed – offered to those who help to rid American streets of crime by providing for their own defense, seems a reasonable and sensible idea.

"I'll remind you that you hold the solution in your hands. In the future, many of you will be called to serve on juries across the land. Some will be asked to make decisions involving the 25,000 gun laws passed despite the clear wording of the Second Amendment, infringing the right of the people – your right – to own and carry weapons. Not one of those laws would have been approved by the Founding Fathers, not one is constitutional.

"Remember that when it's time to exercise your 1000-year-old right and duty to judge the law, as well as the so-called facts of the case.

"Thank you, ladies and gentlemen, and good night."

Chapter Seventeen:
UNCLE BOB ANSON

> *The only certain way to put a stop to the "politics of personal destruction" is to show the other side, vividly and in microscopic detail, how it feels when it's done to them.*
>
> – Alexander Hope, *Looking Forward*

"What the hell does this mean, 'full faith and credit'?"

The Mayor of Los Angeles looked down at the letter in his hand. It had been personally delivered to him by Faith-Anne Hope, Alexander Hope's daughter, a truly vicious anti-government lawyer he'd learned to despise years ago. She hadn't smirked or gloated when she handed it to him – somehow that made it worse – but simply said that it was an order having to do with civil rights, the equivalent of President Eisenhower's order in the 50s to integrate the public schools in Little Rock.

Then she'd left.

The letter was passed from the Assistant Mayor to the Chief of Police to the current head of the City Council. "This is a disaster!" said the city's top cop. "Everywhere else they've done this sort of thing, violent crime has dropped like a shotgunned pigeon, and now the taxpayers're wanting to reduce their police forces by 50, 60, 80 percent!"

"Full faith and credit," the Mayor repeated.

"It's a legal doctrine," said his chief legal counsel, "under which local jurisdictions in America are required to respect the laws of other jurisdictions. We can't arrest a tourist, for example, for driving in the city and county with a Nebraska driver's license. And Nebraska has to recognize marriages that have been licensed here in California. It makes sense."

"But the Second Amendment!" complained the City Councilwoman. "Do you all realize that this invalidates all legal requirements to buy a gun except those that survive the Hope Administration at the federal level?"

"You're not getting the whole picture, here, Beverly," said the Assistant Mayor. "Ever hear of Vermont? There's no licensing requirement in that state, no carry permits. The gunfreaks call it 'Vermont Carry' – and that's what we have to recognize in Los Angeles! It's chaos! It's anarchy!"

"It's effective," said the legal counsel. "Vermont is the safest state in the union."

"Damn that Hope!" shouted the police chief. "He'd better never try to make a speech in this town again!"

"Careful, Sidney," said the mayor's lawyer. "I think you just threatened the President – and that's a felony."

* * * * * *

"Mr. President! Mr. President!"

Forty people screamed at him, all at once. Happily, he'd watched one of his favorite movies last night, *The Outlaw Josie Wales,* holding hands with Dana. He'd had a full night's sleep – something that, any pressure to the contrary, he'd continue to insist on during his tenure here – and a wonderful steak-and-eggs-and-hashbrowns breakfast with a tall mocha, a liter of tomato juice, and lots of melon and other fruit.

He felt as if could face anything this morning, taken care of like that. He lifted his good hand and pointed to a reporter he recognized vaguely from TV.

"Mr. President, certain experts – including the president of the National Rifle Association – have declared that your 'Beyond Vermont Carry' program is a bad idea, and that it will never pass in any case. What's your reaction to that – and wouldn't you have expected more support from the NRA?"

Alex raised his eyebrows. It was a bad move. Strobes flashed and cameras clicked and whirred. He'd be on the cover of the *Washington Post* or the *New York Times* this afternoon, looking like he'd sat on a tack.

"I've learned not to expect anything from the NRA, Mr. Bushmill, but cowardice and treachery. They're the ones, after all, who insisted on giving us their thoroughly unconstitutional background check system."

"But Mr. President – "

"I'm sure you'll appreciate, Mr. Bushmill, that whatever happens to our Second Amendment rights could just as easily happen to our First Amendment rights. How would you like it if your government decided that it had to check into your background before they let you file a story? Believe me, there are politicians who want exactly that. But try and tell it to the NRA. Over the past 70 years they've turned themselves into nothing more than America's biggest and oldest gun control organization."

"But isn't it true that the Second Amendment is only a collective right, so that the states can't be prevented by the national government from forming militias?"

"Nope," Alex said, "not even close. You need to brush up on your grammar, Mr. Bushmill. The first clause of the Second Amendment states a purpose for its having been written, not any kind of limitation on the right it seeks to preserve."

The shouting started again, but Alex raised his hand.

"Be assured, Mr. Bushmill, plenty of real Second Amendment groups – Concerned Citizens Opposed to Police States, Jews for the Preservation of Firearms Ownership, the Libertarian Second Amendment Caucus, the Western Libertarian Alliance – have praised my 'Beyond Vermont Carry' program and solemnly pledged to see it enacted into law, even if it takes 20 years."

"Mr. President," a young female reporter began. "Your surprising offer to pardon every criminal in America ever convicted under the nation's gun laws – "

He held a hand up and stopped her. "Say it right, Miss MacIntosh. That's 25,000 demonstrably *unconstitutional* gun laws, so the people accused or convicted of having violated them are hardly criminals. They're victims of police state policies. But please go on."

"Er, well, Mr. President, it's brought certain reactions – "

He laughed. "You mean it's evoked bellows of wounded outrage from all of the professional victim disarmament groups on TV from the thugs at the United Nations, to Gun Control Incorporated, and the pickled old harridan who runs it, amplified by useful idiots in the socialist mass media."

"Useful idiots ... " she began to object.

"Present company excepted, of course," he lied gallantly.

She shook her head as if she were suddenly dizzy. "Er, my question, sir ... "

"I beg your pardon, Miss MacIntosh. Please, ask away."

"What would your response be, then, to the Secretary General and to Mrs. – ?"

"My response, Miss MacIntosh, is this executive order." He held up a piece of paper. "All personnel connected in any way with the Bureau of Alcohol, Tobacco, and Firearms must report for work as usual, but sit at their desks and do nothing, pending the taking of depositions and an examination of their records for evidence of violations of their victims' civil, constitutional, and human rights. I've already sent federal marshals to their offices in 23 cities to seize those records."

That caused something of a stir. The young woman sat down in her folding chair, tape recorder still held aloft in her hand, and her mouth wide open.

"Mr. President?" It was another reporter he recognized from TV, Jonathan Daniels. "Tell us what will happen to those BATF personnel at the end of the investigation?"

"The same thing that will happen to any official, anywhere in the country, Mr. Daniels, who tries to enforce unconstitutional gun laws in the future. They'll be arrested, tried, and with any luck at all, convicted, fined, and imprisoned. Even more importantly, they'll be required to make restitution to their victims at their own personal expense."

The reporter blinked. "Even if they were simply doing their best to enforce the law in good faith?"

Alex shook his head. "No good, Mr. Daniels – isn't that exactly the same excuse the Nazi concentration camp guards tried to use at Nuremburg?"

No response.

"Well, Mr. Daniels, isn't it?"

"Er...uh..."

"Look: when you get right down to it, my first and foremost job as President is to help people to attain freedom from their fear of government. The only way to do that is to get government officials to see the Bill of Rights as a law to be enforced, rather than a laundry list of arbitrary rules they have to get around. If I can accomplish that without sending anybody to jail, fine. But as Lucky Ned Pepper put it in *True Grit,* 'it's enough that you know that I'll do what I have to do.'"

"Mr. President!" the same forty voices shouted a once.

He ignored them. "I want to say one more thing and we'll put this subject away. For 50 years, various administrations have used the BATF to wage a campaign of terror – what amounts to a *pogrom* – against American gun dealers. Only 10 percent of the number of dealers that existed when I bought my first gun are still with us. Yet everything points to them as social benefactors, suppliers of the machinery of freedom, the source of our plummeting crime rate. I mean to see their numbers *double* by the end of the year, through a massive reduction of regulations, with a view to eliminating dealer licensing altogether in the very near future."

"Mr. President," asked another woman, "there's a rumor that you carry a gun, yourself. May we see it?"

"No, you may not, Miss Jamelle. You can't see my toothbrush, either, or paw through my underwear drawer. I ought to be asking you where your gun is, since, under the law, no individual has a right to expect to be protected by the police – look it up, I'm not kidding you for an instant – and therefore each of us has an absolute legal, not to mention moral obligation to defend his or her own life. Next question? Let's talk about something else – yes, you in the yellow and green paisley dress."

A little old lady with a twangy west-Texas accent spoke up. "Mr. President, the leaders of both major parties in both houses've publicly denounced your list of proposed cabinet appointees. They say they're all nothin' but a bunch of radical libertarians or libertarian leanin' ultraconservatives, and they've promised t'reject their nominations."

"That's what I hear, too. What's your question?"

"What'll you do without a cabinet?"

Alex laughed again. "Well you know I had to have been thinking about this from the moment I was nominated. I guess I could rescind my nominations in favor of hacks that they'd approve of from Socialist Party 'A' and Socialist Party 'B' – but I don't think I'll do that, do you?"

Despite themselves, most of the people in the room laughed.

"Or I could change all of my choices to *interim*

appointments," Alex told her, "and run the government, for the next four years, without any official department heads at all. I've had my legal counsel look into that option for me and I'll certainly take it if I'm forced to."

The woman scribbled furiously in a tiny notebook.

"Or I could just tell the leaders of both major parties in both houses that I'll veto every bill that comes across my desk until they approve my nominees. Of course I'd pretty much planned to do something like that anyway, and said so, openly and often, during my campaign. But the leaders of both major parties in both houses probably mistook me for a politician, noticed that my mouth was moving, and naturally assumed I was lying – providing, of course, that they paid any attention at all to a minor third party candidate."

That remark brought general laughter to the room.

"Mr. President, you make a habit of ending every address you give, on TV, the radio, or the internet with a reminder to the public about jury nullification."

Alex laughed and clapped his hands. "Ah, you *noticed!*"

Everybody laughed. The reporter went on. "Already juries in the western states, encouraged by your rhetoric, have begun to dismantle the welfare system, and several of them just this week threw out the entire EPA concept of 'wetlands', under which that agency has been terrorizing ranchers and farmers who dare to modify their own land to suit their need. Those juries are declaring that private property rights are absolute."

"I'd like to think," Alex nodded, "that I had something to do with that. Your question?"

"Your supporters have started pushing in the state legislatures for tort reforms that would greatly reduce the number of liability suits filed. My sources tell me that the National Association of Trial Lawyers have privately sworn to have their revenge – it's said they're drawing up impeachment papers as we speak."

"And ... ?"

"And it's pretty clear that judges and lawyers hate you. In some states, they're trying to alter the jury system to allow majority verdicts instead of unanimous ones. Do you plan to do anything about this?"

"You mean like withholding highway funds?" Again there was laughter. "My Attorney General, once I have one, will give the higher courts a chance to slap such legislation down. I'm sure they'll be worried that such a practice would greatly damage the credibility of the justice system. If that fails, then we'll figure out where to go from there.

"Any more questions? Very well, then, one more announcement. As I promised shortly after I was elected, I have signed an executive order – another executive order! – requiring each and every employee of the federal government to justify his job under Article I, Section 8 of the Constitution, and the Bill of Rights. All subdivisions of the government will comply, as well. The deadline is five working days from tomorrow.

"No questions about that? Well, then, I'll remind you, as well as your readers, listeners, and viewers, of their 1000-year-old right and duty as jurors to judge the law, as well as the alleged facts of the case."

The room erupted into good-natured laughter and he left it feeling good.

* * * * * *

The conference room seemed awash in a sea of blue, green, black, and white uniforms. The only individuals present in civilian dress were Alex himself, his daughter Faith-Anne, John, and Agent Smith – who always seemed to be in uniform no matter what he was wearing. Alex had learned only recently that the man was an ex-Marine.

Down the sides of the long, polished hardwood conference table sat the Joint Chiefs of Staff of the United States Army, the Navy, and the Air Force, their broad chests bedecked with ribbons. Alex had insisted on summoning representatives of the Marines, the Coast Guard, and the National Guard, as well. His two right hands, John and Faith-Anne sat at the far end of the table, helping him to "surround" the generals, admirals, and their aides.

The brass had stood ceremoniously when he entered. He'd invited them all to sit down, but remained standing, himself. "Gentlemen, this meeting will be extremely brief. I want you to make detailed plans for the withdrawal of all American troops from anywhere they may be stationed today, outside of our borders – "

"Now, now!" He held up a hand. The uproar had been tremendous, considering who these men happened to be. "I want you to do this for me in absolute secrecy. I want you to bring your plans to me for review one week from today. If any among you feel that you can't comply with my orders, you may resign now, with no prejudice toward you on my part."

There was a long moment of stunned silence.

He went on. "Gentlemen, it pains me to agree with a man I disagree with most of the time, Patrick J. Buchanan, but he's right about this: America wasn't cut out to be an empire. It's very bad for us as a people and bad for the people of the world, who don't hate us without good reason. That's why I'm ordering our troops home from Siberia, from Korea, from Bosnia, from Germany, from Central America, and from everywhere else around the world where they've been sent, including places – like Mali, for example – where most Americans have no idea their military has a presence."

"Mr. President," a man in a green uniform with three stars on his shoulders spoke. His silver hair was close-cropped and his eyes were steely blue. "I feel a duty to advise you that the only result of this would be world chaos – "

"General, people who hate freedom always call it chaos." Alex shook his head. "You don't hate freedom, do you? Haven't you been defending it all your life? As it happens, I'm familiar with your distinguished record as a soldier and administrator, and I don't wish to be rude or disrespectful, but I'm your Commander-in-Chief and I'm giving you a lawful order. If you can't show me, in the Constitution, where the leaders of this country have acquired a legitimate right to appoint themselves the cops of the world, then you're obligated to obey that order or resign."

He waited.

The general said nothing, but nodded.

Still Alex waited.

The general suddenly sat up in his seat, startled.

"Uh, yes sir."

"Been a long time since the Point, General?" Alex asked him. "Okay, then, I'll see you all here in a week."

As he and Faith-Anne left the room, John whispered, "Or call it 'Seven Days in January'."

Alex laughed.

* * * * * *

Alex hadn't quite dared to wear pajamas and a bathrobe. The light sweater and comfortable slacks were casual enough for this setting, he thought.

The Marine non-com who had shown him the way departed, leaving him alone in the enormous kitchen – or as alone as a President ever gets in the White House. His movements were being tracked, he knew, by Agent Smith's people or by John or Cap. He wasn't sure how he felt about that.

He'd wondered how his executive order, placing John in overall charge of security and relieving any Secret Service agents unwilling to follow John's orders would be taken by Agent Smith, but it hadn't made much difference that Alex could see. Maybe it was because the younger man had made the older man his mentor and was content to learn at his feet.

Although his Marine guide hadn't said anything, it was obvious that the young man approved of having a fellow leatherneck in the Oval Office. Army and Navy Presidents hadn't worked out all that well.

It was extremely odd, being on his own this way after months of close-quarters campaigning with his friends and family. Almost a week had passed since the inauguration. Ernie, Rick, Katie, and Mick were back in school in Colorado, although he intended to see they had jobs in his administration if they wanted them. (Secretly he hoped they wouldn't – they were good libertarians and belonged in the private sector.) His daughter had leased a house outside the Beltway and was probably there now, since it was well after midnight. She thought he was going to make her chief White House counsel. If they could find somebody to run the Hope Corporation for a few years, he would appoint her Attorney General.

Dana had departed – such sweet sorrow! – an hour ago, escorted by Agent Smith. He wondered how many telephoto pictures they'd take of her tonight on her way out of the White House. She was staying with Faith-Anne. He hated sending her away like this every evening, but tongues were wagging already, mostly in the "liberal" media, about the President's girlfriend being only half his age (which wasn't quite true), or in more viciously "liberal" circles, about the interracial nature of their relationship. Funny, he thought, how the world's worst racists invariably turned out to be on the left.

Not even the worst of them had dared to call her his mistress – yet – but it was coming; he could feel it in his bones. He had plans to head it off, and he and Dana had discussed them at some length this evening.

They'd begin by encouraging the media to photograph Faith-Anne and Dana together as often as possible. There wasn't a cameraman alive who wouldn't find that prospect irresistible. (One of them had caught them together talking to Linda, and labeled the resulting magazine cover, "Alexander's Angels".) The two complemented each other perfectly, one a fair, freckled redhead, the other a golden-hued brunette, both approximately the same height and build. They liked each other and it showed. Then they'd invite Dana's parents to stay at the White House for a weekend. Let the media make what they would of that. Before they had a chance to recover, he and Dana would announce their wedding date.

Randomly, Alex began opening the big stainless steel refrigerators (there were a dozen of them lining the walls) and peeking at what lay inside. Mostly tonight it was hundreds of desserts, puddings of some kind, chilling for tomorrow. He didn't know of any special event being planned, but the White House was like a big hotel, with thousands of people coming and going in any given week, and the kitchen looked the part.

He finally found what he wanted, a big covered platter of roast turkey, chose several slices of white meat with crunchy, salty brown skin still on their edges, and began looking for some bread to put it between, some cranberry sauce (the jellied kind, not the other), and some sandwich spread. He'd been raised on Miracle Whip and couldn't stand mayonnaise.

A happy (if slightly corrupt) thought struck him. Now that he was President, he wondered if someone could get him some really small sardines.

"Oh, Mr. President, please let me do that for you!"

Alex turned to see a small, solid-looking black man in his 60s, wearing a crisp white apron with the White House logo, over a white shirt, black tie, and suit pants. What was left of his hair was steel gray. His tone and expression were civil, but appraising, and not at all subservient.

"That's what I'm here for, sir, after all. I'm Robert

Anson – people call me 'Uncle Bob'. I'm the night kitchen man here in your house, sir."

"And have been for a long time, I'll bet," said Alex. He wondered how many presidents had had this first-week midnight-snack talk with Robert Anson.

The man grinned broadly. "That's right, sir, a long time. It's a good job and I like it. Now what can I get for you – was that gonna be a turkey sandwich? You like multigrain bread? We bake it ourselves, you know."

For all his wealth, Alex had always lived rather modestly, and he had no idea at all how to deal with... he even shied from the word, "servants". What he said was, "That would be fine, er, Uncle Bob. You can call me – "

"I'll call you Mr. President. There's reasons we do things this way, sir. You'll see."

Alex watched Uncle Bob as he prepared the plate. White House china with an embossed paper doily. Four slices of rough, wonderful bread he could smell six feet away. Miracle whip – the man was a wizard. Two generous piles of turkey, with a dollop of jellied cranberry sauce in the middle. Both sandwiches sliced across the corners to make neat triangles. A sprig of parsley that seemed to come from nowhere. It was a lot like watching one of those nightclub sleight-of-hand magicians who work up close.

"Now I'm guessin' you're a barbecue potato chip type," the older man said. "Or I could cook you up some French fries in about three minutes."

"That would be nice some other evening, thank you," Alex answered. "Barbecue potato chips will be just fine tonight. Can I get a Coke, too?"

Uncle Bob raised his eyebrows. "You're the

President, but ... this time of night, sir?"

Alex laughed out loud. "Caffeine never bothers me that way, Uncle Bob. I used to drink Jolt before I went to bed, back in California in the 70s."

"Mister President, you are one lucky man, sir. Here's your sandwiches. Would you like me to call somebody to carry it back for you?"

Embarrassed, Alex shook his head. "No, thank you, Uncle Bob, that would just be silly. If I get lost, I'll just ask a Marine for directions."

Uncle Bob laughed. "You do that, sir. And come back soon, hear?"

"Count on it. And thank you."

The man waved negligently and grinned back at Alex, who nodded and left the kitchen humming a little tune under his breath.

Life was good, sometimes.

CHAPTER EIGHTEEN: *CARLOS HATHCOCK*

> *Never forget, even for an instant, that the one and only reason anybody has for taking your gun away is to make you weaker than he is, so he can do something to you that you wouldn't let him do if you were equipped to prevent it. This goes for burglars, muggers, and rapists, and even more so for policemen, bureaucrats, and politicians.*
>
> – Alexander Hope, *Looking Forward*

"You know there are those in the community – my community – who compare you to Hitler, Mr. President."

Albert Mendelsohn leaned back in the comfortable chair he'd been offered, took a sip of 30-year-old single malted whiskey, and drew on the Cuban cigar he'd just lit.

Alex liked watching Albert and his friends enjoying themselves. In his day, Jimmy Carter had prissily decreed there would be no alcohol served in the White House, not even wine at state dinners. Later, a certain First Lady, now deceased, had banned tobacco. Alex had decided that his ban, if any, would be on self-righteous prohibitionism. He took pleasure offering his guests Glenfiddich and tobacco from the formerly communist island south of Miami. He paid for both from his own pocket. The label on this particular brand of cigars showed Fidel Castro in his final moments, swinging by the neck from a lamppost in downtown Havana.

"You *are* Hitler, to them," Albert's brother Ruven shrugged. "In their view, you're *forcing* them to be free." Albert and Ruven were a study in contrasts, the former tall and thin, the latter short and plump, rather like Sherlock and Mycroft Holmes. Yet nobody could ever mistake them for anything but brothers. It was something in their eyes and the grim set of their mouths. Both had "seen the elephant" and had taken lives, not just to defend themselves, but to defend liberty for everyone.

They had that in common with their host. As a teenager, Alex had believed it was what he was fighting for in Vietnam, at least in the beginning.

They also had it in common with his third guest, the Rabbi Ascher Liebowitz, who had celebrated his *bar mitzvah* in the woods, stalking and killing German soldiers. The hugely bearded Ascher stood somewhere between the Mendelsohn brothers in height, but was a broad bear of a fellow. Ascher would have made a terrific nose tackle, Alex thought, a hockey goalie, perhaps even a Sumo wrestler.

"And you know why, too," Ascher offered. "The late, great Austrian economist Ludwig von Mises was right about the way the socialist mind works. In his heart of hearts, each of them sees himself, personally, at the tip-top of the pecking-order once the revolution has come and gone. And you, Mr. President Hope, are spoiling their employment prospects!"

Alex's fourth guest laughed. Father Joseph Spagelli was too young to have fought in a real war (he'd been attending a Catholic seminary during the Persian Gulf campaign), but he'd grown up in the toughest, grittiest, most dangerous neighborhood in Chicago. If he'd never had to kill anyone, it was a matter of pure luck. In any case, he wouldn't talk about it.

Today, sponsored by the Ralston Foundation (which nobody here knew Alex funded), he taught teens in that same neighborhood and others how to defend themselves, beginning – and how the left-wing media loved to howl about it – with a weekly excursion to the nearest shooting range. Five of his former students were now at West Point, Annapolis, and the Air Force Academy in Colorado Springs. Three had scholarships to Stanford, MIT, and the University of Chicago. One had recently been sentenced to prison for having been caught carrying a concealed weapon – but had applied for and received executive clemency from the Hope Administration.

These four were Alex's first informal guests in the Oval Office. He'd considered inviting them to the residential section of the White House; technically, it would have been a greater honor, and heaven knew the place was empty enough without any kind of First Family (yet) to fill it with the warmth and light of love. But Alex thought his guests would get a bigger kick out of being in this world famous and historical room.

"I must be a masochist, then," Joseph told them. "Force me to be more free some more, will you, Mr. President, please? I don't really need to get an Illinois firearms certificate or pay income taxes. Be cruel. Take them all away from me. Or how about if I give them up for Lent?"

Ascher laughed, "Now *that* kind of Lent, I could observe!" He was examining the fancy Bill of Rights .45 from Alex's desk.

"How very multicultural," Albert told him. "You suppose you could get a famous liberal like the Democratic leader of the Senate to go along with you?"

"That one!" Ascher exclaimed in disgust. "He's no liberal!"

"There's no such thing as a liberal!" everyone but Alex recited loudly, quoting one of his more famous public statements.

"He's just another post-Holocaust Jew," Ruven said, "who doesn't get it. How can Jews visit a Holocaust memorial or museum and not recognize a responsibility to plan for their own safety and that of their families? How can they walk through a death camp and believe they should not have a gun to defend themselves? Why are Jews so reluctant to defend themselves?"

"No, no," Albert shook his head. "It's only the ones you hear of constantly. The media won't talk about Benjamin Kaufman in World War I, who captured a German machinegun nest with a smashed arm, a couple of grenades, and an empty pistol. They won't talk about Hyman Rickover or Generals Rose and Klein in World War II, or Benjamin Prager, Joseph Heller, and Adolph Marix, three of Teddy Roosevelt's Roughriders – Jewish Roughriders! – in the Spanish American War, or the 12,000 Jews who fought on both sides in the War between the States."

Ruven interrupted his brother. "For that matter, Jefferson Davis' right-hand man, Judah P. Benjamin, served as Confederate Secretary of State and the Treasury. Everybody called him 'the brains of the Confederacy'!"

"There's Uriah P. Levi," Albert went on, "and John Ordroneaux, two fighting ship captains in the War of 1812, or even the 'Great Rebel', Captain Mordecai Scheftel, in the Revolution."

Joseph's eyes lit; the Mendelsohns' enthusiasm was contagious."And who could forget Haym Solomon, who raised money for his friend George Washington. He even talked his way out of it when the British captured him. There would never have *been* an America without him!"

"Not to mention Jack Jacobs in Vietnam or Tiber Ruven in Korea," Ruven added.

Ascher said, "It's the professional victim syndrome. Without their precious victimhood, people like the Democratic leader of the Senate are lost. They're shmoos – remember shmoos? Those little whiskery bowling-pin-shaped guys in Al Capp's *Li'l Abner* who gave milk and laid eggs? You could slice steaks off them? The more you did it, the better they liked it. Trouble is, people like the Democratic leader of the Senate all want *us* to be shmoos, too."

"You're right," Ruven told him. "Look at Elie Wiesel, the writer who watched his own father die at the hands of Nazis butchers at Buchenwald. Yet he refuses to take any wisdom from his experience, or from the testimony of survivors in places like Vilna and Warsaw, who were able to defend themselves with guns. He refuses the lesson history offers and supports victim disarmament, instead."

"Or Abe Foxman," Joseph added, "of the Anti-Defamation League, a child Holocaust survivor, raised by a Catholic nanny. His parents miraculously survived the war and claimed him. Then they came to America, where he spouts off for victim disarmament – and socialism in general – although they've both done untold damage to Jews."

Albert shook his head. "Or Paul Lantos, another Holocaust survivor and advocate of victim disarmament. It's as if Jews didn't remember what was done to them. You'd think a people who'd been through all that would be the very first to learn that you can't conduct genocide against an armed population. It didn't take *me* long!"

"You know," Ascher told them, " I've been trying to figure out this particular form of suicidal stupidity for decades, and I'm no closer to it now that I was during the war – World War II, I mean. I think maybe people like that have some vague, semiconscious, and certainly unexamined, notion that the *Shoah* was possible because the German government had guns, and 'therefore' – "

"The idea's so dumb it doesn't *deserve* a 'therefore'!" Joseph snorted. "How can Jews – or anybody – say 'Never Again' without having the power to enforce it?"

"Tell me about it," said Ascher. "They think if they make guns go away, it can't happen again. Trouble is, it wasn't private guns, but government and police guns that did it to them."

"And governments will *always* have guns," observed Alex.

"Maybe the shmoos *want* it to happen again," Joseph mused. "Maybe this is their way – disarming everybody who might fight back – of getting started."

"Only Nixon could go to China," Albert muttered, as if to himself. "Only the Democratic leader of the Senate can bring about another Holocaust."

Alex said, "Well, maybe we can spoil their masochistic plans. In my weekly address next Saturday evening, I'm going to announce another Presidential Commission, this time to look into the late Senator Thomas Dodd and the Nazi roots of his 1968 Gun Control Act."

Joseph sat up straight, "I hadn't heard about that!"

"The victim disarmament crowd was hot in '68," Alex said. "Like the vultures they are, they swooped down on the steaming carcasses of Bobby Kennedy and Martin Luther King and used them to ram through a bill Dodd copied from Hitler's gun laws a couple generations earlier."

Joseph was still aghast. "Copied from Hitler? How do you know that? How could Dodd ever think he'd get away with it?"

Alex replied, "Well for starters, we have a letter from a law librarian, Lewis C. Coffin, at the Library of Congress, returning Dodd's copy of the 1938 Nazi law, promising him the translation he'd asked for would be ready soon. And we have the resulting 1968 American law, itself. He *did* get away with it, Joseph. Who was going to blow the whistle on him, the national socialists at the *New York Times?*"

* * * * * *

"Look at that!" Alex pointed to a convoy drawn up to receive him in a "secret" underground carpark near the White House. It had all the makings of a parade, consisting of his limousine – a lumbering beast with an armored hull, bullet-proof windows, run-flat tires, and a powerplant that would have done justice to a locomotive – and several of the black Suburbans Alex didn't like, to haul the Secret Service and their hardware wherever Alex (code-named "The Professor" – Dana was "Mary Ann") went.

Add to that, unmarked cars of various colors and descriptions to parallel his course, motorcycle outriders, and helicopters to overfly the whole expedition. One of them was ready at all times to rush his presumably broken and bleeding body to Bethesda. Pleasant thought.

This afternoon, it was out across Chesapeake Bay to Maryland's famous Eastern Shore, where he'd been asked to open a new recreational facility named for a fellow Marine, and underwritten by the Ralston Foundation. That was why advisory board members Ascher and Albert and Ruven and Joseph were here. Kitch Sinclair, had been invited as well, but Kitch was giving final exams for the quarter. John planned to meet them there. Dana was working. Faith-Anne and Cap had gone to a meeting of the Space Colony Foundation to help them clear the way for a first private launch.

Today was a first for Alex, too – his first day with a cane instead of crutches. He felt it was long overdue. Agent Smith was standing with them on a catwalk overlooking the parking area. "I guess I knew what I was signing on for," Alex sighed. "But it still seems silly that I can't go anywhere without two dozen vehicles to precede and follow me, plus droves of advance men to 'sanitize' wherever it is I'm going. Makes it damned awkward to step out to the 7-11 for a Squishee."

"It's a Slurpee, sir," Agent Smith corrected him. "Squishees are what they have on *The Simpsons.*"

"Right," Alex chuckled at the mental image of Agent Smith watching the Simpsons. "Still, you know how all this happened, don't you?"

"I do, sir," Smith replied, keeping his eyes on the floor of the garage. "With 300 million people in this country, the President can't draw a breath without somebody, somewhere, taking offense."

Alex shook his head. "It goes deeper than that, Agent Smith. There's a big difference between offending someone and having the power to destroy him. It's no coincidence that the first president to be assassinated was the architect of the American superstate, Abraham Lincoln."

Agent Smith cleared his throat nervously, "I'm not sure I follow you, sir." To men like him, Alex understood, Lincoln wasn't merely a hero, he was a demigod.

"Before Lincoln," Alex explained, "no president had the power to hurt anybody much. Lincoln wiped out a whole culture – or gave it a good try – and used up half a million of his own 'boys' doing it. He imposed conscription and income taxes – both forms of slavery themselves – claiming it was to *end* slavery. John Wilkes Booth believed Lincoln was a tyrannical mass-murderer from whom he was either saving the south or avenging it."

"I'm kind of interested," said Father Joseph, "to see where you're going with this, Mr. President."

Alex nodded. "Well, since Lincoln there have been three successful presidential assassinations – Garfield, McKinley, and Kennedy – and how many botched attempts in between and after?"

"I'm afraid that's classified, sir," said Agent Smith.

"Everybody knows," Alex told him, "about Teddy Roosevelt, Franklin Roosevelt, Harry Truman, Gerald Ford, and Ronald Reagan. Whether you happen to like them or not, unlike Lincoln's predecessors, they had an absolute power over, not just the lives, but the very hopes and dreams of their fellow Americans, a power I don't believe the Founders would have wanted their successors to have."

"Officially speaking, sir, I wouldn't know about that." Agent Smith cleared his throat again. A glance back showed his four guests stifling their amusement.

"I understand," Alex nodded. "But that's only the domestic side. Media and government portray 'terrorists' as crazy or evil. But except for a communist dinosaur here and there, I can't think of one group like that that wasn't worked over thoroughly first by some government or other. What the bloody Brits did to the Irish and the Scots, for example, rivals anything Hitler, Mao, or Pol Pot ever did."

Agent Smith suddenly alert, listened to his earpiece, and mumbled something up his sleeve. "They're ready for you down there, sir." He seemed relieved, as he often did at this point in a conversation.

"Okay. But the point – its relevancy to you – is that I can't think of a way to put the genie back in the bottle. Presidents before me were in danger, they needed elaborate (and to my way of thinking, unAmerican) safety measures because they were always taking something – life, liberty, property – away from somebody. All I want to do is give it back, and I'm in danger because those who've grown accustomed to receiving stolen property see me as taking it away from *them.*"

Alex and his cane setting the pace, they started down a concrete ramp toward the long line of vehicles. "Well, sir," Agent Smith said, "I'll do my best to keep you alive while you get it figured out."

Alex laughed. "I guess that's all I can ask, Agent Smith."

* * * * * *

The driver slowed, stopped, turned in his seat, and said to Alex,

"We're there, Mr. President."

"Good." Alex folded his laptop – he'd been writing next Saturday evening's address – and put it away. He still had a dozen overseas calls to make before the day was over and several hundred executive clemency forms to sign; he didn't feel right using autograph machines for that.

His second meeting with the Joint Chiefs was coming up this Friday and he had another surprise to hand them. "Sorry, gentlemen, that I had to be a bad host and get some work done. It's either double up or lose sleep. I hope you all enjoyed the ride."

"What's not to enjoy, Mr. President?" Ascher asked him. "This is without question the most comfortable automobile I've ever ridden in." If I were the leader of the free world, I'd go for a ride every day!"

"It should be," Alex told him. "It weighs two and a half times as much as any other car its size. It's sprung like the bunkers under Cheyenne Mountain, and it takes a real bump to disturb the passengers. I'm ashamed to tell you how many gallons per mile it burns."

Father Joseph laughed and barely restrained himself from clapping his hands. "It has satellite TV! Ascher, I'm watching winter baseball in the Mexican League!"

The side door opened, making everybody's ears pop, and a cold, salty draft entered the car. In this part of the country, Alex thought, March came in like a toothache, and went out like a wet sponge. Agent Smith was standing at attention. Behind him, John was visible with a long, black plastic case of some kind in his hand.

"Hail to the Chief!" John said.

"He's the one we all say 'Hail' to," replied a stone-faced Agent Smith. Alex suspected he was developing a sense of humor. He stepped out of the car, under the watchful eyes of a hundred heavily-armed men, and looked up at the sign over the facility's unopened gate.

White Feather Shooting Range
Dedicated to the Memory of
GYSGT CARLOS HATHCOCK, USMC

Alex reached back to retrieve two boxes of pistol cartridges he'd been keeping beside him on the seat. "Agent Smith, will you please help these gentlemen get their weapons out of the trunk?"

The look that passed over the Secret Service agent's face was painful to behold. Alex knew just what it meant. All his professional life, Agent Smith had done his best to keep people with guns away from the president. Now the president was opening a new, private shooting range and he was taking his friends shooting. Even worse, while they'd stowed their long arms in the trunk, Alex had insisted that they carry whatever sidearms they were used to, on their persons.

Alex drew his Witness from under his coat, extracted the magazine and chamber round, and slipped the pistol back into its kydex holster with the slide locked back. This was to be a "cold" range – loaded weapons on the firing-line only – and he was observing the custom.

He shrugged inwardly. Sooner or later Agent Smith and every other government employee like him, down to the cop on the beat, was going to have to get used to the notion – which the Founders had thought well of – of a populace that carried as much armament as he did. After all, he quoted Heinlein to himself, an armed society is a polite society.

Each of Alex's guests politely refused Secret Service offers to carry their gun bags into the range. Alex watched the process with amusement. The agents weren't being courteous, they simply wanted control of those guns. Trouble was, this four had been resisting government offers to take their guns for most of their lives.

The ribbon-cutting ceremony was short. Half of those who had not arrived here with the President's party were middle-aged Marine Corps veterans who had been taught to shoot – or to become better shooters – by Gunnery Sergeant Carlos Hathcock. Alex never learned why the man's nickname had been "White Feather". In the only context Alex was aware of, the white feather was a token of cowardice. He kept meaning to ask John about it and kept forgetting.

The other half were two buses full of teenage kids from deep in the District, here to learn from the retired Marines the noble discipline of ethical self-defense.

Alex called them all, young and old alike, "children of the Revolution". He spoke briefly on the desirability of having as many shooting ranges all over America as possible. The closer shooting came to being the national sport – and America a nation of marksmen – the safer America would be. It worked for Switzerland. He even let his listeners wonder whether he was joking about an Executive Order mandating that exactly as much public money be spent on shooting ranges as golf courses. He reminded them of their rights and duties as members of a jury, cut the ribbon, shook a few hands, and two hundred eager individuals followed him through the gate.

Alex believed you could tell something of a person's character from the weapon he (or she) chose for self-defense. Albert traveled light. In a zippered nylon case, he carried a Dan Wesson .357 Magnum revolver, unique in that one could easily change whatever barrel it came with to a shorter or longer one. Today, Albert had selected a six-inch barrel, but he had four-inch and two-inch barrels in the kit. (Alex would have added an eight or 10-inch barrel, too.) The grip was a one-piece black rubber Pachmayr product.

At the bench next to Albert's on the 50-yard pistol range stood Joseph. From somewhere about his person he produced an original alloy-framed 9mm Colt Commander. He'd also taken a venerable old .30 M1 Carbine from the limousine trunk. Alex decided he'd shoot with Joseph and Albert. All he'd brought with him was his .40 caliber EAA Witness Longslide Sport.

Ruven had an FN FAL, one of the world's great battle rifles, using the 7.62mm cartridge Americans call .308 Winchester. He also had a Heckler & Koch P9S, a futuristic looking pistol that one usually saw chambered in 9mm. Ruven's was a .45.

In some ways, Ascher had the most interesting weapon today, a 98 Mauser bolt action infantry rifle rechambered .308 Winchester, issued by the Nazi government to its troops. This one had been overhauled by the victors who had seized it, and ironically bore Israeli arsenal makings. Poetic justice, Alex thought. In the same case he carried a Model 10 police .38 Special revolver. It was a plain, no-nonsense, old-fashioned choice, Alex thought, and reflected Ascher's character perfectly.

Ruven and Ascher allowed themselves to be escorted by a pair of the retired Marines running the place, to a 200 yard rifle range named after the late firearms activist Hap Baker, where they could use their weapons to best advantage. John had brought his customized Fulton Armory M1A with him, a highly refined civilian version of a military M14 in .308, but he'd laid the unopened case across one of the benches, muzzle pointed downrange, and simply stood where he was, arms folded, one hand near his Glock, keeping a protective eye on the President. Alex glanced around, but didn't see Agent Smith.

Gunfire was heard on some of the other ranges now, a sound George Washington had found "charming". Alex, too, thought it the sweetest music on earth. Suddenly, he discovered he'd left his ear-protectors and shooting glasses in the limousine. Without thinking, he called to Albert and Joseph that he'd be back, and, leaning on his cane, headed toward the gate where he'd cut the ribbon. John was right behind him.

Birds sang in the nearby scrubby trees. In the graveled parking lot, he stumbled into an odd scene. One of the female Secret Service agents assigned to him was sitting on the running board of one of the Suburbans, sobbing with her hands over her face. Agent Smith stood beside her, obviously torn between gently trying to comfort her and gruffly ordering her to pull herself back together.

As Alex approached, the two of them and a dozen others gathered around looked up. Her ravaged eyes grew wide; she pointed at Alex's hip. He'd left his jacket on a shooting bench and his pistol was in plain sight. Some agents looked hostile before they regained control. She gabbled something incoherent, and collapsed in tears again.

Agent Smith came to the President, his voice low. "I'm extremely sorry, sir, it's the guns. Not just yours, but those of your guests. To her, guns and VIPs don't mix. We're the only ones supposed to be armed. I think she's having some kind of nervous breakdown."

Alex nodded. "Reassign her, then, Agent Smith, and anybody else on this detail who can't tolerate the full implications of the Second Amendment. Let her guard the Democratic leader of the Senate."

CHAPTER NINETEEN:
CHARLES K. PONZI

> *A con-game is a con-game, and a criminal is a criminal, whether you're Charles Ponzi with his infamous pyramid scheme or Franklin Roosevelt with Social Security. Simply putting on the Funny Hat of Government does not release you from the moral obligation to be a decent human being instead of a crook.*
>
> – Alexander Hope, *Looking Forward*

Dana gave Alex an encouraging hand-squeeze before crossing the room to sit, the makeup lady gave him a final ceremonial dusting – thank heaven for air conditioning; July in Washington was worse than anyone had ever warned him about – the cameraman and director gave him the customary finger-count: five, four, three, nod, nod, and he was on the air.

"Ladies and gentlemen, fellow children of the American Revolution, sometimes I feel that it's my job to say the words – and to state certain unpleasant facts – that nobody else has the courage to say. There are a great many people who get angry at me for doing this, when what they really should be angry at are the unpleasant facts – or, more correctly, the unpleasant individuals originally responsible for making them facts."

He glanced over at Dana, leaning beside his daughter against a back wall of the Oval Office. At moments like this, he wondered if he really was robbing the cradle. Although they were both well out of their teens, late 20s and early 30s, standing together like this, the girls (his daughter and his wife-to-be) looked like they could be college roommates.

But he shrugged off the distraction and drove onward. These were the words that needed saying, words that should have been said over half a century ago.

"The unpleasant fact that I need to address this evening – the unpleasant fact that you need me to address, ladies and gentlemen – is that the Social Security system is bankrupt. There are no other words for it, there is no avoiding it, and there is no funding available, from anyone or anywhere, to bail it out again, nor to refund anybody's money."

There: it had been said. Faith-Anne was miming a cheer. Dana gave him an encouraging smile. Everything else would be easier now.

"Of course you may choose – irrationally – ladies and gentlemen, to be angry with me for stating a simple fact that's been obvious, to anyone who cared to investigate the situation, for more than 60 years. Or you may choose to be rational, to accept the fact for what it is, and be angry with those who knew it would turn out this way when they created the program three quarters of a century ago."

Dana's darkly-bearded boss-man Alan was behind the pool camera once again for this Saturday evening's address, an address that his outfit NetPlanetNews.com had advertised – only slightly misleadingly – as the most significant Oval Office speech since Nixon's resignation. Alex felt that it was even more important than that – a crook folding his tents and stealing away into the night – but it wasn't about his resignation.

Not yet, anyway.

He took a deep breath. "Social Security is – and always was – a fraud, a hoax, a criminal confidence game. It was, in fact, copied from several criminal con-games, including the popular Ponzi pyramid scheme – that were in operation in the 1930s. When you take a little money from a lot of people and then offer to give a bit of it back to a few (pocketing the difference), it looks pretty tempting – until, year by year, decade by decade, the number of people available to take it from grows smaller, and the number who expect it to be given to them grows ever larger."

He paused for a moment to let it sink in. This one speech wouldn't do the job – drive a slayer's wooden stake through the heart of the bloodsucking Social Security system – he knew, nor would the next dozen speeches, or possibly even the next hundred. But the truth had to begin being told somewhere, and the cowardly politicians of the Republican and Democratic parties had been putting it off for several lifetimes.

"I say again, Social Security is – and always was – a fraud, a hoax, a criminal confidence game. Now ordinarily, when the authorities become aware that a con-game is operating in their jurisdiction, they try to capture the thieves, but the chance of recovering even a tiny fraction of their ill-gotten gain is almost nil. It would be irrational, once again, for the victims of a con-game to expect the police to reimburse them. Yet that's what previous Congressional and Presidential plans to 'save' Social Security have promised to do, and that's why they've failed so miserably."

Another glance across the room. His fiance, listening to her cell phone, gave him a thumbs-up. That would be from John, taking a break at home. There went Dana's unconflicted interest again. He returned a look that wasn't quite a smile, but close. If tonight's address turned out to be the end of his presidency, he would make the most of it. He and Dana would hop in the Durango – he'd get his old one back, the peacock blue – and go live in southern Colorado, probably around Montrose, where people openly carried rifles in the back windows of their pickup trucks.

"What I propose – although admittedly it falls far short of 'saving' Social Security or reimbursing its victims – sets things right to the fullest degree that they can be set right. The Social Security Administration will be shut down immediately, and its authority to collect 'contributions', from you or anybody else, abolished.

"Now look at your last paycheck. How much of your earnings were confiscated to keep Social Security alive another week? My new policy will cut your federal tax in half. What's more – this is the essence of my plan – Social Security victims will be permitted to apply the 'credit' in their Social Security 'accounts' to their future income taxes. They will be exempt from all federal taxes until their accounts are cleared."

For many older people, Alex knew, this meant paying no federal taxes at all for the rest of their lives. For Ruven Mendelsohn, a United States citizen since the 1960s (Alex had been surprised to learn), for Julia

Greenwood, the adoptive mother of the Berriganista socialist priest turned libertarian freedom fighter and martyr, for all older individuals like them, it meant blessed relief – and the knowledge that their great-grandchildren wouldn't be impoverished to pay their bills

"Please do with your tax savings whatever you wish," Alex told his audience. "It's *your* money, after all, and it always was. Spend it, invest it, stuff it under your mattress. And before either of the other two parties asks about it, any revenues 'lost' under this new program will be 'made up' through steep reductions in unnecessary – and unconstitutional – government programs, most obviously and immediately by closing down the Social Security Administration itself, and allowing – perhaps even assisting – its tens of thousands of employees to seek new opportunities in the productive sector of the economy."

Now Alex took something of a gamble. Although public attitudes toward smoking had significantly softened over the last decade, what he did now was still a risk. From his desk he picked up a plain dark briar pipe that had been prepacked with aromatic tobacco, lit it with a disposable Bic lighter, and puffed on it. Most of his predecessors had smoked – Kennedy, for instance, had preferred cigars – but Franklin Delano Roosevelt, with his long cigarette holder, had been the last to do so in public.

Alex believed it was time to alter the image of the President of the United States again, to one more like the people he was addressing tonight.

"Although I anticipate strong emotional and political reactions to this new policy from many different directions, I'd like to warn those individuals and groups inclined, for example, to enjoin or sue to stop it, that, as President, my job description consists of little besides enforcing the letter and the spirit of the Constitution, especially the Bill of Rights."

He knew that Alan's camera would be boring in for a closeup now. "The Social Security system is blatantly unconstitutional, and violates the rights of those it has victimized. Any attempts to continue such a violation are themselves a violation of the law – notably of Title 18, Sections 241 and 242 – and they will be promptly and vigorously prosecuted."

He could almost hear the gasps of outrage and indignation – and perhaps a little fear, he hoped – from those who considered themselves heirs of the New Deal. He took another puff, then held the briar in his hands. "In closing, allow me to remind you of your 1000-yard-old right and duty as a juror to judge the law, as well as the so-called facts of the case.

"Thank you, ladies and gentlemen, and happy Fourth of July!"

* * * * * *

One of the marshals pushed him from behind, urging him forward.

For the past 15 years, ever since he'd entered the federal Witness Protection Program, he'd been known as "Arthur Middleton", a somewhat incongruous name for an individual of Japanese extraction. For 15 years he'd believed that he was safe from the neofascists, libertarians, and other right-wing crazies who were anxious to exact bloody revenge for what he'd had a part of at Ruby Ridge, Idaho, and later on at Mount Carmel, near Waco, Texas.

What "Arthur" had never figured on was the election of a President who didn't belong to either wing of the single party in America that pretended it was two – the party that had sent him to do its dirty work in the first place, and protected him ever since – a President who regarded what "Arthur" had done at Ruby Ridge and Waco not as his solemn duty, not as simply following the orders of his superiors in the hierarchy like a good soldier, but as the coldly-calculated murder of innocent and helpless men, women, and children.

The first tall chain-link gate opened at the entrance of the El Reno federal penitentiary near Oklahoma City. The air was somehow dusty and humid at the same time. Everything today seemed charged with irony to "Arthur", from the name of the prison he was entering, with his hands cuffed together in front of him and his feet hobbled with an 18-inch chain, to the city near which the prison had been built. He'd never imagined he'd be wearing the same orange coveralls the surviving Davidians had been given.

He'd learned in the 80s to shoot a scoped rifle more accurately than any other man alive. He'd employed that skill to advance the interests of his government, including nipping certain rebellious bloodlines in the bud, before they had a chance to breed again (which was why he had no compunction about killing a woman or a child). His employers had called him a hero and showered him with medals and other rewards. But now that Alexander Hope was President, all of that was over. His superiors were in prison, too, or dead by their own hands, or at the hands of arresting officers. And he would probably die here, himself, between these gray, concrete walls.

The outer gate shut behind him with a horribly final metallic clash, the inner gate slowly opened, and the federal marshals at his elbows guided him into the prison, proper.

What he saw there wasn't good. The inmates crowded along both margins of the sidewalk were wearing black baseball caps with white embroidered letters that said "The F.L.I.R. Project". FLIR – Forward Looking Infrared – was the system used by his idiotic employers to record everything that had happened at Waco. Unfortunately, the FLIR system had caught "Arthur" and his team firing their automatic weapons into the building to keep the people inside trapped, where they would eventually burn to death.

And *The F.L.I.R. Project* itself was the name of a documentary film that had finally exposed this crime to the public – the new President had shown it in its entirely during one of his Saturday evening talks – and landed "Arthur" here in prison for life.

As long as it lasted ...

* * * * * *

Uncle Bob said, "Well, good evening, Mr. President! Glad you could join us here again. How's it going up there, and what can I fix for you?"

It was well past midnight and the end of an unusually long October day. Alex had made a habit, over the past several months, of coming down to the White House kitchen a couple of times a week to chat with his new friend. It was one of the few ways he had of getting some kind of feel for what people like him – real, productive people – were thinking.

"Well, today," he told Uncle Bob, "I ordered the

declassification of everything that has anything to do with UFOs, Project Blue Book, swamp gas, the bizarre incident at Roswell in 1947, and so on. Any use of the shredder or the bulldozer will constitute a felony. I'll be very interested to see the results. I've always been curious about them, myself."

Uncle Bob wiped his hands on a towel tucked into his waistband and offered Alex a seat at the big stainless steel worktable in the center of the room. "Me, too, sir. That mean you're gonna put Mulder and Scully out of work?"

"And the Men in Black," Alex grinned. "At least I'm going to try. I also signed an executive order rescinding all the stupid regulations about politically incorrect toilets – you know, the regulations that limit the number of gallons in the tank so you have to flush two or three times? The ones that have people smuggling their new toilets in from Europe?"

Uncle Bob laughed and nodded. "We ran into that situation when we built our new house in Maryland. Took Mr. Gordon Liddy's advice and had some decent plumbing smuggled in from France – my wife liked that, having toilets from France, and smuggled, too. Can't I fix you anything at all, sir? I have some excellent stuffed bell peppers left over from lunch."

"And they were wonderful. That would be just great, Uncle Bob. I also removed federal support for 'reformulated' gasoline, which should eventually lower the national cancer rate, if nothing else. Let the midwestern farmers who want to sell their corn-fed alcohol as fuel, set up their own filling stations and compete on an open market. I'll cooperate as much as I can with them, in principle, by hamstringing the

BATF for them."

"Hamstring 'em for me, too, sir. I'm a cook. I always had a hankering to make my own whiskey."

"I'd be happy to," Alex grinned. "In general, now, Congress has begun to understand what the New Media are calling the 'BoRT' or 'BoRTest' – that a proposed bill has to be justifiable under the Bill of Rights before I'll even think about signing it, and that I'll veto anything that doesn't pass. At the moment, legislative activity is at its lowest volume since sometime around the Spanish-American War, and the socialist media are screaming their nasty heads off about a 'do-nothing' Congress."

"Always music to *my* ears, sir." Uncle Bob had gone to one of the huge stainless steel refrigerators and removed a tray of the meat and rice and cheese-filled delicacies. "Now what color would you care for, sir, I got plenty of red and yellow and orange and purple ones, and of course, green."

"Orange, thank you." Alex found the orange peppers especially sweet. "China's been rattling its *ken* again, so I spoke briefly with a private group who've raised enough money to air-drop tiny earplug radios all over China and build orbital transmitters to broadcast the works of Thomas Paine, Thomas Jefferson, and other Founding Fathers into a land hungry to have them. Ayn Rand, too, and Robert Heinlein. Now the real trick will be to talk both Congress and the Pentagon into cooperating with them."

Uncle Bob put a couple of the big stuffed peppers into a microwave oven. He'd finally – very reluctantly – gotten used to sharing these midnight snacks with the President, although both of them joked about getting fat. "You might think about including some Frederick Douglass, too, sir."

"You can count on it, Uncle Bob. Later this week, I'm planning to deal once and for all with *La Reconquista.*"

Uncle Bob turned from watching the oven. "*La Reconquista,* sir? I don't believe I've heard about that."

A wonderful aroma had begun to fill the room, and Alex's mouth watered. He'd been busy and hadn't eaten since six this evening. Dana wasn't here to watch him; she was in California with Faith-Anne, looking at wedding gowns.

"Not many people have. A lot of them swear it doesn't exist, and you'll never hear about it in the socialist mass media, but it was endorsed publicly by the previous President of Mexico, long before I was elected. I became conscious of it because I was running a business in San Diego, and a lot of the people who worked for me were Mexican immigrants."

"So what is it?" asked Uncle Bob.

"It's a plan, or a plot, or maybe just an idea, that if all of the American states bordering Mexico are flooded with illegal immigrants, and the illegals can somehow demand or be given the vote, then those states – California, Arizona, New Mexico, and Texas – and all the wealth they contain – can be 'returned' to Mexico. The border leaks like a sieve and there have been calls in Congress and several state legislatures for years – from politicians way to the left – to give illegal immigrants the vote."

The microwave dinged. Uncle Bob opened the oven and removed the hot, aromatic peppers, transferred them to plates, brought them with silverware and linen, and a plate with homemade bread and butter to the table. He brought himself an oversized cup of decaffeinated coffee and the President an ice cold Coke. "So what do you plan to do about it, if you don't mind my asking?"

Alex shook his head. "I don't mind at all, Uncle Bob. In fact, I'd like to know what you think of the idea. You see, I think I understand something that the conservatives don't – that you can't build a wall high enough, or dig a moat deep enough, to keep people from voting with their feet for freedom. It didn't work in Berlin, where they were trying to get out, and it won't work in Nogales, or a hundred other border towns, where they're trying to get in."

"I see, sir." Uncle Bob began to eat as Alex talked.

"I also understand something that the so-called liberals don't – that you can't separate economic refugees from political refugees. We're the most prosperous nation in the world *because* we're the freest. People want to come here from countries that are impoverished *because* they're oppressive. There's a correlation there that the left doesn't want examined. And it's not only impossible to stop these immigrants, it's morally wrong."

Uncle Bob buttered a piece of bread. His eyebrows were raised. This President never failed to surprise him. "So what are you going to do about it, sir?"

"Uncle Bob, I'm going to take the things that people emigrate for, to the places that they immigrate from. I'm going to offer American statehood – or at least my all-out support for it – to any Mexican state that ratifies our Bill of Rights by a two-thirds majority vote."

He dug into the steaming pepper and had a bite of its aromatic contents, washing them down with a swig of Coke.

"You're the only person I know who ever puts enough cheese in these things! Anyway, I'm thinking of making the same offer to the Canadian provinces."

Uncle Bob shook his head and whistled. Then he took a big gulp of his black coffee. "That oughta help out diplomatic relations," he observed.

"Congresswoman Alvarez," Alex said around a bite of bread and butter, "has had an excellent Spanish translation made of the Bill of Rights, as part of a pamphlet explaining what it means for freedom *and* prosperity. She'll have volunteers distributing it at every Mexican border crossing the minute I finish making my speech this Saturday. We're planning a big radio campaign, as well, 150,000 watts, right into the heart of Mexico. I figure that ought to start a few hundred brushfires that the Mexican government will be so busy putting out they won't have time or energy or money left for any *La Reconquista.*"

Uncle Bob laughed heartily. "Say you know, Mr. President, you ought to try the same thing here in the District – maybe in L.A. and Detroit, too!"

"Good idea," Alex replied, "do we translate the Bill of Rights into Ebonics?"

"People who push that garbage," the older man replied, suddenly serious, "got some sad, sick reason they want their own folks to fail. I gotta warn you, sir, that some of them won't be able to handle all this freedom you're shoving at them with both hands. Some of them are just plain too stupid – I hate to say it – after generations of the welfare state and public education. Some have forgotten (assuming that they ever knew) what it is to be free. Some truly fear freedom. They believe it's too dangerous. They think it means a return to some kind of 'survival of the fittest' civilization and that they're going to be wiped out."

Alex nodded. "I know, Uncle Bob, and it doesn't help that the individuals who could help them, Walter Williams, Thomas Sowell, Ken Hamblin, have never been 'anointed' as black leaders by the white mass media."

"The white mass media!" Uncle Bob repeated. "You know I put the *Washington Post* in the bottom of my parrot's cage, and my parrot died!"

Alex laughed, "In the end it doesn't have anything to do with color, Uncle Bob. America was built by people of all kinds who intuitively understood the enormous difference between 'survival of the fittest' and 'survival of the fit'. People who were willing to work hard for what they wanted and then take a risk with it. The only question in my mind is how do we get more Americans back to that way of thinking."

Uncle Bob sighed. "Well, sir, I wouldn't ever claim to speak for everyone, but for black people, you might start by reminding them that they once had heroes – not the whiny socialists we got today – who stood straight and tall for what the American Revolution promised, although in most cases they were a little bit late getting their own piece of it."

Alex said, "You're talking about people like Crispus Attucks, the first person to die in the Revolution..."

"I am not, sir." Uncle Bob shook his head. "Poor Crispus, through no fault of his own, he's sort of gotten to be the token Negro of the Revolution. No, sir, I had somebody a little more controversial in mind, a little more radical, who also died for freedom. You ever hear of Denmark Vesey?"

Alex scowled in concentration. "The name sure

sounds familiar. Something about a slave rebellion...?"

"South Carolina, sir, Charleston in 1822. I guess the thing that's most important – and impressive – about Vesey is that he already had his, if you know what I mean. He'd been born into slavery in the West Indies and bought his freedom – he won the money in a lottery! He'd built a carpentry business and gotten rich. He had a wife and family and a great big house. He was a respectable member of the community. And he even preached in his own Methodist church, which had about 3000 members."

Uncle Bob began gathering up the plates and silver and glasses, and then paused. "But what Vesey preached about in his church, mostly, was slavery. He hated it, and he wasn't content just to have his own freedom, he wanted slavery ended forever for everybody. As a boy, he'd gotten all fired up about the Haitians overthrowing their masters and taking over their country and he had visions of doing that in South Carolina."

"I remember now," said Alex. "Vesey wanted to kill every white person in the state. Kind of a public relations problem for him as a hero for today, wouldn't you say?"

Uncle Bob laughed. "Mr. President, Thomas Jefferson was an amateur scientist who didn't believe in meteorites. As governor of Virginia, he wanted to bore a half inch hole sideways through the noses of all convicted female adulterers. But being wrong about that didn't stop him from being right when he *was* right, did it? Anyway, the whites eventually shut Vesey's church down, and that's when the revolt began. Vesey convinced somewhere between 6000 and 9000 blacks to join him. The planning took four years. They even imported weapons from their supporters in Haiti."

"But the revolt was betrayed from the inside, by a house-slave who was comfortable with his servitude," Alex said. "Vesey and his lieutenants were caught and tried and hanged – and 'Remember Denmark Vesey!' became a battle-cry for the first black regiment in the War between the States."

"'That's right.' Uncle Bob nodded enthusiastically. "You see, sir? It's like I said. People need real heroes. You know what shocked them in South Carolina? That black people could plan and organize a huge long-term operation like that. They were accustomed to thinking of blacks as some kind of animal – it made the institution of slavery so much more palatable for them, morally speaking. But Vesey spoiled that for them, and they never forgave him for it. In fact they almost wiped him right out of history."

"And you want to bring him back. Are you willing to see it done warts and all?"

"Warts and all, sir, that's the only way. You ever hear what Sam Adams and John Hancock were doing up there in Concord when the British came to arrest them the night Paul Revere and his friends did their thing?"

Alex grinned. "Sure. They were at John Hancock's girlfriend's birthday party, getting drunk."

"Warts and all, sir, warts and all."

Alex laughed.

CHAPTER TWENTY: *KITCH SINCLAIR*

> *Those who profit politically by setting the races at each other's throats are wise to declare ethnic humor "politically incorrect". As long we can manage to laugh at the differences among us, we're unlikely to kill each other over them. People of every sort, forbidden to laugh, reflexively turn to hatred and violence.*
>
> – Alexander Hope, *Looking Forward*

The bride was beautiful in white.

Alex knew she'd have been beautiful in burlap, but nobody asked him. Weddings are not held for the benefit of the groom.

For once, reporters and TV cameras had arrived in force, ABC, CBS/NBC, CNN, MSNBC, FoxNews, the *Washington Post,* the *Los Angeles Times,* the rest of the Old Media. So had NetPlanetnews.com – Dana's former boss wore a tuxedo as he handled the camera – Matt Drudge, Lew Rockwell, J.D. Tucille, NewsMax.com, and several of their other competitors.

Alex stood at the front of the room with Father Joseph, feeling nervous, his injured leg, even after all these months, threatening to fail him. At his right was his best man John (his pretty wife May had come down from North Carolina to be here). Cap was keeping an eye on the room. As promised, he'd been offered the job as flower girl, but had declined.

On the groom's side of the room sat the original Austrian Mafia. Katie was still dry-eyed, but well prepared, kerchief in hand. Ascher Liebowitz sat on the outside aisle, ready to deliver a little address Alex and Dana had requested. Ruven, Albert, and Rachel Mendelsohn sat in the same row, behind Julia Greenwood, Kitch Sinclair and Sheila Hensley.

Dana's mother sat on the bride's side, already sobbing into her lace handkerchief. Although technically a friend of the groom, Linda Alvarez was sitting with her, speaking softly and patting her on the shoulder.

The traditional music started, played by musicians from the Marine Corps Band, resplendent in their dress uniforms. Alex turned to watch Dana coming toward him down the aisle on the arm of her proud father, Faith-Anne following in their wake as maid of honor. When they reached Alex, Dana gently kissed her father on the cheek; he released his daughter to go sit with his wife.

The music stopped. Father Joseph said, "Dearly beloved, we gather together to witness the marriage of Alexander Hamilton Hope and Dana Elise Li." Murmurs arose from the congregation. Alex didn't much like advertising the middle name his parents had imposed upon him. As a libertarian historian, he'd never had much use for the dictatorial Mr. Hamilton.

"Marriage is a sacred institution," Father Joseph said, "not to be entered into lightly. In recognition of this, Alex and Dana will now exchange their vows to one another, and we shall all be witness. Alex, please repeat after me: I, Alex, take you, Dana, to be my wedded wife, to have and to hold from this day forward, for richer as for poorer, through sickness as in health, and, forsaking all others, to love, honor, and cherish until we are parted by death."

Face aching with an expression of sheer joy, Alex held Dana's hands in both of his, lost himself in her eyes, and repeated word for word: "I, Alex, take you, Dana, to be my wedded wife, to have and to hold from this day forward, for richer as for poorer, through sickness as in health, and, forsaking all others, to love, honor, and cherish until we are parted by death."

Father Joseph nodded. "And now, Dana: I Dana, take you, Alex, to be my wedded husband, to have and to hold from this day forward, for richer as for poorer, through sickness as in health, and, forsaking all others, to love, honor, and cherish until we are parted by death."

"I Dana," her voice was shaky; reassuringly, Alex squeezed her hands around the base of her bouquet, "take you, Alex, to be my wedded husband, to have and to hold from this day forward, for richer as for poorer, through sickness as in health, and, forsaking all others, to love, honor, and cherish until we are parted by death."

"May I have the rings?" John handed them to Father Joseph, a tear trickling down one cheek. John handed one to Alex, who placed it on Dana's finger. He handed the other to Dana. Father Joseph looked toward the groom's side of the congregation. "Rabbi Liebowitz, would you care to come forward, now?"

Ascher got up from his chair and joined them.

"Alex and Dana," he began. "I can't express my delight at being at your wedding today, Bill of Rights Day, December 15, 2009. Yours is a marriage of historic proportions, of brains and beauty, talent and determination, principle and practicality, prosperity and power in the best of causes. May your lives be blessed with happiness and accomplishment together as they have been separately so far. May you grace our future and the cause of liberty with children as wonderful as you are."

"Inasmuch," Father Joseph told the congregation, "as Dana and Alex have given their vows to one another, and exchanged rings in token of those vows, by the power vested in me by the Archdiocese of Chicago and the, er, President of the United States, I pronounce them husband and wife. Alex, you may kiss your bride."

* * * * * *

"There you have it, the first White House wedding of the century. The groom, President Alexander Hope, the bride, e-columnist Dana Li, her parents witnessing their daughter's marriage to the President, who expressed a wish that his own parents had lived to see the moment. The first couple were wed in a brief ceremony by Father Joseph Spagelli of Chicago, with words from Rabbi Ascher Liebowitz, underscoring the Presidential wedding by calling for December 15th – Bill of Rights Day – to become the winter equivalent of the Fourth of July.

"I spoke via internet to Vice President Forrey Nadalindov earlier today, from Paraguay, South America, where he is attending a trade conference. His view: 'maybe she (meaning the new First Lady) can calm Alex down, and return him to the sanity we all need him to have'."

"Pritchard Evans-Evans, *London Daily Telescope.*"

* * * * * *

"Ladies and gentlemen, fellow children of the American Revolution, I'm speaking to you today on the 218th anniversary of the ratification of the Bill of Rights. My remarks will be brief because, as some of you know, the beautiful and brilliant Dana Li became my wife today.

"In a few moments fireworks will begin on the White House Lawn. I understand similar festivities are planned in several cities across the country. Public displays, however beautiful and impressive, are no substitute for fireworks in the hands of free and private citizens. The enemies of liberty have cut the Fourth of July at its root. They must not be allowed to do the same to the Fifteenth of December.

"The British considered bagpipes to be weapons of war and forbade the Scots their use. Many cities, counties, and states have ruined our summer freedom holiday with 'safety' regulations. Laws forbidding the possession or use of fireworks must be repealed or nullified, and fireworks protected under the Second Amendment. It is an obscenity that the celebration of American freedom has become so heavily regulated.

"Safety is not a sufficient reason to stifle the celebration of individual liberty. Nor can you encourage individual responsibility – the real source of safety – in adults or children, by denying them the opportunity to exercise it. There is nothing worthwhile that doesn't involve some risk. Henceforward, I will include fireworks in my executive clemency program – but I will remind you that you can change things yourself through your 1000-year-old right and duty as a juror to judge the law itself, as well as the facts of the case.

"Thank you, and goodnight."

* * * * * *

"You're *what?*"

"I'm ending the War on Drugs," Alex informed his old friend and colleague Thornton "Kitch" Sinclair. "Otherwise known as the War against the Bill of Rights. That's a second reason I asked you to join us this weekend. You're the first libertarian I ever met, Kitch, and as a direct, if somewhat delayed consequence, this coming Monday morning I'll be ordering all government agencies involved in waging the War on Drugs to stand down."

"It's a dream come true!" Faith-Anne grinned at both men.

"Even if it is a century late." Dana nodded her agreement.

A young Marine knocked and entered, presenting the president with a clipboard. Alex took the pen attached to the clip, scratched out two lines, made a note in the margin, signed it, and handed it back. The Marine saluted, turned smartly on his heel and left.

They were meeting in the residential section of the White House, in a little sitting room traditionally reserved for the First Lady. It was no coincidence. Dana was fully as responsible for this decision – or at least its timing – as anybody else. She and Alex sat, holding hands, on a small antique sofa, their aluminum canes leaning parallel to one another against a carved arm. To their right, Faith-Anne sat with her computer on her lap.

Kitch occupied a comfortable, if overly feminine chair. Sheila was elsewhere in town, visiting friends. Alex's commitment and integrity had apparently shaken her out of decades of cynicism and torpor.

"I wanted to apologize," Alex told him, "for not asking you to be my best man. We've been friends a long time, but John – "

"Piffle," replied Kitch. "I'm grateful you invited me. Besides, there was a secondary benefit: weddings make women sentimental. I proposed to Sheila immediately afterward, and she accepted!"

Both females exclaimed and congratulated him, but Kitch raised sandy-colored eyebrows. "This program of yours will increase the number of your enemies a hundredfold, Alex. Do you plan on justifying it legally, or simply by brass gall and sheer force of personality?"

Alex shrugged. "Neither. The Drug War's come close to destroying this country; everybody knows it but the politicians. It's corrupted every level of government from the cop on the corner to the Supreme Court. It's obliterated the Bill of Rights. Most of our children – subject to warrantless searches of their cars, lockers, bookbags, clothing, bodily cavities and fluids – have no concept of individual sovereignty. It's turned us into the world's largest banana republic – or a cheap plastic replica of communist Bulgaria."

"So you write another Executive Order..." Kitch didn't approve of what he regarded as Alex's tendency to write Executive Orders. Another knock. This time an elderly secretary from one of the offices downstairs brought a complicated-looking cordless telephone. She approached Alex from behind and whispered something to him.

Alex shook his head. "I can't now, Eloise, I'm sorry. Please give Senator Peters my apologies and tell him I'll return his call first thing in the morning – you'll remind me, won't you?"

She grinned like a girl and nodded, then left the room.

"No, no executive orders," Alex picked up the thread with Kitch again. "Although in this particular instance, I could declare a Constitutional Emergency and suspend a whole laundry list of laws and regulations that are doing the most damage. But I plan to do it on the grounds that I've sworn to uphold and defend the Constitution against all enemies foreign and – especially in this case – domestic. Drug laws violate Ninth Amendment rights, however unpopular, to make, import, sell, possess, and use recreational Drugs – "

Kitch interrupted, his tone a bit contemplative. "Or to practice self-medication... I see where you're headed. You'll say you're just doing the job that you swore to do on Inauguration Day."

"Exactly," Alex nodded. "The enabling legislation – and the imperative that goes with it – was ratified more than 200 years ago. Can you imagine what Jefferson – or even Alexander Hamilton – would make of being asked to pee in a bottle? I *am* doing the job I swore to do on Inauguration Day."

"Self-medication – that's a good phrase," Faith-Anne typed on her laptop. "We'll add that to the initial announcement."

"Credit Dana's colleague," Kitch told her, "internet columnist Vin Suprynowicz. We know Congress and the Drug War establishment will oppose you bitterly. You should have John double up the guard and keep an eye on the Secret Service. How do you think voters will take it?"

Alex grinned, nodding toward Dana. "By addressing them directly," she said, "through press conferences and his weekend TV addresses, Alex has built a relationship with the public that hasn't been seen since Franklin Delano Roosevelt and his fireside chats. It helps that he never fails to explain the reasoning behind his policies, and he never assumes – as other presidents have – that the public is too dumb to understand them."

Kitch smiled, "Sheila and I certainly watch them all."

A third knock at the door brought a man in a sparkling white uniform – not Uncle Bob – from the kitchen. Alex was putting on a dinner in three days for the ambassadors of a dozen countries to whom he planned to cut off foreign aid. He'd given orders that he wanted to check the menu himself. He examined each item, stopping to ask a question or offer changes – ordinarily, he'd leave it up to others; this time he wanted to let his guests down gently – and then gave it to Dana, who said nothing, but handed it back with an approving look. For the first time, she would be his hostess. He winked at her and passed the menu back to the chef, who nodded and departed.

Dana went on. "Alex opposes the minimum wage, for example, not just because it violates the rights of employers and employees to bargain freely, but because it cruelly destroys entry-level jobs by pricing 'marginal employees' – young minority workers just getting started – out of the labor market, adding to the poverty, crime, and gang warfare of the inner cities."

"So opposing the minimum wage," Faith-Anne said, "isn't an evil capitalist plot, but the moral and compassionate thing to do."

Dana nodded. "And because Alex has the ear of the public – "

"Thanks to the internet and independent news services," said Alex.

"That's right," Dana agreed. "The socialist opposition can't distort his intentions as easily as they once did the few courageous others who took the same position."

"The biggest part of the boss's 'secret strategy'..." John entered from an adjoining room carrying a sheaf of papers that he handed to Faith-Anne; he sat on another sofa, making a complete circle of the conversation, "...is that he keeps the opposition guessing at the same time that he catches the public's imagination."

Dana's eyes crinkled delightedly. "He puts the BATF on furlough, and while the bad guys are deciding how to react, he declassifies UFOs. He ends the War on Drugs, and while the drug warriors are reeling (and they will!) he offers a Constitutional amendment to separate science – especially medicine – and state. He stays completely within principle, but they never know where he's coming from."

Kitch nodded. "Because they have no principles themselves, and they're hopelessly stuck in a collectivist mindset. I hadn't heard about the science and state thing, Alex. The religious right will go along with it, because they'll see it as establishing parity with regard to the separation of church and state."

"Praise from Caesar," Alex said. "It's true, I struggle every day to keep seeing things the way Americans do who don't happen to be President." He paused suddenly, felt at his waist, withdrew a vibrating pager, and held it up for his daughter to see. "Could you deal with this, kiddo?"

She nodded, arose, and took the pager, then retreated to her chair and began working with her laptop. After a while she got her father's attention, tossed the pager back, and said, "All taken care of!"

"Good. Blasted doctors don't need to see me *every* day any more!"

"It isn't the public Alex has to worry about, anyway," John told Kitch. "Enforcing drug laws has become a vast *industry* employing millions and enriching thousands. They'll very cheerfully have Alex assassinated rather than lose their power, their livelihood, and their demented sense of mission."

"And they'll sleep soundly afterward," Dana added, "having spent the last several decades dehumanizing – in their own minds, that is – drug users, sellers, distributors, manufacturers, anybody else who opposes their reign of terror, exactly the way Roosevelt and the World War Two generation dehumanized the Japanese."

Kitch turned to Dana, to John, to Alex, concern written on his face. "Decades of dehumanization... what will you do about that?"

"Well, Professor," John said, "we'll take the carrot-and-cliché approach. After the former drug warriors in the DEA, FBI, BATF, CIA, and so on have been 'processed' – "

Kitch blinked. "Processed?"

"Investigated for violations of the highest law of

the land," Faith-Anne explained, "perhaps even tried for them and convicted."

"The President," John continued, "will officially order them to reorganize themselves into a Bill of Rights Enforcement Agency, give them an opportunity to redeem themselves, legally and morally."

"BoREA," Kitch tried the acronym. "I like the sound of that. More executive orders, I presume?"

Alex pretended to ignore him. "A lot of them will quit rather than go along. As for the rest, they'll spend all of their professional time and energy spying on and busting elected and appointed officials and leaving the rest of their fellow Americans alone."

Kitch asked, "And that'll keep them from wanting to kill you?"

Another knock on the door: the same secretary, this time with a form for Alex to sign. Once again, the President made amendments, affixed his signature, and then politely dismissed the woman.

Faith-Anne said, "It'll help. Since we quietly leaked information on this plan early last week, three prominent advocates of internet censorship and victim disarmament appear to have committed suicide. Hard to tell: one was a bullet to the head, but the other two were single-car accidents. About a third of those are suicides, according to the insurance industry."

"We expect others to resign," John added, "from Congress and the bureaucracy, the Old Media – and maybe even leave the country."

"That's why I'm suspending all the Drug War and IRS regulations," Alex told him, "limiting how much money an individual can take out of the country – to encourage them to go. Look, Kitch, this isn't any more dangerous than what we're doing with cold fusion – "

"Cold fusion? That crackpot scam – "

Alex shook his head. "Not at all. It's the most thoroughly and viciously suppressed technology in human history, one that will change everything, very much for the better. The physics and chemistry make perfect sense; I've known that since Pons and Fleischmann did their thing back in the 80s, But in terms of 21st century American institutions, it gores every ox there is."

"Balderdash!" Kitch exclaimed. Alex's respect for him increased in that moment because he'd had the courage to say it.

Alex laughed. "Imagine a footlocker-sized device in your basement that lights your lights, warms and cools your home, heats your water, cooks your food. Another like it in your car takes you anywhere, at any speed, without refueling or recharging, silently and almost for free. No power lines overhead or underground, no oil or gas pipelines. Who wouldn't like it? Oil and gas companies, power generators and electric grids, car manufacturers ..."

"I've heard it all before," Kitch replied. "200 mile per gallon carburetors, cars that run on water, perpetual motion, Nikola Tesla's long lost radium kidney belt ..."

"Kitch, you're wrong. This is like iron pipe and cotton fabric, which – because they allowed people to wash themselves and their clothing – doubled human life expectancy in the 18th century. It's like the Industrial Revolution, or the advent of cybernetics. And there are old, established interests out to stop it at all costs."

"Surely you don't want the government to develop it?"

"No – and don't call me Shirley. I'll appoint a commission of courageous scientists, engineers, lawyers, and historians to look very publicly into the suppression."

"I see."

"But my point is that ending the War on Drugs is less risky than that. Even if it weren't, I'd still ask you to be my Drug unCzar, or my unDrug Czar, or whatever you want to call it."

"You what?" It was several moments before Kitch stopped laughing. "I get it: like putting Yamamoto in charge of the Pearl Harbor attack. Mr. President, I'm flattered. But I know nothing about administering a program like that. Absolutely nothing!"

Alex laughed. "You're not administering, Sgt. Schultz, you're shutting it down. We'll find bureaucrats to help. What I can't find so easily is principled, intelligent, incorruptible people like you."

Kitch raised his eyebrows. "Can I put that on my résumé?"

"Carve it on Mount Rushmore, as long as you make sure the War on Drugs is shut down everywhere, domestically, internationally, at every level of government."

Something went *ping*!. Kitch jumped as if it were a gunshot.

"They're talking about you, Daddy." Faith-Anne turned her laptop so that the others in the room could see the screen. At the moment it showed a rather contrivedly windblown female news "personality" in a trenchcoat, outside what appeared to be a rural courthouse.

Dana retrieved her own laptop from the floor

beside the sofa and found the same website, a recent competitor to NetPlanetNews.com.

"...threatening to convert the White House into an 'executive clemency factory' again, with pardon forms stacked to the ceiling, ready for his signature, Hope has begin emptying America's jails and prisons of more than three-quarters of their populations – "

They cut to an interview Alex had given some time ago in the White House briefing room. " ... these are decent, productive people," he watched himself saying into the camera, "who never harmed anyone, and whose only crime was an – often unknowing – violation of laws and regulations that were grotesquely unconstitutional to begin with."

Alex had been speaking to the media that day – back when he was still on crutches, he noticed – of pardons he'd just granted various farmers and developers convicted under draconian EPA wetlands edicts of filling in ditches and muddy sinkholes on their own property. He'd asked several of them to Washington to join him at the podium. He was returning their land and in some instances ordering the prosecution of the runaway bureaucrats and field agents responsible.

"With fully intended irony," the woman went on, "usually reliable sources close to the President tell us he has selected Nuremburg, Pennsylvania for a series of legal actions that will accuse – and possibly convict – thousands of officials of 'crimes against the Constitution'. The Hope Administration plans to emphasize the point, first made in Nuremburg, Germany, at the Nazi War Crimes tribunals following World War Two, that 'just following orders' is no excuse."

"Nuremburg!" Alex shook his head. "I wish I'd thought of that!"

CHAPTER TWENTY-ONE
SENATOR PETERS

> *Henry David Thoreau used to speak of leaving every individual free to "step to a different drummer". Today, more and more Americans find themselves marching in lockstep to a single drummer, one who is deaf to any cries for decency or sanity, let alone individual liberty.*
>
> — Alexander Hope, *Looking Forward*

The limestone cave in the Arkansas hills was secret, such a good secret that not even the US Geological Survey knew of its existence, and a lot of blood and money had been spent to keep it that way. There had originally been signs that it had once been used as a hiding place, a century and a half ago, by runaway slaves, and then a hideout for bootleggers during Prohibition that had never been discovered by the Revenuers. Before that, paleo-Indians had lived here. Its present owner wore a Clovis-style arrow point he'd found here, on a gold chain around his neck.

But the feature that made this cave most valuable was that it was dry. It sat up in the middle of a small mountain, high above the local water table, and the floor and the walls and the air inside betrayed no trace of dampness, even when it was raining heavily.

Jorge "Pencils" Aguilar had no idea what kind of geological upheaval could carve out a big cave like this and then toss it up, out of reach of the water that had carved it, and he didn't care. He was no scientist; in fact he was much more an accountant than a gangster. All he knew was that it was perfect for his purpose, which was the storage for later distribution of illegal drugs.

He enjoyed looking at the great white bales of cocaine that lined the walls on one side and marched up to the ceiling, where the stalactites had been knocked out because they took up too much room. Stalagmites were gone from the floor, as well. On the other side, greenish-brown bales of marijuana took up more space than the cocaine, but was a perfectly salable product all the same. It was possible, he thought, that there was a billion dollars worth of drugs in this chamber, which was about 100 yards in diameter and probably 60 feet high in the middle. A billion dollars, and it was his.

His and his partners'. It had arrived here from further south, where it came in by small aircraft from South and Central America, and occasionally from Asia. It had arrived here by truck. From here it would go to cities and small towns across America. This cave and its secrets had survived many changes of administration and policies, both local and national. It would support him in his old age.

"Boss! Boss!" Slider, one of Aguilar' flunkies, careened into the cave from a tunnel that wound along for two miles, 50 feet below the surface, and came out in a clearing near the Interstate. "Lookit this! Lookit this!"

In his hand he held a tiny combination television set and 8mm video tape player. Lately, it was his favorite toy. Aguilar took the unit, but had to put his glasses on to see what was happening on the screen.

Alexander Hope was speaking at some kind of luncheon. "As soon as we stop enforcing drug laws," he was telling his audience, "the value of those drugs will plummet. Drugs that presently sell for 100 dollars a baggie, will fall to 50 cents or a quarter, and all of the people who cultivate, process, transport, and sell those drugs will have to find a different profession."

"What?" Aguilar looked around him. If that man had his way, the billion dollars worth of drugs in this cave would be worth less than the plastic bags they were stored in. Hope was a menace, and he had to be –

"That's why," the President said, "I'm issuing an Executive Order within the hour to cease all drug law enforcement for the foreseeable future. I have appointed my friend and colleague, Dr. Thornton Sinclair, to supervise this process. There was no drug problem in America before there were drug laws – look it up, you'll find I'm right. Without drug laws to drive the price up, there won't be any drug problem ever again."

Panic sluiced like icewater through Aguilar' body. What could he do? He was stuck with a cave full of perfectly legal drugs! Was there any time left to move this stuff?

"I don't know about you, Boss," Slider told him, bringing him back to here and now. "I'm gettin' outa here! There's no tellin' what the local cops'll do when their payoffs dry up! They're gonna hate Hope, but they'll take it out on us!"

Aguilar shook his head to clear it. "You're right, Slider. Let's clear out of here. Just leave the stuff and clear out. Our uniformed friends will steal it out of sheer reflexive greed, and maybe leave us alone. By the time they figure out that it's worthless, we'll be somewhere else. I hear Calgary's very nice this time of year."

"Y'gotta be kiddin'! I was thinkin' maybe Costa Rica, Boss. I got a cousin with a seaplane, an' a little money goes a long way down there. They got pretty senoritas, Boss."

"We've all got cousins with seaplanes, Slider, but pretty soon there isn't going to be any gas money for them. I like pretty senoritas. Costa Rica it is, then – oh, wait, there's something I want to do before we go."

He went to the wall, opened a hidden panel, turned a dial, and closed the panel again. "There," he said. "Four minutes after the first person enters this cave, 10 pounds of C4 distributed throughout the walls will blow up, and Arkansas will suddenly be missing a lot of crooked cops."

"Pretty good, Boss – you're a social benefactor!"

"That's me all over, Slider, that's me all over."

* * * * * *

"Your visitors are here, Mr. President."

Alex sighed inwardly. It was a cold and soggy April in DC. He missed his good old Austrian Mafia – Katie wouldn't have called him 'Mr. President', she would have called him by his first name. He also missed Dana – she was off suffering through some kind of physical therapy and planned to do some First Lady work afterward. His only consolation was that Faith-Anne was here to help him deal with 'visitors' this morning.

She still called him 'Daddy'.

He arose and walked around his desk. "Please send them in, will you, Louise?"

There were three of them this morning, and even if he hadn't been expecting them, their faces were extremely familiar. They were the assistant Republican leader of the United States Senate, the assistant Republican leader of the House of Representatives, and the Republican Senator to whom the topic of this morning's discussion was the be-all and end-all of his political existence.

"Good morning, gentlemen!" He strode forward and took each of their hands in turn, as warmly and sincerely as he could manage. "Congressman Blue, Senator Commack, Senator Peters, good to see you. You all know my daughter and good right hand, Faith-Anne? Excellent. Would you all care to join me over here, where it's more comfortable, at the coffee table?"

Blue was a tall man in his late 30s, with strong features, deeply sunken eyes, and prematurely white hair. Alex found himself thinking of the man as "young Boris Karloff". Commack, Blue's opposite number from the Senate, was fiftyish, short, plump, and florid, with a low, rasping voice.

Peters – the individual who'd organized the meeting this morning – was of medium build, appeared to be in his early 60s, and had what Alex thought of as that "lean and hungry look". Peters had founded a national anti-abortion lobby group and led it since his earliest days as a state legislator. He still published a weekly newsletter on the subject.

Coffee had been poured, sugared, creamed, and the first sip taken. Cigars had been offered and refused. All of these social amenities having been taken care of, it was time, Alex thought, to get down to business.

"Now what can I do for you gentlemen today? Perhaps I ought to inform you that CNN is already reporting that a delegation of 'irate Republican leaders' is visiting the White House to remonstrate with the President over what they refer to as his 'lackadaisical' position on abortion."

There was an embarrassed silence, which was exactly what Alex had intended. These three, of course, were the ones who had planted that story with CNN and he was letting them know that he knew it. It was interesting to him that straight talk, an extremely rare commodity in this city – in an apparent contradiction of the basic economic theory known as the Law of Marginal Utility – had no value at all to most of its inhabitants.

The first of them to recover his aplomb was Senator Peters, who shook his head. Alex realized that Peters reminded him of the columnist Robert Novak, whose mortal enemies had called him the Republican "Prince of Darkness".

"No, Mr. President, that's not why we're here. I'd never call any of your policies 'lackadaisical', I'm sure they're all extremely well thought out and energetically pursued. We're here because the nation has arrived at an important crossroads in history. You see, we Republicans – along with a small handful of conservative Democrats in each chamber – we Republicans believe that we finally have garnered enough votes to outlaw abortion altogether ..."

"And?" Alex asked.

"Not 'and'," said Senator Commack. "*But.* But certain conditions have been imposed on us by our potential supporters both Republican and Democratic. Among the conditions, many of those supporters don't want to risk exposing themselves publicly on this issue, only to have you veto the effort. Which means that we can't get this work done without your endorsement."

"I see." They didn't have enough votes to override his veto.

As Commack looked on, Congressman Blue handed out a single Xeroxed sheet to each of them. Faith-Anne glanced over the sheet Blue had given her with a carefully neutral expression, and stuck it in her notebook.

Alex read the proposed bill before he commented. "Well, if nothing else, gentlemen, its brevity is commendable. It simply bans abortion anywhere within the United States, their territories, on US military bases overseas, or on American ships at sea. So where's the rest of it?"

Senator Peters looked confused. "The rest of it, Mr. President?"

"That's right, Senator, the rest of it. When I was a schoolboy, before the Roe vs. Wade decision, something like 50,000 women a year were dying from botched abortions of one kind or another, either self-inflicted, or at the hands of some back-alley butcher. What that tells us, is that, whatever the law may decree, women will still take huge risks to control their own destinies."

"Excuse me, Mr. President, I'm afraid I don't follow you."

Alex nodded. "Well for example, you don't want American women skulking off to Canada or Mexico to get their abortions, do you? So where's your provision for physical examinations at the borders to detect pregnancies leaving the country, or terminated pregnancies coming back in?"

The man reddened. "I...we never thought of that, Mr. President."

Alex nodded. "I wondered whether you gentlemen had thought this matter through completely. Here's another thing: if you seek to outlaw abortions, you're going to have to add an enforcement clause to this legislation, aren't you? And you may even have to create a whole new federal bureaucracy to do the enforcing. I certainly can't imagine any existing law enforcement agency that I'd care to see doing it, can you?"

Alex was morally certain that they *had* thought of those two points, hoping the president would overlook them. The looks on their faces tended to support his suspicions. Whoever had said the devil was in the details had been right. Heaven knew what details these three had in mind.

"And then," he added, "there'll have to be agency regulations that go along with the law and sustain it. To begin with, I suppose you gentlemen realize that you'll have to insist on mandatory monthly pregnancy testing for every female in the country, from puberty to menopause."

"M-mandatory – " Peters sputtered to a stop.

"I don't know what it'll cost, gentlemen, but it's going to be horrendously expensive – and extremely unpopular," Alex mused. "Maybe you'll want to require women to show up once a month down at the local offices of the...well let's call it the 'Pregnancy Enforcement Administration', shall we? Or maybe you can just issue them a home pregnancy test kit every month and they can use it and send in the results – although can you trust them to be that honest? You'll also have to accept the fact that you'll be creating a whole new underground market for false test results."

"Mr. President, I – "

Alex interrupted. "All pregnancies, of course, will have to be registered immediately with the PEA, and every pregnant woman in the country will be required to undergo frequent psychological evaluation to determine whether she's become an abortion risk during the past couple of weeks. And of course she'll have to report for regular compulsory physical examinations to make sure she and the baby remain healthy. Here I thought you three gentlemen were *against* socialized medicine."

Commack tried to say, "Well, that's not so – "

"Naturally," Alex went on, "the mother-to-be will be criminally prosecuted if she drinks or smokes while pregnant, or exposes herself or her baby to secondhand smoke or to any other politically incorrect influence – perhaps even if she eats too little or too much of the currently right or wrong thing. It will probably be called 'unborn child abuse'."

"Mr. President!" Congressman Blue was furious. He held up a hand to stop Alex, who raised his eyebrows, pulled his battered old pipe from a jacket pocket, tamped it with a tool made from a .30-06 shell, struck a match, and puffed it into life. Sweet-smelling smoke filled the room.

"Yes, Congressman Blue?"

"Mr. President, we didn't write any of these things you're saying into the bill. They don't have anything to do with what we're trying to accomplish."

"Ah, but there we disagree, Congressman Blue," Alex puffed. "How can you outlaw a thing without taking steps to make sure that people don't do it? Even if you don't write those provisions into your bill, others who come along later will try to make political hay of their own by tightening up all the 'loopholes' that you left for them so thoughtfully."

"'Loopholes'," for the first time, Faith-Anne spoke up, "being a technical term for the few remaining freedoms that the government hasn't gotten around to crushing yet."

"Well, I certainly don't – "

"I know you don't," said Alex, "But there's no way you can avoid it, Senator. Here's another example: a woman who's obviously pregnant – involuntarily – or has a history of attempted abortions, or who happens to fail a psychological evaluation will *have* to be subjected to various kinds of physical restraint, ranging from house arrest with an electronic anklet to keep tabs on her whereabouts, to the local jail where she can be watched, to a federal prison, to forced hospitalization, to a padded cell in some lunatic asylum, to a straitjacket. She might even be forcibly sedated – turned into some kind of zombie – for the term of her pregnancy."

Peters protested, "But that's not – "

"Yes it is," Alex replied. "You just don't realize it yet. Of course you may have to outlaw all wire coathangers, knitting needles, chopsticks over a certain length, or anything else that can be used to induce a self-abortion. Maybe registering these items and licensing their owners will be enough. Although in that case, the coathangers, knitting needles, and chopsticks will all have to have serial numbers."

Faith-Anne stepped in again. "Any contact between a woman and her health providers will naturally be suspect. If she goes to her doctor, even to have an ingrown toenail removed, they'll have to be ready to prove they weren't planning an abortion, possibly by recording every word they say together. If she discuss the weather for too long with her pharmacist at the drugstore, they'll be subject to interrogation by PEA...greenshirts...who'll want to know if what they talked about was RU486."

"Greenshirts?" asked a puzzled Congressman.

Faith-Anne said, "As in medical greens."

"Likewise, each and every miscarriage, however tragic, innocent, or accidental," Alex said, "will have to be investigated like a homicide, with all of the invasions of privacy and violations of rights any homicide investigation entails. And there's plenty of room in there for another kind of miscarriage – a miscarriage of justice. If a woman can be shown to have taken one vitamin pill too few – or one vitamin pill too many – when she was pregnant, some ambitious prosecutor will make her life even more miserable than it is, by trying to nail her for manslaughter."

Peters tried again. "Mr. President, this is – "

"The direct consequence of what you're trying to do, Senator, nothing more, nothing less," Alex told him. "But it gets much worse. The Democrats will fight this legislation tooth and nail, but once it gets passed, you can count on your opposite numbers in that party to exploit what you've done, and use it as a springboard to push through little items like the parental licensing laws they've wanted at least since the Clinton Administration."

Faith-Anne said, "When that happens, when couples fail to qualify for a government license – maybe because they own guns, or drive an SUV, or smoke, or like to barbecue red meat – their unlicensed kids will be seized by the state and raised in the creches socialists are so fond of."

"Think it can't happen here?" Alex stood, walked around behind the chair he'd been sitting in, and put his hands in his jacket pockets. "Folks probably thought Prohibition couldn't happen. But a million marching morons – well-meaning do-gooders and busybodies – couldn't be wrong, could they? Never mind that they were screwing people's lives up beyond all recognition. Never mind that it brought us the first turf wars, drive-by shootings, poisoned booze, cement overshoes, and the Bureau of Alcohol, Tobacco, and Firearms. Never mind that, once it was repealed, the enforcement boys still needed their jobs, so we got the war on guns, the war on drugs, and eventually, the war on tobacco."

He shook his head. "Gentlemen, I will *not* allow this bonnet-bee of yours to devolve into simple-minded 'feelgood' legislation that makes you look noble to your right-wing constituents, while it ruins the lives of countless individuals whom you never have to look in the eye. The only way I know to keep liberty from being destroyed is by making the government – in this case, that means you – accountable for *all* of the consequences of *all* of its actions, intended or otherwise."

There were grim expressions all around the table. Alex believed that he had failed to win them over or to move them even an inch. He'd been resigned to it from the outset, but that didn't make it any easier to bear.

"No, gentlemen," he told them, "if you outlaw abortion, you'll have to pay a price for seeing your convictions into the law: you're going to have to live with the *unintended* consequences as well as those you had in mind. If you bring me a bill that fails to cover even one of the points I've made, I'll veto it in a New York nanosecond. You might as well go all the way; I'm going to tell the public it's what you propose, because you can't claim to outlaw abortion without it. There's a midterm election coming in seven months. How's that going to go over with the voters?"

All three looked incredulous. Commack said, "You *want* to pass these laws?"

"Of course I don't, Senator. It will give rise to a reign of terror like nothing seen before in America. You'll be enslaving no less than half the population. It will create a new army of armed and armored nannies. It will devour your wives, your sisters, your daughters, and your granddaughters. It will destroy all that's left of what America was supposed to be about. But you'll have made your point, you will have passed your law, and you and your constituents will be happy."

Now it was Peters who stood up. "So we're to assume that you're pro-choice."

"You're to assume nothing of the kind, Senator Peters. I've never said where I stand on the issue personally, because it doesn't matter. Outlaw abortion, and – no matter what anybody hopes or thinks or fears – that's where the country's headed, right into the black abyss of totalitarianism."

There was a long silence. Alex and Peters stared at

each other without blinking.

Then: "As I said in my book *Looking Forward* several years ago, abortion is the issue that the Left counts on, gentlemen, *counts on* to keep the freedom movement divided. And here we all are today, proving it."

Another long silence.

"Look: I shouldn't have to be the one to tell you that you're going to have to grow up, swallow hard, and do your best accept the fact that, as fervently as you loathe abortion, a great many other people in this country disagree with you just as fervently. It's absolutely vital that we shut down this endless, pointless argument, and move on with our real work – fulfilling the promise of the American Revolution."

Blue stood, then Commack. "Maybe that Revolution went too far."

"As I recall, Senator Blue," Faith-Anne told him, "the last one to say that was Bill Clinton.

Commack said, "Even a broken clock is right twice a day."

Alex was ignoring the byplay between the politicians and his daughter. "I plan to end this debate forever, gentlemen, in a manner that will probably be satisfactory to everybody but the *leaders* on both sides."

Senator Peters stiffened, but said nothing.

"Abortion," Alex said, "will remain legal. But not one red cent of federal tax money will ever be spent on it again, and I will do my level best to persuade the authorities at the state, county, and municipal levels to follow my example. As you know, gentlemen, I can be pretty persuasive."

But not with this lot, Alex thought.

In a few more moments there were hands shaken all around, promises made to think over what had just been discussed, and goodbyes said. The three Republicans left, and the President breathed an audible sigh of relief.

"Momma would have been very proud of you, Daddy," Faith-Anne told him with teardrops threatening to fall. "I know I am, and Dana will be, too."

Alex shook his head. "I'm going to brush my teeth, sweetheart. If I'd said 'gentlemen' one more time to that crew, I'd have thrown up for sure."

* * * * * *

The President said, "Government schools continue to exist in America because they serve a dual purpose..."

"There he is again, going on about nothing, the way he always does!" Agnes Cromwell wrinkled her face to signify disgust, but it was hard to notice, because she was old, her face was wrinkled all the time, anyway, and so many things these days disgusted her that there was little difference between how she looked now and the expression she usually wore.

"Agnes, we have to give the young man a chance." Her companion, Enid Throckmorton, shook her head. They sat together in one of the common rooms of the Ivan Montmorency Assisted Living Center, of West Palm Beach, Florida, watching TV on a Saturday evening. Alexander Hope had just begun his customary address for the week. "I've been chatting with some friends of mine about him on the internet, and – "

"The internet!" Agnes interrupted. "The internet! There you go again about the filthy internet! I don't know why they even allow you to have that computer in here, at all! I watch Rosie and Oprah and Tipper! I know what the internet is really about! All that vile pornography and right-wing hate propaganda piped straight into our home! Enid, you should be ashamed – "

"Agnes, there's no 'allow' to it! My apartment is my private property – heaven knows I pay enough for it – and nobody has a thing to say about what I do in it. I don't know why you waste your time on those fat, ignorant sluts on TV."

"Why, I – " She stopped. What Enid had just said bordered on...well, blasphemy. The only programs more important were her stories – *A Brighter Morning, My Children's Children,* and *Look for the Silver Lining.*

"The government has a need," said the President, unaware of the debate raging over him at the Ivan Montmorency Assisted Living Center, "to indoctrinate the nation's children with socialism and turn them morally, politically, and socially against their own parents."

Enid was firm. "The internet is just a different, better way to use the telephone, Agnes. I started playing with computers when I retired from the Broward County public school system, and I got more interested when President Hope pointed out the many benefits the internet and the world wide web offer even the most antitechnological '50s guy', as he put it. Certainly keeps me from going out of my mind with boredom in this place. Why, I played backgammon with another retired school teacher last evening – only she was in New Zealand! Just imagine!"

"Parents," the President went on. "need a storage facility for their children, because both of them have to work full time to pay taxes..."

Agnes was a retired Broward County school teacher, too. "I suppose you voted for the man!"

"Who else was I going to vote for, Agnes?" Enid shrugged. "A child pornographer? A dead woman?"

"So you voted for a monster who's destroyed Social Security, instead, and now wants to destroy the public schools we both dedicated our lives to?"

"In some contexts, I suppose this might be called 'symbiosis'," said the President.

"I don't know about you, Agnes, but I dedicated my life to the children, not the schools. And you know perfectly well that Social Security was *already* destroyed, long before President Hope took office. He just called a spade a spade, and because of that, I won't be paying income taxes on my rental properties any more!"

"Rental properties! And I have to live on the charity of my miserable failure of a son and that horrible daughter-in-law of mine! They voted for Hope, too!"

"Agnes, your son is a network communications consultant who makes six figures a year. He wears Allen-Edmonds shoes and drives this year's Porsche Boxster."

"But he could have been a doctor! Instead, against my urging, he foolishly quit medical school and married – "

"Another network communications expert who makes six figures. And together, Agnes, they support you handsomely."

The president said, "I prefer to think of it as *parasitism.*"

"But it isn't real, Enid! It's all going to collapse!"

Enid sighed. "That's what they said during the Panic of 2001, Agnes, and now it's bigger and better than it ever was. And as a direct result, you have your apartment, and your privacy, here, instead of having to live with your daughter-in-law."

There wasn't anything Agnes could say to that, instead, she changed the subject, whispering out of the side of her mouth, "Your so-called President married a yellow slant-eyed woman half his age, didn't he, Enid? And God knows what they did in the Oval Office *before* they were married!"

Enid laughed out loud. "I believe that you're confusing President Hope with one of his predecessors, Agnes, the one *you* voted for. Twice."

* * * * * *

An hour later, Alex was downstairs inspecting new construction. There had been a swimming pool down here in Kennedy's day. Johnson had ordered it filled in, almost as his first spiteful act as President, and the room had been a great many things since then. Alex was having the pool restored.

Across the hall, he was having an indoor shooting range put in, ostensibly for the Secret Service. He still hadn't taught Dana to shoot, as he'd promised when she was in the hospital. He looked forward to it.

There wasn't much to see right now except for a big hole in the floor and a maze of concrete pouring forms. Agent Smith had come down with Alex – in case one of the construction crew turned out to be a Western Siberian assassin, Alex assumed. John, he understood, was outside at the loading dock, inspecting materials the workmen were bringing in.

The foreman was a broad-shouldered man wearing a beat-up yellow hardhat. At the same time the man felt obliged to stop his own work and explain what was happening to the President – there was a great deal of noise and he had to shout – he clearly was less than happy at the interruption and made little effort to conceal it. Alex sent him back to work and simply stood and watched. Over some 30 years of running a corporation, he'd had a lot of construction done and always liked to watch.

Suddenly, he felt a light tap on his shoulder. He turned to see Dana, still wearing a heavy coat, looking up at him with those big brown eyes of hers. He started to grin and embrace her until he noticed her anxious expression. She had an open laptop in her hand, and was pointing at the screen. Reaching for his glasses, he signaled to Agent Smith that he and Dana were headed for the hallway where it was quieter.

"Okay," he asked her outside the hardhat area, "what's up?

"This was 20 minutes ago. I watched it being recorded." She set the laptop on a hallway table and manipulated the keyboard until there was a moving image of her replacement at NetPlanetNews.com on the screen. The young, attractive black woman was standing by the big wrought-iron fence with the White House in the background.

"...at a press conference on the capitol steps. Republican House and Senate leaders announced, following what they termed 'unsuccessful negotiations' with President Alexander Hope, that they have introduced a bill to impeach him for what they call 'his multiple extralegal and unconstitutional acts'.

"Libertarian Vice President Forrey Nadalindov, who was also there, has publicly approved the Republican effort. This is Marla Hoskins, NetPlanetNews.com."

CHAPTER TWENTY-TWO:
THE CABAL

> *Whenever you're tempted to believe that those who are responsible for all of the world's problems are involved in some vast conspiracy, consider the far likelier possibility that they're just stupid.*
>
> – Alexander Hope, *Looking Forward*

It was a beautiful Saturday morning in Flagstaff, Arizona. They were all beautiful Saturday mornings, here – which was why he and his wife had left Pittsburgh – and the rest of the week generally wasn't too bad, either.

The owner of the little white frame house pushed the screen door open, stepped onto the front porch and stuck a hand in his mailbox. As soon as they were through with their chores, he planned to take his three small sons fishing. He'd even talked his wife and two daughters into coming, too. They were packing a picnic lunch and...

What was this? A long, brown, official-looking envelope from the Internal Revenue Service addressed to Maxwell J. Covelskie. Ah, jeez, thought Max, as his stomach muscles tightened up suddenly, what a way to spoil a perfectly good Saturday morning! He wondered what he'd done now.

Heart thudding leadenly in his chest, he tore the envelope open, to find a letter.

> Dear Mr. Coveleskie:
>
> Owing to:
>
> [A] the new Basic Necessities deductions for food, clothing, shelter, and transportation, along with
>
> [B] deductions now in place for items and activities protected by the Bill of Rights, such as free speech and self-defense, coupled with
>
> [C] recent elimination of the Social Security Administration, the abolition of taxes connected with it, and
>
> [D] the credit already in your account which will be applied to your future federal taxes, and, finally,
>
> [E] the direct dollar-for-dollar tax credit you qualify for because you and your spouse home-school your five children,
>
> It has been determined that you will have no federal tax liability for the foreseeable future, and that, in order to conserve Departmental resources, you will have no need to file again until further notice from the IRS.

The letter was signed by a deputy director of the IRS and there was an 800 phone number he could call to confirm the authenticity of the letter, which he was advised to copy and give to his tax accountant and attorney.

For a moment Max simply stood there on the porch, too stunned to know what to think or feel. As a self-employed machinist, he'd always had trouble paying his taxes and worried constantly about a lien being filed against his income, or this house he and his wife had built with their own two hands.

Suddenly, a happy thought occurred to him. He turned, opened the screen door, and stepped back into the house. "Marilyn!" he shouted, "forget that picnic lunch! We'll go fishing tomorrow! Today we're going to buy a boat!"

* * * * * *

The bar was dark and smoky, just the way its habitues preferred it. It was hard to see who else was here and, maybe more importantly, who they were with.

Darkly complected, with slicked-back oily hair, the Democratic leader of the United States Senate sat at one end of a high-sided horseshoe-shaped booth, upholstered in red leather, sipping a martini and smoking a cigar.

In the same booth, the short, fat, deceptively harmless-looking, Democratic leader of the House of Representatives scowled into the seedy depths of his third strawberry daiquiri. From time to time, he conspicuously wrinkled up his nose at the Senator's acrid cigar smoke, but he said nothing about it, and the Senator returned the favor by ignoring him.

Between the two men, drinking a whiskey sour and a screwdriver, respectively, sat their most closely-trusted political lieutenants, a harsh-featured female

Senator from California, and a droopy-jowled, plump and matronly Congresswoman from Colorado. The California Senator was chain-smoking cigarettes to the resentful glares of the Colorado Congresswoman.

Between the women, the Hollywood producer of movie spectaculars that usually grossed a billion dollars or more was drinking a Shirley Temple.

The female Senator spoke. "Well, boys'n'girls, here's our chance! Those butt-stupid conservatives are gearing up to impeach Hope for us, and all we have to do is sit tight and keep our mouths shut!" She was the kind of liberal who got a lot of mileage from her Jewish surname, even though it had been acquired by marriage and meant nothing more to her than that. She was also famous for advocating stringent victim disarmament for everybody else while she carried a short-barrelled .357 magnum revolver in her handbag and hired bodyguards with machineguns.

The slick-haired Senator shook his head. "It isn't that simple, Diane. I've seen the articles of impeachment. They make a lot of all the executive orders Hope's issued. But you know what it's really all about?"

The Democratic House leader accepted his fourth strawberry daiquiri from a waiter who had arrived. He spoke with a lisp and turned his Rs into Ws. "Didn't Bwue and Commack and Petewth pay him a vithit thith mowning?"

"You've got that right, Bee" replied the female Senator. "And if it was Senator Robin Peters, you can bet there's only one thing they talked about!"

"*Abortion,*" everyone at the table said simultaneously.

"Doeth anyone heaw happen to wemembew," the

House leader lisped, glancing around at his comrades, "what Hope'th pothition on abortion ith?"

The female Senator lit another cigarette with a flourish intended for the Congresswoman and sneered, "Bee, dear, just what makes you think that anyone pays any attention to what libertarians think about anything?"

The Congresswoman who'd come here with her leader spoke at last. She was the ultimate collectivist, proud of the fact that she had never had an original thought in her life, and frankly incapable of making a decision without first consulting somebody – anybody – else. Her voice was pitched half an octave higher than it should have been and was affectedly girlish. "Well, with one of them occupying the White House, now, Diane, dear, maybe it's time that we started. As I recall, the position they take in their platform is some kind of a compromise."

"That's right, Diana," said the female Senator. Both of the women secretly hated the fact that their first names were similar. "Abortion is perfectly peachy with them as long as it isn't paid for with tax money. Isn't that just like them? And they're worse than Republicans because they can't be made ashamed of it! How are poor and minority women going to – "

"Save it for the media, Diane!" The Senate leader snarled and shook his head in disgust. "This is serious! If we go along with this impeachment, it's going to get out that we helped the right-wingers get rid of him over *abortion*! How'll that look on regular TV, let alone what the internet trash will make of it? They'll chop us up like chicken liver!"

"The never-to-be-sufficiently-damned internet," said the Senator from California. She signaled to a passing waiter to bring her another whiskey sour and lit a fresh cigarette from the butt of the previous one. "We were a little too late recognizing the threat it represented. If only we'd nipped it in the bud. Now if we do what we need to do, they'll make it look like we're against a woman's right to choose – "

The movie producer wore nylon running shoes, a sportscoat over a t-shirt, threadbare Levis, and a baseball cap crammed down over bushy gray hair that matched his bushy gray beard. He was well known for his huge personal collection of "assault rifles" and "black guns". Whenever a guest asked him how he squared that with his energetic advocacy of victim disarmament laws, the producer always replied "The laws are for *them*!"

Just now he replied to the California Senator, "If they do, it'll be the end of any contributions you hope to keep receiving from our industry."

The Senate leader retorted, "We don't need to hear this right now, Steve!"

"Hey, Charlie, don't kill the messenger – I'm just stating a plain fact."

"Don't bwow a gathket, darling," lisped the House leader. "One of thothe internet twash happenth to be the Prethident'h mithtreth – they won't dawe – "

"Wife," said the Senate leader.

"What?"

"You heard what I said, Bee! Where have you been for the past week? The lovely and talented Dana Li is Al Hope's *wife*, now, all neat and tidy, with a great big South African rock on the delicate third finger of her dainty little left hand, her doting parents' smiling approval, and all the Ozzie and Harriet trimmings! If we try to make something questionable out of that, we're likely to come off publicly as bitter, resentful, unromantic, and probably *racists* in the bargain!"

"You're right," the Congresswoman said. "You *have* noticed that the President's blushing bride is of Asiatic extraction, haven't you, Bee?"

The female Senator added, "They just celebrated the first White House wedding in two generations. The whole country loves them for it – especially all of the women's magazines."

"Okay, you'we wight," complained the House leader, whose personal indiscretions were an everyday topic of hilarious discussion on talk radio. "I could have paid clother attention. You know, they wewe weawy caweful. Wong pewiodth in the hothpitaw fow each of them. Chapewoned by the Thecret Thervice motht of the time afteward. As faw ath anybody knowth, they nevew even – "

"Enough!" barked the Senate leader. "I hate this! That man is cheerfully dismantling everything we've ever worked for, as we sit by and watch it happen – " The Senator had been a child prodigy and had entered the university in his mid-teens. He still thought of himself as an intellectual, and when he said "everything we've ever worked for," he meant as far back as the 18th century French communitarian, Prodhoun.

"I know what you mean," the Colorado Congresswoman said. "Look at all these highly publicized presidential commissions he's created. The latest one would demilitarize police departments nationwide – no more federal money, or federal control, for local cops – outlaw 'dynamic entries', and limit the police to weapons that are lawful for ordinary citizens. He plans somehow to jawbone local authorities into abject compliance."

This was an especially sore point for her. Her middle-aged jowls flopped up and down in agitation and her artificial little-girl voice squeaked with annoyance. Her goal – and the linchpin of her political career – was to make sure that *no* weapon was lawful for ordinary citizens.

"He's got another commission," added the producer, "to rate federal judges in terms of what he calls 'adherence to the plain language of the Bill of Rights'. He's recommending that pressure of every kind be brought against judges who presume to disagree with the intent of the Framers, or who've used their courtrooms to advance the Progressive cause."

The Senate leader winced at the euphemism. In private company like this, he preferred to be direct, and the word the producer should have used was "socialism". It was a word with an honorable history 200 years long and it was past time that its advocates were free to use it openly.

The Colorado Congresswoman nodded. "I've heard that the pensions of all federal judges found 'guilty' – along with their houses, their cars, and so on – will be used to compensate their 'victims'. Our party will resist, of course, and so will the Republicans, but all the polls say that the people want it. We may have to go along with it or be discredited!"

"What *really* worries me," whispered the female Senator, "is this commission that Hope's organized to investigate all these crackpot claims that the 16th Amendment was never properly ratified by the state legislatures, and that the federal income tax – and the IRS along with it – are illegal! The rabble will love that one, too! We could lose control over the population that we've worked nearly a century to gain!"

The Senate leader regained control. "I appreciate your concerns, ladies and gentlemen," he told them, "and believe me, I share them. But I'm afraid that we're going to have to *stop* this particular impeachment. Bee, Diane, that means you two have to find out who it is on our side of the aisle in either chamber that Peters is counting on, and make them see the light. I mean it." He gritted his teeth at them. "Make. Them. See. The. Light."

The House leader slurped up the rest of his daiquiri. "Count on me, Chawie."

"I will, Bee, I will. Maybe we can impeach this SOB ourselves, later on."

* * * * * *

Ernie Hanover scratched his head and said, "How about...'the graverobber tax'?"

"You know, I think I like 'the ghoul tax' better," replied Katie Harris.

"What, precisely, is a ghoul?" Rick Thomas wanted to know. He was a stickler for correctness.

Mick Douglas grinned and said, "What's a nice ghoul like you doing in a place like this?"

"Shut up, Mick," Katie pretended to be annoyed. "You'd clown at your own funeral. I think it's creature – a demon or a goblin, or a human being with extremely low standards, I don't know – that eats dead bodies."

"Then how about 'the eaters of the dead tax'?" Rick suggested. The four of them looked around at one another, then at their host, the President.

"I don't know," he said. "It doesn't fall very trippingly off the tongue, does it?"

Katie shuddered. "Given the context, Alex, I think that may be a plus!"

Everybody laughed. They were using the same small, comfortable sitting room in the residential section of the White House that was supposed to be reserved for the First Lady. The First Lady herself was up in Alaska at the moment – "the Delta Quadrant", Mick had called it – cutting the ribbon on a brand new oil refinery. She wouldn't be back in Washington, to Alex's dismay, for several days. Sometimes it felt like he'd seen her more often before they were married, when she'd worked for NetPlanetNews.com.

He'd missed her the moment she left. School was out, so he'd asked the Austrian Mafia here to the White House to help him with a problem, then delightedly flown out to Colorado himself to pick them up. They were obligated, he'd told them as they'd boarded his private jet at the Jefferson County airport, after all, they'd gotten him into this mess.

John, who'd flown out to Colorado with the President and acted as Fred "Launchpad McQuack" Gorski's co-pilot, had wanted to know what kinds of weapons the Austrian Mafia were carrying, gave one of them a hard time for not having brought a gun at all – John never told Alex which one it was, but simply provided the culprit with "a loaner" – and another of them for toting what he termed "one of those puny little nines".

At the White House he'd escorted them through all the security barriers, not allowing the Executive Protection Service to search them. They'd spent an hour this morning down in the new shooting range.

"What kind of civilization," Alex asked them now, "punishes its productive classes by taxing the wealth they work so hard to create three, four, five times – and then robs them of the chance to pass it on to their own children – gives it instead to those who are neither willing nor capable of earning it? They pay property taxes, corporate taxes, personal income taxes, capital gains taxes, a hundred kinds of excise taxes, and finally this inheritance tax – this *death* tax – that can wind up taking more than half of what's left. Cannibalism, that's what it is. Maybe 'eaters of the dead' is the thing to call it, after all."

Suddenly serious Katie asked, "Alex, why are we talking about the inheritance tax? Aren't you concerned that the Republicans are trying to impeach you?"

Alex smiled. "You know, in some ways it would be a relief. Despite my best efforts, I haven't had a decent night's sleep since I got here. I'd certainly see a lot more of Dana, and she wouldn't have to quit her job to avoid a conflict of interests. Where's the losing outcome, here? But think, Katie, if they're going to do it, it'll take a few weeks. Which is all the more reason to work hard and fast on issues like this one."

"It doesn't make you angry, what they're trying to do to you?" Ernie asked.

"No," Alex shook his head. "I guess it might if I thought they had any more intelligence than a common laboratory flatworm, but they're Republicans, after all, no brains, no backbone. I do something they don't like, they try to get rid of me in one of the only two ways they can, even though I've never committed so much as a single high crime or misdemeanor.

"The other way is ... ?" Ernie formed a pistol from his fingers and dropped the "hammer" – his thumb – while pointing it at the President.

"That's where the 'no backbone' part comes in, silly," Katie told him.

There was a knock at the door. One of the Marine guards entered, strode to a television set, and turned it on. "Ms Louise said you'd want to watch this, sir."

"Thank you, sergeant." It was C-SPAN, showing the floor of the United States Senate. The overlay, tallying the votes, was labeled "Impeachment, Yea, Nay".

"So much for a few weeks," Rick observed.

The vote was 51 for impeachment, 52 against. Apparently one state had asked to be passed over while some last-minute negotiation was being done. But now the president of the Senate – the Vice President of the United States, Forrey Nadalindov – hammered his gavel into the bench, demanding that the last state vote. He was highly motivated. If the vote went "for", Nadalindov would be the next occupant of the White House.

"How say you Alaska?"

Alex's personal laptop made tweeting noises. Only three people had the e-mail address that could make it do that. Alex went to the 18th century desk where he'd left it on its induction charger and opened it up.

"Alex!" It was Dana, exactly as he'd expected, probably calling to congratulate him on his likely non-impeachment. The coincidence of where she was calling from hadn't struck him yet, perhaps because he'd been a trifle more anxious over what had just happened in the Senate than he'd let on to Katie and her friends. What he hadn't expected was to see was

Congresswoman Linda Alvarez, the only libertarian in the House of Representatives, smiling into the video pickup beside his beautiful wife.

"Greetings, from Juneau, Alaska!" the Congresswoman told him. "And congratulations, I assume. We're standing here in the public park at the Alaskan capitol. You're probably still President of the United States, and you have this lovely creature shivering here beside me to thank for it!"

"What?"

"Please don't be mad at me, Alex," Dana pleaded with a worried look. "Linda's right, I meddled. I heard a rumor from of my former coworkers at NetPlanetNews.com. Linda had flown up here to check it out, too, and I joined her. It was almost – but not quite – true, so we went to work making it happen. Linda actually deserves most of the credit, She–"

"What rumor?"

"I'm getting to that, darling. We talked and argued and twisted arms and made promises all night and most of the day – we hocked your immortal soul, Mr. President – and as a result .. do you want to tell him, Linda?"

"Tell me what?"

"No, dear, you should tell him."

"You really think so?"

"Tell me what?" The two of them were enjoying this. He wondered what it would be like if they ever teamed up in their mischief with Faith-Anne.

"Okay," Linda said, "I'll tell him. The Governor of Alaska, the Lieutenant Governor, the Secretary of State, the State Treasurer, about half of the state legislature, and the entire Congressional delegation, including both Senators, have joined the Free

Libertarian Party of America!"

Behind him, Rick, Katie, Mick, and Ernie had begun whooping and yelling.

"Quiet!" He hated to shout at them, but he couldn't hear Dana and Linda.

"...so I'm not the only libertarian in Congress anymore!" the latter was saying.

Dana added, "So the Alaskan Senators will vote with the Democrats, against the Republicans!"

On TV, the answer finally came. "The state of Alaska votes ... nay!"

CHAPTER TWENTY-THREE:
PHIL OCHS

> *It has been truthfully said that it's the military's job to kill people and break things. Fair enough. It's the job of the militia to keep those people and things from being killed or broken.*
>
> – Alexander Hope, *Looking Forward*

"No," the President said, "I don't want you – any of you – to resign, General. But you can't go on fighting the last war, or the last three wars. It's a brand new century and a brand new situation, domestically and globally. That calls for a brand new way of looking at lots of things, including our national defense. If you think you're up to it, I'd much rather that you stayed on."

The Chairman of the Joint Chiefs of Staff blinked. His colleagues, resplendent in their blue, green, white, and brass, were agitated, as well. "But the first that thing you mentioned, Mr. President, was a massive and wholly unprecedented Reduction-in-Force, and – "

Washington's May weather was unusually hot. Today's meeting was being held in a cool "situation room" deep beneath the White House in an artificial cavern that every government official denied existed.

Unlike movie representations of such rooms – perhaps beginning with *Dr. Strangelove* – it was decorated as cheerfully as possible, with sunlight and views of the White House gardens and lawns conducted below on fiberoptic lines and rear-projected on the walls.

"Hardly unprecedented, General." Alex spread his hands, as if confronted by a classroom full of students who had somehow skipped the course prerequisites. He'd have expected at least one or two of these assorted generals and admirals to have read his book, once he'd been elected. "Until the Second World War, the nation was used to standing down, following a war, reducing its investment in the military, and returning joyfully and wholeheartedly to civilian life."

The room filled with a low grumbling that couldn't be localized. Perhaps it was the Joint Chiefs reacting to his remarks. More likely it was the pumps that kept the Potomac out of this subbasement. Any potential enemy could probably hear this room and the machinery necessary to support it from their submarines far out at sea.

"But Mr. President," the Chairman pleaded, "that's exactly what brought on Pearl Harbor. At any time after World War II, any sort of relaxation on our part, the slightest lapse in our preparedness – "

Alex shook his head. "General, as you know, I'm an historian by trade. I was also a marine officer – just barely – and I know the party line well enough to spout it in my sleep. Franklin Delano Roosevelt is what brought on Pearl Harbor; it was his only way out of the mess he'd made of the Depression – which itself was a result of government meddling, in the form of the 1913 Federal Reserve Act. Thanks to

Roosevelt's wrongheaded interference, there were more people unemployed in 1941, than when he first took office in 1933."

"Mr. President," the Navy's top admiral was offended. "Do you imply he was to blame for the Japanese attacking Pearl Harbor?" For a moment Alex had forgotten that FDR had been Secretary of the Navy.

"I'm not implying it, Admiral, I'm stating it as a fact." He turned again to face the Chairman. "And history, General, clearly shows that there are many forms of national preparedness that don't require stealing half of the country's wealth from those who created it and pouring it down the military-industrial rathole."

The reference to a rathole could hardly been lost, ten floors underground as they happened to be at the moment. All of the officers tried to answer Alex's remarks at once. Good teacher that he was, he remained standing at the head of the table, allowed them to babble at each other, and said nothing until they noticed and shut up.

Then he began again. "This is 2010, gentlemen, the War Century is over. Yet although we're nominally at peace – despite the Founders' qualms over maintaining a standing army – we find ourselves with three million individuals in uniform, inventing swarthy, mustachioed comicbook super-villains overseas, and beating up on dusty little Third World countries, primitive and incapable of fighting us off, simply to keep the Department of Defense in coffee and doughnuts."

Veins showed on the Chairman's forehead; Alex realized that he was probably shortening a life or two, and wondered what medical facilities were maintained down here. “Mr. President, that’s – “

“That’s wrong, General. It’s also illegal. The Pentagon has been operating unconstitutionally since its cornerstone was laid. It’s time this country had a national defense appropriate to a limited republic, rather than an empire. No more foreign adventures, making the world safe for Democrats, no more ‘peacekeeping’ – nothing more than a euphemism for stripping people of the natural rights we’d be pledged to protecting if they were Americans – no more ‘meals on wheels’.”

“I protest!” said the Chairman, “I’m proud of our peacekeepers and the thankless job they’ve been bravely trying to do for 20 years.”

Alex shrugged. “General, I stand corrected. Feel free to resign. But did the possibility ever occur to you that the job is thankless because the people it’s being done *to* don’t want it done?”

For a long time they stood and listened to the pumps work and the ventilation system operate. Alex, who had made a lifelong habit of thinking the unthinkable, had now spoken the unspeakable,

The Chairman was clearly in some kind of pain. Alex found himself wondering about the medical facilities again. “I...well, to tell the absolute truth, sir, it hadn’t occurred to me.” The poor fellow looked like someone who’d been struck between the eyes with a telephone pole. That reaction told Alex that he was probably an honest man.

The President understood. Kitch had put him through something like this two decades ago. “Well, then, General, maybe you’d like to try sticking around and be a part of what happens next.”

The Chairman took a deep breath. "And what would that be, sir?"

Alex nodded, happy to finally be getting down to business. "Let's talk about that Reduction-in-Force I have in mind. It isn't what you think – it's much worse. And it will change the American military forever. But I guarantee there's a method in my madness."

He watched them stiffen and hold their collective breath. Most of them had their arms folded across their highly-decorated chests. He pressed a button recessed at his place at the table – he'd pushed the chair away when he'd arrived – and asked for coffee all around from the Marine orderly who materialized as a result. For the first time, he glanced at John, standing with his back to the wall beside a potted Norfolk pine. His old friend gave him a microscopic thumbs up.

"You see," he told his audience, "we've failed to learn a lesson that our own Continental Army – and a bunch of smugglers and pirates – taught the British in the Revolution and the War of 1812, that the Mujahideen taught the British in the 19th century and the Russians in the 20th, that the Vietnamese taught the Japanese, the British, the French, and later on lots of other folks, including yours truly."

The coffee arrived with startling alacrity. Alex poured a cup and watch the Chiefs sugar and cream their own. He glanced at John, raising his eyebrows. John shook his head and mouthed, "No, thanks."

He took a sip and set his cup down. "You can only do so much with high technology, and it seems to work best with enemies – the Iraquis for instance – who don't really want to fight. Against a worthy opponent, unless you're willing to render the planet uninhabitable, you've got to have a man on the ground with mud on his feet and some kind of weapon, a *pilum*, an *assagai*, or an M-14 in his hands."

With satisfaction, he saw expressions of approval bloom on the faces of the older officers who knew he was speaking a Great Truth.

"That's why I want a plan from you, on my desk within two weeks, to combine all of your extreme combat schools – Army Green Berets, Navy Seals, Air Force Escape and Evasion, Marine Corps boot camp – "

He grinned and there were dutiful chuckles all around.

" – into a single, coherent, perfectly horrible two-year program. Then I want you to start putting all of our current military personnel through it, regardless of their age or rank – unless they wish to retire or terminate their enlistment voluntarily within two years."

The Marine Corps commandant spilled his coffee.

Alex politely ignored it. "Individuals who fail to make it through the program – the vast majority, I assume – will leave the military, as well, with the sincere thanks of their grateful nation. After that, with due respect, I plan to empty the Pentagon and turn it into the world's only five-sided, multilevel roller-skating rink."

He'd expected polite laughter there, as well, but he was mistaken.

Undaunted, he plowed onward:

"That's only the tip of the military-industrial-congressional 'iceberg' that has to be resculpted – dismantled – in a way that will prevent corrupt procurement programs (like the late, unlamented

Osprey) from happening again. And counties can be just as susceptible as nations, when mass-marketing methods are applied to them.

"Even more important than that are the obscene 'military labs' and 'think tanks', where, ostensibly, leading-edge development is taking place, but where, in reality, high ranking civil servants plot and scheme, creating irrelevant systems and building bureaucratic empires, not only without regard for (or input from) the end user – the ground-pounder – but actually have the unmitigated gall to assert that they know what's best for him without ever, in most cases, having spent a day in the field, much less in the heat of battle.

"Sorry. That last represents years, decades, of the most intense frustration you can imagine, in my life as a defense contractor whose mission, for an honest buck, was to give soldiers, sailors, airmen, and marines what they wanted and needed. I was consistently stymied not only by the brass hats, but even more by their civil service sycophants. My plan is for corporations to develop systems out of their own pockets, and then try and sell them to the military as they did in the 19th century."

He cleared his throat. "But back to the subject at hand. The personnel who make it through will be the most ruthless and efficient warriors in military history. They'll also be trained as the most ethical and devoted to individual liberty. And they will be expected to teach everything they know. By statute, their numbers will never exceed 30,000 – or one percent of the current military – so they can never be used to run roughshod over the rest of the country. They will be known as the 'national cadre', the vital core who remain fit and ready to defend America at need."

There were nods of approval around the table. This was more like the military some of them had signed on to be a part of.

"At the same time," Alex told them, "the government will recognize – not certify or license – militia companies organized at the county level that meet certain extremely minimal standards. (There will be nothing to prevent other militia companies from forming that will not seek government recognition.) Basically anyone of a responsible age or either sex will be eligible who can walk, crawl, or roll a wheelchair to the firing line and shoot acceptably straight – and maybe perform other functions appropriate to operating a county militia company."

The Army general asked, "Why *county* militias, Mr. President?"

"It's natural, General, traditional, even neighborly; it hearkens back to English Common Law and J.R.R. Tolkien – and in my experience, it's about the biggest swatch of countryside an average individual can know 'like the back of his hand' – or conceive of personally as his territory. Science amply demonstrated that a defender occupying his own territory has an anthropological, or psychological, or, I don't know, an ethological advantage over an invading aggressor, of somewhere between two and four to one."

The general nodded. "I see, sir, thank you."

"You're welcome, General. Militia members will be given weapons outright – a pistol and a rifle (or in some cases a shotgun) – out of money previously spent on $600 toilet seats. Or they may be offered a tax credit to pay for them. In either case, the serial numbers will be obliterated at the factory, so that militia weapons can never be registered. Militias will have total autonomy in their choice of weapons and almost everything else. No national registry will be kept of their members, any more than of their weapons."

"Excuse me, sir," asked the blue-uniformed Air Force general, "In what ways will these county militia companies *not* be autonomous?"

"A fair question," Alex replied. "Militia members will be trained from time to time by members of the national cadre, sent around the country in twos and threes. That will be the cadre's principle task. The cadre will exercise itself at a greatly-reduced number of bases around the country – one for each major eco-system – and perhaps go abroad to observe techniques at use in foreign wars."

"In groups too small," the Chairman suggested, "to become Vietnam style 'advisors'?"

"You're way ahead of me," the President grinned. "Meanwhile, county militias will probably operate something like volunteer fire departments most of the time. They'll perform search and rescue work, offer an armed neighborhood watch, make citizens' arrests, and help with local disaster recovery. If they make themselves the pride of the community, they can be financed with bake sales, bazaars, charity dinners, fund drives, and exhibition baseball games.

"It will be the full time job of the militia to educate the public, especially children, on their rights – and that fact that, according to courts across the land, their rights do *not* include police protection. Local schools will be required to add the safe and effective handling of weapons to their curricula, and the instruction, more than likely, will come from the militia."

The Army general spoke again. "Sir, you'd put the defense of America – our National Security – in the hands of rank amateurs!"

Alex nodded. "Exactly where it belongs."

"It sounds to me like the Swiss national defense system," the general observed.

Alex nodded. "There are similarities, but the differences are significant. Military service is compulsory in Switzerland. Our 13th Amendment forbids involuntary servitude. A great many administrations have brushed past that; this one will not. And although Swiss males keep a fully-automatic battle rifle and a supply of ammunition in their homes at all times, the weapon is registered, the program is compulsory – and sexist. No girls allowed. Most importantly, unlike the Swiss, our militia companies will not exist to serve the state, but to defend themselves, their families, their neighbors, and, as an accidental side-benefit, the entire nation."

"But what about our our bombers, our tanks, our aircraft carriers, our submarines ... "

Alex planted his hands on the table and leaned forward. "Have you ever known any of those items to be used for genuine national defense, General? For anything but aggression – pardon me, 'projecting power' – around the globe?" He waited for half a dozen heartbeats. "Don't worry, we'll keep the missile submarines, at least for a while, and the hardware to defend them.

"We'll still need naval assets for river work and coastal defense. Mind you, these will *not* be blue water missions, nothing beyond the 50 fathom curve. Still, it's easier to defeat an amphibious invasion before it establishes a beachhead. This force will represent far less than 10 percent of current naval expenditures; it will carry no air arm, no large-scale transport, and attempt no 'projection of power'.

"In time, with training, the militias may take some of these responsibilities over, maybe financed through corporate sponsorships. They'll be able to buy their own fighters and tanks, designed purely for defense and to sell at market prices. I expect that there will eventually be intramural war games – exciting publicly broadcast competitions between the militias to help restore respectability to the concept and get folks 'rooting for the home team'.

"And we'll add something new, gentlemen, 'Backyard SDI'."

"Backyard what?" Several of the men said it at once.

"'Backyard Strategic Defense Initiative'. It's a notion first discussed in the 80s by a science fiction writer and a software engineer, based on a piece of World War I German artillery called 'Big Bertha' or the 'Paris Gun'."

He saw looks of recognition, even delight, around the table.

"You recall: it could throw shells more than 75 miles by shooting them up through the stratosphere – the Germans had meteorologists on their firing teams. The first shot, from German turf, destroyed a church full of people one Sunday in Paris. The French thought they were being bombed by a dirigible so high up it couldn't be seen."

He had their undivided interest now. There were grins on their faces. They loved some hardware – but so did he, for that matter.

"BSDI – we'll call it that – can only be used

defensively. It can't be used for aggression. Instead of 2000-pound bronze shells full of explosives, BSDI will use 800-pound fiberglass containers filled with a million BBs, designed to reach 100 miles above the Earth's surface and burst in front of oncoming ballistic missiles, about one BB per cubic meter forming an impenetrable – if temporary – shield."

He saw several puzzled looks. How could BBs form a shield?

"Compared with the missile's 18,000 miles an hour, the BB will be stationary. It'll make a BB-sized hole going into the missile, and a Volkswagen sized hole going out. End of multimillion dollar missile, for the price of a World War I cannon and a bushel of BBs. Or make that 3088 cannons, owned and operated by 3088 county militias."

"What happens," asked a general, "when the 999,999 BBs that didn't hit the missile come back down?"

"That's simple," said the admiral, "they'll burn up harmlessly."

Alex said, "No, they won't, Admiral, because they'll never achieve anything like the velocity they need to do that. Stationary, remember? I'm no ballistician, but the terminal velocity – the maximum speed it can achieve free-falling in the atmosphere – of a .177 caliber sphere is way too low to hurt anything or anybody. It might make a really interesting souvenir, though, a BB that's been up in space."

"And the militias will be in charge?"

"There will be some cooperation with the government, which will maintain a missile warning system, tell the militias where to aim their cannons and when to fire. In time, cheap orbital technologies, developed by private corporations, will allow our BB guns to be based on manned space platforms – I hope I live to see that. Meanwhile, total cost of the BSDI militia program: roughly eight hundred million dollars, mostly *not* from the federal budget. Quite a difference from the 25 *trillion* the Reagan program was supposed to cost."

"In the meantime, sir, how is America supposed to defend itself?"

"The meantime," Alex said, "is likely to be fairly long, Admiral. I have to convince the people, they have to convince Congress. I'll do it if it requires my whole term and 20 years after that. Through all of it, we'll have the missile submarine fleet to protect us."

The Army general was unsatisfied. "Mr. President, what are the Russians going to make of this? What about the Chinese or Iran or India or Pakistan? You're changing the order of things without consulting them. What about the United Nations?"

"I don't give a damn about what any of them think, General," Alex told him. "I'm doing what's best for America, as I promised I'd do."

The general stood, his chair making a screeching noise on the polished floor. "Then I guess I will withdraw, Mr. President, without prejudice. There's no place for me in this amateur small-arms military you envision. But I'd like to ask you a question, if I may."

"Ask away, General."

"What made you confident that, hearing your plans, we wouldn't just arrest you and pull off a coup?"

Alex smiled. "As in *Seven Days in May?* It was the oath you took to uphold and defend the Constitution. It's my experience that – despite Hollywood propaganda to the contrary – military people like you take that oath a lot more seriously than politicians do."

"But, sir, wouldn't that be all the *more* reason ... "

Grinning now, Alex shook his head. "Not at all. I'll bet you know the Constitution better than the average politician. If the folksinger Phil Ochs were alive today, he'd want to know what I want to know: where does it say we're supposed to be 'The Cops of the World?"

Chapter Twenty-four:
BRADY, BRADY, BRADY

> *If you're not a little bit uncomfortable with your position, it isn't radical enough. How can you be* too *principled? Take the most extreme position you can – you're claiming territory you won't have to fight for later, mostly against your "allies".*
>
> – Alexander Hope, *Looking Forward*

"...amid rumors he's about to give the United Nations '24 hours to get out of town', President Hope will speak to the National Congress of Law Enforcement Officers tonight in what promises to be another tense confrontation. The President has already done what he can at the federal level to bring the War on Drugs to an end. Now, White House spokesmen say he'll address 'other badly-needed police reforms'. This is NetPlanetNews.com. I'm Alan – "

Alex laughed. "The UN is a public nuisance – not to mention a criminal conspiracy to violate everybody's rights as a prelude to enslaving them." He turned to Dana. "That's a good idea your ex-boss has, giving them 24 hours to get off of American soil. Considering how much they've bilked taxpayers out of, I could have their buildings in New York seized and converted into a 'museum of tyranny and state terrorism' – created entirely at private expense, of course."

Dana grinned up at him. "Of course."

"Careful," Faith-Anne closed her laptop and watched the traffic outside the limousine window without really seeing it. Traffic was heavy and the going was slow. "They'll be laying for you, Daddy. I can't imagine what possessed you to accept this – "

Alex chuckled. "'Go straight to the heart of the enemy's greatest strength...'" he quoted.

"Admiral Lord Nelson?" Faith-Anne guessed. Her father seldom caught her out with famous quotations.

"No," John answered. The man looked uncomfortable in what he called his "penguin suit". Alex had insisted that he wear the chest full of combat ribbons he'd won in Vietnam. "The same guy who said, 'Great men don't move to the center, great men *move* the center.'

"He certainly moved *my* center," Dana said. "I thought I was going to die an old maid. And I very nearly did!"

Alex laughed with his wife and then turned to his daughter. "They're not all against me, sweetheart. Not every cop supports the militarization of the police that's been going on for 20 years. I have a decent relationship with street-level cops. It's their deskbound 'superiors' who have an investment in maintaining a police state."

"Darling," Dana told him. Sitting beside him on the seat, she squeezed his hand. "I hate to say it, but it's your street-level cops who'll come confiscating our guns if they're ordered to by those deskbound superiors. At least that's what the surveys tell us."

"Not after tonight," he replied. "Tonight I'll take the next step in demilitarizing the police. I'm not only going to tell them they don't have to follow orders like that, but that they'll be prosecuted if they try – I plan to mention Nuremburg a lot – and that the law will offer them no protection when the people shoot back."

* * * * * *

"Ladies and gentlemen...." Chair-scraping, coughing and clinking of silverware and glasses began to die down. "Ladies and gentlemen, children of the American Revolution, we have a problem, the gravest problem confronting America today. It's a police problem, one that everyone outside your profession seems hesitant – if not downright afraid – to talk to you about."

Leaning on the lectern, speaking off the cuff, as usual, the President glanced from side to side before he went on. He could see that Agent Smith's nose was still out of joint. Alex had forbidden the Secret Service to disarm the 3,000 convention attendees. Counting backup guns, there could be 5000 pistols and revolvers out there in the audience, affecting Smith the way Alex's gun-toting friends had affected the young female agent at the shooting range.

"Every day, we hear of some unthinkable act of brutality carried out by federal, state, or local 'law enforcement' against individuals or groups whose crime is the exercise of their unalienable individual, civil, Constitutional, and human rights. Police officers have become – more than the military ever could – the 'standing army' that was hated and feared by

America's Founding Fathers."

The murmuring began again, low, inimical. These people were used to overcoming problems with physical force; they had a low tolerance for public discussion of their shortcomings. Alex took a deep breath. It was one thing to contain the media, who might otherwise tear his administration to pieces, by confronting them as individuals. It was hard for a reporter to ask loaded questions, or write lies about a President who made it clear he knew about the little blonde secretary, the embroidered expense account, the poor old neglected mother stored in a substandard facility. Media people were more guilty of racism, sexism, every sort of prejudice and bigotry, than anyone they covered. And they were careless how they talked about it in hotel bars.

"Much of the freedom movement occupies itself trying to identify the reasons this happened and reverse them. Mostly, it was a failure on the part of the Founders to provide enforcement of the first 10 Amendments to the Constitution, commonly known as the Bill of Rights."

But confronting 3,000 police officers on what amounted to their own turf, telling them they'd done wrong morally, legally, for decades, was something else altogether. He didn't intend to make enemies where he didn't have to, but he wouldn't shrink from telling the truth to those who needed to hear it most. He looked out over the vast, dark, table-filled ballroom, wondering what would happen next.

"As long as the cause of a problem is being addressed, there's no harm in soothing the symptoms, as well. You may get a CAT-scan to see why you suffer migraines, but you also take an aspirin. I plan to suggest to Congress certain steps to treat the symptoms by which we know we've all begun living in a police state."

The murmur rose to an outraged buzz. The President put a hand up, palm out, demanding silence, a listening ear, an open mind. The quiet he received for his troubles chafed him somehow. It felt tight and hot, like a noose, just before the trapdoor opens.

"Congress may prove reluctant. If so, any of these remedies (or all of them), may be pursued by concerned individuals and groups who find them worthwhile, as conventional legislation, as constitutional or charter amendments, as initiated referenda, or as a part of settlements in lawsuits. I have little power to change what happens at the non-federal levels of government – although I can guarantee that not one cent of federal money will ever be spent again to finance local 'law enforcement' – but I mean to be as persuasive as I can."

This time there was booing and it took both hands to quiet them. Thoughts of lead balloons and screen doors in submarines went through Alex's mind.

"It's time to find answers," he said, "for ourselves, and for our children, so they won't have to live in a police state that, by accident and ignorance of history, we've erected over the past several decades." He hurried on, before they had a chance to react.

"First, there being no Constitutional provision for a national police force, in accord with the Ninth and 10th Amendments, federal 'law enforcement agencies' – the FBI, DEA, ATF, EPA, OSHA, and so on – will be abolished and their present and former employees subjected to legal scrutiny of their current and past activity. They will be forbidden to carry or use weapons of any kind, and will be permitted to operate at all, only under close supervision by local police."

A faint cheer went up and there was a smattering of applause.

"All military weapons, vehicles, and aircraft in use by these agencies will be surrendered to the population who paid for them in the first place, for use by county militia companies."

The applause died as if someone had flipped a switch. The police thought that *they* were the militia.

"Independent civilian review boards will be established to insure future federal compliance with the Bill of Rights. No plea of secrecy or 'national security' will be allowed to impede their investigations. Any willful misunderstanding of any article of the Bill of Rights on the part of elected or appointed officials will be considered evidence of an intention to commit crimes against the Constitution."

This time, having been up and down the conceptual roller coaster a couple of times, his audience waited to hear what he would say next.

"There have been local abuses, too, and there will be local reforms. I have no power to enforce such an edict, but I will do my best to see that police officers at the state, county, and local levels are required to wear uniforms while on duty, and forbidden to act in an official capacity when off duty or wearing non-uniform clothing. These uniforms will bear large individual name patches, and badge numbers readable from a distance of fifty yards. It will be a serious offense to cover or obscure them in any way. It will be a felony for officers to conceal their faces with a helmet or mask, or to wear military-style clothing."

Alex gathered that what he heard now was stunned silence.

"Vehicles used by local police must be marked and identifiable, with highly-visible registration numbers. Government agencies will be forbidden the use of helicopters which have become an instrument of state terrorism and oppression."

More stunned silence. In cartoons and situation comedies, this was the moment you heard the crickets. Alex pressed on.

"Bullet-resistant clothing, which has become a barrier between the police and the public and encouraged a contemptuous disregard for the lives, property, and rights of ordinary citizens, will be forbidden. You all were much nicer people before you started wearing Kevlar. Nor may police officers possess, carry, or employ any weapon prohibited to the public, nor carry a weapon of any kind off duty, concealed or otherwise, until laws in their jurisdiction that forbid ordinary citizens to do so the same thing have been repealed."

Someone to his left shouted, "So you *want* us to get shot?"

"I want those laws repealed," he replied. "And something else: it may seem a small thing, but you have to get rid of those Nazi-shaped helmets. Believe me, any safety they offer is offset by the fear and hatred they engender among the people whose lives, property, and rights everyone assumes you're protecting. Some of them remember what happened in Germany, even if you don't, and they know how close we are to repeating it, if somebody doesn't do something now."

He thought about the three pounds of steel hanging below his left armpit and knew what he had to say next.

"Whether you like it or not, it's time you got used to the idea of an armed citizenry. Mere possession of a weapon is no crime, no matter what local laws assert, nor is carrying it without asking anyone's permission. It's a sacred right protected by the highest law of the land. You know better than anybody else that courts in every state have ruled that no individual has a legal right to police protection, and that a choice to dial 911 – instead of defending yourself – is often a decision to die at the hands of a criminal before the police have any possibility of arriving."

Silence. What could they say to that? What were they thinking? Was he going to make real changes, or was he like the first monotheist, the pharaoh Akenaton, shouting into the wind of history and fated to be erased from it by those who came afterward?

"Things will change, now. Police departments – and 911 operators – will be required to admit, in all printed matter they distribute, on their websites, in the phone book, and in their telephone-answering messages, that nobody has a legal right to police protection. You'll be required to have it printed on your business cards, and your cars will bear the warning, as well, that the police department only 'protects and serves' the public at large.

"To avoid a continuing conflict of interest analogous to the 19th century practice of paying police for each prisoner they locked up, and to prevent overzealous enforcement of statues and ordinances, all fines and traffic revenues will be divided between the American Civil Liberties Union and Amnesty International, provided they adopt a view of the Bill of Rights which is consistent from article to article.

"There will be no more 'dynamic entry'. Possession or use of a battering ram will be a felony. You will serve warrants, seize evidence, and make arrests during business hours, by knocking on the door, not smashing it in. Handcuffs or other restraining devices may not be used on those arrested for nonviolent crimes, or for propaganda purposes or public display. Arresting officials will be held responsible under civil and criminal law for any humiliation to which arrestees, later proved innocent, are subjected.

"Our culture has learned too much, acquired too much 'technology', about restraining people – handcuffs, leg irons, belly chains, straitjackets, concrete boxes, razor-wire – like something out of the Dark Ages or the Inquisition. It's time we unlearned, forgot most of that technology, and arranged rehabilitation for those who've made a lifelong career of keeping their fellow human beings in cages.

"In 'seige' situations (which, in the future, may not be initiated simply because an individual expresses a wish to be left alone, locks himself in his house, or possesses weapons guaranteed to him by the Second Amendment), authorities will be prohibited from interrupting telephone or other utilities, or from restricting access by the media to the subjects of the operation. Nor may they play music, obnoxious sound-effects, or use lights to deprive the subjects of sleep. Such measures impair good judgement and raise the likelihood of unnecessary bloodshed before the situation can be resolved.

"In a broader sense, what's required to restore the balance is that individual officers of the military and police come to understand – and reinforce to one another – that the Bill of Rights isn't just a list of no-nos they have to find a way around, but the very thing it's most important for them to 'protect and serve'. What's more, they must prove themselves all over again – to a people who have lost any other reason to trust them – by taking a new oath to uphold, defend, and enforce, without reservation, each and every separate article of the Bill of Rights in its most radical interpretation.

"To that end, this afternoon I approved a course of study for those in your profession that will allow them to renew their commitment to the Bill of Rights."

He reached into an inside pocket, pulling out a small, stiff, colored piece of fabric.

"This uniform patch, a scroll symbolizing the Bill of Rights, superimposed on the American flag most of you already wear, indicates a promise, informed by that course of study, that you will never violate the rights of those you serve. I'll be asking the military to adopt the same insignia, and to wear their uniforms in public, to display it, as often as possible. In return, those among you who refuse to obey an order that, in good faith, you consider unlawful or unconstitutional, will receive executive clemency and, should the order prove to have been unlawful or unconstitutional, reinstatement to full pay and benefits – and promotion.

"The American people will have liberty and privacy again, whether the government wants them to or not; it will be your job to protect it. Due to an established pattern of abuse by police agencies and individual officers, all wiretapping, internet surveillance, and other invasions of privacy – or any procedure of any kind, including taxation, that requires disclosure of private financial data – will be forbidden. It was a grave mistake to grant such privileges to government in the first place. For far too long, we've erred on the side of 'law enforcement' and generated a police state as a result.

"Given the unmistakable injunction of the Second Amendment against the slightest restriction of the individual right to own and carry weapons, government possession or use of devices for detecting weapons will be illegal, punishable by fines and prison sentences.

"It is inappropriate for sovereign individuals to be sorted and tracked like breeding stock or government property. There is no provision whatever for it in the Constitution. Therefore, fingerprint records and other identification systems now maintained by the government will be destroyed and practices like fingerprinting, voiceprinting, and retinal photography forbidden.

"Beyond that, issuance of drivers' licenses, license plates, and vehicle registration will cease. They were once intended to improve the safety of the road – or prove you'd paid a vehicle tax – but like Social Security numbers, they've been abused. They've become nothing more than police state tracking devices, and are no longer worth whatever good they were supposed to accomplish.

"For individual members of the police and military, I have a personal message: the time for denial is over. If any of these proposed measures angers you, remember who did it to you. Remember that you let them do it. Until you prove the contrary to people you swore to protect and serve, you're the same as those among you who:

"Firebombed and burned a neighborhood out of existence when residents were accused of nothing more than disturbing the peace;

"Assassinated a harmless old man to steal his valuable estate;

"Shot a little boy and his dog to death, then blew his mother's head off with a high-powered rifle as she held her baby in her arms;

"Confined, terrorized, gassed, and machine-gunned 80 innocent men, women – two dozen little children – in a church that was their home;

"Shot a young goat-herder on the Mexican border because he was carrying an ancient .22 rifle to defend his flock from predators;

"Tortured and tried to dispose of political prisoners by denying them prescribed medication and proper medical assistance;

"Threatened, and confiscated evidence from, investigators who questioned a cover-up of an airline crash that killed hundreds;

"Stomped kittens to death in an attempt to intimidate innocent victims of an illegal raid against an gun show promoter;

"And committed thousands of other acts that have transformed a once-free country into a horror-filled abyss. Think back to when you playing with your whistle, toy handcuffs, and plastic revolver. Did you want to be a cop more than anything so your fellow human beings would be *afraid* of you, or did you have something nobler in mind?

"It's time to stand down. Just as the Cold War is over and it's time for the Pentagon to stand down, the War on Drugs – intended to destroy the Constitution you all swore to uphold and defend – is over, too. Don't allow socialists to use your body and mind to force illegal, immoral, *alien* ideas on an unwilling populace. From now on, you are no longer 'law enforcement officers', you are keepers of the peace, stewards of the American way of life. Your goal must be to enforce the highest law of the land, the Bill of Rights. Indeed, it's the justification for your existence and that of the government.

"Don't let your overpaid 'superiors' tell you what the Bill of Rights means. Remember your oath. Don't let judges and lawyers – who stand to benefit from the destruction of the Bill of Rights – tell you what it means. Remember your oath and do what most public officials haven't done for half a century: think for yourself.

"Begin by asking yourself a question: if you were one of America's Founders and you'd just fought a successful revolution against the most powerful, ruthless, and heavy-handed government on Earth, and the last thing in the world you wanted for yourself or your children or your grandchildren was to find yourself beneath the brutal heel of its jackboot again, what would you want the Bill of Rights to mean?

"If that powerful, ruthless, heavy-handed government's first act had been to try to take your guns, would you have written a Second Amendment to guarantee its 'right' to own and carry weapons? Or would you have forbid it from ever having anything to say about your guns?

"The War on Drugs is over. Think back: every dime ever spent on it has made the problem worse. Millions of decent folks believe that, from the outset, it was never meant as anything but a war against the people of America. It's time to end that war, to abolish the FBI, DEA, ATF, and every other federal agency not mentioned in the Constitution, and for that reason alone, is illegal.

"As of this moment, hiring for these agencies is shut off. Those who survive scrutiny of their past activities will be made US marshals and assigned to Bill of Rights enforcement. As such, they will be turned loose on politicians, bureaucrats, and judges, instead of – "

Somebody screamed, "You're not gonna take my pension!"

A shot rang out – Alex clutched at his chest.

Chapter Twenty-five: *LINDSAY ROGERS*

> *Those who lead through authority have rivals on whom they must expend as much energy and attention as they do on their enemies. Those who lead by example have enemies, but no rivals.*
>
> – Alexander Hope, *Looking Forward*

It was more pleasant inside the little country post office than out, where the summer rain fell in fat, cold, wind-driven drops. Mrs. Revets, on crutches the past six weeks, was recovering from a long-overdue operation on her knees, and wasn't looking forward to venturing out into the weather, even if it was just to get to her car.

Opening her glass-fronted rental box with a key, she pulled out a bundle of papers – she hadn't collected her mail in a couple of weeks – and was annoyed when a small yellow booklet in a clear plastic envelope fell onto the muddy floor. As she stooped to pick it up, an awkward and painful task with her crutches, on the booklet's cover she read the words, "UNITED NATIONS IS KILLING YOUR FREEDOMS!"

"Let me do that for you, Mrs. Revets."

As he handed her the booklet, she looked into the

kindly face of the local postmaster, Rex Frederick, a man she'd known for 50 years. They'd gone to high school together in this little town; she'd taught each of his three children in turn at the local public school; his grandson had been in the last class she'd taught before retiring.

"'Mrs. Revets?'" she repeated. "Since when did you stop calling me by my Christian name, Rex Federick? As if we hadn't grown up together, as if we hadn't made that unchaperoned trip to Springfield with Warren and Henrietta and the McNulty twins, back in the summer of '62!"

The postmaster blushed. He still wondered sometimes how they'd gotten away with that. She'd married Warren four years later – they'd all graduated 1964 – and he'd married Henrietta when he came back from the Navy. The McNulty twins had moved to California and nobody here had seen or heard from them again.

"You've got me there, Viola. Anything else I can do for you this morning? How about a cup of coffee – it's terrible tasting but hot."

"No, thank you, Rex. But you could tell me what this thing is." She held out the yellow booklet in its transparent wrapper."

"That," he replied. "You'll find one in every box this morning, and in every residential mailbox, too. It was all over the news. They were sent out by a private foundation backed by the Hope Corporation, which means they're actually from President Hope. Other billionaires – Bill Gates, Warren Buffet – seem to spend their money trying to cram socialism down everybody's throats. Too bad they can't be more like Alexander Hope."

"That man!" Dead or not, Viola had voted for the former first lady. "Rex, I was a teacher for 30 years. I collected money for UNICEF at Hallowe'en, and celebrated Human Rights Day. This...this..."She held the booklet out at arm's length, at a loss for words.

"Yes, Viola, what about it?" Truth was, he was enjoying this.

She was exasperated. "It's right-wing propaganda!"

The postmaster sighed. Half a century ago, he'd briefly considered going steady with Viola instead of Henrietta. She was prettier and had a certain style like nobody else in their tiny high school. Not for the first time, he was glad he hadn't. Viola couldn't see a difference between her feelings and her thoughts, between the way she wanted things to be and the way they actually were. She was kindly, generous with everyone, but Warren had died a decade ago, old before his time.

"Viola, you haven't read it yet. Did you ever compare the UN's Universal Declaration of Human Rights with our own Bill of Rights?"

"Why, no, Rex. I know the Bill of Rights pretty well, of course. And I read through the Declaration once or twice, a long time ago. I guess I just assumed they were the same thing, more or less."

"Mostly less, Viola. Under the Bill of Rights, government exists only with the permission of the people, whom it was created to serve. Under the Declaration, there are no rights, in fact, only privileges to be granted (or withheld) by governments that people are obligated to obey without question or hesitation."

Handing the rest of her mail to Rex, she tore

open the plastic bag and extracted the small booklet. "Why, it's a comic book! Apparently part of a series produced by a group called Jews for the Preservation of Firearms Ownership – they must be a minority within a minority!"

The full title was *Gran'pa Jack Exposes How the United Nations Is Killing your Freedoms!* Inside was the story, in comic book form, of a patriot striving to undo the "brainwashing" the public schools had imposed on his grandchildren.

"What's wrong with a comic book?" Rex asked. "I understand that next week, they're sending one out about how to get a fair trial in America – it's about that jury nullification the President is always mentioning at the end of his speeches."

"Nothing at all. I always thought it was a terrible shame Classic Illustrated went out of business before I got started. It would have made teaching *Silas Marner* easier." She leafed through the little book. "It says here the Declaration fails to protect us from state established religion, or from government quartering troops in our homes. Why would they leave out a thing like that, Rex?"

He shrugged. "I imagine for the same reason it forgets to mention search warrants, grand juries, and rules against double jeopardy, excessive bail, or seizure of property without compensation. For the same reason it fails to guarantee a speedy trial, the right to an attorney, a jury trial in the same venue where the crime occurred, the right to subpoena witnesses, and to confront your accuser."

They walked slowly to the counter, where he lifted a section and went to the coffee pot. Viola indicated that she'd changed her mind. He brought a stool out for her, poured two cups and offered her sugar and half-and-half he kept in a tiny refrigerator.

"Remember," he began again, "that this Declaration was written specifically to please UN member states, the very sort of monsters who rounded up and murdered millions of Jews in Germany, farmers in Russia, property owners and people who were literate in China and Cambodia, and so on. The whole idea is to subordinate individual rights to the power of the state, and impose socialism on everybody by inventing 'rights' – to the wealth, time, and energy of others – that don't actually exist."

She made a clucking sound. "Rex, you sound just like our old Civics teacher, Mr. Sullivan."

"He was always my favorite. He would have pointed out that the Declaration fails to protect citizen militias and the individual right to own and carry weapons. In fact it's a major objective of the UN to seize and destroy every privately-owned weapon in the world."

"That might not be such a bad thing. There are too many guns out there in the wrong hands, and children killing children with them."

"That's what the Jews said, Viola, just before they were rounded up and sent off in cattle cars to camps where they were murdered!"

Viola laughed. "I was just pushing your buttons. I know how you feel about gun ownership, the whole town does. Besides," she patted her oversized handbag. "I practice a little gun ownership, myself!"

They laughed together and drank their coffee.

* * * * * *

John Pondoro and Agent Smith both plunged

into the audience and a jungle of 375 tables and 3000 chairs. Cap was already out there somewhere. Men shouted hoarsely at no one in particular. Women made a lot of high-pitched, silly noises. Most of them were crouching on the floor, many with their guns drawn.

Alex had his Witness out of the nylon shoulder holster before he thought about it. He preferred his plastic hip-holster, and hadn't realized he'd acquired the reflex to snatch across his chest at a gun under his left armpit. As he crouched behind the lectern (they'd brought it with them, it was lined with half an inch of steel), there were flashes that didn't quite startle him enough to shoot at them. Tomorrow's websites and papers, he knew, would show him armed, ready to fight. Some, even in his own party, would think that was a bad thing.

John and Cap returned to the podium, accompanied by a tall, angular 60ish man, with a walrus moustache, receding hairline, and a face that had seen a lot of outdoors.

"This is Deputy Sheriff Lindsay Rogers," John told Alex.

"*Retired* deputy sheriff," the man corrected. "Larimer County, Colorado." He thrust a weathered, long-fingered hand up, toward the President. Alex came out from behind the lectern, stepped down from the dais, shifted the Witness to his left and took the man's hand.

"Retired deputy sheriff," John conceded. "He saved your life, Mr. President. That shot we heard was his and it almost got him killed by the Secret Service. Some guy was drawing a bead on you."

Cap added, "Faith-Anne, once she got her .38

back in her purse and her hands stopped shaking enough to consult her laptop, says he wasn't a cop. Rogers blew his head off with a great big Para-Ordnance .45."

"The Secret Service took my gun," Rogers complained. "How do I go about getting it back?"

Alex reversed his hold on the Witness and thrust the grip at the stranger. "I'll get it back for you, Deputy. Until I do, take mine."

* * * * * *

"Look at this! Just look at this!" The California Senator opened a huge manila envelope and spilled half a bushel of yellow pamphlets over the table they were sitting at in the bar they all occupied between sessions in the House and Senate.

The Senator from New York jerked back as a dozen booklets spilled into his lap and onto the floor. "For heaven's sake, Diane, you nearly spilled my drink! What are these things, anyway?"

"Constitutionalist propaganda," said the Colorado congresswoman, jowls bobbing as she talked, "sent to every household in America – a hundred million of them – printing and postage paid by our beloved President. And there wasn't anything we could do to stop it."

The California Senator sat down at one end of the horseshoe-shaped booth. "We stopped these!" she boasted. "Part of a truckload that postal workers in the District refused to deliver. Imagine millions of black residents of Washington, D.C. being told they have a right to own guns, after all the work we've done, taking them away!"

"Why do I have," said the Democratic leader of

the House. “no inclination to take off my Kevwar when I go out at night? And by the way, do thothe postaw workews know they’we going to jail?”

“Shut up, Bee!” the California Senator demanded. “We’ve got to do something about this!”

“Well somebody tried something this afternoon,” the New York Senator measured his words carefully. “But it doesn’t seem to have worked. We need to try something else, and I know just the thing ... “

* * * * * *

Agent Smith blocked the way, hands at chest level, palms out.

“I can’t let you do that, Mr. President! My bosses will have my eyeballs poached on toast!” There was pleading in the man’s voice. Alex felt genuine sympathy for him. But like all professionals, sooner or later – doctors, architects, literary agents, lawyers – he’d forgotten, momentarily, who worked for whom.

“Refer your bosses to me, Agent Smith,” Alex told him, feeling suddenly very silly. All he wanted was to cross a room – a downtown Washington, DC hotel ballroom – on his own feet. Having to beg somebody or make a fuss to get it done was ridiculous. “I mean to have a look at that body before the city, or whoever, carts it away. You can come with me if you want to. If not, stand aside. Please.”

Agent Smith sighed, cast his gaze down at his highly-polished shoes, and shook his head. “Very well, sir. I’ll come with you.” He started whispering into his left jacket sleeve.

“Good,” declared the President. “You watch my back and John can watch my front, since I was foolish enough to let somebody borrow my gun. Dana?

Faith-Anne? Cap?" Dana put her hand over her stomach and rolled her eyes, but nodded. His daughter gave him a reluctant but willing look. Cap put a hand on her shoulder and together, they proceeded toward the center of the big room where the corpse, by now, was the center of attention for paramedics – who were just packing their equipment up, there having been no use for it – police photographers, and the medical examiner, working under the scrutiny of a dozen Secret Service people.

The well-dressed body of the would-be assassin lay on its back, the legs and arms splayed on the carpet. Between the corpse's feet lay an enormous stainless steel Colt Anaconda revolver with ".44 Magnum" stamped along its six inch barrel. The head was turned toward the right and was the center of a huge dark, glistening stain that was still spreading. Alex had seen dead bodies before – and smelled them, as well. This one had relaxed everything completely.

There was a neat circular entrance wound as big as Alex's thumb, roughly an inch higher than the midpoint between the right ear and eye. Although it was turned away, Alex could see matted hair on the left side, and white matter – brain tissue – leaking from an exit wound hidden in the matted hair. There would be suits, uniforms, and evening dresses at the drycleaner's tonight. Or in the dumpster.

He wondered what had become of the bullet.

Alex turned to look at his companions. Dana was pale and shaky, but grinned at him gamely. She came to him and he put his arms around her. Faith-Anne shrugged. "It isn't as bad as I thought. He's dead and you're alive, Daddy. That's about as good as it gets."

"Have you ever got that right!" Dana said.

"So who is he?" Alex asked nobody in particular. He thought the man looked vaguely familiar, but couldn't be sure, given the condition of the corpse and the circumstances in general.

"Not one of us," a voice behind Alex declared. He turned to see an individual of about 65, in Tony Lama python cowboy boots, dark slacks and a western-cut sportscoat. What hair he had left (mostly what he had was shiny pink scalp) was white and trimmed neatly. He affected a moustache rather like Deputy Rogers'. Around the neck of his pinstriped white shirt was a string tie with a badge-shaped silver slide.

The man put his hand out toward Alex. "I'm Gabe Henderson, Mr. President, former sheriff of Laramie County, Wyoming, and President of the National Congress of Law Enforcement Officers. I don't want to bother you, but they hauled Lindsay Rogers away, and I wanted to find out if the man who saved your life is in trouble for doing it."

"He'd better not be." Agent Smith had been listening. He talked into his cuff again, then listened. "They've turned around and are bringing him back. They found your pistol on him, Mr. President."

"Tell them to give it back right now – and if he doesn't have his own piece back in 24 hours, tell them heads are going to roll. See that he gets that .44 magnum, too, once they're through with it – he certainly earned it."

"Yes, sir." Agent Smith went back to his radio.

"Will that do, Sheriff Henderson?" Alex asked.

"That'll do, sir. I didn't vote for you – in fact, with the Republican candidate in jail for kiddie porn, I didn't vote at all – but I will next time."

Alex nodded. "Thanks."

* * * * * *

One of the few changes Alex had made to the Oval Office was to install a large computer monitor in place of the traditional four TV sets, each tuned to a different network. Alex seldom paid attention to the networks, which were dying the slow death of the unwatched in any case, although he could have if he'd wished, cybernetically dividing the screen he was watching now into several parts.

Faith-Anne and Dana were watching with him. If Dana had ever missed doing the job she was watching now, she'd never said so to him. Alex admired her and worried about her at the same time.

"As expected," intoned a commentator who did not represent any of the traditional networks, "one Hope legislative proposal after another has met with blistering opposition from both major parties, and the establishment mass media – none more so than his recently-announced decision to take the US out of the United Nations."

Stock footage of Alex was run briefly, speaking to an audience about the threat the United Nations posed to America and the Bill of Rights. The sound-byte had him warning them that the UN's Universal Declaration of Human Rights was a fraud that failed to guarantee any of the rights Americans take for granted. When the view switched to the studio, the graphic in the background over the speaker's shoulder showed the familiar UN buildings, with the red circle and slash of the European "forbidden" sign superimposed over it.

"However – most disappointingly for the President – his own Free Libertarian Party of America is sharply critical of him, as well, a few of its members attacking him for not effecting change quickly enough, and a majority, ironically, for effecting it too quickly."

The bearded image of Dana's former employer was replaced with that of a thin, sharp-featured middle-aged woman labeled NORAH YASSER, FLPA NATIONAL CHAIRPERSON. She wore a severe gray suit, white blouse, and pearls.

"Correct, Alan," she said, apparently responding to a question asked earlier. "By moving so hastily, and in such a radical direction, Hope is taking too many chances. If any of his programs fail, they could all be tarnished, and the credibility and future aspirations of the FLPA could also be damaged, possibly beyond repair."

"What credibility? What future aspirations?" Faith-Anne exclaimed. "Before Daddy came along, the FLPA wallowed for 40 years without electing a candidate to any office higher than dogcatcher!"

"But Ms. Yasser," the off-camera interviewer replied, unaware he was making the President's daughter furious, "isn't withdrawal from the United Nations a longstanding plank in the FLPA platform?"

The woman seemed genuinely startled that anyone had actually taken the time to read the FLPA platform. "Yes, Alan, it is. We'll withdraw ...eventually...when the time is right."

The camera switched to an earlier incarnation of the interviewer, sitting opposite the FLPA official, a three-ring notebook open in his lap. Alex made a note to send the man a state-of-the-art laptop. "And you feel that President Hope's timing of this matter is wrong?"

"It's all wrong, Alan," Yasser replied. "And, apparently, I'm not the only one who thinks so. I understand the Democrats in the House introduced a formal bill of impeachment against Hope this afternoon."

He was incredulous. "On the same day as an assassination attempt? With his picture above the fold on the front page of every paper on the planet, and on every newssite on the World Wide Web, gun in hand, heroically prepared to defend himself? Talk about bad timing!"

Yasser shook her head. "In the end, that picture is bound to do him – and us – more harm than good. That's why the FLPA has deemphasized the Second Amendment over the past few years – the polls are all against it. Who does Hope think he is, anyway? James Bond? John Wayne?" She sighed, "I suppose it could be worse. At least we have another libertarian – a better libertarian – to replace him."

The interviewer blinked. "And who would that be?"

"Why, Vice President Forrey Nadalindov, of course! He'd be here with me, except that Hope sent him to Siberia earlier this week to observe our troop withdrawal there."

Alex, Faith-Anne, and Dana laughed out loud.

* * * * * *

Meanwhile, in New York City, in the United Nations offices of the representative of an eastern European member nation who had watched his communist President's bodyguards neatly executed by the country's Olympic team, using their .22 caliber target pistols, sensitive documents were being shredded and reshredded, while everything else was being packed.

CHAPTER TWENTY-SIX: *GENTLEMEN OF THE CLUB*

> *The most dangerous and successful conspiracies take place in public, in plain sight, under the clear, bright light of day – usually with TV cameras focused on them.*
>
> – Alexander Hope, *Looking Forward*

The Democratic leader of the United States Senate felt out of place. This was Republican territory. He was probably the least likely member of his party to seek Republican company, let alone Republican cooperation. But it was absolutely vital, and he was the only one who could do it.

The entire building smelled faintly of very expensive cigar smoke. The hallway where they'd agreed to meet, to which he'd been guided by a member of the uniformly young, attractive facilities staff, was very expensively carpeted, a gallery, one long side constructed entirely of very expensive tinted glass that looked out onto a well-manicured, sparkling emerald, very expensive lawn, in the center of which lay an azure jewel sparkling in the August sun, a large, very expensive swimming pool with an enormous transparent plastic canopy.

That must have been very expensive, too.

Swallowing his distaste, the Democratic leader of the Senate stuck out a hand. "Tom! Good to see you!"

"Charlie!" His opposite number in the Senate smelled of gratuitous exercise. The fellow was wearing a sodden sweatshirt, gym shorts, a bright yellow terrycloth headband, and a pair of matching bands on his wrists. He looked like an exceptionally bad impressionist doing Olivia Newton-John. He even had a racquetball racquet tucked under one arm.

Despite the absorbent wristbands, the hand he offered was damp. The Democrat released it, resisting an urge to wipe his own hand on the pants of an Armani suit that cost more than most American families earned in three months.

He sighed inwardly. This shrine to elite privilege and obscene wealth annoyed him deeply. Democrats could live like this because the people wanted them to, because they had all the right intentions, but not vicious, greedy Republicans. "Let's go somewhere quiet and have a drink, Tom, we've got business to discuss."

"So I've heard, Charlie, so I've heard. But your money's no good here, This is my club. Just name your poison." The Republican hailed a passing waitress in establishment livery and ordered himself a bloody maria – spicy tomato juice and well-aged tequila with a big sprig of celery.

"Glenfiddich, neat," the Democrat mumbled to the waitress, hating himself for noticing that she was very young, extremely wholesome, and predictably beautiful. "My club," the Republican Senator had bellowed at him crudely, "my club" – exactly what anyone would expect from a Neanderthal Man.

"We'll be in the dressing room," the Republican

added, taking the Democrat's elbow – the Senator worried about his suit again – and steering him in the proper direction. "It's a mite cozier than it may sound, Charlie."

* * * * * *

"What do you *mean* you won't help?" The Democratic leader of the United States Senate was incredulous. He felt that he'd sacrificed his purity and integrity by coming into enemy territory like this, and now he was being betrayed for it. "Didn't you vote to impeach the man just a few weeks ago?"

"Now, Charlie..." The Republican Senator knocked a long ash off his cigar and settled deeper into the overstuffed, leather-upholstered chair he occupied. A servant, male this time, since it was the men's dressing room, had brought him a terrycloth robe and taken the head and wristbands away. The Republican Senator's tall drink sat sweating on a little stand, beside the crystal ashtray and a tasteful reading lamp. On the tiny table lay a folded copy of *The Wall Street Journal*, and on a nearby computer terminal, the front page of NetPlanetNews.com was visible.

"Don't 'Now Charlie' me, Tom!" The Democratic leader of the Senate was suddenly furious. If anything, this room was making him even more angry than the rest of the club. Called the "dressing room", it was more like the reading room in an old-fashioned English men's club, with its dark woodwork, its wainscotted walls, and its comfortable, heavy furniture. The ceiling was low, however, acoustically tiled, and there were engineered partitions and air-curtains scattered around to assure privacy.

"Al Hope is a menace to both our parties! We can

get rid of him, only if we agree to work together! The Vice President has shown a willingness to – "

"To what, Charlie? Sell him down the river? Word is, Nadalindov wanted to do that before Hope was ever nominated. Haven't you noticed how the man cuts his own Administration down every chance he gets, or that the President returns the favor by sending him on one 'goodwill mission' after another to royal hellholes like Nepal and Tierra del Fuego?" The Republican chuckled to himself. "I'd do the same thing. Hope's pretty funny, at that!"

The Democrat sniffed. "Of course I'd noticed. But that only makes Nadalindov more – "

"Nadalindov's an idiot," the Republican said, "who couldn't make it in the big Republican Party, and switched to the little libertarian one where he thought he'd wind up being the Big Frog. The trouble is, Charlie, in my part of the country, big frogs get gigged and cut up and their legs eaten. Same thing's about to happen to Nadalindov, by and by, I expect."

The Democrat shook his head. "But surely that's not why – "

"No, that's not why, at all, Charlie. I've just been looking at the polls, is all. You want to carve Hope's gizzard out because of what he's done about the UN, your beloved BATF, or because, very gradually, he's presiding over the shutting-down of the public school system. Shucks, we wanted to impeach him over what he's done to the DOD and what he plans to do to the police. But Charlie, there's a huge, huge problem."

"The polls?" asked the Democrat.

"The _people_ – at least enough of them to make a difference. I admit, I never had any idea how much contempt the United Nations is held in, where the heartland of this nation – what you Democrats call 'flyover country' – is concerned, or how much people out there loathe and despise the public schools, or enjoy the power of a 'fully informed jury'. It isn't the kind of thing we ever thought to ask about before this."

The Democrat took a big gulp of his drink. "Not to mention this blasted militia thing he's so hot about – a bunch of overgrown Boy Scouts with guns!"

"You need to learn to relax, son. That's no way at all to respect a single-malt whisky." The Republican puffed on his cigar and took a sip of his own drink. "In my day, Charlie, Boy Scouts all had guns and could use 'em. Kinda like the idea, myself. When I retire I might just join a militia company. While you, on the other hand, will have to go back to selling used – "

"I *never!*" The Democrat was outraged.

"You will, now, Charlie, my lad," the Republican Senator chuckled, childishly pleased to have gotten a rise out of his Democratic rival. "You will now."

* * * * * *

"Uncle Bob?" It was well past midnight. Dana was fast asleep, but he'd stayed up to write his Thanksgiving address to the nation, and now he was hungry.

For some reason, at least half of the lights were off in the White House kitchen. One far corner in particular lay in almost complete darkness.

From that corner came a voice. "Don't you come in here...Mr. President."

"What?" Alex was astonished – and confused.

The voice had been that of Uncle Bob, though, the last two words preceded by a sort of gasping wheeze.

The man could be heard taking a deep, labored breath. "I said, don't come in here, sir. I don't know if I finished him off or he's just playing possum."

"Playing – " Alex suddenly understood. He drew his Witness .40 from beneath his jacket. Deputy Rogers' Para-Ordnance .45 had been returned in considerably less than 24 hours – the authorities having determined, unnecessarily, that it was, indeed, the very gun that had been used to stop a would-be presidential assassin – along with the assassin's revolver, letter of thanks from Alex, and a brand new box of Federal Hydrashock .45s.

Behind Alex now, the young Marine corporal who had accompanied him down to the kitchen – he'd been looking forward to a bacon, lettuce, and tomato sandwich he'd been promised – unfastened the flap of his dress holster and extracted the .45 caliber SIG-Sauer P220 automatic he was carrying in it.

Alex felt himself being pushed aside as the corporal put himself between the President and whoever the "he" was that might be playing possum. Alex grudgingly let it happen. He probably had more combat experience than this kid, but he was also 40 years older and had much slower reflexes.

"John," he addressed the air inside the big room. "Or Cap. I hope you're listening and watching. It appears we have a situation here in the kitchen."

Just then, Uncle Bob began coughing. The sound, a rasping gurgle, was horrible and painful to listen to. It was clear that the old man was badly hurt.

They found him sitting on the floor, slumped against a cabinet, a nine-inch chef's knife in his left hand. The knife, his arm up to the elbow, and his midsection were black and slick with blood. Alex grabbed the nearest thing he could find – a big dish towel – to press against the center of the bloodstain.

"A little more to the left, if you don't mind, Mr. President," Uncle Bob wheezed. "I think I've been shot in the liver." The last word was a whisper.

"Here it is, Mr. President!" The corporal flipped a light switch. Lying on the floor less than 10 feet away from Uncle Bob was the body of a younger man dressed in kitchen whites. Part of the man's insides had spilled out onto the floor. A Ruger Mark II .22 pistol – with a noise suppressor on the barrel – was still clenched in his hand.

"Is he ... ?" the President began. He knew the answer already.

"He sure is, sir! Dead as Kelsey's – I mean, dead as a doornail, sir." The young Marine sounded almost admiring. "Uncle Bob, you sure did a job and a half on this guy. Why, he's opened up like a brook trout!"

Uncle Bob made a noise that may have been a satisfied chuckle or sigh of pain. Alex kept pressure on the wound – there was no exit wound as far as he could tell. He'd dealt with injuries like this – and the one 10 feet away – in Vietnam.

Suddenly, there was a lot of noise just outside the kitchen entrance. Two more Marines with guns drawn came though, followed by a pair of Agent Smith's finest with submachineguns. (Agent Smith himself had taken a rare week off to visit his ailing mother.) Next came paramedics with a gurney and big red plastic boxes. One knelt and slid his hands under Alex's.

"I've got him, sir – if we could have a little more

room, now, please?" The paramedic's touch and voice were surprisingly gentle for a football player-sized figure with heavy, almost blue five o'clock shadow.

Alex nodded and stood, suddenly aware for the first time that his hands and the sleeves and front of his shirt and jacket were drenched in sticky crimson, his favorite J. Garcia necktie would never be the same, and the odor of the blood took him right back to Southeast Asia. He looked around, found his big autopistol where he'd laid it on a worktable, and hesitated. Blood is immensely destructive to fine steel machinery.

"Got it, Boss," John told him. The big man put his equally big .45 caliber Glock Model 21 away in its shoulder holster. He picked up the EAA Witness .40 and pushed it into his waistband. A few feet away, Cap watched two more of the paramedics finish their examination of the apparent assailant, determine to their own satisfaction that he was as thoroughly dead as the young Marine had said he was, and turn their attention to Uncle Bob.

As soon as they were away from the body, one of the Secret Service detail staked himself out over the suppressed Ruger .22 autopistol, now lying on the bloody tiled floor beside the body, making certain it remained untouched.

Another was watching the big knife that Uncle Bob had wielded so effectively. It lay on the floor beside him now.

"Thanks, John," Alex said. To the paramedics: "How is he?"

"Don't know yet," said the senior emergency team member, a short, tough-looking middle-aged woman with a New York accent and her gray hair cut in a pageboy. She patted Uncle Bob gently on the shoulder. Incredibly, the man was still conscious. "I've treated much worse that lived."

"Through your treatment?" Uncle Bob wheezed up at her.

The paramedic turned to Alex. "He's okay if he makes lame jokes. And that was lame, Uncle Bob, real lame. But you're going to owe me a soufflé, at least."

"At least. Have 'em check the cake." Uncle Bob closed his eyes and exhaled.

"He's resting easy, don't worry," said the paramedic. "He's saying silly things, but his vitals are stable. He's lost a lot of blood, but we're getting it replaced as fast as we can. Get him to Bethesda and he'll be fine. And Mr. President, you're pretty lucky, yourself. It looks like Uncle Bob here forced himself to stay conscious, just so he could warn you."

Alex nodded. "It does, at that. I hope he lives so I can give him a medal."

They had the unconscious man on the gurney now. The President, John, Cap, and what Alex thought of as the original cast of World War II followed the paramedics out to where they could watch Uncle Bob being loaded onto Marine One and whisked away. There was nothing in the world, Alex realized again, like the high-pitched keening of a helicopter's turbines, and the pounding of the rotors through the night air were like the beating of a giant's heart.

They went back to the kitchen – Cap excused himself to make some investigative phonecalls – to watch the forensic people going over the room. The body would remain here for a little while longer. City police had been notified and their detectives were going through security now.

November 5, 2010, Alex thought. Twenty-three months in office. And this was the third – no, make that the fourth – violent assault on his household in two and a half years, counting what Chip had done to Dana, later to Alex himself, and then the banquet attempt in June. Alex meant to get to the bottom of it.

"He wasn't saying silly things – look at that." John pointed to a worktable in the corner. On a plate lay a small chocolate torte of a kind that Alex liked very much, and which Uncle Bob occasionally made for him. Apparently it had just been iced, because a bowl of frosting and the used tools were still lying there. There was also a glass or plastic vial about the size of an AA battery, filled with an oily-looking yellow fluid.

"My guess?" John answered the unasked question. "Uncle Bob got done and stepped away for a minute. This guy tried to poison the cake and got caught."

Alex nodded, suppressing a cold internal chill and a shudder. "Doesn't rycin look like that?"

John raised his eyebrows. "The stuff the commies used to kill that Bulgarian freedom broadcaster in London in the 60s? If it is rycin, there's enough in there to wipe out the whole District of Columbia!"

"Let me know what's in the vial, and what fingerprints are on the outside."

"You got it, Boss," said John. He paused and glanced down at the PDA he held in his left hand. "It's Cap. We have some information on the dead cook, now. He was one of several extra hands the White House took on when the you were originally inaugurated, and was cleared by the FBI and the Secret

Service. He worked out so well that they kept him on after that. According to Bob Anson's wife, he liked the new kid very much and even took him home to Thanksgiving dinner with my family."

Alex shuddered.

"Unfortunately," John went on, the person he said he was – and a copy of whose birth certificate he used to get a Social Security number – actually died 25 years ago at the age of 18 months and was buried in El Paso, Texas."

"Makes sense," said the President.

John wasn't through. "You do realize that every ounce of food in this place is going to be thrown out and the kitchen scoured for poisons, don't you? Until it's done, we're all going to end up eating Scottish food."

Alex blinked. "Scottish food? Like haggis? Why?"

"No, Scottish food, like MacDonald's. I could use a Big Mac right now."

Alex nodded. So could he.

* * * * * *

Elsewhere in the city, the Democratic leader of the Senate sat up in his bed, pointed the remote control at the TV set across the room, and turned it off. So *that* was why his Republican counterpart had refused to have anything to do with the most recent attempt to impeach the President. Why bother, when you have a method in mind that's much more direct?

Of course they were Republicans. They'd bungled it again, getting their own agent killed in the process and injuring some kind of White House menial, but then you can't make an omelette without breaking eggs, he quoted Mussolini (or whoever it was) to himself, and it's the thought that counts.

The Senator grinned, settled into his pillows, and turned off the light.

* * * * * *

Meanwhile, in rural Maryland, the Republican leader of the United States Senate turned to his wife, beside him in bed, reading a romance novel. "Well, my dear," he said, "I guess the Democrats gave up on that impeachment idea of theirs, after all, and cut straight to the chase. Very messy."

"Is that so?" his wife said, ignoring him.

"It sure is. I'd feel responsible – for turning 'em down, you see – but they're such blithering incompetents, it's almost fun to watch 'em work!"

Chapter Twenty-seven: *NORAH YASSER*

"The perfect is the enemy of the good," you say?
I say that if nobody ever insisted on the perfect,
there'd never be *any good.*

– Alexander Hope, *Looking Forward*

"Relax, Forrey," said the President. "I didn't ask you here to chew you out. You're doing such a swell job as this Administration's ambassador of good will, I have a new and challenging assignment for you."

Standing at a sort of parade-rest in front of the large, circular table, Nadalindov gulped back his anger and humiliation. "New and challenging?"

Dressed in t-shirt and jeans and a faded levi jacket that he hadn't worn since before the 2008 FLPA convention, Alex leaned back against the fake leather upholstery in the booth he occupied, one eye on a TV monitor hanging from the ceiling nearby. Somewhere in the world they were playing baseball tonight, instead of politics. He didn't care who it was or where they were, he just wanted to get this over with and watch.

"That's right, Forrey," he informed the Vice President. "New. And challenging."

Handmade stained glass lamps hung low on

chains over every table. There were ski poles, baseball bats, and tennis rackets along the walls, up near the ceiling, pictures of sports and movie celebrities, and a cheerful young woman was going from table to table making balloon animals for the children. The Muzak was playing eviscerated renditions of Bob Dylan protest songs. The Vice President looked about desperately for a chair to drag up to the table, but the loose chairs all seemed to be taken by Secret Service agents in shockingly informal attire – for them.

They'd taken their ties off.

He couldn't sit in the booth with the President. One end of the big circular bench was occupied by Agent Smith, wearing Dockers, Hush Puppies, and a crisp blue buttoned-down office shirt – no tie – under a sportscoat at least a decade out of style. Looking very uncomfortable while he did it, he was pretending to be sipping at a glass of iced tea.

The other end was taken up by John Pondoro who looked natural and comfortable in his worn bluejeans, cowboy boots, and colorful western shirt. The tall amber beer before him on the table hadn't been touched yet. Nadalindov noticed he had a big hand inside his African-style bush jacket. The whole thing felt horribly to Nadalindov like a scene from *The Godfather.*

Cap Pondoro sat away from everybody else in the Presidential party, at the oval bar in the center of the room, pretending to be a civilian. He wore a Hawaiian shirt. In front of him was a drink with a little paper parasol in it.

He stood, instead. "Mr. President, I've been to the Isle of Skye as your representative, and every other postage stamp-sized island in the world. I've been to every village within a stone's throw of the Arctic Circle and milked reindeer with Laplanders, Samoyeds, and Siberians. I've climbed Mount Kenya and Mount Kilimanjaro, visited Madagascar, toured ancient ruins on Sri Lanka, Edmund Hillary's base camp near Everest, and the Krakatoa crater. I've had 589 inoculations since I was sworn in – 589! – and had to take long, painful cures anyway, for at least three dozen diseases there aren't any inoculations for! I've been to *Borneo!* What American Vice President has ever been to *Borneo?*"

Alex grinned and nodded reassuringly at the man. Dinner hadn't been ordered yet. He had a tall Coca-Cola in front of him, but wished it was one of the wonderful "Perfect Margaritas" the restaurant chain was famous for.

"You're certainly the first, as far as I know, Forrey, and let me tell you, you're doing a great job! But as I say, now you can relax. All I want you to do now is go down and pay our American scientific research stations in Antarctica a visit. Spend a few weeks there, and let our lonely scientists know what a great job I think *they're* doing, too."

Nadalindov blanched. "A few weeks – "

"Play baseball, Forrey." the President told him, gesturing toward a bat and ball and fielder's glove that had been stapled to the wall. "I hear that baseball's very big down there. When the weather's warm enough and the sun is shining – 24 hours a day, right now, seven days a week – and there's no wind, they play shirts and skins, right out there on the ice. I saw it myself once, Forrey, in a Walt Disney documentary."

The Vice President stood silently for a moment, breathing, with his eyes closed, and his fists lightly clenched at his sides. Then: "Mr. President, on my left ankle I have scars from a snakebite I got in South Africa. A black mamba. Or a krait – opinions vary. They tell me I'm lucky to be alive, in any case; another eight seconds and I wouldn't be. I had surgery last September on my right elbow where a crocodile bit it in Mali – that's in Africa, too. I have fingernail scars down the back of my neck from an overly affectionate chimpanzee – more shots! And I was very nearly mauled by a big yellow tiger in Vietnam!"

"Well, then, there you are," said the President. "I said you could relax. There isn't any dangerous wildlife in Antarctica. There isn't any wildlife at all – the men complain about it – excepting for the odd penguin."

The Vice President crossed his arms stiffly and took a rebellious stance. Alex could see that the man's elbow and neck still hurt him. "And you know what, Mr. President? There isn't any Forrey Nadalindov in Antarctica, either, and there never will be! Because I'm not going!"

Alex looked to Agent Smith, and then to John, who gravely winked an eye at him. "That's fine, Forrey, just fine. Of course I'll expect your letter of resignation on my desk, the very first thing tomorrow morning."

"What?" Nadalindov was taken aback.

"You heard me, Forrey, you're through. You could have had a part in accomplishing everything that you've ever claimed you've wanted to accomplish all of your adult life. Number two position in the first libertarian Presidential administration? You might have wound up being President, yourself – although I personally doubt it. Instead, you wasted my precious time, and your own, trying to sabotage my efforts and backstabbing me in the media. Now you've refused a direct order from your Commander-in-Chief, and it's over at last. Get out of my sight."

Nadalindov's face was raw with anger. "I warn you, the FLPA won't be happy about – "

Alex chuckled. John grinned ruefully, looked down at the table, and shook his head. Even Agent Smith surprised himself, emitting a tiny snicker and then covering his mouth. "I guess that's just a chance I'll have to take. Goodbye, Forrey."

The man turned on his heel, stamped past a dozen "undercover" Secret Service agents, and out of the restaurant. Dana, Faith-Anne, and Linda returned from the ladies' room, where they'd gone for tactical reasons, rather than biological ones, when the Vice President had arrived. They were just in time to see Nadalindov push the door at the entry out of his way and step through it.

John and Agent Smith got up politely to let the ladies into the booth, Faith-Anne and Linda to the President's right, Dana to his left. She loved this restaurant chain, she'd confessed, mostly because many of them had carousel ponies built into arches that partitioned it. She took Alex's arm, cuddled close, and laid her face on his shoulder.

"He didn't want to go to Antarctica?" She asked with imitation cuteness.

Alex shook his head grimly, but said nothing.

"He's going to resign?" Faith-Anne asked, batting her eyelashes.

Alex nodded the affirmative grimly, but said nothing.

Linda began, "So – "

Alex held a hand up, stopping her. "Congresswoman Alvarez, if you have no objection, I'm going to appoint you Vice President in his place."

A smile flashed on her face, switched off suddenly by a thought. "I'm sorry, Alex, the Senate will never agree. Don't you remember in 2001, when I – "

Dana reached across the table, past Alex and Faith-Anne, and put her graceful, gentle hand on Linda's. "But this time, Madame Future Vice President – and unlike last time – you'll have a President behind you who actually has measurable testosterone in his endocrine system."

"Thank you, my dear," said Alex. "Somebody get Cap over here. Shall we order dinner? I'm starving!"

* * * * * *

Meanwhile, as far away as they could be from the President and his companions – and still be in the restaurant – a well-dressed and highly attractive couple sat together in a small, dimly-lit booth for two.

He was a senior columnist for the *Washington Post.* She was an anchorwoman for CNN's Washington Bureau. Both of them were married – but not to each other. Nevertheless they sat together holding hands, sipping their Perfect Margaritas, and greatly enjoying each other's company.

They'd chosen this particular restaurant in an out-of-the way Virginia suburb, because they'd calculated that no one important enough to do them any damage could possibly see them here, in this aggressively middle-class establishment. Of course they'd known that the President and all of his senior staffers would be eating out of the White House for a couple of days, but they'd never dreamed that it would be here, instead of at some elegant downtown DC hotel dining room.

Now, despite their romantic (if illicit) assignation, all their instincts as news people – and political animals – had been piqued. They'd seen the Vice President come and go, and now they saw Linda Alvarez.

What did it all mean?

They looked at each other, their eyes meeting in a predatory flash that they were both astonished – and delighted – to discover was vastly more stimulating than alcohol, candlelight, and flowers. Both of them wondered what they should do about seeing the President. If they reported it, gave it the weight they should, it would end their marriages.

They each whipped out a cell phone. "Let's do it!" she said. "I think the angle I'm going to take is to praise Hope for his common touch."

"You're right. We'll share the by-line," he agreed.

"My name first," she insisted.

* * * * * *

The setting was a small convention meeting room in one of the less expensive Washington hotels, decorated in a gray-green pastel plastic wall covering and ropy indoor-outdoor carpet on the floor. Hanging on the wall behind the speaker were an American flag and the stylized figure of the Statue of Liberty, silkscreened in yellow on a Navy blue banner.

Not surprisingly, given the circumstances, many more than just the usual NetPlanetNews.com, DrudgeReport, and WorldNetDaily cameras had shown up. FoxNews was present, as well as CNN, MSNBC, NBC, CBS, and ABC. They'd been told more or less what was coming and many of them relished it.

The speaker, the same thin, middle-aged woman who had criticized the President for moving too fast – to implement the policies and principles it was assumed by everyone she agreed with – stood behind a cheap folding table covered with a coarse white tablecloth supplied by the hotel. The portable lectern before her was emblazoned with the same Statue of Liberty graphic as the one displayed on the banner behind her.

"My name is Norah Yasser," she told the microphones and cameras pointed at her. Her voice was nervous. Still camera shutters clicked, as well, and automatic winders whirred. "It's possible you remember that I'm the National Chairperson of The Free Libertarian Party of America."

She took up a condensation-beaded plastic carafe of ice water beside the lectern, poured herself a glass, drank a little, and set it down.

"I'm speaking with you today because, responding to the forced resignation of Vice President Forrey Nadalindov late last night, at his request, the National Committee of the Free Libertarian Party of America met this morning in an emergency session at their headquarters in the Watergate office complex, to formally withdraw the 2008 Free Libertarian Party of America's presidential nomination of Alexander Hope."

There was a small stir in the room, but no reaction of any kind of astonishment.

"That nomination was, of course, Hope's first step on the way to the White House. Without it, he never would have become President. We of the Free

Libertarian Party of America believe that because that nomination has now been withdrawn, Hope has a real and absolute moral obligation to step down in favor, not of Congresswoman Linda Alvarez, whom he has illegally named as his "interim Vice President", but of the duly-elected genuine people's choice as Vice President, Forrey Nadalindov."

"Ms. Yasser!"

"Ms. Yasser!"

"Ms. Yasser!"

A dozen voices shouted at once. The Chairperson let them shout, took another badly-needed drink of water, and then indicated one of them.

"Pritchard Evans-Evans, Ms. Yasser, *London Daily Telescope.* Isn't it fair to say that President Hope has accomplished nearly everything any libertarian would want him to accomplish in his first term?"

"Yes, but – "

"Hasn't he established presidential commissions to terminate what he terms 'the unconstitutional campaign of terror' waged by the Bureau of Alcohol, Tobacco, and Firearms, for example, which he says should never have existed in a country with a Second, Ninth, and Tenth Amendment?"

"Yes, but – "

"Or the Food and Drug Administration, whose powers, he pointed out in last Saturday's address, are illegal under Article I, Section 8, or the Environmental Protection Agency, which he says has become another Gestapo, or the Occupational Safety and Health Administration, which he claims has made a bureaucratic nightmare of the American workplace, or – "

"That's enough, Mr. Evans – "

"That's Evans-Evans, Ms. Yasser, and I'm the voice of the people here. I'll say when it's enough."

"Evans-Evans." She gave a small, forced laugh. "Are you his press secretary?"

"No, Ms. Yasser, I'm a journalist, trying to ascertain the truth, in this case, why, when it has benefitted to an infinite degree from the sheer fact of his presidency, when he has put an end to arbitrary property seizures, and 'civil forfeitures', while declaring 'peace with honor' in the War against Drugs, and restoring those victimized by it to their previous condition, when he has defanged a Securities Exchange Commission which distorts the economy beyond recognition, as well as the environmentally destructive Army Corps of Engineers and many another such 'alphabet entity', the man's own party demands his resignation."

"Mr. Evans, I – "

"That's Evans-Evans, Ms. Yasser. Understand, I *oppose* most of what the man has done. I'm a Tory of Burkean philosophy and quite proud of it. But President Hope told us what he was going to do – he keeps telling us every Saturday evening – and he has kept his word remarkably well."

"See here, Mr. – "

"You're not going to tell me anything I need to know. I'm going home." With that, the British reporter shut his notebook, slid crabwise through the maze of gray-enameled folding chairs filling the room, and walked out.

Half the camera lights went out; others began filing from the room.

The press conference was over.

Chapter Twenty-eight:
DANAL G. PRABDORRID

> *Understand from the minute the fight begins that you're going to take damage. Accept it. (You'll always suffer more from the idiots and cowards on your* own *side than from any enemy.) Keep your overall goal in mind above all. Those who swerve to avoid a few cuts and bruises defeat themselves.*
>
> – Alexander Hope, *Looking Forward*

Using the remote control, Dana switched the television off. "I wish I'd been there."

She sighed. Her old injuries were bothering her today, as they did whenever there was bad weather. Too many broken bones, not all of them healed perfectly despite Alex's wealth and power. Dana would take ibuprofen, but she wouldn't take anything stronger, saying what she always did, that she didn't want to miss a single minute of a single day of her life with him. It made Alex angry to see her in pain. She was a wonderful, beautiful young woman who didn't deserve to suffer.

"So they want me to resign," he mused. They sat together in bed, holding hands. "I suppose I could call a press conference tomorrow and denounce the

FLPA right back – maybe even reveal the full truth about what they – "

Dana shook her head. "I like a good fight, darling, but that would put you down on their level: mental microbes. It doesn't sound like your style."

He shrugged and squeezed her hand – careful not to hurt her. "It doesn't, does it? Then I guess that leaves a little something that I should have done long ago, something that's very definitely my style. It's going to take a while to organize"

She turned to look into his eyes. "What's that?"

"You'll see. It's a surprise."

* * * * * *

It took six months, in the end, and it had all the hallmarks of an award ceremony.

Sprouting a bouquet of microphones, the lectern stood on a raised platform at the front of the room, the Presidential seal it was emblazoned with, the focus of bright lights and a dozen television cameras. At the back of the platform hung neutral-colored drapes. Agent Smith and his dark-suited minions bracketed the platform and stood in corners at the back of the room.

John and his son were present, as well.

The first two rows of theater seats in the small White House auditorium, ordinarily reserved for the print media, were occupied today by several dozen upper-echelon civil servants from the United States Forest Service, some in uniform and some in civilian clothing.

Acting as his press secretary, the President's daughter entered the room briskly from a door at the left, climbed two steps onto the platform, and, standing beside, rather than behind the lectern, announced, "Ladies and gentlemen, the President of the United States."

Alex entered from the same door, following Faith-Anne's footsteps until he stood behind the lectern. She retreated to the back of the platform by the drapes. He allowed his photograph to be taken by the still cameras, then took two long white envelopes from his inside jacket pocket, put them on the lectern, held up a hand, and spoke.

"Ladies and gentlemen of the media, fellow children of the American Revolution. I invited you here today to accomplish two not entirely unrelated objectives. The first is to appropriately acknowledge the lifework of Mr. Danal G. Prabdorrid, the retiring director of the United States Forest Service, who has been an active officer of that agency for some 35 years. I'd be pleased to have you join me up here on the platform, ."

An elderly overweight man wearing a dark green uniform stood up in the front row and allowed himself to be escorted onto the platform by two Secret Service agents. Agent Smith's men brought the senior Forest Service director around to stand at the President's left side.

"My goodness, I most certainly did not expect anything like this, Mr. President," he told Alex and the microphones in an Anglo-Indian accent. "It is such a big surprise, I do not know what to say."

Alex grinned. "I'm sure you'll think of something in the next few minutes, Mr. Prabdorrid." Everybody laughed politely. "But first, there's someone else here I want to introduce, Ms. Dia Luppina. Please bring Ms. Luppina in."

The same two Secret Service agents brought in a small, stooped, middle-aged, Hispanic-looking woman from the same door Alex had entered by. On the platform, they left her at the President's right.

He introduced them. "Ms. Luppina, Mr. Prabdorrid. Mr. Prabdorrid, Ms. Luppina. Mr. Prabdorrid, I wonder if you'd do me a favor."

He nodded his head vigorously. "Yes, certainly, Mr. President."

"Fine. Take this, if you would, and present it to Ms. Luppina." He handed one of the envelopes to Prabdorrid. The man looked confused, but stepped around the front of the lectern and did as Alex requested.

"An explanation is in order," Alex said. "Once upon a time, Ms. Luppina had what most of us can only dream about, the proverbial 'little cabin in the woods' originally a Colorado homestead dating from the 1860s, which now found itself entirely surrounded by Forest Service property, an 'inholding', protected by the same legislation – passed by Teddy Roosevelt – that established the Forest Service in the first place, from being taken by the government."

He turned. "I see you're starting to recognize Ms. Luppina, Mr. Prabdorrid." Despite air conditioning, the man had begun perspiring.

"Unfortunately," Alex went on, "the Forest Service wanted to tie up what it regards as loose ends. Their policy for decades has been to close more and more federal lands to human use. Now they wanted Ms. Luppina's property, but they couldn't just take it. So instead, they told her that before she could use the only road that connected her land to the public highway, she had to pay a fee – and just incidentally sign her property over to them.

"Being the sort of person who chooses to live in a little cabin in the woods, Ms. Luppina told the Forest Service where to go and went on using the road. They arrested her and charged her under a law written to deal with terrorists. A federal judge fined her and threatened her with prison unless she signed her property away. Under the terms of her probation – for terrorism! – she was locked out of her home, but under the terms of her mortgage she was still required to make the payments on it. But the legal bills she ran up meant that the payments didn't get made, and the bank foreclosed on her home."

He pointed to the envelope. "This – which I thought Ms. Luppina would appreciate receiving directly from the hand of Mr. Prabdorrid, who is responsible for her misfortunes – contains papers granting her executive clemency and immunity from any further prosecution in connection with this matter. It also contains title to her own property, and an easement giving her full use of the road for access, and all surrounding federal land for recreational purposes. I've also seen to it that her little home, a 150-year-old structure the Forest Service saw fit to demolish, will be rebuilt."

Ms. Luppina began weeping. Faith-Anne stepped forward and put an arm around her gently. Her father turned to a very pale Prabdorrid.

"I have something for you, too, Mr. Prabdorrid." he extended the second envelope to the man who raised a shaking hand, but couldn't quite bring himself to take it. "What it contains is notification that you've been dismissed from the Forest Service and deprived of pension and benefits owing to your abuse of the power of your office and the violation of your oath to uphold and defend the Constitution. You're also being criminally charged – gentlemen?"

From behind the drapes, a pair of burly federal marshals emerged with handcuffs, belly chains, and leg-irons, and started to lead Prabdorrid away.

Alex stopped them. "If it's any consolation, Mr. Prabdorrid, you're not the only federal employee – and the Forest Service certainly isn't the only agency – to suffer this fate, you're only the first. And Ms. Luppina isn't the only abused individual who's going to be compensated for what you did to her – preferably at your personal expense.

"Take him away."

At those words, a dozen powerful-looking uniformed federal marshals entered from both side doors at the front and arrested each and every individual sitting in the first two rows of the little White House auditorium.

"One more thing, and we'll move on. If anyone happens to be on federal land and sees a sign declaring it part of a United Nations Wildlands Project, or subject to the UN's Convention on Biological Diversity, or anything like that, tear it down and destroy it. The UN has no authority of any kind in this country and never will as long as I am President."

* * * * * *

"Now to the main reason for this conference: as I'm sure you know, a few months ago, the national committee of the Free Libertarian Party of America attempted to excommunicate me." He laughed. "They voted to retroactively revoke their 2008 nomination of me as President of the United States."

Laughter, quiet at first, but growing moment by moment, filled the room. Faith-Anne returned to the platform, having taken Ms. Luppina somewhere to lie down, and recover from her surprise.

"I've since had my lawyer," he indicated Faith-Anne, "check the FLPA's by-laws. She found they can't do what they claim they did.

"No matter. The reason it took me so long to respond is that we're here today to announce the birth of a *new* political party, founded on the principle that guides this administration, the stringent, energetic, and enthusiastic enforcement of the Bill of Rights that you've just seen.

"We're going to call it the Bill of Rights Party. The initial organizing effort has been undertaken by four good friends of mine from Albert Gallatin Memorial College, Mick Douglas, Ernie Hanover, Katie Harris, and Rick Thomas."

"Bear with me now, I'm not digressing. Among the many other abuses she suffered, Ms. Luppina was denied her right to a jury trial and became, instead, the subject of what's called an 'administrative court' – created specifically to get around the Constitution's strict limits on government power and to deprive Americans of their liberty and property without due process of law. This morning I issued an executive order abolishing all such courts.

"I'd like to end this now by introducing a proposed Constitutional amendment – it will be the 29th – that will require judges to inform juries of their 1000-year-old right and duty to judge the law, as well as the alleged facts of the case. Adding it to the Constitution will be the first objective of the Bill of Rights Party. I ask each and every one of you for your help and support to get it ratified.

"Thank you."

* * * * * *

"Mostly by employing internet TV, radio, and other 'new media' to directly address the American people, President Hope has begun to win friends. Membership in the Free Libertarian Party of America promptly imploded as most of its members followed him over to the new Bill of Rights Party. What began as an historically unprecedented change of parties quickly has now become the early opening shots of the campaign of 2012.

"Gradually, a trickle of congressmen – and across the nation here and there, a few state legislators, a handful of city councilmen, even a mayor or two – have declared themselves members of the Bill of Rights Party. A couple of prominent labor leaders have crossed over, as well, sending a cold chill December down the spines of Democratic Party leaders. Labor has quickly been joined by academics and the leaders of a handful of influential corporations.

"With both House and Senate equally divided, and the old parties themselves in increasing disarray, next year's coming election campaign should prove extremely interesting. This is NetPlanetnews.com. I'm Alan – "

The Democratic leader of the Senate turned the TV off with a vicious snap of the remote, beginning to be sorry that he'd returned a favor by inviting his opposite number to his favorite bar. His presence, the cheerful Christmas decorations, and the holiday Muzak were quickly becoming intolerable. "Well, what are we going to do now?"

"What we always do, Charlie," the Republican leader of the Senate sipped his bloody maria. "What we always do: by now, you know who's been trying to do our work for us. We simply get them to try again. Sooner or later they'll get lucky."

* * * * * *

A bell went, *"ding!"* and the elevator door opened.

John and Cap stepped out, looked right and left, up and down, then stood aside for Alex, followed by Dana. The corridor was deserted, as had been arranged in advance, but the Secret Service detail had agreed to let the hospital have it back as quickly as possible.

"I detest sneaking around like a criminal," Alex observed wearily for the hundred thousandth time since he took the oath of office.

"You'd hate being dead a whole lot more, Boss" John gave the same answer that he always did. The corridor was long and led to a pair of heavy glass doors that opened onto a parking lot John had joked was the size of an eastern county.

"Uncle Bob didn't think very well of the prospect," Dana told them. They'd come back down to the ground floor after visiting the badly-injured chef, who'd been in and out for half a dozen operations over the past several months, and was looking forward to returning to work. He'd been a night shift worker for 40 years, was having trouble adjusting to the hospital's schedule, and had complained about it during a phone call from the President. Alex had taken this as an opportunity to get out of the White House in the middle of the night with a minimal escort.

"He doesn't seem to care for the food here, either," John replied. They walked a dozen paces further down the hall, then he said, "Which hardly surprises me, having spent some time in the hospital, myself – but it's past time we got something to eat."

"I'm hungry, too," Alex nodded as they reached the doors. They'd had a light meal earlier, but it was only a memory. "You remember how it was when we were 'forced' to eat out. Uncle Bob isn't going to be running the kitchen tonight, no matter how much he wishes he could be. How about it, sweetheart, could you eat something at a restaurant?"

She laughed. "I could roast and eat an elk! Is there someplace we could get a steak at this time of night – no, make it morning?"

John pushed the heavy doors aside and nodded at the pair of Secret Service agents waiting just outside, one of them a worried-looking Agent Smith. The President's limousine was some distance away (Alex had forbidden them to block the entrance) and there were no escorting Suburbans. The five began to walk 100 yards to the waiting car, across a dark and empty parking lot.

Agent Smith was the first to get there. He knocked on the glass for the driver to unlock the door, heard the answering clunk of the electric door locks, grabbed the handle, and pulled.

Suddenly the door burst open of its own accord, and Agent Smith was engulfed in deafening noise and blinding flashes as somebody inside the car cut him nearly in half with a submachinegun. He was dead before he hit the ground.

At the same time, someone inside the car fired a heavy caliber handgun at the other Secret Service

Agent, standing ten feet from the car beside Dana. That agent was lifted off his feet and died, too, but not before both John and Cap and Alex dragged Dana to the ground behind the almost nonexistent shelter of a concrete parking bumper and had their guns out.

Three dark forms emerged from the car in a corona of muzzle flashes, spraying the ground before them with their weapons. Bullets ricocheted like a deadly hailstorm from the tiny barrier the President's party hid behind. He and John fired several times, and a submachinegun stopped working as the man who held it was thrown back into the car. One figure with a shotgun had run around, trying to flank them, but Cap, in an exchange of fire, had put a stop to that.

Before they could turn their sights on the one with the heavy handgun, they heard four shots and were surprised to see Dana firing a Browning Hi-Power at the assassin.

They waited several long heartbeats, then John got up – Alex stayed with Dana until he got the all-clear – to check on the bodies.

He returned. "Hate to say it, Alex, but Agent Smith is gone. He was turning into a pretty good guy. His partner's dead, too, and the poor driver. I'm not sure how they got to him inside an armored car."

"And the assassins?" Dana asked.

"Two dead – I didn't know you could shoot like that, Dana! I could cover all four of those bullet holes with my pocket watch!"

"This one's still alive!" Cap shouted. "And it's a woman!"

"And here comes hospital security," John added. "Don't let them take your weapons, either of you."

Alex sat up and grinned. "I think I can handle

that." As John strode to meet them, Alex turned to Dana. "Is that a South African magazine? Seventeen shots. I didn't even know you were carrying a weapon, let alone capable of such marksmanship."

"Agent Smith taught me," she said, putting her Browning in her lap and taking him tenderly by the hand. "I had to be good, darling. These days I'm shooting for two!"

CHAPTER TWENTY-NINE:
WILLIAM LI

> *Tell me what you think, not what you think other people think. If you voted in terms of what you're ready for, rather than what you've convinced yourself others are ready for, we'd have had Constitutional government, a libertarian society, and eradicated socialism half a century ago.*
>
> – Alexander Hope, *Looking Forward*

My dear Three-Dee,

Thank you for your call this morning. It warms my heart to see that you're well and happy, and I'm sure your mother will be pleased, as well, once she "recovers". I couldn't tell you over the internet that she has taken to her bed and will hardly speak to me, because she believes that I am somehow responsible for everything that makes her unhappy.

Part of the problem, I suspect, is that your mother still thinks of herself as a young woman – which, believe me, is quite wonderful most of the time – but I'm afraid she was not quite ready, because of that, to become a grandmother. I know that she'll get over it the very first moment, a few months from now, when she holds your baby in her arms.

Another problem, although she doesn't dare to put it in words, is that, setting your happiness aside and considering only the bad things that have happened, the terrible injuries you suffered in 2008, and this latest violence, she feels deprived of a mother's right to shake a finger at you and say you should have listened to her and married What'shisname the doctor. Instead, you thoughtlessly ran off with an extremely wealthy man who also happens to be President of the United States.

What's a mother to do?

But I think the heart of the matter is that she can't get up, go back out into the world, and face other members of the faculty and her friends at the American Association of University Women, knowing that they know that you have successfully defended yourself – and trust me, you are more precious to her than anything else on Earth – not to mention her grandchild-to-be, with the very sort of high-capacity semiautomatic pistol that all "right thinking" people believe must be outlawed.

Personally, I'd have gone with a little bigger caliber.

One reason I'm writing this is that I want you to understand, even decades from now, when I can no longer tell you in person, that I have always been proud of you, my dear. I was proud of you when you were a straight A student here in Manitou and the cutest little figure skater at the Broadmoor Skating Club. Later I was proud to see you every day on NetPlanetNews.com. I am proudest now, when you have become the most beautiful and intelligent First Lady this nation has ever been honored with.

Be well, let us know how you are feeling. I promise I'll get your mother to the terminal next time you call. Please tell Alex I never knew it was possible for a man to respect and admire his son-in-law so much.

Your loving father,

William

* * * * * *

"Three-Dee?" Sitting at his desk, Alex raised his eyebrows.

Still holding the letter her father had faxed her, Dana laughed. "'Darling daughter Dana' – he's called me that for as long as I can remember."

Alex nodded approvingly. He'd called his daughter "my little" until he'd handed the family business over to her. Then he went back to work. It was an unusually busy morning in the Oval Office.

In addition to the Presidential workload that was to be expected on the best of days, Faith-Anne had told the media what had happened last night at the hospital. Now they wanted to know in the President's own words if there had been yet another assassination attempt.

They appeared to be trying to twist things around, so they could blame these events on Alex –

better yet, on his "radical" policies. They wanted to know if it was true the chief of the President's Secret Service detail had been killed in the line of duty.

They wanted to know if it was true that Alex had used that huge, high-caliber, high-magazine-capacity assault pistol – the one he'd recently been photographed waving around – to kill one of the assassins.

They wanted to know if it was true his wife, the former pinup girl of the right-wing government-hating anti-establishment internet website NetPlanetNews.com had killed one of them, herself, as well.

They wanted to know if it was true that the son of the President's bodyguard had shot and wounded a woman.

They wanted to know if it was true that the President's perverse hankering to sneak out of the White House without his usual complement of keepers was responsible for what had happened at the hospital.

Expressing a desire "to tell the plain truth without a lot of loaded questions from the stilted hacks of the Old Media", Alex had spoken exclusively to Dana's former boss at NetPlanetNews.com.

Yes, Alan, there had been another assassination attempt.

Yes, Alan, Agent Smith had been killed bravely protecting the life of the President. He was a good man; Alex and Dana had grown to like him very much. Smith's mother, his only living relative, was in the hospital, under treatment for shock. Dana and Faith-Anne were taking turns at her bedside. Two other Secret Service men were dead, as well, but Alex would see that they and their families were never forgotten.

Yes, Alan, Alex had fired several shots in his own defense. They wouldn't know how effectively until they had reports from the medical examiner. The same was true of Dana, she had fired several shots. Her father, Professor William Li of Manitou Springs, Colorado, had sent his hearty congratulations and a big bouquet of flowers.

Yes, Cap Pondoro had shot a woman – who was firing a 12-guage shotgun at him at close range. She was in the prison ward of a local hospital, under constant guard, and had agreed to tell them anything they wanted to know about what had happened.

Was it true, NetPlanetNews.com asked, that this tragedy would never have happened if Alex had chosen a different time of day, with more cars to escort him and a larger Secret Service detail?

It wasn't a tragedy, Alan. That's an expression reserved for acts of God, like earthquakes and hurricanes. It was the work of murderous criminals. And it wouldn't have happened, either, if he'd just stayed home and hidden under his bed. But that would make him a pretty poor sort of a human being, wouldn't it now, let alone a President?

"One of my first acts as President," Alex told the camera, "was to reopen Pennsylvania Avenue in front of the White House to vehicular traffic. The Old Media criticized it then as an unjustifiable risk. But it was something that should have been ordered by my predecessor – and the street should never have been closed by his predecessor."

"Well, then, Mr. President," asked Dana's former boss, "what do you see as legitimate precautionary measures you should take?"

Alex spread his hands. "I've tried to be the kind of President that Americans don't want to see assassinated, by not threatening anything – their lives, their property, their rights – that's legitimately theirs. I believe I will ultimately succeed, and that this attempt was carried out purely on behalf of those few who don't want to lose what they have taken by force and fraud."

* * * * * *

One of the "hidden" doors to the Oval Office swung aside, and John barreled into the room, peering with some difficulty at the screen of a small "personal digital assistant" he held in one big outstretched hand. The device bore the Hope Corporation flying horse logo on its back.

"I swear," the man said, "my arms get shorter every day. Is Dana here? She wants to know all about last night; she could read this for me."

Alex laughed, offering a pair of glasses to his friend. "Try these – Long's Drug Store, $15.99. Dana said she was going to go learn to knit. I'll believe that when I see it. She wanted to catch up on the latest New Media gossip with her old boss while he's still here in the house."

"Got my own, more's the pity," John told him, taking a case out of the inside pocket of his jacket and adjusting the wire-rimmed lenses on his nose. "Here's what we've got on the former thugs last night. There was no ID, and no labels in their clothing. Fingerprints say they were one Henry Augustus Galen and one Willem Fuhre, old-time wetwork specialists who'd done this and that for the CIA and the FBI from time to time over the past 25 years, usually carried on the payroll as accountants."

"And the woman?"

"Our old friend the 'professional lady' who deflected our first investigation onto Horrwyrn and Moure, I wonder if we should tell them it's okay to come back."

Alex laughed.

"Fuhre sometimes bragged that he was at Waco during the entire siege, attached to the 'Hostage Rescue Team'. They'd also worked with some anti-Semitic groups in the middle east and may have eliminated that priest friend of Kitch Sinclair's."

"John Greenwood," Alex supplied. "Also known as Johann Gruenwald and Abram Herschel Rosen, depending on who's talking about him. I speak with his mother from time to time. Joe Spagelli asked me to, says it helps. I suppose we have no idea who these goons were working for this time."

John grinned. "We could stake their mailboxes out and see who sends 'em a pink slip. I think our professional lady friend will eventually tell us. She's bargaining for immunity right now, but has dropped enough hints that I could probably send federal marshals to visit the Democratic and Republic leaders of the Senate. On the other hand, she could be lying. Time will tell. We do know who they *weren't* working for, though."

"Oh? Who's that?"

"The Free Libertarian Party of America. Your friend Norah Yasser called this morning pathetically desperate to tell us – on the assumption we'd find out for ourselves – that Galen and Fuhre are listed in their computer files as FLPA members in good standing, with dues paid back as early as the 1990s."

"Somebody hacked their database."

"I have experts checking right now, but I'm sure it's what they'll find. I don't know if the other side actually expected us to swallow a cover story so obviously phoney, or they have something better in mind."

"Such as?"

"Well, not wanting to depend entirely on the testimony of a fake prostitute, I've been listening to pressure groups complaining bitterly today, mostly on Spanish-language talk radio, about the Vice President getting a translation of the Bill of Rights, and a proper explanation of it, into every Spanish-language newspaper in America. Throughout Mexico, too – our Linda doesn't take small bites! They say she wants to try to have it printed in every telephone book in the country, too, right along with the English version."

"That's what she tells me. You think someone wants to kill us over that?"

"I don't know, Alex, I'm just trolling at the moment. If more Hispanics could be made to see the promise inherent in the Bill of Rights, and especially your policy of Bill of Rights enforcement, a lot of left-wing politicos and rabble-rousers would find themselves unemployed."

The camouflaged door opened. Faith-Anne strode in, laptop in hand.

"Good morning, Daddy, you were right."

"I was right?"

"You were right."

"What is this?" John complained, "a rerun of *Dragnet*?" Alex and Faith-Anne laughed. "So what was it that your father was right about this time?"

"Well, you know that Daddy – the President, I mean – has used executive orders, or the threat of executive orders, to pressure the Congress into repealing capital gains and corporate taxes, which he referred to on one of his Saturdays as 'economic double jeopardy'. He also attacked death 'duties', which he called the 'grave-robbers' tax'."

John nodded. "Yes, I remember. I recall that we had champagne that night."

Faith-Anne laughed. "Then he wrote another order that would have exempted life's basic necessities – food, clothing, shelter, and transportation – from taxes of any kind. The Democrats hated that, since they're supposed to be the friends of the poor. But they're even better friends of my money and they want as much of it as they can steal."

It was John's turn to laugh. "That night it was margaritas!"

"So it was. And then just to make them even madder, he added a second program to exempt anything protected by the Bill of Rights – including firearms and ammunition – and told them he planned to 'pay' for the cuts by reducing all government programs evenly, across the board."

Before John could respond, Alex said, "Pina coladas."

"That's right, Daddy. Well, you predicted correctly. Congress says it's tired of being pushed around. The Democrat and Republican leaders of the House and Senate have gotten together. They say they're passing legislation to curtail the President's power to issue executive orders."

"I can hardly wait to see the exact wording," Alex replied. "You can't run a government without the

Chief Executive instructing his departments on how to carry out mandates that originate with Congress. Of course I don't mind that at all – but I assume that they will, eventually. In any case, I'd be bound by my oath to veto any such legislation."

"And they say they have the votes to pass it again, over your veto."

"I get it," John exclaimed, turning to Alex. "Whereupon you claim a victory in tricking Congress into eliminating one of the most evil, liberty-damaging practices in modern politics. Is that good judo, or what?"

"Only if we can trick them into it," Alex agreed. "Once they've done it, I can easily operate on a strict 'veto-and-repeal' basis, allowing no new legislation to cross my desk unless it's approved by two thirds of Congress – unless it's a repeal of some previous legislation."

"My Daddy's a genius!" Faith-Anne declared exuberantly. "By the way, Daddy – Uncle John – Cap and I are getting married Saturday afternoon."

* * * * * *

"So, by the power vested in me by the Archdiocese of Chicago and the, er, President of the United States, I now declare you husband and wife."

Father Joseph folded his hands. "You may kiss the bride."

For once, Cap performed exactly as he was instructed, and with considerable enthusiasm, coming up for air only to get a face full of dried rice from his laughing stepmother-in-law. Dana's former boss stepped out from behind the tripod supporting his tiny camera long enough to kiss the bride, not before

Alex. John surreptitiously wiped a tear from his eye, embraced Faith-Anne, and hugged her until she squeaked.

"Not 'Uncle' any more," he told her.

"No," she agreed, "I'll call you 'Pappa'."

CHAPTER THIRTY: *THE PROPHET SAMUEL*

> *The shortest path to victory is a* straight line.
> *He who remains most consistent wins.*
>
> – Alexander Hope, *Looking Forward*

The gantry was small, Alex thought, and the rocket caged within it even smaller. It wasn't at all like the massive Apollo operations of the 60s and 70s, or the NASA shuttle launches. More than anything, it reminded him of the V-2/WAC Corporal shots of the 50s, but there weren't many here today who would remember those.

John would be an exception. He and Dana stood beside Alex as they watched through the observation slits of the Space Colony Foundation bunker, here on what had been renamed Open Sky Island, not far from Brownsville, Texas. The site had been chosen because it was almost as far south as it could be in the United States – SCF was negotiating with Belize to build a second launch site – and it was the location of Impey Barbicane's giant moon-shot cannon in Jules Verne's *From the Earth to the Moon.*

The field had been cleared, and the countdown was at T-minus two minutes. The rocket out there, 500 yards from the window he was looking through was a surplus Russian SS-18, originally built for the Soviets' mobile strategic defense system. It had been hauled around on the back of a big truck for years, until satellite surveillance had rendered it obsolete, then it had been warehoused. SCF had bought it "for a song" and rebuilt it for this mission.

Atop the formerly Soviet rocket was a sophisticated capsule bound for Ceres, largest of the millions of asteroids circling the sun between the orbits of Mars and Jupiter. Most asteroids were a mile in diameter or less. Ceres was 620 miles in diameter and had the same surface area as the Indian subcontinent. SCF's "bird", as they called it, would fly to Ceres, go into orbit, and photograph every square inch of the little world, with an eye toward terraforming it – giving it an Earthlike atmosphere under a plastic envelope – and sending settlers. All of that was still decades away, but today's launch was a bold first step.

"T-minus 30 seconds," came a female voice over the loudspeaker. Dana moved closer and squeezed his hand. He could feel his own heart racing. Glancing over his shoulder, he saw the launch team at their consoles, headed by the young Electrical Engineering student he'd met so long ago at the FLPA convention four years ago. She happened to glance up. He gave her a wink, and returned his attention to the window.

"T-minus 10 ... "

He wondered if his children would get to see Ceres up close, or maybe even live in a colony there. He even wondered if he and Dana might ...

"T-minus five ... four ... three ... two ... one ... "

An enormous noise filled his consciousness and shook his bones. Dana hugged him tightly and tried to say something but he couldn't hear. It was as if something gigantic were being torn in half by even more gigantic hands. The gantry was enveloped in smoke and billows of rising steam, and the light at the base of the rising rocket was too bright to look at directly.

"We have ignition, friends and neighbors! We have lift-off! SCF EV1 – Exploratory Vehicle Number One – the *Robert A. Heinlein* is on its way to Ceres! Thank you, Mr. President, for getting the government out of the way!"

* * * * * *

They stood on the platform together, hand in hand, the air around them almost solid with confetti, balloons, and a thousand cheering voices. At Alex's left, Dana was radiantly beautiful and as pregnant as a human being can get without giving birth. Technically, she'd been due day before yesterday, but she'd said she wanted to hold out for today.

About an hour from now, Alex figured nervously.

At Alex's right stood Vice President Linda Alvarez, the woman who would almost certainly become the first female President in American history. The knowledge that he could trust Linda to carry forward what would now amount to a 16-year reform plan filled him with joy. He had just won the 2012 election with one of the highest voter turnouts on record.

Dana's parents were beside her, tears streaming down Jesse Li's face. She wouldn't be able to go back to the Jane Jefferson Club now, Alex thought. William seemed so happy Alex worried about his health. Beside Linda stood John, who had agreed to be his new Chief of Staff. Behind Alex and Dana stood the

Austrian Mafia, Rick Thomas, Katie Harris, Ernie Hanover, and Mick Douglas. All four would be on his official staff now, with time out for a couple of them to go to law school.

The only ones missing – and Alex couldn't really blame them – were Faith-Anne and Cap, on their honeymoon in a faraway location he and Dana and John were sworn not to disclose. They'd called Alex only a few minutes ago to congratulate him, he wearing an outrageous aloha shirt, she wearing a grass skirt. Alex suspected that he'd wind up a grandfather before long – the thought of Dana being a grandmother was ridiculous.

The Old Media were still at it, of course, claiming that Alex had cynically used his daughter's wedding – netcast in real time on NetPlanetNews.com – his beautiful pregnant wife, and three attempted assassinations to win the sympathy of the voters. Alex countered that he didn't want the voters' sympathy, but their agreement with his policies.

"Three things won this election for us," he said now, addressing a hotel ballroom full of supporters and campaign workers. "The first is that we kept our word. Even those who disagree with us know exactly what to expect from us – these days, they just consult the Bill of Rights."

The crowd cheered. It was five minutes before they were quiet again.

"The Hebrew prophet Samuel warned us many centuries ago, about the excesses government is inclined to, predicting that it would take our crops and our sons and our daughters from us. And so it has, for an unconscionably long time. But that's over now, and it occurred to my charming bride that it is inappropriate for a free country filled with individuals equal under the law to build and maintain a Presidential Mansion."

More cheering. He had to wait until they stopped.

"And so ... " He waited. "And so we will keep another promise that brought us to this moment. Dana and I will begin – as soon as our baby comes – to move out and convert the White House into a national museum."

This time the noise was almost painful. Dana gave him an odd smile and put a hand on her belly. It suddenly dawned on Alex that the extra cheering was for their baby, who had moved inside her in response to it. He took her hand. She squeezed his almost hard enough to make it painful.

His throat seized up and it was difficult to begin again. "The third thing that brought us here is a promise I made to introduce and ratify yet another Constitutional Amendment – the 30th Amendment – which will impose an absolute moratorium on all legislation for 100 years."

More cheering, almost equally enthusiastic. Here was his historic departure, the concept that was about to transcend all previous politics, right, left, and center, and that he'd be remembered for longest.

"I'm told," he finally said, "some New Media observers are calling it my 'political masterpiece', and I'm far too polite to contradict them."

Polite laughter, followed by an expectant hush.

"We will make a happy exception, of course, for the repeal of laws that already exist, so that a century in the future, whenever the Old Media complain about a 'do-nothing' Congress, what they will have no choice but to mean is a Congress that hasn't repealed enough laws lately."

More cheering, mixed with laughter. The only happier day in his life was Election Day four years ago, when he'd learned Dana loved him.

"The great libertarian philosopher and teacher Robert LeFevre used to point out that there were more than 15,000,000 federal laws – over fifteen million! – and that was way back in the 1970s. Nobody knows how many federal laws there are today, more than 20,000,000 certainly, surely more than 30,000,000. But knowing that, our judges continue to lecture us, from time to time, that 'ignorance of the law is no excuse'."

Laughter rocked the ballroom.

"Whatever the correct number is, it is *enough*. If the size of government were reduced by 99 percent, it would still be too big. If it were reduced by 99.99 percent, it would be too big. I will spend the next four years reducing it as much as I possibly, humanly am able.

"As much as you'll let me."

The room erupted in a thousand voices cheering. Nothing else could be heard.

Alex took Dana – and his child – in his arms and let the crowd cheer.

APPENDIX ONE: *ALEXANDER HOPE WANTS YOU!*

In all the excitement, it appears that President Hope neglected to name a Cabinet. Now he needs your help. Write to us at one of the adresses below and tell us what Cabinet position you'd accept, and in 100 words or less, why Alex should appoint you.

Keep in mind that most of these positions are not authorized by Article I, Section 8 of the Constitution, so that your principal job would be to abolish your department and put yourself out of work.

You may nominate someone else, of course, but you must have their written permission. Only one entry per individual will be permitted, so if you nominate someone else, you can't nominate yourself.

All entries will be judged by Aaron Zelman and L. Neil Smith, who (after conferring with President Hope, of course) will have the final say in the matter. The authors, their families, employees of Mazel Freedom Press and J.P.F.O. and their families are not eligible to enter. Entries will not be acknowledged or returned (except as specified herein), will remain the property of Mazel Freedom Press, and may be published (with proper credit) on its website or related sites, and possibly included in future editions of *Hope*.

Winners will receive a signed certificate officially appointing them to President Hope's Cabinet. A grand prize will be announced later. Deadline is November 1, 2001, and winners will be announced on Bill of Rights Day, December 15, 2001.

These are the Cabinet positions:

Attorney General
Secretary of Agriculture
Secretary of Commerce
Secretary of Defense
Secretary of Education
Secretary of Energy
Secretary of Health and Human Services
Secretary of Housing and Urban Development
Secretary of the Interior
Secretary of Labor
Secretary of State
Secretary of Transportation
Secretary of the Treasury
Secretary of Veterans' Affairs

Write to "Hope Cabinet", c/o Mazel Freedom Press, P.O. Box 270014, Hartford, WI 53027, or send e-mail to lneil@ezlink.com

Appendix Two: *CELEBRATING BILL OF RIGHTS DAY*

Aaron Zelman and L. Neil Smith, authors of *The Mitzvah* and *Hope* would like to know how you plan to spend December 15, Bill of Rights Day.

As Alexander Hope points out, the politicians and bureaucrats have coopted July 4th, Independence Day, and transformed it into a gruesome celebration of safety fascism and unanswerable authority, the exact opposite of everything it was meant to be. Sooner or later, we'll take July 4th back, but until then, December 15, Bill of Rights Day is *ours*.

Will you write a letter to the editor of your local newspaper? (Sample letters and model op-ed pieces appear on The Bill of Rights Day page at www.jpfo.org). Will you contact your local radio and television station? Will you call a press conference? Will you hold a rally in your nearby park or meeting hall?

Let us know, and we'll post your Bill of Rights Day plans on the J.P.F.O. website.

Thanks!

Aaron Zelman and L. Neil Smith

Appendix Three: *A FEW OF ALEX'S FAVORITE THINGS*

These and other fascinating websites may be linked to conveniently through http://www.jpfo.org.

Allen-Edmond Shoes
https://aeshoes.allenedmonds.com

Concerned Citizens Opposed to Police States
http://www.ccops.org/

Cold Fusion
http://world.std.com/~mica/cft.html

Dan Wesson Firearms
http://www.dan-wesson.com/

Dodge Durango
http://www.4adodge.com/durango/
http://www.durangoclub.com/

European American Armory (Witness Pistols)
http://www.eaacorp.com/firearms/pistols

Fuel Cell Technology
http://www.fuelcells.org/

Fulton Armory
http://www.fulton-armory.com

Glock Pistols
http://www.glock.com/home.htm

Jews for the Preservation of Firearms Ownership
http://www.jpfo.org/
LearJet
http://www.learjet.com/
The Libertarian Enterprise
http://www.webleyweb.com/tle
Lucchese Boots
http://www.lucchese.com/
Montana's Yellowstone Trail Boots
http://www.montanasyt.com/
Private Spaceflight
http://www.space-frontier.org/
Sardines
http://www.crownprince.com/
Omega Watches
http://www.omega.ch/

About the Authors –

Aaron Zelman learned about freedom and self-reliance growing up in the Arizona desert. A Vietnam veteran (he was a Navy Corpsman assigned to Fleet Marine Force, Third Marine Airwing) he's also the co-author of *The Life Insurance Conspiracy, The Consumer's Guide to Handguns, "Gun Control"; Gateway to Tyranny, Death by Gun Control, The State vs. The People* and *The Mitzvah,* now being made into a motion picture. Aaron is the creator of the educational series of "Gran'pa Jack" freedom booklets, and publisher of the *Bill of Rights Sentinel.* He's perhaps best known as the founder and Executive Director of Jews for the Preservation of Firearms Ownership, regarded by many as America's most aggressive civil rights organization, and director of its sister organization, Concerned Citizens Opposed to Police States (CCOPS). *Hope* is Aaron's second effort at fiction. He lives with his wife and children in the Kettle Moraine region of Wisconsin to which he says they've successfully escaped from "Naziwaukee."

Former gunsmith, ballistician, reserve police officer, and likely the most widely-published and prolific libertarian writer in the world, **L. Neil Smith** produces fiction which is often compared to the works of Robert A. Heinlein and H. Beam Piper. Author of countless essays and articles, as well, he's been called "the most frequently crossposted writer on the internet." Neil has also performed as a professional musician, playing banjo and guitar. An enthusiastic competitor in the long-range sport of handgun metallic silhouette shooting, he lives in Fort Collins, Colorado with his wife Cathy, his daughter Rylla, and two striped orange cats named Amber and Ambrose. *Hope* is his twenty-fourth book.

"Aaron Zelman and L. Neil Smith have written a compelling, visionary novel about how life in America would be radically improved if we had a President who actually believed in the Bill of Rights."

James Bovard
author of
Lost Rights and
Freedom in Chains

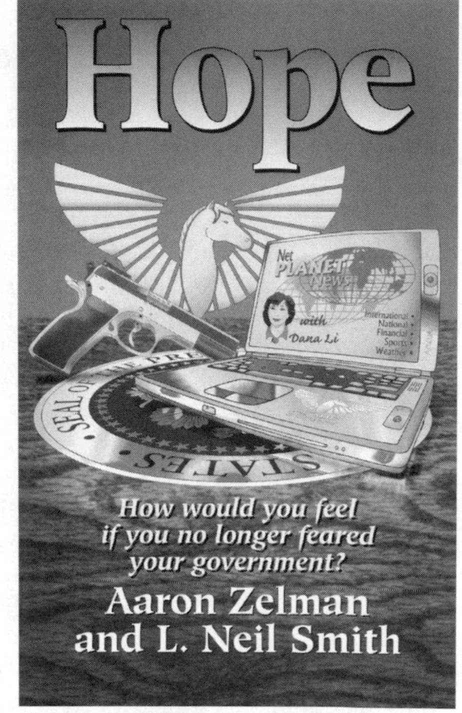

$14.95 each • 6 copies **$55.95** • 12 copies **$99.95**

Buy *Hope* and *The Mitzvah* OR *Dial 911 and Die*

and save $3.00 on the total order.

Prices include shipping.

For delivery to Canadian addresses, please add 10% to cover additional postage cost.

ORDER FORM

JPFO • P.O. Box 270143 • Hartford, WI 53027 • 262-673-9745 • fax 262-673-9746

www.jpfo.org

Total enclosed $ _______

Wisconsin residents add 5.6% sales tax

AMEX / VISA / MC # ____________________________ Exp. Date __________

SHIPPING LABEL – PLEASE PRINT CLEAR BLOCK CAPITAL LETTERS

Name ________________________ Phone ______________________

Address ____

City ________________________ State / Province _________________

Postal / Zip Code ____________________

The U.N. "Declaration of Human Rights" places NO POWER into the hands of individuals, or the people... even if the government turns oppressive!

PRICE CODE "A"
Gran'pa Jack #5
(24 pages)

1	Copy US $3.00 ppd.
25	Copies US $15.00 ppd.
50	Copies US $20.00 ppd.
100	Copies US $38.00 ppd.
250	Copies US $93.00 ppd.
500	Copies US $180.00 ppd.
1000	Copies US $350.00 ppd.

Read one of Alex Hope's favorite booklets — "Gran'pa Jack #5"! FREE when you order HOPE

JOIN JPFO TODAY! *Only $20.00 – Tax deductible!*
(Jews for the Preservation of Firearms Ownership, Inc.)
For delivery to Canadian addresses, please add 10% to cover additional postage cost.

ORDER FORM

JPFO • P.O. Box 270143 • Hartford, WI 53027 • 262-673-9745 • fax 262-673-9746
www.jpfo.org

Total enclosed $ ________ ❑ **Membership**
Wisconsin residents add 5.6% sales tax

AMEX / VISA / MC #______________________________ Exp. Date ____________

- -

SHIPPING LABEL – PLEASE PRINT CLEAR BLOCK CAPITAL LETTERS

Name ______________________________ Phone ____________________
Address ____
City ______________________________ State / Province _______________
Postal / Zip Code ____________________

Get one copy of #2 and #5 FREE when you order HOPE

PRICE CODE "A"
Gran'pa Jack #1, 2, 4, 5, 6 & 7

(24 pages)	Booklets #1	#2	#4	#5	#6	#7
1 Copy US $3.00 ppd.						
25 Copies US $15.00 ppd.						
50 Copies US $20.00 ppd.						
100 Copies US $38.00 ppd.						
250 Copies US $93.00 ppd.						
500 Copies US $180.00 ppd.						
1000 Copies US $350.00 ppd.						

PRICE CODE "B"
Gran'pa Jack #3
(48 pages)

1 Copy US $4.00 ppd. ______
25 Copies US $20.00 ppd. ______
50 Copies US $30.00 ppd. ______
100 Copies US $49.00 ppd. ______
250 Copies US $120.00 ppd. ______
500 Copies US $210.00 ppd. ______
1000 Copies US $390.00 ppd. ______

All seven booklets FREE when you order three or more books of your choice.

JOIN JPFO TODAY! *Only $20.00 – Tax deductible!*
(Jews for the Preservation of Firearms Ownership, Inc.)
For delivery to Canadian addresses, please add 10% to cover additional postage cost.

ORDER FORM

JPFO • P.O. Box 270143 • Hartford, WI 53027 • 262-673-9745 • fax 262-673-9746
www.jpfo.org

Total enclosed $ ______ ❑ **Membership**
Wisconsin residents add 5.6% sales tax

AMEX / VISA / MC # ____________________ Exp. Date ________

SHIPPING LABEL – PLEASE PRINT CLEAR BLOCK CAPITAL LETTERS

Name ________________ Phone ________________
Address ________________________________
City ________________ State / Province ________________
Postal / Zip Code ________________

THE STATE vs. THE PEOPLE

THE RISE OF THE AMERICAN POLICE STATE

by Claire Wolfe and Aaron Zelman

Introduction by James Bovard

Coming soon –

The State vs. The People;

The Rise of the American Police State,

by Claire Wolfe and Aaron Zelman

Reserve your copy today! Send the information below to:
JPFO • P.O. Box 270143 • Hartford, WI 53027

- -

PLEASE TELL ME WHEN THIS BOOK IS PUBLISHED

Name ______________________________ Phone ________________

Address ____

City ______________________________ State / Province __________

Postal / Zip Code ______________________

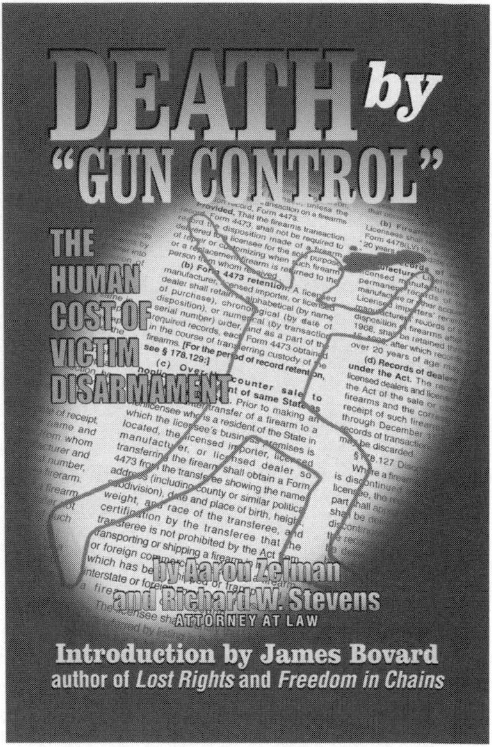